SWEET THUNDER

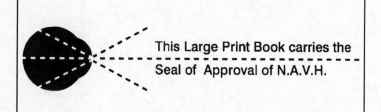

This Large Print Book carries the
Seal of Approval of N.A.V.H.

Sweet Thunder

Ivan Doig

THORNDIKE PRESS
A part of Gale, Cengage Learning

GALE
CENGAGE Learning

Detroit • New York • San Francisco • New Haven, Conn • Waterville, Maine • London

GALE
CENGAGE Learning®

LIBRARY OF CONGRESS CATALOGING-IN-PUBLICATION DATA

Doig, Ivan.
   Sweet Thunder / by Ivan Doig.
     pages cm. — (Thorndike Press Large Print Core)
   ISBN-13: 978-1-4104-6133-9 (hardcover)
   ISBN-10: 1-4104-6133-5 (hardcover)
   1. Newspaper editors—Fiction. 2. Montana—Fiction. 3. Western stories.
4. Large type books. I. Title.
PS3554.O415S84 2013b
813'.54—dc23   2013028746

Published in 2013 by arrangement with Riverhead Books, a member of Penguin Group (USA) LLC, a Penguin Random House Company

I was with Hercules and Cadmus once,
When in a wood of Crete
they bay'd the bear
With hounds of Sparta . . .
I never heard
So musical a discord,
such sweet thunder.

— WILLIAM SHAKESPEARE,
A Midsummer Night's Dream

And we worked at the writer's trade,
Many a magical book we made.

TO MY WRITING BUDDIES
David Laskin
David Williams

AND OF COURSE, THEIR MUSES
Kate O'Neill
Marjorie Kittle

1

"Morrie, don't fall off the cable car, please. At least not until we reach the top of the hill."

Grace's flash of smile and dimple reassured me her warning was of the teasing sort, although hardly the usual honeymoon endearment. Indeed, standing precariously on the steps of the crowded conveyance as I had to, I nearly lost hold in my startled reaction to what I was seeing. Not the fancy San Francisco shops bedecked with holiday wreaths nor the picture-book view of the dusky bay and its ferry fleet like bright water bugs, arresting as those were. No, what caught my eye as the cable car climbed the steep street was the bowler-hatted figure evincing sudden great interest in the cooked chickens hanging by their necks in a Chinese grocery storefront. My heart beat with the question: Could it be? After the gambling mob in Chicago all those years ago, after the goons of Butte, another one?

Another window man.

The species was unmistakable, in my experience. Someone tailing an individual of interest by blending in with other pedestrians until the individual happened to glance around, as I had just done, forcing an about-face to the nearest display behind plate glass. But why now, why here? What perverse kind of luck was following me through life like a secondary shadow?

"I thought I saw someone I recognized," I vaguely made my excuse to Grace.

She craned to peek past me from where she sat. "Somebody from Butte? We should have said hello."

"No, no, I must have been wrong. A case of mistaken identity."

The cable car clanged to a stop atop Nob Hill and I helped her down, my mind still taken up with that sighting. Grace slipped her arm through mine, gay as a Parisienne on promenade, as we strolled past the flivvers and delivery vans lining the manicured driveway of our hotel. "I can't wait to hear Caruso tonight," she snugly pressed my arm to her side. "What's he singing, again?"

"Mmm? *Pagliacci.* The clown who cries."

"Oh, my. What for?"

"Effect."

"Those Italians. Remember Rome?" An even more fervent squeeze of my arm. "But this tops it all, you man of the world, you. Caruso. *Polly-whosis.* Deluxe hotel on Snob Hill." She laughed her delight. "It's like a dream, don't you think?"

"Very like." Knowing what I must do, I stopped short of the columned entrance, where the doorman in gaiters and ruff waited to bow us in. "My dear, you go on up to the room. I'll just nip around the corner for today's papers."

"Don't be long, darling," she dimpled in a way more than wifely, "we don't want to be late for the singing and crying."

The newspaper vendor, Blind Tony, was ensconced in a hutch, practically buried in stacks of newsprint. Throughout our stay I had always made generous with a silver dollar for the day's two bits' worth of the *Sporting News* and either the San Francisco *Call* or *Bulletin.* This time I gave him an amount that clinked in his hand.

"That old silver eagle seems to have company, guv'nor."

"Let's regard it as rent on a sense of hearing, shall we, Tony," I responded. Keeping my voice low, I asked whether his keen ears

11

had picked up any footsteps following my own.

The sightless eyes squinted in recall. "Funny you should mention it. Right after your last couple times here, there been a set of leather soles and Cat's Paw heels that go by, slow like."

I had to think fast. "Here's what those pieces of silver and I want you to do . . ."

Having enlisted the news vendor, I turned to saunter off toward the hotel as usual, but as soon as his booth concealed me at an angle from anyone down the street who might be watching, I ducked back and into the structure, hiding behind the bulky torso of Tony and stacks of newspapers. Fresh ink of headlines permeated the close quarters. **Harding Vows Era of "Normalcy"** . . . **Carrie Nation Buries Hatchet in Prohibition Victory** . . . **Congress of Soviets Sets Russian Economic Goals** . . . **Earthquake Kills Untold Thousands in China** . . . Nineteen-twenty was going out with sound and fury, as human annals tend to do. But I had no time to dwell on that as Blind Tony, significantly cocking an ear, alerted me to the approach of the man in the bowler hat. I dove a hand into my side pocket for the precautionary item I carried there by habit.

"Help me find my house key where I dropped it, can you, guv'nor?" Tony called him over.

As the stranger obligingly stepped up to the booth, I reached out and grabbed him by the necktie, flourishing my brass knuckles in front of his nose and demanding to know who he was.

The man managed to fumble a business card into sight:

BAILEY PRIVATE
INVESTIGATIVE AGENCY

HELENA, MONTANA

WE SEEK AND FIND

"I'm Bailey," he choked out.

Blinking, I asked the requisite question, namely what on earth he wanted of me.

"I have something for you," he squawked the gist of it as best he could, "from Sam Sandison."

At that name, I released my grip on his necktie and let the set of brass knuckles slip back into my suit coat pocket. My surprise not lessened in the least, I inquired: "Why in heaven's name didn't you simply walk up to me like a civilized human being and

13

deliver whatever it is?"

Sulkily adjusting his tie and what composure he could find, the private detective replied that he liked to get a sense of the person he was dealing with before getting down to business.

Very well, then, I was glad to oblige. "How did you" — I wasn't going to dignify Seek and Find — "track me down?"

That met with a snicker. "There aren't any too many Fancy Dans trotting around to places like this who pay off in Montana cartwheels."

I looked sharply at Blind Tony, who was communing with the heavens. "His money is as good as yours, guv'nor."

"So anyhow," said Bailey, "let me give you what's coming to you." He darted a hand into his suit coat, and I froze at the glimpse of a shoulder holster and its resident revolver. What he produced, however, was a set of papers. A legal document from the look of it, and as I speedily read through it, a confounding one.

While I was trying to digest the contents, Bailey, piqued at being snaffled by the necktie, huffed that he almost hadn't taken this cockamamie case, since Sandison was the client. "He's the Strangler, you know."

"Yes, yes, I do know," I said absently, still

14

deciphering legalistic thus-and-therefores. "I am also fully aware that vigilante justice, to call it that, against cattle rustlers happened a long time ago, and ever since then Sandy —"

The detective rocked back on his heels. "Holy cripes, you get to call him that? Maybe that explains something like this."

Thinking hard, I tapped the document against the palm of my hand. "You know what this is about, do you?"

"Have to," Bailey replied cautiously. "I never take a case blindfolded."

"Then with this proposition of his, would you say Sam Sandison is of sound mind?"

"Are you kidding? He can run circles around either of us in the brains department."

That at least was no surprise. Pocketing the document, I parted with the private eye. "Enjoy San Francisco."

"Have a ton of fun in Butte," he called after me sardonically.

Grace was gussying up for the opera when I stepped into the hotel room. Fixing her hair, although her crown braid of flaxen tresses always looked flawless to me. Her compact form filled the latest gown as effectively as a dressmaker's form. In the dresser mirror

15

she gave me her best smile, bright and teasing, as I came up behind her and put my hands on her silken shoulders. How lucky you are, Morris Morgan, deservedly or not, to have this woman in your life, I told myself yet again.

I stood rooted there, weighed down by a pocketful of legalese, as Grace with a little hum busied herself at her hair again. There are times in life — this most definitely was one — when you can feel fate and destiny pressing on you like a heightened law of gravity. Add in some unknown measure of danger, and deciding becomes a burden like no other. To do or not to do; try that on, Hamlet. A surreptitious telegram to Sandison turning down his madcap proposition would mean Grace's lustrous head need never be bothered with this; other vulnerable parts of either of us as well. That would be prudent, no doubt wise. The other choice, though. What a chance. What an intriguing gamble. What a wink of fate.

"I have news," I announced, although I had totally forgotten to buy newspapers. "Down in the lobby, I met up with an emissary from Butte. The long and short of it is, Dora Sandison has passed to her reward —"

"Oh, what a shame," Grace expressed

16

proper respect. "She was such the lady."

"— and Sam Sandison has bequeathed us their house."

At those words, I felt something like electricity go through her. "In the West End?"

Aren't mansions always? "Very nearly as far in that direction on the compass of social climbing as one can go, I suppose. Ajax Avenue."

"Is it," her eyes were large with trying to take the prospect in, "one of the show-off ones?" Her boardinghouse, where all this began, was considerably down the scale in every way from the profligate showpieces erected by the early generation of Butte copper barons.

"Mmm, in reasonably better taste. I was only ever there a time or two, but I remember it as roomy and done in a style of its own." Much like Samuel Sandison himself, I did not bother to add.

Grace absorbed that for a moment. Then flung herself into hugging me. "Morrie, you rogue! What a wonderful Christmas present!"

As I regained my breath, she ran her fingers up and down my lapel and confided with a bit of a blush: "I have a confession to make. It's awful of me, but . . . I'd begun to

17

wonder how you are as a provider."

That made two of us. For the fact of the matter was, our money was evaporating fast. Just prior to winning Grace's hand, I had attained a junior fortune on a sporting wager. More like a sure thing, actually, for who in his right mind would not have bet against the heavily favored Chicago White Sox in the 1919 World Series, intuiting as I did that the team would not play its best for owner Charles Comiskey, known in sporting circles back there as Cheap Charlie. I admit I did not foresee that his baseball minions would succumb to bribes and deliberately let Cincinnati win, but it came to the same, which is to say a satchel of cash for Grace and me to embark on married life. With that wherewithal, our honeymoon had turned into a honey year. Europe, New York, New Orleans, and of course San Francisco, we hit the world's high spots in the manner to which we were all too soon accustomed. The document beneath the fabric Grace was so fondly fingering had spared me a confession of my own, namely that I possessed not the foggiest notion of how to support us, in high style or low, once the satchel was empty. Now, whether or not we had any money, we at least had a mansion, ready and waiting for the claiming.

"Ah, Grace," I tucked a stray tendril into her interrupted hairdo, "there is one slight wrinkle in Sandison's bequest that I should perhaps mention."

"Fire when ready, you sneaky provider, you."

"The house comes with Sandison."

2

The train — which had royally whisked us away to more comfortable climes not so many months before — deposited us now onto the wintry platform of the Butte depot. Snowbanks of apparently arctic depth lined the railroad tracks, and the depot eaves showed long teeth of icicles. One of us at least was unbothered by the cool reception; Grace's cheeks bloomed in the frosty air. "As they say, there's no place like home," she smiled encouragement to me, each of her words a smoky puff of breath, "even at ten below."

I merely nodded, distracted as ever by the eye-popping view. The Richest Hill on Earth, always bragged of with capital letters, did not look the part as it hunched at the back doors of the wintry city. Rather, it appeared to be a conglomeration of belching factories and bizarre steel towers leading to nowhere and grim gray dump heaps pocking a misplaced hump of earth, which, with a fresh covering of snow, gave the startling impression of having risen like bread dough. Looks can be deceiving, never more so than in this instance, for the Butte hill contained unmatched deposits of copper, at precisely the time when civilization was wiring itself for electricity. Some twenty billion dollars of the conductive metal had been mined from the Hill. As for the community that had exploded from rough western mining camp to a secular capital of political power and cultural aspiration, Butte was no beauty but held an allure of its own. Literally sitting on riches, the unlikely mile-high metropolis, which always appeared to be trying to catch up with itself in sporadic skyscrapers and flung-together neighborhoods, had drawn seekers of wealth, from miners to moguls. I myself first arrived practically penniless in the tumultuous year of 1919, and while my path to good fortune was not the standard one, I had to grant that Butte had been a lucky diggings, as the saying was, for me as well. Although, as is too often the case where men battle for control of the earth's yield, not without risk attached. What a crime, on what a scale, for a city of such treasure to be forever squirming under one mighty thumb. Even in the innocence of snow capping the distant roofs and cornices of tall downtown businesses, it stood out to me: the top floor of the Hennessy Building, where power resided. Where the offices of the Anaconda Copper Mining Company looked down on the city and, for that matter, the state that it had long ruled like a corporate fiefdom. Where suspicions ran high against interlopers of whatever sort.

With a well-learned sense of caution, I glanced around for anyone taking undue notice of our arrival. Window men, if any, would have stood out like penguins against frosty glass backdrops, and passersby swathed from the crystalline cold all seemed to have their heads down to watch the tricky footing on the tilted streets. Nothing unwelcome about our welcome, so far. Still, certain shards of memory from 1919 sent an occasional quiver through me.

Shivering more than a little herself as we waited for our luggage, Grace murmured in wifely concern, "You look bothered. You aren't nervous about the Sandison house, are you?"

"No, no, just wondering at the whereabouts of our belongings," I alibied, looking around for the baggage handler. With sinking heart, I spotted him emerging not from the baggage car but the depot, claim check in hand.

I groaned. "Not again?"

"That trunk of yours got sidetracked somewhere between Frisco and here, I'd say," he cheerfully proffered the claim check. "It'll catch up with you sooner or later, you can just about bet."

"Not if experience is any guide," I protested hotly, citing my own previous trunk lost when I first arrived to Butte, and still missing after all this time. I was well launched into an impassioned lecture to the unimpressed baggage man about this trunk of ours having accompanied us uneventfully on railroads around half the world until this accursed one, when Grace tugged at the sleeve of my overcoat. "Morrie, never mind. I have my overnight case and you've your satchel, we can get by."

Resigned to the loss, evidently my own personal admission ticket to Butte, I sighed heavily and accompanied Grace out to the street. A jitney sat chugging at the snowy curb, and the bundled-up taxi driver poked his head out to ask, "Where to, folks?"

I said with what I hoped was the air of a mansion owner, "Ajax Avenue, please."

"Horse Thief Row it is," the driver said nonchalantly. "Hop in."

■ ■ ■ ■

Probably since the villas of Pompeii, palatial homes are ornaments of wealth, and Butte had more than its share of fanciful big houses. Our route swung past the monstrosity built by the early copper magnate William A. Clark, a many-gabled Victorian monument to vanity that took up half a block. More ostentatious yet was the château his son had imported from Europe and reassembled to the last cubit. Housekeeper that she'd had to be in operating her own boardinghouse, Grace peered apprehensively through the frost-flowered windows of the taxi as we passed other West End behemoths, her gloved hand gripping mine harder and harder. "Grace, Sandy's residence as I recall it is not as gargantuan as these," I sought to reassure her. To no avail. More firmly, I tried again. "It's only a house, remember."

"Around here, that's some 'only,' " she said with a swallow.

Now I was the apprehensive one. "I hope you're not getting —"

"No! I'm fine. Fine."

The driver called out, "This's the street. Which shack is yours, pard?"

I pointed over his shoulder to a stonework architectural mix with a peaked tower room predominating. Draped in snow and icicles, the three-story house looked like a polar castle.

"There, see?" I soothed Grace when the taxi left us off outside the gray granite manse. "Smaller than Versailles."

"A little," she allowed doubtfully, as we negotiated the frosty front steps and porch. The second time I rapped the brass knocker in the shape of a helmeted warrior's frosty-eyed visage, Ajax on guard duty, a familiar gruff voice called from somewhere inside. "Coming. Don't wear out the door."

"Morgan," the figure that flung it open and loomed there almost filling the doorway issued, as if identifying me to myself. As commanding as Moses, he rumbled, "It's about time you stopped gallivanting all over the landscape. Heh."

Samuel Sandison himself was nearly geographic, the great sloping body ascending from an avalanche of midriff to a snowy summit of beard and cowlick. Glacial blue eyes seemed to see past a person into the shadows of life. Attired as ever in a suit that had gone out of fashion when the last century did, and boots long since polished by sagebrush and horsehide, he appeared to be resisting time in every stitch of his being. Description struggled when it came to his mark on history, cattle king turned vigilante turned bookman and city librarian, who had bent every effort and not a few regulations to provide a rough-and-tumble mining town with a world-class reading collection. And always, always, the long shadow of the hangman's tree followed him, carried forward from when he'd owned the biggest ranch in Montana. Having shared an office with him in something like companionable exasperation — the feeling may have been mutual — I always connected this outsize man with those lines of the poet Cheyne: *Greater than his age was he / Story and legend his legacy.*

Right now, he was some manner of unprecedented tenant ushering us into a sprawling residence newly ours. Parlor, drawing room, music room with piano and peach-and-plum wallpaper wrongly inspired by Gilbert and Sullivan's *Mikado,* living room, dining room, nameless others, kitchen somewhere in the distance. Fine-grained oak here, bird's-eye maple there, Turkish carpets everywhere. "Bedrooms and such are upstairs," he waved toward the heavens, "there's a mob of them. Help yourselves." With Grace wearing the wide-eyed expression of a first-time museumgoer, he trooped us on through the downstairs until we reached a conical room at the base of the substantial tower, practically submerged in books. "Library," he pronounced, probably just for the satisfaction of the word. Spying a rare-books catalog open on the overflowing desk, I couldn't help but ask, "How's shopping, Sandy?"

"About like dealing with pirates, as usual." He frowned at me a certain way, book lover to book lover. "What do you think of *The Song of Igor's Campaign?*"

"Where 'the wolves in the ravine conjure the storm,' if I am translating rightly? The poetic flavor of that might not be received as well as it should by your library patrons, this time of year." I inclined my head to the depths of snow and thermometer, which evidently were here to stay through the Butte winter.

"You maybe hit on a good point there," Sandison drawled. "I'll hold out for something less Siberian." Noticing Grace biting a finger — I could tell she was trying to tally the number of rooms encountered so far, with floors yet to go — he addressed her with elephantine gallantry. "My hat is off to you, madam, for turning this hopeless case," he indicated to me, "into husband material."

"What? Oh, yes. I mean, Morrie had a hand in that, too." The topic of matrimony reminding her, she paid her respects to the late Dora: "I'm sorry about your loss."

He bobbed his head in almost schoolboyish fashion, evidently not trusting his voice. Clearing his throat, he returned to eyeing me critically. "What are you doing with all that foliage on your face? Hiding the mud fence?"

There is quite a philosophy to growing a beard — or a mustache, as I occasionally resorted to — but in this instance, I'd done so simply as a precautionary measure. That winning bet on the corrupted World Series may have upset the Chicago gamblers who lost their shirts to some smart aleck with too much of a hunch, as they no doubt saw it, and I thought it best not to fit my description while Grace and I hit the high spots of the world. I had also added some pounds in our sampling of national cuisines; advancing from lightweight to middleweight, as I preferred to think of it. A bit of camouflage never hurt, in my experience.

"I think it's very becoming on him," Grace said loyally, of my carefully tended whiskers. "Hmmp," Sandison grunted, himself bearded as a Santa. The glint in the gaze he gave me showed he was restraining himself, barely, from asking, "Becoming what?" Before he could hold forth about me any further, Grace put in, "I'd like to look over the kitchen, if I may."

"Madam, be my" — he halted the sweep of his hand toward the rear region of the house — "I started to say guest, but landlady is more accurate, isn't it. Heh." Grace flinched ever so slightly and left us.

"That brings up something, Sandy." I strolled the circle of the room for the pleasure of running my fingers over the valuable books. "Exactly how is this living arrangement supposed to work?"

"Easy as pie, simpleton. I'll hole up here when I'm not downtown at the public library," he deposited himself in his chair at the heaping desk, "and use a stray bedroom. The rest of the place is yours and hers. Signed, sealed, and delivered."

"That leads to my next question." The chair groaning under him as he shifted haunches, Sandison waited for me to ask it. I gestured to include everything from ancient Ajax guarding the entrance to the mansion to the gift of title in my pocket. "Why?"

"You don't think I'm going to live forever,

do you?" he said, mildly for him. "You might as well have the place instead of the taxman."

That seemed to sum the matter up, at least as far as he was concerned. It was only the start of it for me. "Thank you very much, I think. But ah, taxes, and upkeep —"

"Coal," he added to the list with a grunt. "The place eats it like a locomotive."

"— and staff —"

"The cook and a couple of maids left, after Dora passed away. I figured you and the missus would take care of all that your own way anyhow."

"— all of which," I drew a needed breath, "leads me to wonder if I might have my old job back. A steady wage would be most welcome at this point, Sandy."

For the first time, he looked less than commanding, the chair groaning some more as he shifted uncomfortably. "Can't be done, Morgan, as much as I'd like to. The trustees have gone off their rocker about the payroll. The idiots won't even let me hire a book-cart pusher, let alone an assistant like you were. It's a damn shame." His turn to take in the mansion with a gesture. "Naturally I'll kick in some rent. I'll discuss that with the landlady," he said with another glint, "she looks like that is right up her alley." From under snowy cowlick and frosty eyebrows he studied me in a way I knew all too well. "The rest, though, you're going to have to provide by putting that head of yours to work, aren't you."

"I see." I wished I did.

That night in bed, an ornate one that must have held Sandison and Dora comfortably enough but was big as a barge for us, neither Grace nor I could close our eyes, let alone sleep. A large arched window at the end of the bedroom looked out over the lights of the city, with the white web of stars above like a reflection. I have always loved the night sky and its desires coded in constellations and comets, but it was not that keeping me awake. It was Grace.

"I have to keep pinching myself that this is really happening, Morrie."

"I know what you mean."

"I'm practically black and blue."

"No doubt."

She turned toward me, her flaxen hair garlanding the pillow. "I have to tell you something. Don't take it wrong. Promise? This, this palace or whatever it is, is a housekeeper's nightmare. I mean, it's wonderful, in all other ways. Everything done so fine. The woodwork. The furniture. The Turkey rugs. But it's so" — I could just make out her face in the dark as she searched for the proper word — "endless."

"Yes, I've begun to notice that."

"Not that His Nibs" — the jocular lordly moniker fit Sandison rather nicely, I had to grant her — "isn't the soul of generosity for giving us the house. But he had reason to, didn't he. Imagine how he must have rattled around in here alone until he had his, his —"

"Epiphany."

"— whatever you want to call it, to pass this barn of a place along to us and turn himself into a high-class boarder. Him and a thousand books." She was gaining speed all the time. "It's too much house even for me, Morrie. I could work myself to a nub trying to keep up with all that needs doing, and it would still gain on me every hour of every day. Can we afford hired help?"

"In a word, no."

"Then I know of only one thing to do. I take that back. Two."

"Grace, love, you're not really going to say —"

"Griff and Hoop. They're the only answer."

With difficulty I held my tongue from asking, "To what question?" Describing themselves as retired miners — "at least the tired part" — Wynford Griffith and Maynard Hooper had been fixtures at Grace's boardinghouse when I alighted there new to Butte, bandy veterans of mine disasters and union struggles and other travails they could recite at Homeric length. It was true, as Grace now was pouring into my ear, that Griff was something of a handyman and Hoop was, well, constantly available; we had left them in charge of the boardinghouse during our honeymoon sojourn without too many qualms. The pair of them as house staff on Ajax Avenue, though? For one thing, they were getting so old they creaked. For another, as I protested to her, if they moved in here, who was going to mind the boardinghouse?

"We'll have to close it until we get this place whipped, that's all there is to it," she said conclusively. "No boarder in his right mind is going to show up in Butte in the middle of winter anyway."

She raised on one elbow, her flaxen hair spilling to her shoulders as she gazed down at me.

"That leaves you, J. P. Morgan."

I matched her wavery smile with my own.

"I don't suppose it's an honor I can decline, hmm?" We had counted on my old job at the library, which Sandison scotched. The void yawned distressingly large.

The fact is, I do not take well to most forms of employment. The acid of boredom sets in insidiously and my mind finds other pursuits. Life among the blessed books of Butte aside, the one occupation I had found to give my head and heart to was teaching in a one-room school, in my first venture into Montana a dozen years before. Grace knew only the vaguest of that brief prairie episode of my life, and the question was what gainful work I could find, and stick to, in the here and now. Her first husband, who perished in Butte's worst mining disaster, the 1917 Speculator fire, evidently had been a paragon of husbandly virtue, uninterruptedly employed, steady as a clock in most ways, right down the list except for an unfortunate habit of betting on greyhound races, the surest way to have one's wages go to the dogs. Given that, I knew what a leap of faith and love it had been for her to risk life with me. Trying to sound as confident as a man can while flat on his back, I gazed up at her. "*Nil desperandum,* my dear. Never despair."

"House rules. English only, in the marital bed."

"What, you've never heard of Ovid?"

"I'll Oafid you, chatterbox," she tickled me in the ribs. And with that, everything else could wait until morning.

"Big."

"Righto."

"Lots needs doing."

"Nothing we can't fix."

Hoop and Griff moved in as though tooling up to attack a rockface in the days when they were a flash team of drillers in many a mine, with a clatter and a magpie glitter of interest in what awaited. Squinting around at the expanse of the house as Hoop likewise was doing, Griff assured me, "Don't worry none, Morrie. We'll pitch in here and there and it'll all add up, you'll see." His tool bag beside their battered suitcases there in the side hall struck me as somehow ominous, but I was in no position to turn down help of any sort. Grace had disappeared to the far reaches of kitchen and pantry, and Sandison had not yet made his appearance for the day. The snow-bright morning practically wreathed our new arrivals in wrinkles, Hoop and Griff having worked underground side by side for so many years and boarded together for so many more that they had grown to resemble each other, wizened and bent as apostrophes and nearly telegraphic in their talk. Mineral, vegetable, or animal, the pair could boil down a topic almost instantly. Grace had great affection for them — as did I, with reservations — and Griff, a lifelong bachelor, and Hoop, a widower, shared a near holy reverence for her; "Mrs. Faraday," as they primly had insisted on calling her up until now, when their tongues were going to have get used to "Mrs. Morgan."

All at once, their speculations back and forth as to which ailment of the house merited most urgent treatment petered out as they looked past me down the hallway, and in unison doffed their hats and clasped them to their breasts.

I scarcely had to turn around to the object of their respect. "Good morning, Sandy. I hope the accommodations" — he had taken over a back bedroom in what amounted to servants' quarters, but handiest to his beloved library tower — "were up to expectation?"

"It'll do. Hell, I've slept in bunkhouses before. What's all the commotion?"

Ceremoniously I introduced Hoop and Griff as new boarders, doubling as household staff. Sandison grunted a greeting to the bandy-legged pair, who returned the sentiment in hushed tones of awe. Reputation is a mighty thing, I was reminded again. Even in this city where justice not uncommonly was meted out by fist, gun, or dynamite, the legend of Samuel Sandison's vigilante days stood head and shoulders over other such episodes. It was an old joke that civic uplift came to Montana with the lynching of the villainous sheriff, Henry Plummer, in the gold-strike town of Virginia City in 1864. Tradition of that grisly but effective sort found expression after Sandison's summary way of dealing with cattle rustlers — hence his lurid nickname "the Strangler," or sometimes simply "the Earl of Hell" — and here he stood before us, wild-bearded and filling a suit that would have held both Griff and Hoop. Practically kowtowing, they said they'd better get at things and disappeared to an inner room, where moments later hammering broke out.

"You keep some strange company," Sandison commented in their wake.

"They'll fit in," I blandly replied.

He gave me a look, but then grunted again and reached for his overcoat and hat. "Walk me to work, why don't you. It'll give you something to do besides idle your life away."

We set off in sunshine that did not take the chill out of the air, as though the sun's warmth was waning with the year. The other residences along Horse Thief Row were as frosted as cakes, and I learned from Sandison's rumbling commentary on the neighborhood that it had been his wife's idea to move there when they left the ranch. "Dora wanted a fancy house for a change," he said of the mansion I still had to get used to thinking of as mine and Grace's. "Myself, I've never been keen about living on a street named for a two-bit soldier in the Trojan War."

"It depends on the version of Ajax you believe in," I protested. "In one telling of it, he was larger than life and a warrior of great prowess. In the other tale, I admit, he comes across as a bit of a peewee and thinking too well of himself. But —"

"That's what I mean, oaf. If he was an unquestionable hero, he'd have his own epic poem, wouldn't he."

"But, I was about to say, if antiquity's penchant for dualism has given us Janus, a god with faces looking in opposite directions, why can't there be a twofold reflection of character in the myth, or myths, if you will, of Ajax? Perhaps representing mind and matter?" I thought I had him there, but

Sandison just snorted.

"Pah. I said he was a two-bit soldier, didn't I? A bit of this and a bit of that. You should learn to listen, rattlebrain."

About then we rounded the corner toward downtown, leaving mythology behind. Like Grace, I nearly had to pinch myself into believing my own senses, for the view ahead stretched like no other in America, with the winter-capped Rocky Mountains rising to the Continental Divide seemingly just beyond the city limits, and every manner of dwelling place and work spot of a hundred thousand people jumbled in between here and there. It was as if a section of Pittsburgh had been grafted onto an alpine scene, the power of industry and that of nature juxtaposed. The contest between the two was in the air, literally. You might think a city dominated by smokestacks and dump heaps would look its best under a covering of snow, but logic did not always apply to Butte. The weather could not keep up with production on the Hill, its low industrial rumble lending to the illusion that the humpbacked rise simmered like a volcano, belching constant smoke and venting muck from dozens of mineshafts, so that the snow being shoveled from paths and doorways as we passed was a mushy gray. "We need a good blizzard," Sandison prescribed as we made our way down the sloping streets toward the business district. Once again I marveled at my benefactor-cum-boarder, as wintry himself in his silvery wreath of beard and breath as Father Frost of the nursery rhyme. How did it go — *King of the whitened clime, ever there / Leaving tokens of wintertime everywhere.* Season in, season out, Samuel Sandison was like no one else I had ever encountered or expected to.

Conversation was a sometime thing with this uncommon man, I knew from experience, and so to keep matters going I pitched in with topics ranging from the weather to politics. As ever, Sandison's responses varied from grunts and silences to pronouncements that snapped a person's head around. As the saying was, life was serious when it made him; in all the time I shared his office, the only real mirth he showed was when he spotted a bargain in a rare-book catalog and would let out a "Heh!" and smile in the deeps of his beard. Yet there was almost no other person, save Grace, whom I found more compelling.

Just now he was grumbling about the recent national election, which had picked as president the most wooden member of the U.S. Senate. "Warren G. Harding is

40

barely bright enough to operate an umbrella. Damn it, what's this country coming to?"

"History reminds us that worse has happened, Sandy. You will recall that Caligula elected his horse to the Roman Senate."

"Hah. The American electorate has chosen the north end of that animal going south."

As we talked on, our breath wreathing our beards, that feeling of being in the company of fate came over me, perhaps just from nearness to Samuel Sandison, a figure monumental enough, Janus-like, to have "The Earl of Hell" inscribed on one side of him and "Progenitor of the Finest Book Collection West of Chicago" on the other. And somewhere between, the unlikely genie who bestowed a mansion as if giving away an old suit of clothes. Impetuously I told him he must inform me or Grace if there was anything we could do to cushion his life at the house. "I know you must miss Dora greatly."

"About like losing one eye," he said simply.

Glancing at me and then away, he turned gruff again. "The natural order of things turned upside down somehow, Morgan. Who would have thought you'd be the married man and I'd be the tanglefoot bachelor."

By now we were approaching his domain, his realm and his scepter, the Butte Public Library, and my heart skipped at the first full sight of it. How I loved that castle of literature, a granite Gothic extravaganza, with its welcoming arches like the entranceway of a cathedral and a balcony neatly cupped above and a corner tower with its peak inscribing the sky. The library's holdings were the even greater glory, with beautiful first editions of the output of authors from Adams, Henry, to Zola, Émile, shelved along with lesser works. Again like a many-sided figure, Sandison as librarian was also the institution's prime benefactor by mingling these treasures on loan from his own collection with the library's standard fare, an act of stupendous generosity that also made it impossible to fire him.

A block away, overtaken by so many memories good and the other sort, I was slowing to such an extent that Sandison looked over his shoulder at me. "Coming in?"

"Not today, Sandy."

"Suit yourself, if you'd rather loaf than improve yourself," he drawled, lumbering off to where the staff awaited him as usual in a line at the top of the library steps. With a pang, I watched him count them in through the arched doorway as he had counted cowboys at the corral in his previous life.

On my way back to the house, it was only when I stopped at a newsstand to buy the *Sporting News* and what passed for a local paper, the wretched Anaconda-owned *Butte Daily Post,* that the odd fact occurred to me. Sandison in our wide-ranging conversation had not bothered to bring up the copper company and its mailed-fist grip on the city at all. Which was a bit like that Sherlock Holmes mystery of the dog that did not bark in the night.

3

I had never been domestic. Which is to say, a householder, owner of a home of any sort — let alone a moose of a house up there with the most grandiose of them on Horse Thief Row, thanks to Sandison's quirky bequest. Back a decade and more ago, my brother and I and the love of his life necessarily dwelled under the same roof during the rise of his career, but the Congress Plaza Hotel in Chicago, when we were in the money, was such address as the three of us had. Therefore, Ajax's pop-eyed stare each time I put a key in the big front door of what was now the Morris and Grace Morgan domicile was apt enough.

The house, the mansion — the manse, as some imp within me couldn't help categorizing it — this home-owning opportunity or burden or responsibility or whatever it constituted, made me look at myself in a new way. To be painfully honest about it, until then I amounted to something like a tourist excursioning through life. Episode followed episode, never uninteresting but somewhat lacking in basic design. I lived by my wits, sufficient company most of the time. But now there was Grace to be thought of. Didn't I owe her, if not myself and my page in the book of life, a more settled and assured existence? In a word, domestication?

It would have been less a test of my resolve if the most perfect example of carrying a house on one's back were something other than the snail.

The pair of them were hard at it, Griff whanging away at a loosened stairway runner while Hoop handed him carpet tacks, when I returned later in the day after a trek around town scouting for employment, a discouraging exercise if there ever was one. With Montana again on hard times — the Treasure State, as it was known, seemed stuck in the mining-camp cycle of wild boom and precipitous bust — any jobs that I was more or less fitted for were scarcer than hen's teeth, which left me facing the prospect I dreaded. The C. R. Peterson Modern Mortuary and Funeral Home. "There'll always be an opening here for you," Creeping Pete, which was to say Peterson, long since had assured me amid the display of caskets with lids up. Briefly I'd served as his establishment's cryer at Dublin Gulch wakes when I first alighted in Butte, but this time around, I would have to plead sobriety and confine myself to the undertaking parlor; the rest of the nation may have signed on to Prohibition, but in this city, three hundred saloons merely turned into three hundred speakeasies and bootleg liquor flowed so freely at wakes that the corpse's brain wasn't the only one being pickled. I had no doubt that Creeping Pete would make room for me on the premises of the Modern Mortuary and Funeral Home, however. Somebody had to put on a fixed smile and sell those caskets. Accordingly, I was not in my best mood as I headed for the kitchen to tell Grace she was about to have an undertaker's assistant for a husband.

"By the way, Morrie," Griff called between slams of his hammer. "You're wanted."

That stopped me as if impaled. The vision of oneself portrayed in every post office in the land with that incriminating word beneath would halt any thinking person. Confusion asked the sizable question: for what?

Griff sized me up as if putting a price on me himself. "Got the note on you, Hoop?"

"Somewhere." The other oldster patted his pockets to finally retrieve it. With no small measure of trepidation, I unfolded the message.

Mr. Morgan —
Welcome back to Butte — we've missed you something awful. Jared needs to talk to you, and you know I always want to. Meet us at the usual place, the usual time, tonight.
Yours until the fountain pen runs dry,
Rab

I checked to make sure. "This was brought by — ?"

"That kid," said Hoop. "Thin as a whisker."

Relieved, I went directly to the kitchen to inform Grace. Slicing onions, she was in tears, but greeted me with a world-beating smile all the same. As Hoop and Griff and I knew and Sandison was about to find out, her years of balancing a boardinghouse budget had made her a canny if unconventional grocery shopper, and today's triumph was a bargain on rabbit. "Those French. Remember that meal, lapin à la something

47

or other?"

Touching her cheek to wipe away a trickle, I managed to look regretful as I told her to set one less plate for supper. "Jared Evans wishes to see me about something."

"Of course you need to go, then," she said at once. The leader of the mineworkers' union inspired almost royal loyalty, and I had been proud to stand with him in a certain episode in 1919. "Still," she sniffled from the effect of the onions, "it's a shame you'll miss the stewed rabbit."

The spacious eatery with the big red welcoming sign NO WAITING! YOUR FOOD AWAITS YOU! was called the Purity Cafeteria. Butte never undernamed anything. I scanned the ballroom-size dining area but could not spot Rab and Jared yet, and so went to the serving counter at the back and, with a mental apology to Grace, got myself a pasty. Fortunately pronounced like *past,* not *paste,* this was a meat-and-vegetables dish encased in pastry crust, introduced to Butte by Cornish miners, and in my experience, that rare thing, a hearty delicacy. It proved to be so, again this evening, as I ate, watching the traffic of customers waiting on themselves, until a wraithlike presence at my side caught me by surprise.

48

"Hiya, sir."

"The same to you, Famine!" The boy had grown in height the past year, but not at all in girth, still skinny as an undernourished greyhound. Straw hair flopping over his pale brow as he stood on one stilt leg and then the other, he retained the personification put on him by schoolmates, Russian Famine, which he greatly preferred to Wladislaw. Close behind the lad, natural authority resting on him as ever, Jared Evans provided me a serious smile along with a handshake and the greeting, "Professor, how you doing?" Then came the whirlwind, Rab, exclaiming, "Mr. Morgan!" and flinging herself into hugging me while I was only half onto my feet.

What a family tableau they made as they settled at the table with me. The boy restless in every bone but his mind at ease, I could tell, in the company of these trusted grown-ups. Jared, lean and chiseled, his dark eyes reflective of battles he had been through, from the trenches of death in France to the sometimes deadly front lines of the miners' union contending with the copper bosses of Butte. To my thinking, Jared Evans always looked freshly ironed, with a touch of starch. Not his clothing; Jared himself. On that score, though, I noticed he was better dressed than I remembered, which I credited to the influence of Rab, frisky clothes horse that she had been since school days. Properly named "Barbara" until in a classroom moment I never regretted I permitted her to flip that around to "Rabrab," and now a teacher herself, she still exuded the zeal of a schoolgirl, albeit one who happened to have the chest and legs of a circus bareback rider. Jared had made a fortunate catch with her. And she him. Russian Famine luckiest of all, nearly a street orphan but for these two as his guardians. I could tell the boy thought the sun and moon rose and set in them, the pair in his parentless life to look up to.

Gratified to be reunited with them so fast, I wondered, "How did you know I was back in town?" Rab only wrinkled her nose as though the whereabouts of Morris Morgan were common knowledge, while Jared winked and said, "Moccasin telegraph," the old rubric for the soft-footed way news travels. Laughing as much as we talked in catching up, we shared quick stories, including mine of the mansion bequest from Sandison. The fidgety seventh-grader doing his best to follow the maunderings of adults brightened. "Ain't he the one called the Earl of —"

"Careful with your language, Famine," Rab admonished.

"I was gonna say 'heck,' " he maintained guilelessly.

I chuckled and asked the boy whether his current teacher was as strict as that stickler last year, meaning Rab.

"Got her again, don't I," he reported with a fresh outbreak of fidgets. "Her and me are in the hoosegow."

I blinked. "He means the detention school, up on the Hill," Rab hastened to explain. "It's a dormitory school, for boys who are truant too much or delinquent in other ways that their families can't handle. They learn some shop work, along with regular classes. They can be a handful — I know what you're going to say, Mr. Morgan, remembering what I was like —"

"Justice is served," I said it anyway with a smile tucked in my beard.

"— but they tame down if treated right." She left no doubt that was her calling, explaining that she was a day matron at the so-called hoosegow. "That way, Famine can come along and go to school under me."

"She's terrible hard, sir," the boy testified.

"So are diamonds, my friend," I said with a fond swipe at the hair perpetually clouding in on his eyes. Now Rab suggested the two of them tend to the matter of food, and Famine in a few bounds sprang ahead of her to the serving line.

Silently proud, Jared watched them go, and then there were the two of us, and the topic always on the table in the shadow of the Hill, it seemed. I tried to put it diplomatically: "As those more statesmanlike than I might ask, how stands the union?"

Jared tugged at his wounded ear, an answer in itself. A German bullet had clipped the lobe neatly off, lending him a swashbuckling look advantageous in leading an organization of hardened miners. He was every inch the combat veteran now, in more ways than one. "The war over here goes on and on," he more than answered my question. "Anaconda just kills us more slowly than the Fritzies did." By that, I assumed he meant the long-standing reputation of the Hill's mines as the most dangerous anywhere, one mortal accident a week on the average, not counting conflagrations such as the Speculator fire, which claimed 164 lives, or the slow burn of silicosis in the lungs of hundreds of other doomed mineworkers. But no. Jared Evans practically blazed with fresh intensity as he leaned across the table toward me. "You missed the fireworks, Professor." I listened in stunned silence as his recital of the happenings of the past year added to the frieze of Butte's historic battles between labor and capital. The mineworkers' union had been ending 1919 on a high note, literally, when Grace and I left on our extended honeymoon. With a newly contrived work song, which I and a highly unlikely collaborator in the person of Sam Sandison had a hand in, to serve as the rousing anthem of its struggle and Jared's shrewd new generation of leadership, the union was intrepidly facing off against the Anaconda Copper Mining Company on the eternal issue of working conditions in the deadly mines. "The lost dollar" of wages, a cruel twenty percent cut Anaconda had arrogantly clipped from mine pay, was won back that year by carefully spaced walkouts — the phrase "wildcat strike" was never uttered on the labor side — and mineworkers ten thousand strong were finding their voice in the words of that "Song of the Hill," *I back you and you back me, all one song in unity.* All in all, matters had been brought to what seemed a favorable negotiating stage by the time Grace and I were boarding our train and bidding farewell to a copper-rich city with a fresh start of decade ahead of it. But in Jared's telling, history brutally repeated itself when an unforeseen circumstance brought in troops again. That circumstance shocked me into exclaiming:

"A general strike? Jared, that sounds extreme of you."

"The Wobblies forced our hand," he said wearily. The radical Industrial Workers of the World whipped up such anti-Anaconda fervor, his explanation ran, that the mine-workers' union had to side with them on the call to strike that past spring. A disastrous showdown followed, with guards outside the emblematic Neversweat Mine opening fire on pickets, killing one and wounding sixteen. Martial law was immediately imposed, miners saw no choice but to return to work, and Anaconda blacklisted anyone suspected of IWW sympathies.

"That pretty well broke the Wobs' power," Jared concluded, "but it left us scrambling for some way to deal with Anaconda besides walking off the job into bayonets and bullets." Good soldier that he was, he wryly credited the enemy who was always there: "Wouldn't you know, they're right back at it again, up there in the Hennessy Building, trying to make us swallow a pay cut. That's right," he registered my reaction, "the hogs are back at the trough." Lowering his voice, he passed me a look with more behind it than he was saying. "I've given them something to think about, though, in who I've got negotiating for us. He not only tears into them about wages, he gives them holy hell every time about conditions in the mineshafts and the company goons who did the shooting at the Neversweat and you name it." He hunched closer. "And that lets me — Professor, are you listening?"

As deeply as if in a séance, with the ghosts rising in the dark streets outside, those shadows that had followed me in my earlier Butte experience, window men in the employ of Anaconda whom I finally outwitted but not with any great margin of safety; oh, yes, I was listening.

"Has he recited everything but the Bible to you, Mr. Morgan?" Rab and Famine came bearing their meals and Jared's. But before my companion in conversation could so much as lift a fork, she leaned in conspiratorially. "Show him." She giggled. "Go ahead."

Perfectly poker-faced, Jared dug out a calling card and presented it to me. The official-looking imprimatur was as boggling to me as the legal scripture in Sandison's missive that produced a mansion.

STATE SENATOR JARED EVANS

REPRESENTING
SILVER BOW COUNTY

AND THE CITY OF BUTTE

Well, that explained his spiffed-up appearance. "Politics now? Jared, you're full of surprises."

Over Rab's proud boast that he was elected by a landslide, he confided to me: "A change of tactics, is all." This least playful of men grinned ever so slightly. "It seems to have gotten Anaconda's attention."

Rab leaned across the table to whisper: "They're scared he'll be governor next." With her racehorse keenness she looked like she couldn't wait for that result, and Russian Famine between shoveling his food down was listening for all he was worth. Still looking at me, Jared sobered. "The idea is to build some bargaining power, for dealing with Anaconda. They've had their way with the legislature and so many other politicians for so long, people are getting fed up. I can at least give the copper bosses a bad time on the floor of the senate and" — the bit of grin showed on him again as he looked at Rab — "beyond, if it ever comes to that. We'll see what the voters think after I raise enough ruckus."

"Intriguing," I had to commend his plan of attack. "And classic in its approach. You draw on the countryside, in this case the voting public, to harass the opponent into retreat, very much as the Russians rose up against Napoleon on his march to Moscow. I wish you every success, Senator Evans."

"There, see?" Rab nudged him.

"The thing is," he confided further, "we need to whip up public opinion like never before for this to work. The power of the press, no less. But that's the catch."

"Oh?"

"Anaconda owns every daily newspaper in the state."

"The snakes got their mitts on everything," Russian Famine echoed that.

"Hush a minute, Sharp Ears," Rab chided gently.

"Except," Jared continued, his grin growing now, "for the one the union is about to start."

"Ah."

"That's where you come in."

I sat upright as if jabbed. "Jared — and Rab, need I say — I am not a journalist. It is a noble profession, but I'm not fitted to scurry around reporting on this and that."

57

"You wouldn't have to." Jared leaned in closer, his voice lowered. "You'd be our editorial voice. We need a wordslinger. Someone to tear the living hide off Anaconda, day after day." He held me in his commanding gaze. "Professor, you're our man."

How does it happen with such regularity? As if intrigue and predicament were the Adam and Eve of my family tree, situations seek me out. With the best intentions in the world, I find myself catapulted into circumstances far out of the ordinary. Chicago; Marias Coulee; Butte; and now chapter two of this city of perils. Was this my role in life, to be a gazetteer of risky occurrences?

My protestations were batted down as quickly as I could bring them up, with Rab pitching in whenever Jared paused for breath. "That is so typical, Mr. Morgan. You're entirely too modest about your wordslinging ability."

I could not even prevail on the central issue of Anaconda siccing its goons on me again if I joined the union cause as its editorial tribune, Jared pointing out that the pair who had shadowed me previously had left town in a hurry after hints in the form of dynamite fuses were dropped on their pillows. "We learned something from the Wobblies there," he said firmly. "Don't worry, we'll play rough if Anaconda gets on your tail. Odds are, they won't pick you out ahead of me or anyone else on the newspaper staff. You'll just blend in and be writing pieces without your name attached." His steady gaze took me in. "Besides, that beard changes your appearance like night and day from the last time around. I had to look twice to be sure it was you."

"Those're some whiskers," Russian Famine backed that up.

Temptation knows how to find me, I had to admit. Caskets for company were looking less and less appealing. Even so, I tried to dodge a newspapering fate with one excuse or another until the accusation flew across the table, "You're fudging."

"Rab, I am not fudging."

"Dancing all around the issue like a troupe of Cossacks, then."

I sighed. "All right, Perseverance." Turning to Jared, I told him I was not promising anything, mind you, but I would take his proposition under advisement and —

"I know what, Professor, you can have a pen name," he forged past all that. "That'll give you one more disguise, in case anybody gets too curious about who's doing the wordslinging."

"There," his partner in scheming declared with a toss of her head, while Russian Famine hungrily took it all in like an apprentice conspirator, "doesn't that sound rosier?"

I sighed again. "A pigment of the imagination, Rab."

Grace was sleeping peacefully when I came in, and had gone to the kitchen by the time I got up. Thus it was at breakfast that I made my announcement.

"I seem to have found employment."

"See," Grace greeted that as though she had never had an iota of doubt, "you are a provider after all. Griff, Hoop? Hear that?" They took turns maintaining they were not surprised in the least that I was employable. Sandison was absent from the table, preferring to start his day with bread and cheese and his books. "Tell us, mysterious," my freshly proud wife urged. "What's the heavenly job?"

"Writing editorials against Anaconda on a regular basis. In the newspaper Jared Evans is starting up."

"Oh, Morrie."

"Yipes," Hoop or Grifflet out.

60

Those were not the kind of exclamations I'd hoped for. "It is steady work that pays a decent wage," I defended, "which is something all three of you were prescribing for me up until this instant, I believe."

"We don't count as much as some," said Griff, glancing sideways at Grace. "Anaconda won't like that sort of thing," he put it, Hoop nodding gravely.

"What is so alarming about public debate in the editorial column of a newspaper, for heaven's sake?" I was provoked into defense of the job I hadn't been sure I wanted. "The discussion of fair wages and safe working conditions and so on is a practical matter, not a declaration of war. I should think Anaconda can stand a bit of give-and-take where clubs and bullets are not required."

"Okey-doke, Morrie. It's your neck." Shaking their heads, the pair of them gimped off to their tasks of the day.

Grace stayed sitting with me, fried eggs and side pork going cold on our plates while we each waited for the other to say the right thing. I noticed a flush come over her. "My love, I really do not see that much reason for concern," I tried to sound soothing. "I'll be writing editorials anonymously. Pseudonymously, to be exact."

She rolled her eyes. "Morrie, you could be

writing those things posthumously and Anaconda would still find out it was you."

I looked at her apprehensively. "Grace, there's one consideration I hadn't thought of until now. Don't tell me this makes you —"

"No! Absolutely not. I'm perfectly fine." She shot to her feet and began ferrying dishes to the sink. "I suppose you know what you're doing. But somebody has to worry about you if you won't."

"Mr. Morgan, if you so much as say one word about 'The Wreck of the *Hesperus*,' I'll bat you."

"Tsk, Rab," I returned her murmur. "Would I do that?"

Plainly, though, the vacant premises of the newspaper-to-be was on the rocks drastically enough to have been long abandoned. The building, down a backstreet in the part of town winkingly known as Venus Alley and next to a Chinese noodle shop, once had been a secretarial school, which accounted for the array of rickety desks and typing stands and abandoned typewriters in the gloomy space. Walls were peeling, light fixtures hung askew, and a musty feel prevailed as though fresh air was a foreign commodity. None of which appeared to faze

Jared in the least, marching from window to window, flipping up flyspecked green blinds. Over his shoulder he called, "What do you think of the enterprise so far, Professor?"

Rab's shoe pressed a warning on the toe of mine. "It, mmm, has possibilities."

Dusting his hands, he marched past us. "This is nothing, come see what's in the back room."

Dutifully Rab and I filed after him into an even bigger and grubbier space, evidently a warehouse butted up against the front structure. It too needed heroic cleaning, but in the middle of the floor sat something new and huge, its every part gleaming like rarest metal.

Even I was at a loss for words for a moment. Reverently I approached the printing press. "Jared, if this wasn't born in a manger, where did it come from?"

He winked at Rab and grinned at me. "We're not the only ones who want to find some way to take on Anaconda. Farmers and ranchers are sick of the copper collar, too." He lowered his voice, even though it was only we three in the cavernous room. "There's a pair of rich cattlemen, brothers, up north. One of them was going into politics, war hero and all," his tone never betraying the fit of that description on himself, "until he ran into skirt trouble, the rumor is. Anaconda is usually behind any funny stuff like that, so he has it in for the copper bosses, and that loosened up his check-writing hand," he finished with a benign smile at the state-of-the-art printing press.

Rab spoke up. "It's the Williamsons, isn't it. The Double W ranch and all the rest." She could see I needed enlightening. "They own everything they can get their hands on," she could not help sounding like the homestead-bred girl she had been in Marias Coulee. Old antagonisms die hard.

"We need all the allies we can get," Jared said with soldierly simplicity.

Rab nibbled her lip. "I suppose."

I was with Jared, in this instance. The enemy of my enemy is my friend and all that. "I'd say equipment like this forgives the Williamson gent some sins." I couldn't resist running a hand over the press, in awe of the complex of machinery that turned lead impressions and ink into news articles and headlines spun onto a continuous web of newsprint and at the end of the process, into beautifully folded newspapers. "What an astounding era of communication we live in," I mused. "Gutenberg would be proud."

Voices were heard out front. Jared gathered Rab by the waist and clapped a hand to my shoulder. "Come meet the staff."

Milling around among the desks and typing stands were a couple of dozen individuals. I stress that last word, for even at first look this group comprised an odd lot. Old, young, predominantly male but including a few women with a Nellie Bly keenness to them, they looked so disparate as a staff that only an inclusive undertaking such as a newspaper could hold them. I marveled at how such a collection of timeworn refugees from journalistic outposts and eager neophytes had been assembled; I was quite sure I recognized a young couple from meetings of the erstwhile Ladies' and Gentlemen's Literary and Social Circle in the basement of the public library. One figure in this crowd stood out for exactly what he was, a hunch-shouldered pallid type, stone bald, as emblematic of the newspapering profession as a wooden Indian is of a cigar store. This was none other than Armbrister, Jared's choice of editor.

While Jared with Rab attached was going around the room making introductions, the sallow journalist and I singled ourselves out as if by instinct. Shaking hands at a careful distance, we studied each other. Armbrister wore a trademark green eyeshade and the expression of a hound dog on a cold trail. From the look of him, he had worn both since time immemorial. He eyed my rather smart tweed suit — London; those tailors — none too neutrally.

"You know beans about newspapering, Morgan?"

"A bit, from a lifetime of reading every scrap of newsprint possible. Do you know beans about arousing public opinion for a good cause?"

"I've heard distant rumors of it," he answered lugubriously, "about like the existence of the unicorn."

"Mmm. I understand that up until now you worked for our rival, the *Post.*"

"City editor on that rag, was all," he snapped, giving me a look I thought of as the Butte eye. It was not a true squint, simply a slight lowering of the eyelids like a camera aperture finding finer focus. I had encountered it at Dublin Gulch wakes, and in a mineshaft nearly a mile deep in the Hill, and on occasion in the woman at my side in life, Butte-born as Grace was. That particular cast of eye perhaps became habitual in a city always enwrapped in conflict. Armbrister maintained it as he grudgingly spoke the next: "I didn't have to run up to the top floor of the Hennessy Building like a coolie and have every word pass inspection with the bastards there, if that's what you're thinking." At the mention of Anaconda's lair on high, his long face grew longer. "A man has to make a living, you know."

"I do know."

Something in the way I said that drew the first twinge of interest from the hound dog face. "Evans swears you're a pip at making the language dance." He sniffed. "Naturally, any paper worth its ink needs a Fancy Dan for its editorial page or readers will never get past the funnies."

"And naturally, you are the crusading editor leading the charge and I am the, ah, working stiff."

He gave me another looking-over to see if I meant that, and by some intuition must have decided I deserved the benefit of the doubt, at least temporarily.

"Hell, man," he rasped, "maybe we're a pair of a kind, jokers wild. We'll see."

I nodded at the eyeshade of green celluloid, prominent as the visor on the helmet of a knight. "I don't mean to be impertinent, but I thought only editors like the one in *Barnaby of Drudge Street* wore one."

That brought a laugh like a bark. "Buster, if I didn't wear this for reading copy under every kind of light except Jesus' halo, I'd be one of the blind cases selling papers on the street instead of editing one. You a book-worm, then?"

I confessed I was.

"Damn good thing," he surprised me. "An editorial writer needs all the ammo there is."

Having observed our colloquy, Jared came over and said it looked to him like we maybe could stand to be in the same office with each other. "So far so good, in getting things set up," he rubbed his hands in satisfaction as the news staff shoved desks into arrange-ment as decreed by Armbrister, and the compositors and pressmen trooped off to ready their work sphere in the rear of the building. Armbrister's lair, besides a strate-gic desk in the middle of the newsroom, turned out to be a tightly glassed-in cubicle that likely had been the instructor's refuge of quiet when the typing school was going full blast. Rab joined us in there, saying brightly, "I have a question for you gentle-men of the press. What's the name of the newspaper?"

Seeing the three of us were stumped, she declared: "I thought so. Let's think. What about" — I could practically hear her mind whirring as if she were trying out an idea on backward pupils — "the *Plain Truth?* That's been in short supply in Butte newspapering."

Jared rubbed his jaw. "It's nice, Rab, but I like something that sounds a little tougher, like maybe the *Sentinel?*"

"That'd do in a pinch," Armbrister said with a grain of editor-to-publisher deference, "but we want something with some real kick to it." He started reeling off feisty possibilities — the *Spark, Liberator,* the *Free Press.* Then, almost bashfully, he confessed: "I've always wanted to have a masthead in type big as what they use on Wanted posters that just goddamn outright says *Disturber of the Peace.*"

"No, no," I exclaimed, the thought ascending so swiftly in me I was light-headed, "it must be something that carries the sound of promise, that resonates across the land, that dramatically bespeaks the coming clash with Anaconda." The two men were set back on their heels, while Rab gleefully watched me balloon off into the upper atmosphere like old times. Passionately I invoked Shakespeare, the magically phrased passage in *A Midsummer Night's Dream* when Hippolyta, queen of the Amazons, with rhythmic zest recounts the great hunt with Hercules and the dragon slayer Cadmus, *"When in a wood* of Crete they bay'd the bear / With hounds of Sparta," concluding with the inimitable turn of phrase, *"I never heard / So musical a discord, such sweet thunder."*

Thus was the Butte *Thunder* born.

4

"So, Morgan, welcome to the den of lost souls," Armbrister initiated me into the ranks as the newsroom full of novitiates turned to their tasks the first frantic day of publication, each hunched over a desk or a typewriter or talking into a telephone. I had much to learn, such as calling the vital opening sentence of any newspaper article a lede to differentiate it in print from the soft metal, and slugging each page of copy, as that term was, with topic and page number in the upper right corner, and noting that a less than urgent writing assignment was referred to as AOT, meaning "any old time."

Besides such lessons learned on the run, simply being around Armbrister was a fast education in journalism, I was finding. The long-faced editor was gruff, salty, uncompromising; from the first minute, the staff idolized him. In the green world of inspiration beneath his eyeshade, he was constantly thinking up angles of coverage and fresh features to dress up the paper; that bald head in the center of the newsroom reflected the adage that grass doesn't grow on a busy street. He passed judgment on assignment suggestions with a swift "Amen" or just as decisive a "Nix" that sent a reporter off either to report or to rethink. Along with the bluer part of his vocabulary was the dreaded utterance that he needed such-and-such column inches pronto, or if a deadline really loomed, prontissimo. It quickly became ritual for the first staff member growled at a certain way to go around the room and warn the rest of us our editor was turning into Generalissimo Prontissimo. With the general air of purpose driven by Armbrister's personality and, yes, deadlines, the newsroom seemed on the point of vibration. And at press time, when the almighty machine in the back room began spinning out newspapers by the thousands, that actually proved to be the case; the thrum could be felt in the whole building, as if the news on the page were a wave of sound reverberating into the waiting world. *Thunder,* indeed.

But back there at the very start, any tremors were confined to those of us clustered around the editor's desk, as Armbrister, a hawk hovering in his element, scanned around relentlessly for assignments ready to be turned in. Jared, looking on with Rab proudly hooking arms with him and myself, kept tugging at his tie, dressed as he was in the sober new suit befitting a publisher and legislator. "Damn this collar," he ran a finger inside the neck of his duly starched shirt, "how do you put up with it, Professor?"

"Just remind yourself it's not copper," I said easily.

"Hear, hear!" said Rab. "Besides, this way you're all spiffed up to celebrate the new newspaper and the new year, both," she brought out a grin on her self-conscious spouse by straightening his tie back from where he had just adjusted it. "The senator here will be kicking his heels up at the union hall — the Serbs are going to show us all some dance they swear won't resemble a polka. What about you, Mr. Morgan — are you and Grace and Sam Sandison going out to paint the town red?"

"Our household is catching its breath tonight, Rab. Maybe a wink at the new year as it slips in, is all."

"Good riddance to the old one," Jared said somberly of the mineworkers' *annus horribilis* that had left Anaconda with the

73

upper hand, and Armbrister dourly added his amen to that. "You're going to have to get us off to a flying start," the editor gave me a certain kind of look from under his eyeshade, "so I hope you've exercised your brain about —" Just then the newsroom door banged open and the stutter of type-writers momentarily stilled.

Turning her head to see who it was, Rab showed surprise. "Did you ask him to show up? Today, of all?"

"Better to deal him in than not," Jared replied softly. "And he's a good reminder to us all what this is about. Look at that — it's like the coming of Saint Patrick, isn't it. Nobody can take their eyes off him."

I'd had my back turned to the man, and faced around to a strapping figure sweeping toward us in a rolling gait, lunch box swing-ing in his hand and the mark of the Hill on him in that slight lean as if stooping under a mine timber. Every shoulder within reach he batted as he progressed through the newsroom, dropping "That's the stuff!" and other plaudits along the way, companion-able yet commanding. Nearing us, his keen gaze fixed on me, he laughed and called out:

"Is it Morgan underneath all that? If whiskers could talk, you'd be Cicero, boyo."

I blinked. "Quin!" The unexpected sight

of him took me back, in both meanings. Pat Quinlan had been the life of the party at Dublin Gulch wakes, and I use that contradictory term advisedly, when I was forced to attend as the representative of the C. R. Peterson Modern Mortuary and Funeral Home. Memories of the bootleg rye that flowed from his pocket flask into me on those occasions washed away most of the rest of my doubts about becoming a newspaper employee, where drinking on the job was merely optional.

"I'd forgotten," Jared was saying to me as Quin's hard hand pumped mine, "you're already acquainted with our negotiator." My surprise redoubled. Beyond doubt, Pat Quinlan was surpassingly capable of giving Anaconda holy hell, and the other kind, too. However, he and Jared had not seen eye to eye on union matters in that other year of trouble, 1919. Quin was perhaps not quite the fieriest firebrand in the ranks of Butte labor, but never that far from flaming up, either. Enlisting him as the union's second-in-command surely was a gamble on Jared's part — shrewd, possibly, but a gamble nonetheless to have a rival so close.

"Morgan, my fellow, Jared tells me you're our editorial scribe." When he looked at a person the way he was eyeing me, Quin had a sort of dark gleam to him, his the so-called Armada complexion, consequence of ship-wrecked sailors blending their Spanish blood with the Irish many generations ago. "A man who's dynamite with words, have we. I like that." He clapped me on the shoulder.

I coughed. "I'm glad I pass muster with Dublin Gulch."

"We'll put you up for pope," he said airily. He glanced past Jared. "And our Barbara! You look like the Rose of Tralee amongst these bog trotters."

"Tsk, aren't you the gravel patch of the Blarney Stone," Rab absorbed the compliment in the spirit given.

Armbrister had been tolerating the disruption to his newsroom about as expected, which was to say barely. "Back to work, everyone," he bawled to the staff, then wheeled to Quin. "Come on over, you need to meet Cavaretta. He'll be covering union matters, such as the ongoing negotiations with Anaconda. They are ongoing, aren't they?"

"Like Niagara." As Quin strutted off in the company of the editor, Jared rolled his eyes and shadowed after them to tamp down whatever the dark prince of the bargaining table told the reporter.

Rab watched expressionlessly, no small feat for her. "The show-off," she whispered to me. "I can't stand him. I'm sorry, I just can't."

"Quin isn't to everyone's taste," I murmured back, "but as I understand it, Jared's strategy is that Anaconda chokes on him worse than the rest of us do."

"Oh, he's useful, in that way," she retorted, her lips barely moving like the skilled whisperer she had been in my classroom. "But I can't forgive him for how he behaved in the big strike. Jared would be trying to keep people from killing one another, and Quin would come around behind him, yelping about striking the blow against Anaconda." She shook her head. "There's always been a union faction at the Neversweat that's out for blood, and Quin's their man." Her whisper turned fierce. "They and the Wobblies drew blood, all right, on themselves when the goons started shooting."

"Hence, Jared taking the political route, instead of taking on Anaconda bare-handed as Quin is inclined to do?"

"Hence," Rab confirmed with a sly twist to the word.

Conversation with the reporter had ended with a grand backslap from Quin, and here came the three of them to us, Armbrister and Quin each checking the clock like a man in a hurry and Jared glancing down at the black lunch box conspicuous at Quin's side. "You're going on shift, you mean?"

" 'Course I am," said Quin as if surprised to be asked. "We don't trade out of shifts at the 'Sweat." He laid it on thicker yet. "It's bad luck, you know, if you don't work the last shift of the year in the same diggings where you did the first. Breaks the chain of fortune, it does."

Looking uncomfortable in a way that had nothing to do with neckwear, Jared said only, "Tap 'er light, Quin," miners' way of saying, So long and good luck, both.

Smiling devilishly, Quin set off on his promenade out of the newsroom, but whirled as if something had just struck him. "Morgan?" He made a fist. "Give them this."

"I shall do my best, Quin."

Watching him all the way out the door, Jared then turned to the case of imminent explosion at his side. "Don't start, Rab. He's a scamp and a scene stealer, we know that. The trick is to give him enough of a stage to keep him satisfied." All business now, he squared around to Armbrister and me. "We need to get out of your hair, you have work

78

to do." He grinned at me. "Thought up that pen name yet?"

"Just now. A *nom de plume* fitting to the promise of the *Thunder,* I think you'll agree. Pluvius."

Rab smothered a giggle, surely remembering the rain-catching instrument I introduced into the classroom when she was a schoolgirl, a pluviometer. The ostensible Latin god of downpour and freshet alike approximated my role as editorialist very well, in my estimation.

Jared puzzled that out for a moment, glancing at her for reassurance, then granted, "Your choice, I guess."

Meanwhile Armbrister was clouding up beneath his green eyeshade, as editors do when deadlines loom. "Let's never mind the fancy Latin and start producing some plain English. I need the editorial piece, dead pronto. You type, dare I hope?"

"Assiduously."

He pointed me to a vacant desk and typewriter in the corner next to his cubicle. The din of the newsroom did not bother me, because in my Butte Public Library phase I had grown accustomed to working in the same office with Sandison and his grunts and snorts and booted prowling of the room. I worked quickly.

A question comes with the new year and the next legislative session, soon to start. Why, do you suppose, is it that every bill proposed in the Montana legislature is always printed in four copies, instead of three, as in other states? Let's do the arithmetic, shall we? One for the House, one for the Senate, one for the governor, and that leaves —

Number four, which goes to the top floor of the Hennessy Building in Butte, headquarters of a certain copper company.

And what does that add up to?

Control of the legislative levers of power and until now, of the daily press of this state.

Oh, it will be said, it is merely a matter of custom and convenience for the largest employer in all of Montana to be kept abreast of pending bills and such. It has been convenient, all right, and customary, for that top-floor monopoly, though not for the rest of us.

No other company has been a worse neighbor than the one whose coils of power extend from Wall Street through that local aperture to the depths of the richest mineshafts on this continent and up again to the legislative chambers of Helena.

Does this mean there is nothing to be done, and the Treasure State is forever doomed to be squeezed this way?

Absolutely not. The remedy does exist, as shall be set forth in these columns in days to come, openly and freely. The black name that slithers down this page has gripped the newspapers of Montana for too long. The *Thunder* is here to speak common sense and justice. Mark it well; what you hold in your hands this moment is nothing less than a declaration of journalistic enterprise that refuses to be choked by the copper collar of the Anaconda Company.

— PLUVIUS

"I'd've said 'snake' somewhere in it."

"Me, too. Kind of people they are."

"Pretty much readable otherwise."

"Not too bad for a start, Morrie."

Griff and Hoop passed suppertime judgment on my editorial debut along with the potatoes and gravy and baked chicken until I had my fill in both respects. Grace had been so occupied with cooking and serving our New Year's Eve feast, to dignify it with that — I looked ahead to the day we could afford roast beef — she'd had time only to glance at the newspaper page and exclaim,

81

"Ooh, it looks as serious as a hymnal."
Sandison merely issued a series of grunts as
he read the copy of the *Thunder* folded open
to my words. But something told me he
wanted to see me alone after the meal.

I slipped into his tower cave of books as
Grace dealt with the dishes and my Welsh
critics hobbled off to their rooms. "And so?
Is my prose up to literary standards?"

The chair groaned under him — it had a
bad habit of that — as Sandison stroked his
beard and considered me. "It's too bad
there isn't a pill for foolhardiness."

"The cure might be worse than the ailment, Sandy," I mounted in self-defense. "I
admit spelling out 'Anaconda' that way may
have been a bit dramatic for a start, but
Jared Evans was happy with it and the newspaper staff honestly cheered. Sometimes a
chance must be taken, wouldn't you say?
Caesar at the Rubicon. George Washington
at the Delaware."

"Quixote at the windmill," he trumped
those without effort. Waving away my further protest, he conceded: "All right, all
right, you're determined to be a hornet up
Anaconda's nose —"

"Actually, I prefer the locution 'bee in the
bonnet' —"

"— but that doesn't mean you can sit

down to the typewriter and torment the company's highly paid thieves up there in the Hennessy Building that same way day after day and get away with it. You're going to have to be ready to be attacked in return, laddie. The *Post* isn't in business just to sell patent medicines and hernia belts."

I took his point. I had to. I'd given no thought to what came next. At such a time, thank heaven for the courage history lends. My gaze lifted to the erect spines ranked row upon proud row around the room. "If I may, Sandy, I would like to call on your friends for aid from time to time."

"Now you're showing a lick of sense. Help yourself." He swept a hand around the wall of books behind him, where I had to hope to find the right inspiration from the likes of Addison and Steele sharpening with *Tatler* wit the debates of England, Horace Greeley defending the Union with the verbal artillery of the *New York Tribune,* and, yes, Tom Paine, ever his own man but speaking for all in detestation of domination. The great typeset voices to bolster my own unfledged one.

The new year blew in with snow that whitened the night, our bedroom far from dark with the blue-silver reflection off the freshly

83

blanketed Hill and the whirling flakes. Sandison's wish for a blizzard to clean the town was being granted in full with the arrival of 1921.

Beside me, Grace raised her head from the pillow to sigh at the storm howling and scratching at the arched window. "Too bad. Someone always climbs to the top of the Muckaroo headframe and sets off whizbangs at midnight. Not tonight, they won't."

"The storm before the calm, perhaps."

She puffed lightly at me and my quip as if putting out a candle. "New Year's is no laughing matter, you. Where does the time go, answer me that." Restless as the weather, she sat up against the bed's headboard, ran her hands through her flowing hair, then hugged her knees as she gazed at the flurries smacking the window. "It seems only yesterday we were being married and going off to see the world, doesn't it?"

"No." I rolled over enough to kiss her elbow. "It seems like many perfect yesterdays ago spent in the best company since matrimony was invented."

"Flatterer." She looked down at me, the dimpled smile I so loved just visible in the pale night. "Are you pleased?"

"With life in general? I have you, I have house enough for several people, I have employment and a living wage, how can I not be pleased?"

"With yourself, I mean, Mr. Pluvius."

"Mmm, that." Assessing whether you are living up to your pen name — choosing one with the mystical properties of a Roman god sets a shamefully high mark — pits one side of you against the other, but try I did. "There too" — she could tell I meant the *Thunder* and its cause — "I feel I'm in the right company. If words can carry the day, as Jared Evans thinks they can, I am not short of words." I smiled up at her. "As you may have noticed."

She did not smile back. "I'd be the last one to doubt you can pluviate or whatever it is until the other party falls down dizzy. But I can't forget what my Arthur always used to say. Taking on Anaconda is like wrestling a carnival bear. You have to hope —"

"— its muzzle doesn't come off, yes, yes, I fully remember the saying." Along with Shakespeare's loftier one about so musical a discord when the bear was bay'd; that was not exactly the tune I was hearing in my debut as a newspaperman. First Sandison, and now my heartmate — I did not lack for concern about my well-being, at least. But if I couldn't sound reassuring on a feather

85

bed, I might as well trade in my tongue. "Grace, this is not like before, when I needed to watch my step every time I set foot outside. Anaconda wins when the battle is in the streets, no question. But a sparring match in newspaper columns is quite another matter, surely. The snakes, to borrow Hoop and Griff's term, would face prosecution if something befell me or any other of the newspaper staff, Jared has enough political power now to see to that. No, our bet is — forgive that figure of speech, my dear — the battle will be fought out on the page, where it can be won."

Still clutching her knees, Grace heard me out to the last word, the only sound for some moments the howling of the wind. Then she patted my hand in the feathery way I had come to know and count on, and gave me the kind of kiss that sealed one year and promised much for the next. "All right, Morrie. I have to hope you're right, don't I. Good night, you."

"Good night and happy new year, Mrs. Morgan."

"Lords and ladies of the press, gather 'round to have our fortune told," Armbrister called out the next day in the newsroom. The *Thunder* staff surrounded him, Jared and Rab and even Russian Famine thrown in, as the fingers-crossed editor opened a *Post* snatched from the earliest available newsboy. "Let's see what the bastards uptown think of us," he muttered. I held my breath, and I was not nearly the only one, as he scanned the rival editorial page for the response to my initial denunciation of Anaconda and its might. Then, it had to be seen to believed, an actual look of satisfaction came over him. "Hot damn, folks. We caught them with their pantaloons down. Listen to this."

Will they never learn, the inkslingers who crop up periodically to decry commercial success and general prosperity? A succession of so-called opposition newspapers have talked themselves to death in trying to pit labor and capital against each other, instead of celebrating the American way of wages and profits going hand in hand. This latest journal of misinformation, with a name that suggests it has its head in the clouds, we predict will shortly follow the others into oblivion.

Amid hoots and cries of derision at that, Armbrister humorously shook the paper as if to make any more invective fall out, and when none did, cast the *Post* into the nearest wastebasket.

During the celebratory commotion, Jared batted my shoulder as if slapping on a brevet of commendation and soundly told me, "Well done, Professor." I reciprocated by saying I could not have written what I did without his disclosure of the copper company's secret set of legislative proposals. He slipped me a glance not without political guile; he was learning fast. "We'll see what other surprises we can come up with," said he. During this, I became aware of an outbreak of restlessness down at my side. Bright-eyed, Russian Famine whispered up to me. "What's pantaloons?"

"Britches that are too big," I gladly defined our adversary as well as the item of apparel.

"But that's awful, what it said," Rab was bursting with indignation, whirling from Jared to me seeking outraged response to match her own. " 'Journal of misinformation,' phooey. 'Head in the clouds,' my foot. Mr. Morgan, why on earth are you looking like you've been paid a compliment?"

To try to settle her down, Jared called Armbrister over. "Jake, am I right that we won the first round because they were only shadowboxing?"

The green eyeshade bobbed. "That load of horse pucky in the *Post* is a fragrant example of the low journalistic art of Afghanistanism. Going as far afield from the topic as the map will allow." His expression took a saturnine turn. "The SOBs are afraid to even say 'legislature.' So we have to make them. Won't you, Morgan?"

And so I went to my typewriter and set off the newspaper war.

5

It is legend locally that President Theodore Roosevelt, in plain view at a window table in the Finlen Hotel, heartily ate a steak as the admiring citizenry of Butte looked on. Not so well remembered is what he wanted for dessert: hearts of monopolists, sauced with justice. It was the late, great Teddy who dubbed them, let us not forget, "malefactors of great wealth."

There is no wealth greater, in this city and state and far beyond, than that of the Anaconda Copper Mining Company. Nor is there a malefaction — mark it well: the word comes from Latin, *malus* meaning "bad, ill, evil" and *facere* meaning "to do" — more unjust than the grip of the copper colossus on the legislative process of the Treasure State.

An appetite for change, anyone?

Grace was even more right than she knew, in remarking that my calling had been found, or as I preferred to think of it, I had been searched out by a fitting profession at last. For I stepped forth from Horse Thief Row and down the sloping streets of Butte to the newspaper office each day with a hum in my heart and words flowing in my head. Oh, I was aware of the old bromide that an editorial writer does nothing more than observe from the high ground until the battle is over, then descend and shoot the wounded on both sides. But that was not the Butte fashion, not the *Thunder* style. I was proud that from the first inked copy off the press, I, or at least Pluvius, was in the thick of the crusade against the Anaconda Copper Mining Company and its despotic power over the mines and the city and the state. And if I could enlist the lately deceased trustbuster Teddy Roosevelt into the cause, so much the better.

Grace dramatically read my latest *Thunder* salvo to the suppertime audience, Hoop and Griff chewing along in agreement, while Sandison sat back in judgment.

Finished, she stretched to pass the newspaper back to me across the huge dining room table, where the five of us spent mealtimes like picnickers at a wharf. "That

91

should give them indigestion at Anaconda headquarters, if that's what you wanted."

"Well put, madam." Sandison turned to me. "Taunting doesn't get the job done in the end. When do you get down to brass tacks?" Hoop and Griff perked up their ears at the phrase.

"All in good time," I said with the air of invincibility fitting to an editorialist. "It is a matter of tactics."

How often does a name fit so perfectly it cannot be improved on? From the very start, the atmosphere around the *Thunder* held that tingle of anticipation that the air carries before a rain. The spell was contagious. With its aroma of ink and paper and cigarette smoke and its staccato blurts of writing machines and jingling of telephones, the newsroom was a strangely exciting place where nothing definitive seemed to be happening, yet everything was. A newspaper is a daily miracle, a collective collaboration of wildly different authors cramped into columns of print that somehow digest into the closest thing to truth about humankind's foibles and triumphs there is, i.e., the draft of history, and no day had yet come when I was not profoundly glad to do my part.

The staff, a high-spirited bunch, raucously

welcomed me into their number. In the newspaper world, you can be a boozehound, a Lothario, a grouch, a moocher, almost anything, and if you can sit up to the keys of a typewriter and play the English language as if on a grand piano, you are prized. So it was with me, none of the usual journalists' peccadilloes attached to my person, and my prose as quick as my fingers — Armbrister never had to hover over me near deadline — was abundantly acclaimed. Moreover, my reputation in the newsroom grew when there was confusion at the copy desk over Thomas Cromwell and Oliver Cromwell, and I rattled off the couplet that distinguished the ill-fated royal minister from the later Lord Protector: *Tommy bowed before the king and lost his head / Ollie stood tall and the king lost his instead.* One of the old hands working the rim cackled and called out, "What are you, a walking encyclopedia?" As a brand-new journalistic enterprise the *Thunder* lacked a morgue, a newspaper's library, and after that I was often called on to fill in. Routinely an outcry from somewhere in the newsroom would be heard, such as "Quick, Morrie, who was the inventor of the guillotine?" and I would furnish the answer. Some wag soon modified Morrie to Morgie, a conflation of name and role that I rather liked, and I felt thoroughly established in the fellowship of the press.

Meanwhile, it was up to Pluvius, among my wardrobe of names, to wage battle with the *Post* and by implication its puppet masters high atop Butte and loftier yet on Wall Street. My editorial-page opposite number went under the inane *nom de plume* of Scriptoris. The fool; he was self-evidently a writer, or at least a typist. Why waste the Latin? That aside, the journalistic exchange of insults was something like the stutter step when you meet someone in your path and each moves in front of the other.

The *Post:*

That organ of propaganda trying to pass as a newspaper seems not to know even the basics of the mining industry, that smelter smoke is the smell of money.

The *Thunder:*

Also of lung disease, the leading cause of death among miners and their families.

The *Post:*

The latest diatribe from that ill-named

broadsheet down by the district of ill fame disputes the right of the largest employer in the state to make itself known in the halls of the legislature. We ask you, what is wrong with proper representation of management and capital in civic debates?

The *Thunder:*

Representation is one thing, colonial domination is another. Anaconda has made Montana the Congo of America.

Yet, in this gloves-off fight, part of the foe was always out of reach. A villain is supposed to have an identifiable face, the more prominent the wicked features, the better the target. Against this classic rule, the Anaconda Copper Mining Company wore the most impassive mask in America: that of Wall Street. Oh, there were names, fearsome ones — the Rockefellers and Henry Rogerses of the dragon's nest of all monopolies, Standard Oil — attached to its corporate ownership, but those kept their distance from Butte and bloody deeds in the streets; and their hirelings, while notorious enough locally, comprised a shifting cast of characters there in the loft of the Hennessy Building. "Quin and I agree on that much — you never quite know who you're dealing with, they 'come and go like shadows," Jared spoke from experience in round after round at the bargaining table over wages and safety conditions in the mines, negotiations that seemed to have no end. The only thing to be counted on was that up on that top floor, men in celluloid collars worked to keep the copper collar tight on the workers of the mines and the rest of society that constituted Montana as well. Faceless as it was heartless, Anaconda to all appearances could be attacked only by barrage, as the *Thunder* was doing, yet any thinking person pined for the one sure blow that would bring a giant down.

"You're doing your part like a real fighter," Jared applauded my free-swinging editorial style. "Just what we need." He now had to divide himself between the ongoing Butte struggle and the legislative session under way in Helena, and the double effort showed on him. His dark, deep Welsh eyes seemed to hold more than ever, calculations on two fronts active behind his gaze when he came by the newsroom to confer with Armbrister and me.

"Unlike Ulcer Gulch, it at least sounds like something is getting done around here," he ruefully contrasted legislative life with the contrapuntal rhythms of typewriters and telephones around the trio of us in session at the editor's desk. Three and a variable fraction, actually, as he had Russian Famine along, fresh from selling the *Thunder* on the street as the newest of our newsboys, while Rab attended to some after-hours task at the detention school. The lad was in motion even standing still, wiping his nose with the back of his hand, taking his cap off and putting it back on, restlessness accentuated by indoor confinement. Absently stopping him from playing with the spindle where Armbrister spiked the overset, stories waiting to be used, Jared thought out loud to the other two of us.

"It's pretty much as we figured, a lot of legislators don't move a muscle without orders from the top floor of the Hennessy Building. But you'd be surprised how many don't like it that way. I get the feeling there are quite a few, maybe enough to do us some real good, who'd turn their back on Anaconda if they thought they could get away with it." His quickness of thought always surprised me. "What's the Latin for that, do you suppose, Professor?"

"Mmm, perhaps most aptly, *Ad rei publicae rationes aliquid referre.* To consider a thing from the political point of view."

"To be scared to death of a kick in the

slats from the voters," Armbrister translated more aptly yet. "But how do we get them panicked enough in Ulcer Gulch to ditch Anaconda?"

"That's the trick entirely," Jared granted. "We'll need to come up with something that'll do it, later in the session, when I learn the ropes a little more." Uncomfortably realizing how much he was sounding like a politician, he made a face. "Some of the old bulls in the cloakroom gave me the wink on how to get anything done in Ulcer Gulch, which is to take it easy, take my time. Save anything big for my maiden speech, is what it amounts to. Oh, I know" — he raised his hands against Armbrister and me reacting as newspapermen were bound to at any letup whatsoever in the campaign against Anaconda — "it's going to be hard for all of us, holding our fire." His face took on the rigid set of a combatant who had learned that in the trenches of the western front. "The waiting is always the worst part." Then he was back from the past, taking the edge off with what could pass for a grin. "In the meantime I have to watch out for what happens to maidens, don't I."

Russian Famine worked on that while the others of us laughed in manly fashion, then Jared sobered into his publisher's role.

"Don't get me wrong, the *Thunder* and the Professor's editorials read like Holy Writ to me, but I wonder if we're getting across to people, or is that going to take until Judgment Day, too?" He jerked his head toward the Gibraltar always to be conquered, the Hill. "I made the rounds through the tunnels at chow time, and I hate to say so, but more men had their noses into the funnies than the editorial page."

I winced at that, but Armbrister merely lifted his hawklike shoulders. "That's what we're up against in this business. Morgie can write in purple and gold and still not get them away from Krazy Kat."

Truer words were never heard, according to Famine's rapid nods. "Krazy's my favorite," he piped up in a voice as thin as the rest of him. "Boy, Ignatz Mouse really knows how to throw a brick, and Offissa Pupp always after him, that's good stuff. I even read the funnies some in school," he confided to us in man-to-man fashion, "if Mrs. Evans don't catch me." Armbrister's sardonic expression said, *There, see?*

The boy's testimonial made me think. "Perhaps what's lacking is some compelling entertainment of our own." I asked Armbrister, "Those small items that fill in the bottom of a page — what are they called?"

"Fillers."

"Exactly, those. Just suppose we were to use that space instead for brief submissions from the miners in their native languages. Say, oh, Finnish one time and Italian the next and on down the line, day by day. Jokes, sayings, bits of song. Perhaps call it 'Voices from the Hill.' It might draw their eyes to the editorial page."

Jared turned to Armbrister. "Jacob, what do you think?"

What the editor thought could be read in his grimace. "It'd be a hell of a headache to deal with in the page makeup. But you're the publisher."

"I guess I am. We'll give it a try." Jared already was half laughing. "Any contributors close to home you happen to have in mind, Professor, just for instance?"

And so we entered the period of what I think of as the skirmishing before the decisive battle, daily editorial blasts of whatever caliber I and my opposite number at the *Post* could come up with, heavy artillery yet to be brought to bear. In the set of reflections where a person reads his or her life, I would not have traded that experience for anything, nor, as it turned out, would anything have persuaded me to

100

repeat it ever again.

The home front, so to speak, was seldom quiet during this. It is scarcely fair to say the Sandison mansion was a white elephant. More like a woolly mammoth, hard to know where to attack. Palatial to live in, mostly — the music room with its *Mikado* wallpaper aside — the spacious residence simply demanded this, that, and the other be done to it, upkeep without end. The furnace tended to balk, the plumbing to gulp. A stair tread somehow would work loose in the night, necessitating a storm of hammering by Griff and Hoop the next morning. The rain gutter over the front stoop sagged in a V under the weight of icicles, daggers of ice as if to challenge Ajax. The ladder work it took the pair of them to repair it practically constituted mountaineering. Grace indubitably had a point about the manse needing them. The best I could furnish was support of another sort, that countenance of a natural-born home owner, even if the snail analogy did keep creeping up on me.

Accordingly, the day I came in after work and saw that the dining room table was not yet set, I made myself hum with apparent unconcern while I went to the kitchen to investigate.

Grace was so engrossed in the volume

open before her on the meat block, she didn't hear me enter the room. Assuming she was looking up a recipe, I cheerily called out, "Hello, chief cook and bottle washer. What's for supper?"

Her head snapped up as though I had broken a hypnotic spell. "Nothing, yet," she moaned, casting a frantic look across the kitchen at the clock. "The time got away from me." She gestured helplessly at the open pages. "Oh, Morrie, it's those books of his. I was just curious about what you and His Nibs see in them all the time, so I took one down to read a little. And now I can't stop."

I edged near enough to peek at the prose. Dickens. I might have known. "My dear, let's trust that David Copperfield will prove to be the hero of his own life, at least long enough for us to put some food on the table, all right?" So saying, I traded my habitual daily complement of newspapers for an apron. "I'll whip up some ham omelets and scalloped potatoes, how's that sound?"

"Music to the ears." Bustling toward the larder, she gave me a grateful peck on the cheek in passing. "What would I do without you, Mr. Morgan? Here, I can at least peel the spuds."

We busied ourselves at the meal preparation, side by side. As the potato peelings flew, Grace regained herself. "Morrie? Now I have to ask you about some reading of your own. That paper." She pointed the paring knife at the tabloid of shouting headlines that lay atop the comparatively quiet *Thunder*. "I didn't say anything during baseball, when you tracked down the *Sporting Whatsis* even in London. Or football, when you would snatch up a copy as soon as we got off a boat or train. But this time of year? Please tell me you're not doing something like betting on racing or" — she wrinkled her nose — "boxing."

"No, no, worry not." I hastened to justify the *Sporting News*. "Basketball, the winter sport. See there, the University of Chicago overwhelmed Northwestern, thirty-four to twenty-six. As a loyal alumnus, I am true blue to the Maroons, in a manner of speaking. I always follow their sporting exploits."

Which was true as far as it went. The fuller explanation, which I was determined to spare her, was that I was keeping a careful watch on the aftermath of the Black Sox scandal. The ballplayers involved were getting the worst of it, banned from major league baseball, but so far the gamblers behind the fixed World Series were evading prosecution, not the outcome I devoutly wished for. If the fixers ever entirely escaped entanglement in the case, their criminal minds might well turn to the fortune lost to some mysterious bettor in the Montana hinterlands, the kind of curiosity I could not afford in more ways than one. That encounter in San Francisco showed that if Bailey could seek and find me, it was hardly beyond the capability of the Chicago gambling mob. My hope had to be that the gangsters were kept busy staying one jump ahead of the investigating authorities long enough for the so-called autumn classic of 1919 to fade into the history books. Time was on my side, at least.

Innocent of such concern, Grace paused in her peeling to tug mischievously at my apron strings. "You men and your games."

With Griff and Hoop proclaiming, "Best meal in ages, Mrs. Morgan," and Grace keeping a rueful silence, Sandison surprised us all by not grunting a good-night as usual when the last bite was done and going off to his lair of books. "Here, madam." He thrust a squarish envelope across the table to Grace. "Morgan can read over your shoulder." He tendered a similar envelope to the other side of the table. "You two can share one, surely." Hoop opened it and Griff leaned over to read.

YOU ARE CORDIALLY INVITED TO THE
ANNUAL ROBERT BURNS BIRTHDAY
AND COSTUME PARTY
JANUARY 25, 8 P.M.–MIDNIGHT
BUTTE PUBLIC LIBRARY

"Sandy," I exclaimed, "I had no idea you are an aficionado of the Ploughman Poet."

"His rhymes are all right if you like wee this and bonny that," Sandison allowed. "But the main thing is his birthday comes at the time winter is driving people crazy. The library has been throwing this party for years. It was — it was Dora's idea."

"And what a nice one," Grace warmly endorsed the notion of a Scottish extravaganza in the Constantinople of the Rockies, even if there were a few more wintry weeks to endure to get to it. "Thank you ever so much for the invitation, Samuel. We'll be there in full regalia, won't we, Morrie."

"Unquestionably."

"Eh, us, too."

"Righto. Wouldn't miss it for the world."

Sandison acknowledged our thanks with a slight bow, or at least his beard seemed to, and he hoisted himself off to his books. As

Grace cleared the table, I headed to the living room to finally peruse the *Sporting News.* However, Griff and Hoop had preceded me as far as the staircase.

"*Hsst.* Can we have a word with you?"

I looked up to two worried faces, ancient as Ajax in the gloaming of the stairwell, halfway to the top. "And that word is . . . ?"

One hemmed and the other hawed, combining into the protestation that they did not want to hurt Sandison's feelings, not the least little bit, understand, and I was beginning to before it came. "This Scotch party of his. Are we gonna have to wear them little dresses?"

"Kilts, you mean?" How mighty the temptation, to see the pair of them, bowlegged as barrel staves, stumping through the social evening in drafty Highland tartans. Somehow I resisted and told them they might well costume themselves as, say, shepherds instead.

After making absolutely sure that sheepherders wore pants even in Scotland, the two of them retired to their rooms and I set out for the living room again. Passing the door to Sandison's library tower, though, on impulse I stopped and knocked.

"Come in, it's on hinges."

Seated at his desk as if moored there, he

106

glanced up from what was evidently the latest treasure, still nested in its wrappings. "Ever seen this?"

Even closed, *Oeuvres Complètes de Buffon* was a true work of art, the leather spine elegance itself and the marbled cover aswirl with blues beyond blue. "Paris, 1885," Sandison said clerically. "Go ahead, have a look." Inside, the steel engravings of Buffon's beasts and birds were the most vivid menagerie imaginable. It is a trick only the finest illustrators can pull off, a bit of egg white mixed into the hand coloring to give sheen and add life. Holding my breath, I turned the folio pages to the peacock. The colors practically preened off the page, so vivid were they.

"Exquisite, Sandy." I thought again what an achievement a book is, a magic box simultaneously holding the presence of the author and the wonders of the world. Ever so carefully I shut the dazzling volume. "A marvelous find." My curiosity couldn't be held in. "Will it live here" — I meant the shelves stocked with his personal favorites, which ran to hundreds and hundreds of everything from fiction to phenomenology — "or downtown?" — meaning the public library.

"Haven't quite decided." He patted the

gorgeous cover and chortled into his beard. "It would make the dimwit trustees sit up and take notice, wouldn't it, to have this in the collection. The only copy west of Chicago." Without looking up at me, he asked, "What's on your mind besides your hat? You didn't pop in here to see if I have *Mother Goose Rhymes* for bedtime reading."

"It caught my attention during supper the other night that the mention of Teddy Roosevelt drew a bit of reaction from you." He had harrumphed like a bullfrog. "I wondered why."

"Of course it set me off, nincompoop. Knew him in the line of business, didn't I."

"What, politics? Sandy! Are you a secret Bull Mooser, you're telling me?"

"Hell no, before any of that nonsense of him trying to be president every time there was an election." Sandison gazed off into the distance of the past. "Teddy was a rancher out here for about as long as it takes to tell it. Had a herd of cattle, over in the Dakotas. One bad winter was all he could take, and he scooted back east to something simpler, like policing New York or conquering Cuba." I waited. Sandison sighed, taking his voice down with it. "Yes, ninny, he was in the cattlemen's association with me, at the time we had to deal with rustlers.

108

Good citizen Theodore lucked out and didn't get known as Roosevelt the Rope Fiend — his cowboys weren't as quick at stringing up cow thieves as mine."

How the strands of fate twine mysterious ways. One man is snared in the reputation of a vigilante, and another dangles free and becomes president. It would take more than leather-bound volumes of phenomenology to contain the workings of chance. Such thoughts were interrupted by the next rumble from Sandison. "You were smarter than you knew, using him in that editorial." That is not a comment I too often get, and I cocked an eyebrow for him to continue.

"He's popular as hotcakes in the great state of Montana, from being out here in boots and spurs," Sandison obliged gruffly. "You'd think he was a top hand with cattle, when he hardly knew which end the grass goes in." He laughed, none too humorously. "How you do it, Morgan, I don't know, but sometimes you plunge in blind and come out walking on water. The Galilee shortcut, ay?"

"It is not a talent I set out to attain, actually."

"It could be worse, you could have a knack for the accordion." He fingered the Buffon bestiary again. "That educate you enough for one night?"

"Amply as always, Sandy."

"By the way, the sliding door in the drawing room is stuck half-shut."

"Righto," I sighed.

Frowning so hard his green eyeshade was practically a beak, Armbrister summoned me into his office on an otherwise ordinary day of editorial mudslinging. "You seen this?" He brandished a galley of overset at me. When I took the freshly inked strip of proof sheet and held it up for a look, the spatters of consonants told me this could only be Griff's contribution to "Voices of the Hill." Armbrister meanwhile ranted that it "practically drove Sully cross-eyed setting it." The compositor Sullivan who had delivered the item from the pressroom did look somewhat woozy on his way out. "What the blazes does it say, anyway?"

"Oh, a joke of some sort, I imagine. I told Griff to keep the item short and light."

Armbrister nibbled his lip. "All those *ff*s, I don't like the looks of it. What if it's a dirty joke?"

"In *Welsh*?"

"Well, not that, then. Code of some kind to the Wobblies? Or something libelous about Anaconda? Those two old hoodoos aren't exactly the souls of moderation."

There he had a point. Now I was nibbling my lip. "We must trust Griff."

"That's not good enough. I'm not slapping something in the paper I can't read a syllable of."

"Jacob, really, it's not intended for us, it's for those miners whose souls still yearn for the sounds of the green valleys and gentle streams of Wales."

"It's still Greeker than goddamn Greek to me and I'm the editor."

"Jake," I tried, "you're being overly suspicious." He merely strummed his suspenders, waiting me out. "You win," I conceded. "I shall take responsibility if anything goes wrong with it."

"All right, we'll run the thing." Calling for a copyboy, the editor gave me a last speculative glance. "You're adventurous, Morgie. That probably has double *f*s and *l*s in it in Welsh."

After that, Griff was greeted on the street for days by fellow Welshmen who would repeat what sounded like a series of gargles and practically fall over laughing. Griff's manner around the manse suggested authorship came naturally to the chosen, and he airily told me anytime the *Thunder* needed another contribution of the language of heaven, to just let him know. At first Hoop grinned along in the reflected glory, but something came over him during this time, I couldn't help but notice. He was saying little at meals and bolting off to his room as soon as possible, and his mind often seemed elsewhere as Griff and he tackled the house's latest ailment.

Finally came the morning when he caught me alone as I was about to leave for work, and hoarsely whispered, "Morrie, got a minute? There's something I need to talk to you about awful bad."

As he took me aside in the back hallway, I braced for the nature of the awful bad. Had I sundered his and Griff's long-standing friendship with my bright idea about funny fillers? Was the something medical, old miners' ramshackle bodies being what they were? Possibly the ailing house itself?

Worry etched in his face, Hoop looked deep into mine and husked:

"Do Huck and Jim make it?"

I blinked that in. "Both of them, I mean," he went on anxiously. "Because if they catch that Jim and do to him —"

"Hoop, you've been reading, haven't you."

"A person can't help it in this place." He gestured helplessly. "Every time you turn

112

around, there's books fit for a king. Pick one up just for a look, and next thing you know, you can't quit." Indeed, there were fatigue marks under his eyes testifying to late nights in the company of open pages. "Griff's got his nose in Kipling poems. Probably safer." He looked at me fretfully. "If the two of them don't get to New Orleans on that raft —"

I laid a hand on the bowed shoulder. "Rest assured, Mark Twain will not let you down."

With the Robert Burns Birthday and Costume Party creeping up on us, Grace pondered what to wear. "Remember Edinburgh? Those plaids. I wish I had that shawl." She paused to size me up like a draper. "And that Harris Tweed blazer you bought on Princes Street. You looked like the laird o' the castle in it."

We both knew where those items of apparel had vanished to. "Say no more," I gave in to the inevitable. "I'll go by the depot after work and see if by some miracle our trunk has appeared."

But nothing that miraculous was produced, the depot agent merely reciting yet again that the lost would be found sooner or later. Given that my own trunk had been missing for practically an eon, that was less than reassuring.

It did not help my disgusted mood that the warehouse district down by the railroad tracks was a snowy mess, and to save my London shoes as I headed back uptown I picked my way along a different street than I had come, past a run-down warehouse where a truck with GOLDEN EGGS POULTRY FARMS on its side was parked out front. I was just passing when I was overcome with the uncomfortable feeling of being watched.

I checked around. Peering at me from the deepest recess of the warehouse doorway was a thickset figure with a face that advertised trouble. Old fear freshly flooded through me. A window man, even where there were no windows? Bundled up in overcoat and gloves as I was, I couldn't reach to an inside pocket for my brass knuckles before he was on me like a springing tiger.

"Boss!" he yelped, grabbing my elbow. "We wasn't expecting you! We heard you'd be in Great Falls about now, fixing the trouble with that speakeasy that got raided. Man oh man, you move fast."

"You are —" I attempted to tell him he was wholly mistaken as to my identity but he cut me off with: "Smitty." He winked. "I know we ain't supposed to know each

114

other's real names, not even yours. But I never got to shake your hand at the big meeting back when Prohibition came in like Christmas all year long, and I been dying to ever since." My hand was swallowed in his. "Boss, was you ever smart! This is the best racket ever." It did not sound as if he meant poultry products.

My confidant stepped back in admiration. "What a slick disguise, dressing up in fancy threads. You look like one of them Vienna professors." With my overcoat collar turned up and winter felt hat pulled down, the beard no doubt was my most prominent feature, not helping any in convincing this enthusiast that any resemblance he saw in me was coincidental. Finding my voice, I tried: "Really, I'm not —"

The engine roar of an automobile navigating the snowy street toward us at startling speed drowned me out. Smitty's broad face registered alarm. Yanking a pistol from a coat pocket, he cried, "Watch out!" Before I could react, he bowled me over, tumbling us both into the snowbank near the Golden Eggs truck, him on top.

His action came barely in the nick of time, as a gunshot blasted over our heads and lead splattered against the brick wall of the warehouse. Gunfire gets your attention like nothing else. I held an aversion to guns. In my estimation, sooner or later they tend to go off, and I did not regard myself as bulletproof. Someone — who? — had just tested that out.

In the shock of it all I went inert as a mummy, but Smitty fortunately did not. Rolling off me where I was squashed into the snow, he swiftly was up and firing back at the vehicle speeding away.

"A shotgun, the dumb clucks," he jeered as the car disappeared around a corner, "what'd they think, they're hunting ducks? Everybody knows you can't reload a double-barreled real quick." Pulling me to my feet, he alternately wiped snow off my overcoat with the barrel of his gun and kept watch around the fender of the truck. "Amachoors. It's that Helena gang. Don't worry," he risked stepping far enough into the street to retrieve my satchel for me, "we'll hijack a couple of their loads on the Bozeman run. That'll make them think twice about stunts like this."

With gunfire still echoing in my ears, I numbly started to ask about the police. Smitty didn't let me get past the word. "Nahh. Cops don't come nosing around here. If they do, we'll tell them we was shooting snowshoe rabbits." He had me by the elbow again. "Come on in, quick, in case those dummies double back."

That sounded prudent. But as soon as he bustled me into the huge warehouse, I regretted it with a nearly audible gulp. From behind file cabinets and desks and every other piece of furniture, a dozen or more men peeked in our direction, holding pistols like Smitty's.

"Put away your artillery, boys," he called out jovially. "Everything's hunky-dory now, the Highliner is here."

Instantly there was a swell of cries of "Yeah, hi, boss, great to see you!"

By now I realized I was in a precarious situation; the only question was, how deep. The picture before me was becoming all too clear. In back of the desks and filing cabinets, nearly filling the rest of the warehouse, stood a sleekly painted fleet of delivery vans, the majority with Golden Eggs blazoned on the sides, others with Treasure State Pork or some such. However, what they were delivering, I could tell at a glance, was not the product of hen and pig, but stacks and stacks of boxes labeled SUPERIOR RYE — CANADA'S TRADITIONAL WHISKEY.

"Them Helena jaspers," Smitty was holding forth to an appreciative audience about our ambush escape, "they couldn't hit the broad side of a barn. You shoulda seen the boss when they jumped us — he never said a word. Cool as ice."

Frozen with fear was the more accurate description, a condition not allayed by facing a gang of gun-toting bootleggers who had mistaken me for their mastermind. This did not seem the right moment to set that straight. Ringed around me like admirers at a banquet, the whole assemblage awaited my words expectantly.

"How's" — my voice sounded high as a choirboy's. I cleared my throat and made a face. "Butte air." They all laughed knowingly. "How's business?"

There was a chorus of "Terrific!" "Great!" "Out of this world!" Then, though, a mustached individual, otherwise a bulky replica of Smitty, stepped forward with a worried frown. "Boss, I hate to tell you this when everything is running so slick, but we got a problem, up at the border."

I cocked my head inquisitively, and he rushed out the news that the crossing point at Sweetgrass had been shut tight by federal alcohol agents. "They're even inspecting carloads of nuns," my mustached informant complained. By now I was putting two and two together and realizing that the Highliner, whoever he was, must be the authority on that northernmost "high" stretch of Montana, where the boundary line with Canada extended for hundreds of miles but roads were few.

A hush of expectancy settled over the assemblage as my solution — that of the evidently all-wise Highliner — to the border-crossing problem was awaited. Looking around the office section of the warehouse as casually as my nerves would allow, I spotted a roll-down map, such as had been in my Marias Coulee schoolroom. Stepping over to it, I yanked it down with a flourish, desperately hoping it was not a Mercator of the entire world.

I was in luck: the long-nosed profile of the state of Montana displayed itself. Still not saying a word, I studied the map. The Sweetgrass portal was like the lip of a funnel from Canada to main roads on the American side, which no doubt was why it had drawn the attention of the government agents. Off westward from there was what looked like wild country with no sign of habitation or roads. The old advice "Go west" had not failed me yet. As if back in a classroom, I seized the nearest item of any length lying around to use as a pointer, which happened to be a sawed-off shotgun. Mutely and gingerly, I held it by the grip and planted the end of the barrel at random on an obscure spot along the western reach of the Canadian border.

The bootleggers flocked around the map like crows at a picnic basket.

I waited tensely as they peered at the geography in studious silence until suddenly one of them broke out excitedly: "I know that neck of the woods, I'm from up toward there! The boss is right, there's an old Indian trail through a gap in them benchlands up there. I bet it would take trucks!"

I nodded wisely, resisting an urge to wink lest I overplay the role. "It's Whiskey Gap now," Smitty declared, rubbing his palms together in satisfaction. "Didn't I tell you the Highliner would have the answer?"

Very, very carefully putting down the sawed-off shotgun, I made a show of glancing at the wall clock as if pressed for time. But before I could make a move toward my departure, the mustached man was asking with urgency: "Boss, how'd that Great Falls mess come out? Did you get those cops that raided the speakeasy squared away?"

"We'll —" I had to think hard for the barnyard phrase — "teach them not to suck eggs."

Around the room a general nod of agreement indicated that took care of that, some-how.

Using the chance, I started to say it was time for me to take my leave, but reworked it in my head and brought out:

"I need to scram."

Smitty put up a protesting hand. "Boss? We know you send Mickey around at the end of the month for it, but you brung your satchel and all — don't you want the take? Save Mick the trip?" He gestured proudly. "We had a good holiday season. Everybody in Butte was busy hoisting drinks on New Year's — boy, was they ever. Show him the dough, Sammy."

I stood rooted, my dumbstruck expression mistaken for quizzical. The mustached thug went to the safe in the corner, knelt and spun the combination. When the safe clicked open, inside were stacked bundles and bundles of currency. Staring at the largesse, I was practically overcome with the memory of the munificent Black Sox bet. Here for the taking lay a similar fortune, sufficient to propel Grace and me back into the high life of the past year. A train tonight would put us and the bulging satchel in Seattle by this time tomorrow, and from there an ocean liner to Hawaii, Siam, Tasmania, any-where . . . It was so tempting it was paralyzing. Like me, the whole roomful gazed reverently at the pile of cash.

Trying to keep the strain out of my voice, I said one of the harder things I have ever uttered.

"Let it sit on the nest and hatch out some more."

An appreciative laugh rippled through the bootleggers. "You know best, boss," said the mustached one, tenderly closing the safe. "While you're here, you got any advice about how to keep the racket going so good?"

I stroked my beard as if in Viennese consultation. "Keep doing what you're doing." Leaving them with the simple wisdom of that, I rapped out, "Smitty?" He jumped like a puppet. "Walk me to the corner."

"You don't know who the Highliner is? Morrie, do you go around with your head under a bushel basket?" Across the table from me, Griff squinted as if trying to see if I was all there.

"Kind of a willie wisp," Hoop propounded about my evident double. "Shows up somewhere and, poof, he's gone."

"This still tells me nothing definitive about his identity," I pointed out.

Griff speedily took care of that. "He's the

number one bootlegger in the state. Most wanted man since Judas."

"Nobody knows who he is," Hoop anticipated my further question. "Drives the cops crazy."

"I imagine." Whatever his pedigree, the mastermind behind the fleet of egg trucks and similar innocuous delivery vehicles was resourceful. And to judge by that stack of cash in the safe, which still smarted to think about, highly successful. In any case, I felt fortunate to have dipped in and out of the Highliner's persona without undue harm, and to have learned not to set foot in the warehouse district again. One shotgun blast was plenty. Not wanting to alarm her, I had not told Grace, or for that matter any of the others, about that episode of mistaken identity, let alone the gunfire. But I could see wifely curiosity being aroused as she followed my exchange with our tablemates. "Why do you ask, Morrie?"

"Merely keeping current. Newspaperman's habit, you know."

"Prohibition," Sandison startled us all with a growl. "They might as well have tried to put a chastity belt on the entire country while they were at it. Pass the spuds."

For days after that, I jumped a little every

time an automobile backfired, but gradually my encounter with warring bootleggers began to fade. Memory shares some of the properties of dream, and as time passed, the episode softened into something like deep-of-the-night thoughts: Was that actually me, turning down a stack of money that barely fit into a safe? What bound me (and of course Grace) to Butte and its backstreet hostilities except a gift-horse mansion? Answer came none, as is so often the case with thoughts that appear in the night, and increasingly I had to put my mind to the field of battle across town, the *Thunder*'s hard-fought contest with our competitor.

Armbrister may have charged me with being venturesome in the matter of miners' fillers enlivening the editorial page, but as editor he showed a bold streak himself. Those of us in the newsroom learned to sit back like pewholders about to hear thunder from the pulpit whenever he would hold up crossed fingers and announce, "Lords and ladies, I have a hunch." From his years of servitude at the *Daily Post,* always referred to on our premises as the *Silly Boast,* he knew Butte inside and out, and so constantly tinkered with our journalistic offerings to entice readers away from our despised rival. One time the hunch, inspiration, mad notion purloined from somewhere might be a gossipy new feature called "Around the Lodges" — the city had fraternal organizations of every stripe and inclination — and the next, "The Homemaker's Helper," solicitously aimed at weary miners' housewives trying to keep a family fed and fit on the pay their husbands brought from the Hill. "Cranking up the hurdy-gurdy," he called such audience-pleasers.

Thus it was that I was manning my typewriter, firing editorial ammunition in the direction of the top floor of the Hennessy Building as usual, when the editor sauntered over, actually looking pleased about something.

"Guess what, Morgie, we're coming up in the world. We're going to start running the weekend stock exchange roundup." His harsh laugh. "We've got a source for it, let's say." He flourished the galley of companies and numbers set in practically flyspeck type. "I have a hunch it'll draw us readers with some actual bankrolls to their name," he said with relish. "Horse Thief Row types and such."

"Devoutly to be wished, I'm sure. May I?" I held up the galley, the better to scan it. "Anaconda, up three, too bad. Chicago,

Burlington and Quincy Railroad, down one, so on and so on," I skipped through. "Hmm, hmm, hmm, here it is." My thumb at the particular listing, I showed Armbrister. "Nelots, unchanged."

"Never heard of the company, but so what?"

"Envision that backwards, as the *Post* is counting on us not to."

His face drooped. " 'Stolen.' " He grabbed back the galley as if it might singe him. "Those tricky bastards. They almost made me fall for it."

"Nosce inimicum tuum," I counseled, "Know thy enemy," and went back to my typewriter to cannonade that foe some more.

Almost like a boxing match, that day held another round of parrying and punching. The presses had run, ours and the competition's, like twin but opposing engines in the daily race for readers, and the rival versions of news and opinion had been dispatched to the streets, to be hawked on every corner by newsboys as usual. Most of the staff had left for the day, except as ever the few nightside reporters and rewrite men, and I was putting on my coat and trying to settle down Armbrister as he shook his head over the latest piece of "Voices from the Hill" overset. From the ranks of the Irish, it ran:

My sweetheart's a mule in the mine,
I drive her with only one line.
On the ore car I sit,
While tobacco I spit,
All over my sweetheart's behind.

"For crying out loud, Morgie, do we have to put this in the paper?"

"Of course we must. Quin sent it in, can't you guess?" Armbrister looked even more pained. "Jacob, it actually serves the purpose quite well. In one regard, it is the very essence of Ireland, is it not?"

"This malarkey? How so?"

"It's a limerick."

The office door banging open ended that, as into the newsroom came Rab and Russian Famine, the one furious and the other downcast. "Hoodlums, that's what they are," Rab said through her teeth as she stormed over to Armbrister and me, "absolute hoodlums. Jared is in Helena or I'd have him find them and, and —" Dire enough punishment failed her. "Just look what they did to poor Famine."

He had a bloody lip. Worse, tear tracks down his cheeks. Worse yet, his newspaper

127

bag slung over one shoulder was torn and empty. "Got run off my corner," the words practically twitched out of the upset boy. "Couple of the Posties slugged me and threw my papers in the gutter. Same thing happened to Abe and Frankie."

And no doubt countless other *Thunder* newsboys, Armbrister and I understood with a glance at each other. "Isn't this swell," he uttered in a Job-like tone. "It leaves us with cigar stores and Blind Heinie's newsstand and not a hell of a lot else to get the word out." He threw his hands up. "Take me now, Jesus! Without newsies, we might as well be whistling down a gopher hole."

As the editor's lament raged on, Rab and I watched Famine test his split lip with his tongue.

After a little, I murmured to her, "Rab? I wonder —"

"Mr. Morgan," she purred in my ear, "are you thinking the same thing I am?"

The detention school amounted to a slightly prettified reformatory, the high brick wall surrounding it garnished with a few flower boxes, growing nothing but icicles this time of year. According to one of Rab's remarks, the soot-gray many-gabled residence on a shoulder of the Hill above Dublin Gulch had been a nunnery — a short journey for pious girls from the mine families, now a holding pen for troublous sons from those same shanties. As I topped the last street rise and left behind the world of downtown, the day was a rare one of winter clarity, the snow-held Rockies beyond the city limits dazzling in full sunshine, while the thirty or so mining operations in full swing along the Hill stood out in every detail of black steel headframe towers and bin cars loaded with peacock shades of copper ore and squat red-brick hoist houses throbbing and thrum-ming with cable work, the entire spectacle as if a gigantic factory had been thrown open for inspection.

The Richest Hill on Earth never ceased to thrill and chill me at the same time, with its powerful manufacturing of wealth and the squalid leavings of that, dump heaps like Sahara dunes and gaping bottomless pits called glory holes. And three times a day, the human equation came into stunning view as shifts changed and miners in their legions poured forth to and from neighbor-hoods gullied into the surroundings of machinery and dumps and pits. I am not subterranean by nature. Only once had I dared to go down in one of these mines, the forbidding Muckaroo on the crest of the Hill not far beyond the detention school, and it took every drop of courage in me to trek through a labyrinth of narrow, unforgiving tunnels. Yet beneath the ground I stood on, beneath all of Butte, around the clock three thousand men per shift drilled and blasted and shoveled in the most dangerous of circumstances to produce the metal that would wire the world for electricity. The old twofold question: What price progress, what cost if not?

With those thoughts in the back of my head, I rang at the iron front gate of what Russian Famine had aptly enough called the hoosegow school. But looking every inch the spirited schoolmistress rather than a jailer, Rab met me with a rush, lowering her voice conspiratorially as she hastened me into the building. "So far, we're in luck, Mr. Morgan. I've sweet-talked the superintendent into it. If the boys can get steady jobs that don't interfere with school, they can be let out for that period of time."

"A perfect fit. You haven't lost your wiles since you practiced them in my schoolroom, Rab."

"Such things as I learned from you," she acknowledged that trace of mischief with the right kind of grin, then turned seriously

130

to the matter at hand. "I chose the seventh grade for this. The eighth are one step short of desperadoes."

I smiled. "That hasn't changed either."

"Although I suppose I should warn you about even these." She paused with her hand on the knob of the classroom door. "If you remember Eddie Turley" — my poorest and most ill-fated student, son of a bullying fur trapper, in that Marias Coulee schoolroom — "I have loads of him for you." I assured her I was not expecting little gentlemen in velveteen.

Still, walking into that room was a step into bandit territory. Row on row, street toughs who looked hardened beyond their twelve and thirteen years — Rab had warned me they'd earned detention terms for fighting in class, petty theft, or chronic truancy, although some were simply from disrupted families that could no longer care for them — the lot of them were coldly eyeing me and my suit and vest. It was all I could do not to stare back. The youthful faces were sketch maps of Ireland, Italy, Cornwall, Wales, Finland, Serbia; early drafts of the mining countenances drawn from distant corners of the world by word of a hill made of copper. In the person of their immigrant fathers and mothers,

Butte's hard-won contribution to the American saga still went on, its next chapter these young lives ticketed, like those, to the mines.

"Mouths closed and eyes and ears open, everyone." Rab swished to the front of the classroom, brisk as a lion tamer. "Today we have with us someone schooled in so many fields of learning it would tire you out to hear them. Except to say I will make anyone who misbehaves regret it to the end of time, I'll let Mr. Morris Morgan tell you himself why he has come. Mr. Morgan, they're all yours," she demurely invited me up to the desk and blackboard, her eyes saying, *Have at them.*

That introduction did not impress the captive audience as much as might have been hoped. At desk after desk, young roughnecks slouched as if they had heard their fill from figures of authority, as they no doubt had. A fortunate exception, up front amid the obvious hellions, was a smaller, redheaded boy with the face of a Botticelli angel, watching as if he couldn't get enough of me. It wrung a person's heart to think of such a one cast out into the world; why someone had not put him in a pocket and taken him home, I couldn't fathom. Meanwhile at the far back sat Russian Famine, prudently away from sharp elbows and random clouts, looking restless but curious. Well, two such were better than none. I cleared my throat and set to work on the rest.

"Your instructor, Mrs. Evans" — off to one side Rab tried to look matronly, not at all successfully — "has invited me to offer this select group a chance for each of you to go into business for yourself."

"Huh, us? That's a good one," a long-shanked tough in the second row jeered. "Who do you want us to knock the blocks off of?"

I forced a chuckle. "I didn't say that, did I. What Mrs. Evans and I have in mind is for you to become individual merchants. With the freedom of the city, at hours that won't interrupt your, ah, education, in which to sell your merchandise."

"Sellin' what?" another sarcastic voice demanded. "Noodles to giraffes?"

"Nah, canary birds, cheap, cheap," yet another member of the unholy chorus was heard from. Retribution in her eye, Rab started for the nearest offender until I held up a hand to stop her. "The merchandise," I went on as if uninterrupted, "is the entirely honorable sort produced at the place where I myself work."

"Yeah? Where's that, then?"

"At a bastion of the Fourth Estate. At Butte's citadel of fair enterprise," I couldn't help getting a bit carried away. "At the pinnacle of journalistic endeavor, the *Thunder*."

In an instant the room rang with wild hoots. "You mean that rag down by Venus Alley? . . . Newsies! Beat that! He wants us to be newsies! . . . That don't sound like no way to get rich."

There was only one thing to do. Sighing, I took off my suit coat and rolled up my sleeves as if for a fight. Stepping closer to the blinking rank in the first row of desks, I singled out a chunky youth who had been one of the loudest hooters. Gazing at him so relentlessly his Adam's apple bobbed, I demanded to know: "What day of the week is this?"

"T'ursday, natcherly."

"What if I told you it had another name?"

"Uh, like what?"

I whirled to the blackboard and wrote in big letters THOR. "Thor's day. In the time of some of your great-great-great-grandfathers, that was the pronunciation."

"Yeah, so?" some skeptic called out. "Who's this ape Thor?"

I glanced around for some kind of implement. The window crank would have to do. Seizing it by the handle, I leaped onto the

134

teacher's desk and brandished the blunt instrument overhead so threateningly that the entire front row reared back in their seats with a sucked breath. "THE GOD OF THUNDER!" I roared. "That's who."

While I had the class's undivided attention, I stayed atop the desk and regaled them with the mighty reputation of Thor and his mountain-crushing hammer in the bloodiest of Viking myths. Rab had her hand over her mouth, eyes sparkling, and Russian Famine squirmed in excitement as I led the lesson around to thunder's inception from lightning. "What we hear as that hammer blow of sound is the air being disturbed by the bolt of electricity. And so," I concluded, still looking down at the pale sea of faces, "thunder comes of a troubled atmosphere. I hardly need to tell any of you that describes quite a lot of life here in Butte as well, hmm?"

While that hung in the air, I hopped down from the desk. "That's why the newspaper is rightly called the *Thunder,* and why I think I've come to the right place for its best possible newsboys."

"Yeah, but," the silence was broken by a high-pitched voice from the end of another row, "my brudda tried that wit' the *Post.* He always ended up wit' a pile of papers nobody'd buy."

"I promise that will not happen with the *Thunder,* which lives up to its word in fairness for the workers. We will buy back any of your unsold newspapers at half the street price," I improvised, with mental apologies to Jared and Armbrister, who would have to figure out the further economics of that. "You're guaranteed that much of a wage, while you're making profits from all the papers you sell."

"No hooey?" This came from the evident ringleader, who had spoken up at the very start. The others again let him speak for them all as he thought out loud, "There's still a catch. The Posties already got the good corners."

"Ah, but — every intersection has four corners."

My questioner persisted. "Then what if the Posties don't want us on any of 'em and gang up to run us off?"

"Streets are a public thoroughfare. You have as much right to be there as they do, if you take my meaning."

"Now you're talkin'." He gave me a sudden wink, and craftily translated for the roomful of waiting faces. "If they try to give any of us a bad time, we all pitch in and knock their blocks off."

136

"Yeah! You bet! That's the way!" acclamation resounded, and with that, Rab moved in, bearing a large map of the city so that the carriers of the *Thunder,* as they now were, could each pick out intersections to claim as their own.

Stepping away from the stampede of newly made newsboys, I wiped my brow and was putting my coat back on when I heard a small, worshipful voice somewhere around my elbow. "That was really something, mister." The cherubic one with the flaming hair was looking up at me with puppy eyes. "How you talked a streak like that."

Resisting the urge to pat him on the head, I warmly thanked him for the compliment and he skipped away as I waited to have a last word with Rab, still busy enforcing crowd control at the map. All of a sudden, I heard a commotion in the hall outside the room.

"Give 'em back."

"Lay off, Famine. Ow!"

"Give 'em back, I tell you." The scuffle escalated until I rushed out and found Russian Famine with the wildly kicking redheaded tyke wrapped in a choke hold.

"He's got something of yours," Famine panted as soon as he saw me, discharging the little kicker in my direction. "He was just gonna pony up, wasn't you, Punky."

"Uh, sure." The redheaded angel without wings shuffled toward me. "I found 'em just laying around." Still with a guileless expression, he dropped into my hand with a clink the set of brass knuckles ordinarily in my suit coat pocket.

As the little pickpocket left us with a beneficent shrug and as I was hurriedly checking for my wallet and watch, Famine moved close and, eyes shining, said confidentially, "I bet knuckies like that are just the ticket in a fight, huh?"

"They can be." I patted the side pocket where the knobbed brass items were safely restored. "But their greater use is in warding off fisticuffs. They serve as persuaders for the other fellow to think twice, shall we say."

He pursed in thought. "That ain't bad, either."

Glancing in at the melee of newly minted news merchants around Rab and the map, I lowered my voice. "Famine, it might be best if my little metal friends stayed just our secret, do you think? Some of your, mmm, classmates could gossip in the direction of the wrong ears if they knew about these, perhaps."

The boy's face squinched in wise agreement. "Yeah. You never know what's gonna happen in a hoosegow like this."

6

If life came with an instruction book, I had reached the chapter on taking stock of oneself without the help of a mirror. Looking at the larger picture, much seemed to have been lately set right in the world of me and mine. With the streets of Butte once again ringing with "Extra! Extra! Getcha *Thunder* here!" there was considerable to celebrate along with Robert Burns's nativity, really. Jared's bold newspaper venture was holding its own against almighty Anaconda, the manse had not fallen down on us, and I could see no lasting effects from my neck-saving impersonation of the Highliner. So let the grand day, or at least night, come, sang my heart.

A Scottish costume party might seem to be overdoing the obvious, merely a matter of showing up in customary garb ranging from those drafty kilts that so unnerved Griff and Hoop to the pulpit black of preachers thumping John Knox and the Covenanters back to life. But that overlooks the wardrobe potentialities in the pages of Sir Walter Scott and Robert Louis Stevenson and, for that matter, Burns himself. No sooner had I enlightened Grace as to the rural nature of much of his poetry than she chose to dress as a milkmaid, saucy bonnet and all. "If that doesn't put me in the spirit, I don't know what will." She looked doubtfully at me in my usual suit and vest and watch chain. "Morrie, excuse me all to the dickens for saying so, but you don't much resemble a Scotch version of a cowboy —"

"Cowherd."

"— who'd be a milkmaid's honey —"

"Swain."

"— see there, we're already running out of vocabulary. Why are you grinning like a hyena?"

I couldn't help it, because Sandison, bless him and his strange ways, was granting me a boyhood dream. From the time I was old enough to take a book in my lap and make sense of sentences, I had loved *Treasure Island.* Robert Louis Stevenson's ruffianly crew aboard the *Hispaniola* as it hoisted sail for the isle where a chest of gold lay "not yet lifted" captured my imagination, and here was my chance, tucked in me somewhere ever since discovering young Jim Hawkins in his classic adventure, to sign on as a sea dog. "I shall be a none too ancient mariner, my dear, knee breeches and all. How does that sound?"

"Overboard."

When the celebratory night arrived, however, she enthusiastically pitched in on my maritime getup, fussing over details as though she were a wardrobe mistress. "My, you do look piratical," she ultimately circled me in inspection. "Isn't the eye patch a nice touch?"

"If I could see better, I might think so."

She powdered my beard to make me appear appropriately grizzled, and one last flourish, clipped a hoop earring onto my earlobe. "There now, you're ready to sail the seven seas."

"I'll be content to navigate whatever Sandison's notion of a party is," I said in all honesty.

Having perfected me, Grace ducked to the dresser mirror for one last primp. I couldn't see that she needed it, her flaxen hair peeking fetchingly from under her ribboned bonnet, her firm figure doing full justice to a maidenly blouse and ankle-long skirt. She caught my watching reflection. "Now what's the grin about?"

"Merely thinking how well you fit the story of Robert Burns and the milkmaid."

"A Morrie story, is it," she turned to me quite coquettishly. "All right, I'm in for it, while you do something with this impossible bow, please."

Going to her, I began, "Our man Burns is strolling along a country lane, no doubt writing poetry in his head by the ream, when who should he meet, a full pail in each hand, but a pretty milkmaid." I tugged the bowstrings of Grace's bonnet and her with it closer than absolutely necessary for tying, and continued. "Naturally he stops and bows and greets her, but she scarcely even replies and keeps on her way. Great one with the girls that he was," I went on as my fingers flew with the bonnet strings and Grace listened with mock soberness, "this would not do, and he calls out after her, 'Lass, d'ye not ken who I am?' "

" 'Nay, sir,' she barely glances over her shoulder at him, 'ought I?' "

" 'I'm Rabbie Burns,' " I finished the bow, and the story, with a flourish. " 'Ay, well,' says she. 'In that case, I'd better put my pails doon.' "

Grace whooped at the tale, poking my chest with a provocative finger. "I knew there must be some way around crying over spilled milk."

Waiting for us at the bottom as we came giggling down the stairs were Griff and Hoop, attired as shepherds in rough clothes and sturdy boots. Not so different from their mining days, except for the tam-o'-shanters perched on their bald heads like tea cozies. Laughing like children playing dress-up, the four of us piled into a taxi where the driver barely glanced at us before setting out for the library.

Would you believe, the heavens sent the old romantic scamp of a poet a present on his birthday, a resplendent full moon, the night on a silver platter. Butte looked its best in the snowy dark, the lofty downtown buildings washed by the moonlight. Grace nudged me in the ribs — "Oh, look!" — as the taxi drew into view of the library itself, lit like a filigreed lantern, every window to the topmost in its Gothic tower an aperture of glow. "Doesn't it remind you of the Rhine? Those castles."

Up the broad steps we grandly went, arm in arm, bandannaed and bonneted, trailed by Griff and Hoop, wordless for once. Striding into the handsomely lit foyer, I had the uncanny sensation of returning to an earlier life, when Sandison for some reason known only to himself hired me as his assistant and the Butte Public Library became my abode. It was as if nothing had changed, the palatial proportions, the Tuscan red wainscoting, the ceiling panels of white and gold interset among the dark oaken beams, the all-seeing portrait of Shakespeare above the Reading Room doorway. Most regal of all, arrayed in ranks as if holding court on the mezzanine were the reds and greens and gilts of those books of Sandison's unmatched collection.

Knowing my helpless affection for this citadel of literature, Grace pinched my elbow and whispered, "Welcome back." But there was too much traffic in the royally decorated hallway for me to dawdle like a tourist. "Looky there, the mayor," Hoop was murmuring to Griff about a stout person-age attired, if I was not mistaken, like Sir Walter Scott's Ivanhoe. "Righto," Griff responded in kind, "and that pack of dea-cons or whatever coming through the door are them trustees Sandy's always grousing about." In short, all manner of costumed partygoers were pouring in, wigs and crino-lines and buckle shoes and tasseled shawls back in fashion, the crowd parting like water around a stationary massive figure, kilted and outfitted with sporran and dirk and a claymore broadsword in a decorated scab-

145

bard, a veritable statue of Highland legend. Except it was Sandison.

He let out a "Heh, heh" at the sight of us, Griff and Hoop chorusing in greeting, "Swell outfit." Pointing with his beard, he instructed us that the festivities were getting under way downstairs. "Enjoy yourselves," he ordered.

The tingle at being back in such familiar surroundings increased in me as we descended to the basement of the library, which was as snug a venue as could be found in a mile-high city with the temperature hovering near zero. The thick stone walls did away with noise from outside, and the curtained stage at one end of the long room nicely turned the space into an impromptu auditorium. In that earlier time, among the countless tasks Sandison tossed to me was juggling the calendar of organizations that met here in evenings, and while bunches such as the Ladies' and Gentlemen's Literary and Social Circle and Dora Sandison's Gilbert and Sullivan Libretto Study Group not infrequently had given me fits with their needs and foibles, I found myself thinking back on them with something like nostalgia. Parts of the past lend themselves to that while others —

"Isn't this a picture!" Grace's exclamation

did justice to the thronged scene we stepped into. Onstage, above the bewigged and bonneted heads of the multitude, was the Miners Band, magnificently embossed and brass-buttoned in their emerald green uniforms as they played a Burns air, "Ye Banks and Braes o' Bonnie Doon." People were clustered thick around the food table, where serving girls dished out oatcakes and scones. Griff and Hoop wisely migrated toward the punch bowl.

"Mr. Morgan, you only lack a peg leg and a parrot." Rab swooped on us from behind, Jared self-consciously following in the uniform of a lighthouse keeper, medallioned cap and all. She herself wore a startling blood-red gown, yards of it, which had Grace and me guessing until we hit upon ill-fated Mary, Queen of Scots.

"That leaves only our youngest member unaccounted for," I said, looking around for Russian Famine.

Rab pointed. "That's him over there, hopping like a jackrabbit."

Off to one side, a number of children were playing peever, an Edinburgh street game that was a cross between rosey toesy and hopscotch. Sure enough, when I squinted my seeing eye, the wraith in a soldier uniform complete with a soup plate helmet was adroitly hopping from one chalked square to the next while lightly kicking the flat-sided peever stone along. "It's one of Jared's old uniforms I cut down to fit him, he insisted so," Rab confided as if it were a family secret. "He absolutely worships this man of mine."

"He's at that age," Jared said soberly. I still watched the boy, remembering the nimbleness of that time of life. While Grace and Rab chatted, Jared accepted attention from constituents dropping by to urge him to give 'em hell in the senate, "them" needing no translation. In an interval, he grinned at me and shook his head. "It's a little different from when we had to hide out down here, wouldn't you say, Professor?" One of my prouder moments had been smuggling him and other union men into this basement time after time to come up with the miners' anthem that the labor movement had sorely needed at an earlier moment of suppression brought on by wartime hysteria. Music perhaps has no battalions, but it conquers worlds, too.

Just then the band struck up a dance tune — the schottische, of course — and Jared and I were practically swept off our feet by our eager wives. The evening galloped on that way for some time until a break in the music, and a chance to catch breath.

But as Grace and I adjourned from the dance floor, what wind I had left was nearly knocked out of me by a slap on the back. I turned around to the nearly coal-black face of Pat Quinlan. In old work clothes and a flat cap, he looked as though he had come straight from mucking out ore on the Hill, except the substance darkening him all the way to the eye sockets appeared really to be coal dust, not the usual grime that went with copper mining. "The Morgans!" he greeted us like the long lost. "Grace, you nabbed yourself a dilly with this one." He winked at me as the worthy successor to her Arthur, one of his mates in the mines.

She recovered from the greeting, but not quite from the sight of him. "Quin, what ever are you supposed to be? A one-man minstrel show?"

"Let me guess," I interposed. "A pitman."

"Right the first try, Morgan my man. Solidarity with our brothers in the coal pits, over there in the thistle patch."

"Very effective," Grace said, still looking at him as if she would like to scrub him down. "A dancing man, are you? I didn't know that."

Quinlan laughed, more or less. "It's Jared's doing, my being here, I'll warrant you. He'll primp me into respectability if it kills us both." He cast a look around at the crowd in its finery of make-believe. "Besides, I had to come to see how the other half lives, didn't I?" All too casually, his gaze returned to me. "That reminds me. Might I have a word with you about when the *Thunder* is ever going to be accompanied by lightning?"

Grace cocked her head as if she had heard a rumble, all right. "You'll find me at the punch bowl, Morrie."

As she left, Quinlan moved in to speak confidentially, arms folded on his chest as he again took in the laughing, talking, dancing celebrants in the great room. "What I was saying to Grace I meant, you know. How many of them have ever been down a mineshaft? Or even up on the Hill, to see the way we live, see what it's like on the hind tit of Anaconda?" He nudged me with his elbow. "You know Dublin Gulch." I did. The sprawl of streets right in amid dump heaps of the mines, shanties with laden clotheslines bucking in the gritty wind. For moments longer Quinlan stared out of his coal dust mask of a face at the other Butte gathered there, then expelled a deep breath. "That's just people, I suppose." Lowering his voice, he came to the point. "I don't mind telling you, the commotion about the copper collar you and Jared are kicking up in the newspaper is all well and good, but from where I sit, it's also slower than the wrath of God." Another wink from under the flat cap. "Tempus fidget, you know." Joke that was not a joke, as he went on: "I don't know how long I can bluff the company lackeys there in the Hennessy Building, in the bargaining. Oh, don't think I mind ranting on a bit and giving them this." He made that fist again. "It makes them squirm in those fine chairs of theirs polished by the seat of their tailored suits. I like that.

"Howsomever," another of those gusty breaths practically up from his toes, "the buggers are starting to push back, more every session. They were on good behavior, for them, for a while there after shooting us down at the gate of the 'Sweat." He laughed bitterly. "Even the so-called authorities, the sheriff and police and whatnot, thought that was a little much." He tapped my arm as if in warning. "But now the company has something up its sleeve, or my mother didn't name me Pat Quinlan. The snakes keep bringing up the dollar we won back in the last wage talks. So far, it's still just dickering, but if they see the chance, they'll take it away again, like that," he snapped his fingers.

Pausing, he looked at me, eye patch and eye, to make sure I saw where this was heading. "We'll have to take to the streets if that happens. Whatever Jared thinks, we'll have to. This time, tear the town down, if it comes to that, soldiers be damned." That came fiercely, then he settled back to merely darkly determined. "So, if you wonders at the *Thunder* are going to get any leverage on Anaconda, sooner is better."

"I see, I think."

"I figured you might. Well, don't let me ruin the party for you. The good woman is waiting for you at the punch bowl."

"Aren't you partaking?"

Not unexpectedly, he slapped a side pocket of his pitman's jacket. "When I want a nip, I carry my own. Tallyho, Morgan." He moved off toward the end of the room, where Griff and Hoop and other old-timers were carrying on. "I'll join the stag line. One thing about Butte, it has enough widows to keep life interesting."

"What's put the wind up him?" Grace wanted to know when I joined her.

"Quin's a man in a hurry. Perhaps for good reason."

"What did he want?"

"For me to hurry Jared along, against

Anaconda."

She pursed her lips in concern. "It doesn't have to be tonight, I hope."

"Lass, for you I'd postpone the end of the world," I gave her my best Burns imitation, and she smiled, dimple deep. Fortified with punch, we moved along to the victuals end of the table, where Sandison had stationed himself in tartan lordliness, knees as big as hams showing beneath his kilt.

"Samuel, you certainly know how to throw a party," Grace told him gaily, fanning herself. "I haven't danced so much in years."

"Scotch parties require a lot of footwork, Dora always said," he responded mirthlessly.

I cocked a look, or at least half of one, at him. "I'm interested, Sandy, that you do not use the prescribed term 'Scottish.' "

"Don't be a jackass. The Dutch don't call themselves the Duttish."

Suddenly Rab swirled in on us, anxiously looking in every direction. "Have you seen Famine? I told him to stay here in the room with us, but he's disappeared, the pup."

Sometimes you just know. "I believe I can find him." Grace granted me leave with the assurance that she wouldn't turn into a wallflower with Hoop and Griff available to dance the light fantastic with her, and I went off in search of a junior wisp.

Fortunately I knew every nook and cranny of the building, from being dispatched by Sandison on every conceivable kind of librarianly chore. And if I were a boy — no, if the daredevil boy haunting my memory were Russian Famine — there would be one place above all others sure to lure him. I took the shortcut of the back stairs and in a minute was in the rear of the darkened Reading Room. Guided by feel and instinct, I worked my way to the central desk, pausing there to listen. Somewhere overhead there was the *hop hop hop* sound of the peever game, although more lightly done.

Quietly as I could, I climbed the stairs to the mezzanine. Sure enough, there were the boots and puttees and helmet he had shed. I peered down the aisles between the lofty shelves of books, but could not make him out in the dimness. Careful to keep my voice down and not startle him, I softly called: "Famine? Your absence has been noticed by headquarters."

Silence for a long moment, then another of the subdued hopping sounds.

"Mrs. Evans is awful nice, but she don't trust me out of her sight."

"I wonder why."

"Beats me. I never busted my neck yet."

"That may be, but she and Jared are naturally concerned when you vanish like that." Still searching from aisle to aisle, I saw nothing but shadows. "All right, poltergeist, I give. Where are you?"

"Up top. What's a poltergeese?"

Startled by the response literally over my head, I shot a look upward past the highest shelf of books. Belatedly remembering, I pushed up my eye patch to make sure of what I was seeing. Squatting on his haunches, gazing down at me for all the world like a stone carving in a cathedral eave, the light-haired boy roosted on the narrow top framing of the nearest set of bookshelves. Directly above the works of Tolstoy, if I was not mistaken. I realized he had been leaping from bookcase to bookcase, traversing the room without ever touching the floor.

"It's a fancy word for 'ghost,'" I answered his question, "which you will find out all too much about if you fall off there."

"Nah. That's why I'm in socken feet. Makes climbing around easier and such."

"I'll take your word on that. But you're being missed at the party."

"Nothing much going on there. I can do that dumb peever game with my eyes shut."

"No doubt. There's the matter of manners, though. Being nice to those who are nice to you."

"I try, but it's a pretty small bunch." Suddenly grinning at me from his perch like a mischievous gargoyle, he asked, hushed, "Sir? Got 'em on you, in that rig?"

I clinked the brass knuckles in the swag pocket of my breeches. "I'm never without."

"Attaway. A guy has to look out for hisself, don't he."

Springing to his feet as if taking off to fly, he toed back and forth along the precipitous top of the shelving like a tightrope walker; it was all I could do not to hold out my arms in the vain hope of catching him. Abruptly he crouched again, flipping the hair out of his eyes to peer down at me. "I figured I had the place all to myself. How'd you know I'd be here?"

"By divination."

"Huh?"

"It simply occurred to me, is all." True, as far as it went. Memory returned me to a first time, one of those markers in life. I had been filling in at the reference desk, answering questions about everything under the sun, when Rab appeared with her restive troop of sixth-graders, consigned to the basement for story hour. Trailing the others was this boy, awkward as if made out of sticks yet quick in every way, gazing hungrily around the holy Reading Room as if desperate to take in the world of grown-ups with their riches of books open before them. Nameless as he then was, I knew him in a flash, the teacher in me recognizing the restless soul, the burning wish to rise beyond his circumstances. Now the roles were reversed, something in my face giving me away as he scrutinized me from his perch. Hesitating, he spoke, more hushed yet. "Can I ask you a thing?"

"Anytime."

"You ever get like me? Itchy to do something but you don't know what?"

"On occasion," I admitted to more than I wanted to.

"That's good. I was afraid I was the only one with those kind of skitters."

I braced for a slew of unanswerable questions, of how to contain wild urges and blind desires, the riptides in the blood. But Russian Famine only gave me that gremlin grin again, a gleam coming into his eyes. "Know what's most fun for climbing around on?" He couldn't wait for any guess from me. "The Hill."

Seeing my puzzlement — the copper-rich rise of land was one of the most dangerous

157

places on earth underground, but hardly any physical challenge above that — he confided further: "Those what-chums that stick up. Gallus frames."

"Good heavens, those?" I should have known. Gallows frames, as the headframes were called that towered over the mineshafts to raise and lower elevator cages by cable and pulley. "Famine, that's too dangerous, with the cable hoist running and all the other machinery that could catch your clothing or —"

"Huh-uh." The expert's scorn for my objection. "I only do it on the dead mines." He looked at me shrewdly. "They shut the Muck a while back. That's a good one. You can see plenty from up there."

The demise of the Muckaroo, the one mine I had ever descended into, or ever intended to, came as startling news to me, an epitaph of a kind, and Famine shifted himself a little as if catching my discomfiture. Suddenly a spine-chilling note echoed through the building, making him freeze like a hunted quarry. "What's that? Somebody getting killed?"

"If my ears don't mislead me, it's a bagpiper warming up. You'd better come on down — you wouldn't want to miss the ceremony of piping in the haggis, now, would you?"

"Depends. What's a haggis?"

"Food. Of a sort."

"Huh. That sounds halfway interesting."

"Now, how do you get down?"

"Easy. Same's I got up." Like a tightrope walker he tiptoed the length of the bookcase to the poetry section, where slim volumes left a few inches of exposed shelves, which he descended as handily as a ladder. Alighted and scooping up his soldier gear and already in motion toward the source of the not yet melodious wails, he glanced over his shoulder at me. "You coming?"

"At my own speed. Don't inquire too closely about what's in the haggis, all right?"

Off he went, scooting down the back stairs, but by impulse I chose to go out through the Reading Room. A pale cast of light from the foyer lent just enough outline to the massive oaken tables and softly conjured the Romanesque clock above the reference desk as I gripped the banister in my descent. If I had been able to levitate like a certain wraith of boy, right then is when I would have, for these old loved surroundings cast me into a spell of my own. My introduction to the Butte Public Library, and to Samuel Sandison and so much else, had taken place in this very room when

I requested the Latin edition of Julius Caesar's *Gallic Wars* — my own copy a victim of the luggage-devouring railroad — and realized from the tanned leather cover and exquisitely sewn binding that I was in a literary treasure house. What a wealth we are granted, in the books that carry the best in us through time. Now, as if in that daydream state between waking and sleeping, I wound through the maze of darkened chamber with my smile lighting the way.

Only to go cold as I stepped into the illuminated foyer. A pair of overcoated figures, hats low on their brows, lurked in the nearby corner of the otherwise empty lobby. They were ogling me with an astonishment equal to mine with them.

"Boss!"

Before I could draw back, the broad face of Smitty loomed into mine. "What a disguise! If we didn't know it was you, we wouldn't know it was you, huh, Ralphie?"

"Ain't that the truth." The other bootlegger goggled at my knee breeches.

Smitty meanwhile was squinting hard at my pirate patch. "I bet I get it. Keeping an eye on the jerks who run the town, right?"

I managed to coarsen what there was of my voice. "You said it."

"Smart." Smitty clucked in admiration.

"They got to get up early to beat you, boss. Wait till we get back to the warehouse and tell the boys how slick the Highliner is, it don't matter where or when." He turned to his sidekick and tenderly took something in soft wrapping from him. "Since you're here, how about you deliver the baby?"

I nearly dropped what he deposited in my arms before I realized the gurgle it made was the liquid sort, not the infantile kind. Peeking inside the wrapping, I read the label on the bottle. OLD BALLYCLEUCH, 90 PROOF. "We had to send all the way to Calgary for it," Smitty said proudly, his fellow bootlegger nodding in reverent affirmation.

"I'll mind the bundle of joy," I borrowed some of Sandison's gruffness without apology.

"Swell, boss, we'll leave you to it." Smitty gave one last admiring wag of the head at my pirate costume. "C'mon, Ralphie, back to the egg truck."

"Wait."

They stopped in their tracks. I glanced the length of the corridor to make sure it was deserted, both of them doing the same. "Tell the boys —"

They hung on my words.

"Keep the hens setting."

"Right, boss!"

"You bet, boss!"

Downstairs, the dancing was breaking up in anticipation of the haggis ceremony. Grace, looking flushed from twirls around the floor with Griff and Hoop, met me with a whoosh of relief. "I'd nearly given you up for lost, you." She touched a curious finger to the parcel I was so carefully cradling. "So, Captain Kidd, what do you have there? Buried treasure?"

A closer guess than she might have thought, actually. Telling her it was a delivery for our host and I would explain later, I sidled off through the crowd, trying to look unobtrusive, toward the punch bowl table where Sandison still presided like a Highland chieftain. His frosty eyebrows cocked slyly when he saw the bundle in my arms. "You look like you're carrying nitroglycerin," he chortled as I edged in close enough for us to talk without being overheard.

"It maybe amounts to the same. Old Ballycleuch, Sandy?"

"Heh." He poked into the wrapping enough to verify the bottle of scotch. "That's the stuff. Strong enough, it probably walked from Scotland by itself."

Glancing nervously toward where the mayor and the police chief stood swapping jokes, I hissed to him: "Need I remind you it is a prohibited substance? As in Prohibition, remember?"

"I must have missed that page in the book of fools. Hand me that lemonade pitcher." Shielding the action with the bulk of his body, he emptied it into the punch bowl, then barked, "Make yourself useful, can't you? Get around here and pour the needful into the pitcher, hurry up."

We got the job done just as a wild skirl of tune announced the bagpiper entering the auditorium, followed by two other kilted figures bearing the haggis platter between them. The contingent advanced in a slow march as the bagpipe brayed and huffed, until reaching the victuals table, where a spot had been cleared for the prize of the night. As was his due, Sandison posted himself there to preside as the wail of the pipes wound down and the red-faced piper awaited his traditional reward.

Grandly Sandison hoisted the pitcher in one hand and a tumbler in the other, then with a generous hand poured what looked for all the world like lemonade, meanwhile booming the customary question, "Piper, wha'll ye ha' in your libation?"

"More libation, mon."

Pouring further, Sandison included a

glassful for himself to toast the deserving bagpiper and then the poet of the land of thistle and heather and lastly the crowd — "Here's to honest men and bonnie lasses!" — with a healthy swig each time. "And now for the food of the gods!" So saying, he advanced to the victuals table, flourished the ceremonial dirk, and grandly cut into the haggis for serving.

Glimpsing the mushy gray contents, Hoop and Griff along with a good number of others faded back, but Grace, ever the provider of meals, and I, incurably curious, tried the haggis. "It's not as bad as you might think," she judged, maybe the best that could be said for a recipe that begins, *Take one sheep's stomach . . .*

Once the Scotch version of feasting was done, the only thing left on the evening's program was a parting message from our host. Sandison, however, showed no sign of mounting the stage and in fact had withdrawn behind the punch bowl again. Something in his manner told me to visit the situation, and I excused myself to the others.

Standing there as pensive as it is possible for a bare-kneed white-maned colossus to look, Sandison was gazing off somewhere in a world of his own. Well, the lord and master of the Butte Public Library and its birthday

164

gala had every right, didn't he. But there was still the matter of an auditorium full of guests starting to mill uncertainly.

"The shade of Rabbie Burns awaits an appropriate good-night, Sandy," I exuded encouragement as I came up to him, "as do the rest of us."

"I can't do it, Morgan." He was clutching the pitcher of scotch to his breast with both arms and I realized a significant amount of its contents must have gone into him. "Dora always did this part," he blubbered, with tears leaking into his beard. "You'll have to."

"Me? Oh, no. I haven't a clue how to end a Scotch soiree."

"Don't quibble." He snuffled. "Just get up there, slowpoke."

Pressed into service, I nearly tripped on the steps leading to the stage — the confounded eye patch — as I tried to think what to do or say. The trouble with Burns is that he is like Shakespeare; everyone's head already was full of language on loan from him. *The best laid schemes o' mice and men. Let us do or die! Nae man can tether time or tide. My love is like a red, red rose. Should auld acquaintance . . .* Why could the Scotch bard not have been less prolific?

Gulping, I took my position at center

165

stage as the audience quieted in anticipation or apprehension, it was impossible to tell which. The faces of Grace and Rab and Jared, at first surprised, were gamely supportive, and behind their backs Russian Famine grinned conspiratorially at the sight of me at that unexpected elevation. The Miners Band onstage in back of me, though, were gathering their music sheets and starting to put away their instruments. Down front, the dignitary brigade, as I thought of them, the whiskery trustees and city fathers, were glancing back and forth in perplexity at Sandison's absence and my presence. Depend on it, in the back of the crowd Quinlan cupped his hands and called out, "Show us your tonsils, man!"

Think, Morgan! I enjoined myself, think how to end this labyrinthine evening. And not for the first time, the library itself came to my aid. One of Famine's toeholds had been that shelf of Tolstoy, the immortal holdings of *War and Peace* and *The Death of Ivan Ilyich* and *The Kreutzer Sonata* and most pertinently *Anna Karenina*. The splendid ball that Anna attends at the Shcherbatskys' palace floated in my mind like a vision, and while Butte was not nearly Moscow except for snowfall, a dance floor bridges many differences. I had only to

166

pluck the right opening note, whatever that was.

"As the strains of the bagpipe have reminded us," I put that as generously as I could, "Robert Burns's native land was a commonwealth of music as well as of rhyme. Therefore, it may be fitting to conclude this evening of festivity with a musical excursion that takes in his Scotland, the old country, and our own land, the new." There is a trick to speaking swiftly and firmly enough that a crowd has to listen to catch up. "This particular promenade dates from 1773, when James Boswell accompanied the learned Dr. Johnson on their tour of the Hebrides," I sped on. "Hosted on the Isle of Skye, the two of them joined in, Boswell tells us, a reel of 'involutions and evolutions,' suggesting the partings and arrivals of emigration. It was, in the wonderfully simple words of Boswell, 'a dance called America.'"

Quickly I hummed a snatch of what passed for a reel to the suddenly alert Miners Band. The bandmaster allowed as how they could probably do something with that. Turning to the crowd, I quickly described the sequence, the first couple addressing the pair behind them before whirling away, the next couple addressing the third, until the entire line of dancers was awhirl in a great circle. "First in procession, fittingly," I extended a gesture as if I were the master of the ball, Shcherbatsky-style, directly at the suddenly sobering Sandison, "shall be our incomparable host, the Butte city librarian!"

While the band worked up the tune and I clapped a rhythm, Grace alertly slipped over to Sandison and separated him from the scotch pitcher, seized him by a reluctant arm, and steered him to the head of the line with her. Rab and Jared stepped lively into place behind them. Hoop and Griff, no slouches, each picked a willing widow, and with some hesitation even Quinlan did the same. The mayor, proving himself a good sport, joined arms with his wife next. On down the procession the couples multiplied, downtowners and those from the Hill, old-timers and newcomers dancing as one in a Rocky Mountain outpost where copper and blood mingled, all in the dance called America.

7

"You really do seem to have found your calling." My astute wife did not mean my impromptu role as dance caller a few nights past, which was unlikely to be repeated unless Robert Burns were to have more than one birthday per year. Snuggled in bed to read, as had become our custom with Sandison's treasury of books to draw from — vintage leather-bound *A Tale of Two Cities* ready on her nightstand and a fine new collector's edition of *My Ántonia* on mine — we first were attending to the day's news, the *Thunder* rustling as Grace flapped it open against the bedcovers. " 'Copper Goliath Shall Inevitably Fall' is today's masterpiece, is it. I don't know how you keep it up, Morrie," she tweaked my ear affectionately, "Anaconda must be getting thoroughly sick of Pluvius."

"They deserve to swallow their medicine, let us say." Armbrister made sure it was a heavy dose, with headlines of screaming boldface atop my editorials. Socratic dialogue conducted in mannerly fashion, the newspaper battle was not.

"Mm hmm. Too bad it isn't poison."

Her harsh words surprised me, and my expression must have shown so. "Sorry to sound that way," she met my eyes, "but it's the plain truth." She heaved a breath. "When it comes to the company and the copper bosses, I want them to burn in hellfire equal to what happened in the Speculator."

"You have every reason," I said quietly, out of respect to the fate of her Arthur.

"And yours?" She cocked a look at me, one that counted for a lot, I could tell. "You haven't lost anyone in the mines." She rattled the newspaper a little. "What brings it out in you, Mr. Thunderer, taking on Anaconda as you are?"

I took time to think of how to say it, but in the end, it just came out. "I hate men who skin other men for profit."

My surprising wife, who to my knowledge did not have a mean bone in her body, patted my pajama sleeve in approval. "Good for you. Don't let up on them." Her hand did not move from my arm. "Speaking of that. Quin, the other night. He's a hothead, but his notion that Jared Evans could stand some prodding — have you?"

"Exceedingly carefully, which I would say is the only way Jared can be prodded. I suggested to him that our readers might like a hint now and then of any weakening of Anaconda's grip on the legislature. You know him — he told me that was not a half-bad idea, whenever he got any of it weakened." I must have caught something from Quinlan, for I very nearly winked in saying the next. "I also put a bug in Rab's ear that possibly, just possibly, the rest of humankind does not exhibit the patience of Jared in this matter. Who knows, the marital bed may be the place to get a message across."

Grace pinched me lightly through the sleeve. "It has been known to, you rogue." Satisfied for now, she went to loyally reading my excoriation of the lords of copper, while I spread open the *Sporting News* for the latest on the Black Sox aftermath, in which only the ballplayers and small fry of the gambling mob still were getting the worst of it, unluckily. To an ironic eye, the pair of us might have looked like one of those comical illustrations of bums bedded down on park benches beneath newspapers, but of course appearances deceive. The mansion with its upkeep demands had not driven us to shivering poverty. Yet.

"Morrie?" A finger holding her place in the editorial, Grace glanced over at me as if she had thought of something else that could not wait. "Do you ever feel . . . singled out?"

Something in me answered before I could think. "All the time." Realizing how that sounded, I hastily reeled off, "There's you. There's all this." I swept my hand as if we owned everything from the creaky floor of the manse up to the stars. "How could I not feel the favors of good fortune?"

"More than that, though." Her glance had turned into a serious gaze, as if trying to read me like a crystal ball. "I mean, things that don't seem to happen to other people somehow pick you out. I know it sounds silly, but —"

"Do you have that kind of feeling, too?" I asked cautiously.

"Around you," she attempted a smile, "how can I help it?"

"Grace, I don't know how to account for luck, good or bad, if that's what it is," I tried to laugh off her concern. "I'm simply me, you're you, and life writes the rest, don't you think?"

"I suppose you're right." With a little frown of concentration, she went back to her newspaper and I to mine.

"Oh, before I forget for the morning," she moved to the domestic topic after finishing my editorial contribution. "Griff needs money to buy coal. A ton wouldn't hurt, he said."

"Of coal or money?" I moaned.

Grace gave me a little swat with the society page. "Don't be so down in the mouth about our home sweet home. We're gaining on it. Hoop and Griff are sure of it." Adding as she traded the *Thunder* for Dickens: "Just as you are making headway against Anaconda, yes?"

"*Labor omnia vincit,* I suppose."

That drew me a warning look.

"Sorry. 'Toil conquers all.' " Thinking to myself, it had better.

Fidget or *fugit,* time restlessly moves on, and in the aftermath of January's rite-of-winter night of revelry as orchestrated by Sam Sandison, February's abbreviated page seemed to vanish almost as soon as the calendar was turned, and here came an early thaw and March with it. Butte coming out from under the snow was not a particularly pretty sight, but I welcomed the lengthening days — each a chicken step longer than the last, Grace assured me — with their gradually warmer weather for walking to work, while the meltwater running down the steep guttered streets made music in its way. Everyone assured me snow could be back anytime and frost would not leave until at least May, but the way things were going, it was something like springtime in my spirit. Bootleggers did not waylay me — although at odd moments I rather missed Smitty and his effusions about my Highliner persona — now that I knew to go nowhere near the warehouse district. At home, as I was determined to think of the temperamental manse, life passed peacefully enough, particularly in the evenings, when up and down the bedroom hallways the only sounds were the rustle of pages and accompanying intakes of breath and occasional chuckles.

At the *Thunder,* similarly, the only thing earthshaking was the daily start-up of the backroom press, sluicing our challenge to the *Post* and its corporate masters into the world. Jared Evans, carrying responsibilities that would have buckled a Samson, I was sure had taken to heart the anxiety expressed by me, Quinlan, and no doubt Rab, but right then time and the times were too much at odds for him when it came to grappling with Anaconda. He and the other legislators were sidetracked in the extended legislative session, trying mostly in vain to deal with Montana's latest hard times. Collapse is a strong word, but the homestead boom that for nearly twenty years had promised to make Montana "the last great grain garden of the world" fell to earth, literally. The climate had turned around, drought withering the dryland crops that had flourished on rains that no longer came. Crop prices plunged after the appetite of the Great War was sated and peace set in. Across the state, banks were going under and towns with paint still fresh on their false-front stores were shrinking away in, I hate to say it, classic decline. Like a sooty dump-pocked mining city emerging from winter, history is not always pretty to watch.

The *Thunder* newsroom, though, like any newsroom, thrived on dire events.

On the unforgettable day, I was fashioning the next editorial lambasting the lords of copper in their downtown aerie, my typewriter thwacking at a measured pace in the traffic of clatter in the newsroom, when kittenish Mary Margaret Houlihan, the society reporter desperate for a lede about oncoming social doings, called out, "Remind me, Morgie, dear, what the Ides were about?"

"Glad to. The Roman occasion derives from *idus,* the Latin for 'middle,' " I warmed to the task of walking encyclopedia, as I sometimes do. "And so, the middle of March, the fifteenth, was traditionally a festive holiday, but thanks to Shakespeare, we now think of the Ides of March as the fateful day when Julius Caesar —"

I was interrupted by a shout of "Jake!" Across the room, Cavaretta was on his feet, still clutching a telephone. "Accident on the Hill. Five whistles." Everyone in Butte, myself included, knew that was the signal to send stretchers.

"Which mine, Cavvie?"

"The Neversweat."

"Get up there, *now,*" Armbrister bawled. "Take a shooter, make it Sammy," he specified the chief photographer. Snapping out orders left and right, the aroused master of the newsroom spotted me sitting in my corner, where, Mary Margaret and the Ides aside, I had been trying to think with my fingers as usual. "Morgie, go with them, see what you can pick up for your page." His green gaze met my startled one. "I have a hunch."

The three of us piled out of the building and into a taxi outside one of the Venus Alley establishments. The driver was used to urgent requests, apparently, and sped us through the business district, honking everything but a streetcar out of the way, until our jitney wound its way through Dublin Gulch toward the landmark mine atop the Hill, the Neversweat, with its line of smokestacks billowing, as had been written, "like the organ pipes of Hell." The storied seven stacks of the 'Sweat, which, legend had it, were address enough to deliver a miner anywhere on earth to this colossus of copper deposits. As the taxi roared toward the mine gate, Cavaretta, who was young but enterprising, leaned from beside me in the backseat to consult with the photographer, crammed with his gear next to the driver. "What's best, Sammy, split up or stick together? I haven't covered one of these —"

"Yeah, you might not this one, either," the photographer let out wearily, "from the looks of that ape." The taxi driver practically overlapped his utterance with his own exclamation, "Hell, it would have to be Croft, he'd jump off a cliff if they told him to."

A rifle-toting guard had stepped into the gateway, holding up a meaty hand that definitely meant *Stop*.

"No soap, coming in here. I got my orders," he declared as he came to the driver's window, one denizen dependent on the workings of the Hill to another. "Better turn this buggy around."

The taxi driver was not swayed. "C'mon, let me make a buck by getting my fare where they want to go. What's the big deal all of a sudden?"

"New policy," the guard stolidly recited. "Nobody not connected to the mine is allowed in until I hear from them downtown."

Out the side of his mouth, Cavaretta implored: "Can't you do something, Morgie?"

I thrust my head out the car window. "It's all right, Croft, that's where we're from — didn't they tell you? These gentlemen of the press are on our side. They're with me."

Whether the beard did it or my oratorical approximations, which were not exactly untrue, the gate guard straightened up in instant respect. "Yessir. I didn't get the word to expect *you*."

"One more thing," I intoned before the taxi started up. "If anyone shows up claiming to be from the *Post,* turn them away. We don't want the wrong kind of people in here."

"I gotcha," he all but saluted. "Any fakers, I'll give them a hard time."

178

There was no question where to go in the huge mine yard, everyone gravitating to the towering headframe and its elevator shaft, where the taxi driver let us out and was generously bribed, my role again, to stand by. Cavaretta, Sammy, and I turned as one to the commotion beneath the headframe's steel strutwork. The scene has been played at mine mouths probably since Roman times, the crowd drawn to disaster, those in authority pleading for order, rumors flying every which way. Sammy, a short but authoritative man, immediately set up shop with his tripod and other camera gear, aiming at the starkly silent shaft for whatever its elevator cage would bring up. Over there a besieged, florid-faced individual who was obviously the mine supervisor was trying to settle down a thick circle of agitated miners and other employees. This was the mine where Quinlan worked and I thought I spotted him in the midst of the turmoil, but under the helmet and grime it was hard to be sure from any distance. Fast earning his reporter's stripes, Cavaretta sized up the situation. "No bodies in sight yet. This may be a while. Morgie, can you find a phone and hang on to it for me?"

It took no great divination to guess that if the person in charge was caught up in the stormy scene surrounding the mineshaft, his office might well be vacant. Head down as if I had urgent business, I strode across the mine yard to the appropriate building and brazenly walked in.

I was in luck. Everyone in any office down the long corridor was caught up one way or another with the mine accident and the interruption of production, and those who did glance at me as I passed presumed from my topcoat and hat — and beard — that I must be someone important sent up from the Hennessy Building headquarters. At the office marked SUPERVISOR, I ducked in.

Aha, unoccupied. And, sitting right there on the desk, a telephone. I at once appropriated both, clapping the receiver to my ear and hurriedly tapping the switch hook for the operator, to place the necessary call to the rewrite desk in the newsroom. Only to be intercepted by a prim female voice at a switchboard somewhere on the Neversweat grounds, "Sorry, what department are you ringing, please?"

I was struck wordless. The telephone system was internal to Anaconda; was there nothing the damnable company did not control to the very last detail?

Swallowing hard, I said with forced casualness, "I'm calling to downtown," gave the

Thunder's telephone number, and hoped.

After forever, a familiar raspy intonation came. "Matthews here, what've you got?"

"Matt, it's Morgan, at the Neversweat," I spoke fast and low to the rewrite man. "Don't use my name or Cavaretta's on here, I'll explain later. I'm holding the line open for him, he's still at the mineshaft getting the story."

"Sure thing, I'll stay on. But he'll need to go some to make deadline."

"He will, we will. Sammy's set to shoot when they bring the victims up, let Armbrister know for the front-page layout."

Just as I finished speaking, the red-faced man from the din around the mineshaft barged into the office, charging toward what was unmistakably his desk, his chair, his telephone.

He stopped short at the sight of me sitting there, dressed to the gills and hat still on, hugging the phone to myself. "Do I know you?"

"Hardly." Which was true enough. The mine supervisor, whose name I fumbled out of memory from 1919 as Delaney, had laid eyes on me, somewhat disguised — and beardless — when he was night overseer at the Muckaroo and Jared had smuggled me into an unimaginably deep shaft to meet with miners on the matter of a union anthem; it's a long story. With deliberate vagueness, I now said, "I'm new at the newspaper."

"Reporters," he said as if the word left a bad taste. "Tell your yobbos at the *Post* to be damn careful how they handle this one, understand?" He jerked a thumb. "Out of the way. I need to use that."

My heart skipped as he rounded the desk and reached for the phone still in my possession.

"No," I startled both of us, holding the instrument away from him. "You can't, right now, this in use. I'll explain later."

"Can't?" Knocked back a step or two by my effrontery, he was turning apoplectic. "Who do you think you are? Get up from there! This is my office, my —"

Before he could finish, a storm burst in the room. No gate guard could keep Jared Evans out. "What's going on, Delaney?" he demanded as he hurtled in, angry to the point of bursting. "Five whistles, and you don't let us know at union headquarters, we have to find out for ourselves? That's a new low, even for your bunch of snakes." Throwing a look my way for an additional target, he did a slight double take at my still presence. Something told him what I was at, maybe the white of my knuckles in my death grip on the phone stem and receiver, so, showing no hint of recognition, he spun from me to the mine supervisor. "Don't stand there like you've lost your tongue, let's hear the accident report."

"It . . . it happened in the Chinese Laundry, that's why it's taking so long." Listening for all I was worth, I blanched. The hottest, sweatiest level of any mine, in this case nearly a mile deep. Delaney hesitated, caught between being cowed and in authority. Jared's shrewdness in entering the political realm was proven again; an incensed union leader who was also a state senator was obviously more than a mine overseer wanted to face. Delaney licked his lips and fumbled out, "It's a nasty one, see, and we —"

"I gather that it is," Jared snapped. Like me, he was dressed nattily, but in the tension of his body and the set of his shoulders, he was once again all miner underneath. "Now, will you quit beating around the bush and —"

"The pair of them were getting set to blast a fresh run of ore, and the charge must have went off on them," Delaney reported in a rush of words. "It's taken some digging to get them out. They're both gone. I'm sorry as hell."

Jared looked like he wanted to throttle him. "Two men *dead* and you don't even have the union shift rep in here to start notifying the families and the rest? It's in the contract, you know that — you're supposed to get our man on the first fast cage for this." He shot a look out into the corridor. "Where the hell *is* Quinlan? Isn't he up yet?"

Blindly defensive, the mine supervisor blathered, "They're bringing him up as quick as the stretchers could get there, I told you it happened in the deep shaft and it takes —"

"Bringing?" Jared turned pale, and no doubt I did, too. "It's Quin, in this?" It was an accusation, not a question.

No sooner had that truth crashed into the room, while I was still sitting paralyzed, than a voice trilled in my ear: "I'm so sorry, but has your party spoken with you yet?"

"No, I mean yes, he's there, he's merely occupied."

"I'm awfully sorry, but other departments are waiting to use this line."

"Things are delayed," I said tersely, hoping that would sound like official business to the switchboard operator and newspaper business to the mine overseer.

184

"I'm just terribly sorry, but the company rule is that an outside line should be used no more than —"

"I am sitting at the desk of the supervisor of the entire mine," I said slowly and distinctly. "Does that tell you enough?"

The voice went away without even saying it was to any degree sorry.

More shaken than I had ever seen him, Jared was hearing out Delaney's pleading try at explanation. "God's truth, Jared, I wish it had been anyone but Quin. I know how this looks, but it was a total accident, it has to be."

"Then it's a sonofabitch of a coincidence, isn't it," Jared said savagely. "The one man, after me, that Anaconda would be glad to be rid of. What's the company trying to pull? Pick us off, the way the goons did outside your gate and —"

Frantic, Delaney interrupted and pointed at me. "Is it all right for him to hear this? He's one of those, you know."

Of course Jared waved that away and went on with his tirade. But that was the moment I truly realized I was one of those. A newspaperman. Fresh to me, the hunger of the newsman to be first with the story, but oh, how I felt it. The same appetite raged in Cavaretta, Sammy, Armbrister, Matthews hunched ready at his typewriter on the far end of the line, every man and woman of the *Thunder,* it was our calling: To tell the reading public this story of the Hill, before the *Post* could bury it away on page eight in the death notices. If we could only get the news out. The time, the time. How I did so with both hands engaged with the telephone, I don't know, but I fished my pocket watch from inside my topcoat, suit coat, and vest pocket, and looked. Deadline was not that far off.

Meanwhile Delaney was still maintaining that Quinlan's fatal accident was only that, sheer chance, until Jared coldly broke in on him.

"Just tell me this. Will you swear to me, man to man, the company didn't have anything to do with it?"

Delaney's face froze. "Them downtown, you mean."

Jared and I realized in the same instant. The Neversweat overseer was frightened. Nervously he rattled out, "I don't see how they — anybody — could have set this up to happen. I make every shift boss inspect the blasting supplies for short fuses, powder leaks, all that. You raise such hell with us anytime anyone's hurt, I come down hard on handling explosives. I swear to you, that's the honest truth."

Still incredulous, Jared asked: "Then how do you explain it? Two drillers, as savvy as anybody on the Hill, get blown up just like that?"

Delaney mustered himself. "You know what Quin was like. He never saw a corner he couldn't cut. How many times did I get after him for chasing into new rock ahead of the timbering crew? He'd laugh in my face and tell me he'd never yet heard the undertaker's music in the rock, he'd back off when he did." He stopped, his jaw working as if deciding whether to say the next. "Jared, you had better know. He was drinking, some. On the job, I'm pretty sure, although I couldn't ever catch him at it."

Jared winced but shook his head. "I can't buy that entirely. Quin could hold his whiskey, he had a hollow leg." I'd have said the same. I watched Jared reach his decision. "Whatever the hell happened, no matter whose fault, I'm calling the men out."

Delaney cursed, then pleaded. "How's a wildcat strike going to help matters any?"

"Nobody said 'strike,'" Jared made the terms plain. "Just this shift, a walkout. We owe Quin that much."

"Do what you must," the supervisor gave up. He glanced uncertainly at me jealously guarding the phone. "I'll let them downtown know, whenever."

No sooner had he said that than a sudden wash of light through the office window startled the three of us, before we realized it was photographer's flash powder going off like daylight lightning. Delaney drew a breath. "I suppose that'll be the cage with the bodies."

Cavaretta came racing in, puffing from sprinting from the mine head and searching the corridor for me. He drew up momentarily at the sight of Jared and the mine superintendent, but swiftly stepped around them. "Don't mind me, just borrowing the phone a few minutes. Thanks, Morgie." He began dictating: "Two veteran miners perished in an explosion of unknown cause deep in the Neversweat mine earlier today. Patrick Quinlan, mineworkers' union representative on the afternoon shift and a well-known figure in the Irish community, and his drilling partner, Terence Fitzgerald, were said to be setting a dynamite charge in the four-thousand-foot level when —"

"— history repeated itself as tragedy," my editorial picked up the story the next day. It went on in this vein:

In rough numbers, the mining operations of the Hill kill a miner a week. This week it was two, one of them the combative presence across the bargaining table from the Anaconda Company in wage and safety negotiations. Pat Quinlan died, insofar as is known, because something went terribly wrong in a routine blasting of a wall of ore. Whatever happened, it fits on the list of mining conditions terribly wrong in the copper monopoly's empire of mines:

Is there enough ventilation at the extreme depth Anaconda has pushed its mineshafts in, say, the greatly misnamed Neversweat, so that a mineworker is not blinded by his own sweat as he handles dangerous materials? No.

Is there medical help, even of the first-aid sort, in place and prepared when the dreaded signal of five whistles goes off? No.

Is there a change of course in the company's administration of its mines since the Speculator fire, when the escape doors that were supposed to be in the tunnels' cement bulkheads somehow were not there and one hundred sixty-four miners died? No.

That's Anaconda history for you. That's tragedy.

"About close enough to the line," Armbrister judged, Jared reluctantly concurring, as they read over my words practically letter by letter before letting them into print. The *Thunder* could not accuse the Anaconda Copper Mining Company of murder, without proof, because of the libel law. But people could read beneath the ink of our version of Quin's death if they wanted. Take that, Scriptoris and company.

"All right, Sherlock. Who do you think did it, them or him?" Grace with her common sense got right to the question, handing the editorial back to me from her side of the bed.

I smoothed the *Thunder* atop the *Sporting News* before setting both away for the night. "I would not put money either way. One is treacherous, one was reckless. Unless something else comes to light, it's anybody's guess."

I attended Quin's wake, and then the burial, for to my surprise I was asked to be a pallbearer. In the nature of things Jared was, too, and it was after the service at the C. R. Peterson Modern Mortuary and Funeral Home while we waited for the hearse that he took me aside. "I've had a word with

190

Armbrister, you'd better know. No more editorials about Quin."

"What!" Funeral home or not, my voice rose to a pitch. "Why not? After what happened, it gives us all kinds of ammunition to —"

Jared squeezed my shoulder hard enough to shut me up. "I found a Wob card on him."

My stunned silence didn't require the hand he now dropped. "Delaney did the decent thing and left me alone to go through Quin's belongings, before the undertaker got there. It was right there in his wallet, big as life, along with his union card." Jared spoke quickly, keeping an eye out for the arrival of the hearse. "Anaconda can't have known he was a Wobbly" — he shook his head as if trying to clear it of Quinlan's plural versions — "if he really was to any extent, or they'd have blackballed him from the Hill, the way they did all the others. And," his face hardened, "painted us Red along with him."

I did not need that spelled out. Since the Russian Revolution, America from the top of government on down had undergone a spasm of fear, not nearly over, of Bolshevism, anarchism, any ism that could be deemed un-American. Only the vegetarians were spared, it sometimes seemed, the epidemic of prosecutions, deportations, jailings, blacklistings, of left-wing activists of any stripe. In the mines and forests and ports of the West, the Industrial Workers of the World and their "radical" philosophy of workers' power had been singled out as a particular threat to the existing order, and crushed. It could keep happening.

"I unfortunately understand," I had to concede, meeting Jared's sober look with my own. "Red isn't the most becoming color these days, is it."

"It clashes," he said with resigned grim humor. "Here comes the hearse. Off to the cemetery, Professor."

There it was left, Pat Quinlan of Dublin Gulch six feet under Butte soil after a life at its deeper depths, the mystery of his death interred with him.

8

A newspaper without a cause is little more than a tally sheet of mishaps local and national and whatever social gatherings and sporting events will fill the rest of the pages. Distinctly like our insipid rival, the *Daily Post,* in other words, and every other docile daily on the Anaconda Copper Mining Company's leash, all across the state. Thank heavens, the *Thunder* never waned to that extent after going silent about the disaster in the Neversweat, but some days it was close. Deprived of Quin as a martyr, I had to reach farther and farther up my sleeve for editorials taking the fight to Anaconda. Over at the *Post,* Scriptoris had nothing much to do but casually snipe back; we could have written some of our exchanges in our sleep. While still putting out a paper people wanted to read — still cranking the hurdy-gurdy, in Armbrister's term for it — our sense of direction was less sure than in the first heady months of publication. The staff sensed it. Journalists have a nose for that. Newsroom morale was helped only a little by Jared gamely introducing in the legislature a toughened mine safety law, doomed to have the life choked out of it by the copper collar, everyone knew.

"What I don't understand," Griff groused at supper during this time, "is how come you don't keep after the snakes about that blast going off on Quin. There's something fishy about that. In our day we handled every kind of dynamite and such, didn't we, Hoop —"

"Enough to wage a war, just about."

"— and you didn't see us blowing ourselves up." He tapped the air with his fork for emphasis. "You just had to have the right touch, know what you were doing. And wouldn't you think Quin did?"

In answer, I could only say cryptically that Jared Evans had a strategy that might take a while, and try to let it go at that. Only he, Armbrister, and I knew — and of course, Grace and Rab — about the incriminating IWW card and Quin's dangerous duplicity to us as well as to Anaconda, if that's what it amounted to. Accordingly, my policy necessarily was *De mortuis nil nisi bonum* — Speak no ill of the dead — and not inciden-

194

tally, keep Hoop and Griff from letting the cat out of the bag while gossiping with their old mining cronies.

The other person at the supper table stroked his snowy beard and said nothing, which in a way said something in itself.

Not since Robert Burns Night had I visited the Butte Public Library, and as ever it was like entering the world as it should be, organized, hushed, welcoming. Good day to you once again, William, I greeted Shakespeare at his post above the Reading Room as I passed on my way up to Sandison's office. He was not in. Back downstairs, I started my search for him at the Reading Room, where Smithers at the periodicals desk and pretty Miss Mitchell in the cataloging section wigwagged fond greetings to me. I knew better than to expect anything of the sort from Miss Runyon, the gorgon of the main desk and an old antagonist from my time as Sandison's assistant in charge of this, that, and her.

Registering unpleasant surprise as I approached, her eyeglasses swinging on the chain around her stout neck as she pulled back in her high chair to increase the distance between us, she whispered forbiddingly, "What can I do for you?"

"I wonder, Miss Runyon, if out of your vast store of information" — I should not have, but I let my gaze graze across her voluminous forbidding chest as I said that — "you can tell me where I might find Sandy."

"Mr. Sandison," the words all but leaned across the desk and cuffed me, "is on the prowl. He spends more and more time in the stacks, with those precious books of his. That man."

Up the grand staircase to the mezzanine and its tall ranks of richly hued books I went. Stopping to listen, very much as I had done when Russian Famine was flying overhead from bookcase to bookcase, I heard a sound faint but distinct as a rippling brook, the riffle of pages being turned.

There he was when I stuck my head around Poetry A–K, open book in hand. I could just make out the gilt title on the spine, *A Life in Verse,* by the sometimes inspired, sometimes pedestrian poet Cheyne. White eyebrows ascending toward his cowlick in surprise at the sight of me, Sandison appeared almost shy at having been discovered fondling the volume. "Caught me counting the herd," he rumbled, reshelving Cheyne and passing a lingering hand over the beautiful leather of the works of Matthew Arnold, Baudelaire, Blake, the two Brownings, and of course, Burns. I was the one surprised as he lowered his voice to ask, "Ever have the urge to write?"

"I thought that was what I do for a living."

"A book, man," he said as if I were simple-minded. "The real thing." The next came out rough as a grindstone, but was nonetheless a confession. "Sometimes I'd like to get it all down. What the country was like when Dora and I came in by stagecoach, young pups that we were, and started the ranch. And everything that followed. It'd make quite a tale, don't you think?"

Possible titles flooded my mind. *We Hung Them High. The Earl of Hell Remembers. Finagling the Finest Book Collection West of Chicago.*

Reading me from the inside out, Sandison sighed and changed the topic. "What are you doing in here this time of day anyway? Aren't you supposed to be saving the world, editorial driblet by driblet?"

"Ostensibly, I'm here to look up statistics on mining production. Actually, I just wanted to get out of the office for a while."

"Statistics, ay?" He glanced at me shrewdly. "Pluvius getting hard up for material, is he?"

"Things are a little dry right now," I had to admit.

With a grunt, he turned in the other direction, his bulk nearly filling the aisle between bookshelves. "Come on out on the balcony where we can talk. I have a touch of the office strain of cabin fever myself."

Cupped neatly in the stonework above the main entrance's keystone arch, the small balcony looked out on Broadway, the Butte version, busy enough with automobile traffic and delivery vans — a Golden Eggs truck casually putt-putting along with the rest, I couldn't help but notice — and the familiar sight of messengers trotting through the more leisurely passersby to run purchases from the Hennessy department store or bank errands or, of course, Anaconda pouches of directives to its managers on the Hill. Winter at least having retreated if not gone, pedestrians had become recognizable as something other than walking piles of clothes, and optimistic bonnets instead of head-scarves could be seen on some of the more fashionable ladies. By now it was April, fooler of a month. One day the weather would be what passed for spring at an elevation of a mile, and the next would feel as if it had come from Iceland. Leaning his elbows on the rim of the balcony as I was also doing, Sandison sniffed the air. "Hmmp. The time of year is doing its damnedest to change, once you get past the smell from up there." Silently we looked past the downtown buildings, even the tallest ones dwarfed by the hill of copper — its serape of snow in its last tatters by now — that was this contentious city's fortune and its curse.

"You've slacked off on Anaconda since right after those two miners were blown up," he said as if still conversing about the weather. "What's that about?"

Why did I feel some sense of relief in unburdening myself to this cantankerous old mountain of a man? Sometimes we need ears other than our own, but there seemed to be more to it with Sam Sandison; there always did with him. In any case, I owned up as soon as he asked. "Don't pass this on to Hooper and Griffith, please, they're better off not knowing. But we found out Quinlan was . . . not quite what he seemed."

He gave me that look of his. "Knew that, almost. Didn't you tell me once he'd pull out the Little Red Songbook when things got too quiet at a wake?"

"I confess, I thought he simply liked a good song."

"Hah. A person can do that and still be a rascal. You of all people should know." Now I was giving him a look, but he only said as if in passing, "Aren't journalists supposed to be students of human nature?"

"On that" — I exhaled a good deal of regret — "my grades perhaps are not always the highest."

"A card-carrying IWW member, what next." He had gone back to musing on Quin. "Some secret threat to society they are." Absently rubbing the stonework of the library as a captain on the bridge of a ship might stroke a railing of familiar oak, he pondered aloud. "Doesn't mean he was wrong about the state of things. The Anaconda Company needs to be leveled to the ground and their bones stomped in." The glacier-blue eyes were perfectly mild as he surveyed the Hill, where the belching smokestacks of the Neversweat were most prominent. "Not that I'm in favor of violence, mind."

It was too much for me. My despair coming out, I heard myself say: "I'm wondering if I'm cut out for Butte." He glanced at me sharply. "Don't take me wrong," I hurried to add, "I am happy to be employed at the *Thunder,* just as I was here in your bailiwick. It's only that I'm not sure I have as much

200

staying power as Jared Evans and the rest. It's their fight, in the end. I'm simply something like a cornerman."

"Odd analogy," he drawled. "I'd have thought you're more like the old hand who knows how the best punches are thrown."

"Yes, well," I could have done without his own analogy, "it may seem that way, but I am about out of combinations with any real jab to them, when it comes to Anaconda."

"Don't give up, Morgan." Sandison leaned back to his full, snowy height, as if sizing up the hurly-burly of busy humanity in the street below us. "You never know what might come along and change the story."

It didn't take long.

"Another box of rocks for the old gentleman."

The postman handed me what was undoubtedly Sandison's latest hefty book purchase when I answered the door the following Saturday forenoon. "Oh, and this for you," he fished a letter out of his mailbag. "Sorry to be the bringer of bad news." Clucking his tongue, he went on his way as I studied the official-looking piece of correspondence.

My curiosity piqued, I at once tore open the envelope. Its contents staggered me.

Flabbergasted as I was, I needed advice at once. Grace was out buying groceries. Hoop and Griff were in the basement, noisily doing something to the furnace. That left only Sandison to consult about what I held in my hand, if I could get over being speechless.

First he spotted the package under my arm, as I stepped into the round library room.

"Hah. That'll be *Moby-Dick,* the deluxe edition with N. C. Wyeth illustrations. Melville is quite the coming author, now that he's been dead long enough. About time it got here," he said as though I had dawdled en route from the front door. As usual on weekends, he still was in pajamas, his idea of leisure being a stroll directly from bed to his book-lined lair. He did not believe in slippers, only a pair of rundown cowboy boots softened by time, which made his toilet trips in the middle of the night a disturbing experience for anyone within hearing. Comfortable as a king in his big boots and striped nightwear, he slit the package as quickly as I handed it over and opened the illustrated tale of the whale, about the size of a breadboard and twice as heavy. The richly colored set of pages depicted Captain Ahab lashed to the leviathan, about to be dragged down to his doom. Which was how I felt as the master of the manse at that moment.

Paying me no further mind, Sandison leaned over the Wyeth handiwork, chortling. "Tells the story right there, wouldn't you say?"

I was too upset to do anything but wordlessly thrust my own piece of mail between him and the book.

Frowning, he plucked the paper from me and gave a hasty read. "The property tax bill," he identified it, as if I couldn't. He handed it back. "A bit steep this year, isn't it," he said, already paging through *Moby-Dick* again.

"Steep? It's, it's precipitous!" I sputtered.

"Welcome to home ownership in the great state of Montana," he replied mildly.

"But it seems to me a terrific sum, for someone of my salary," I protested, my spirit still sinking like Ahab.

Sandison sighed. "Morgan, do I have to spell out the facts of life to you? The tax is based on what you own, ninny, not what you make." He swept an arm expansively toward the bulk of the manse beyond his private room. "And this place is quite a bit of property, you know. Horse Thief Row doesn't come cheap."

203

"Sandy, just this one tax year, I wonder if you could possibly —"

"No, I couldn't possibly," he scotched that. "My funds, such as they are, are tied up in the account book dealers need to draw on. I thought I'd made that plain, back when I signed over the house to you and madam. Good Lord, man, can't you manage to own a piece of property and pay up like a normal person?" he all but stamped his nightwear boots at me.

"I am willing, but the cash is weak," I would have paraphrased that into Latin if I'd had the presence of mind. "How am I — Grace and I — supposed to pay up, as you so casually put it, and still afford the upkeep on this omnivorous house?"

Sandison stroked his beard in a wise way. "Maybe you ought to take up bootlegging. There probably aren't taxes attached to that, don't you think?"

Doubly dumbfounded now, I gawked at him. How did he know I got away with impersonating the Highliner at the warehouse? Yet if my ears were not playing tricks on me, what was the Earl of Hell suggesting but — "That Old Ballycleuch, you certainly produced in timely fashion on Burns night," he drawled, to my utter relief. "I still take a dram when the spirit calls, heh, heh." He reached toward his bottom desk drawer. "You look like you need one now, laddie."

"No. No, thank you. I need to think."

"Oh, dear," Grace groaned, settling at the kitchen table when I gave her the bad news about the size of the property tax bill. "And that's just the half of it."

"Just the — what do you mean?"

"The boardinghouse, Morrie. Surely you haven't forgotten about it?"

"How could I?" Although, truth be told, I had. A second weight of domicility on my back — on our backs, to be fair to Grace, although I was the wage earner — bent me to what felt like the breaking point.

"So," she was saying with resignation, "there must be a tax notice in my old name waiting at the post office — we should fix that with the recorder of deeds, Morrie."

"Yes, yes, all in good time. But as to the tax bill, *bills,* I mean —"

"Here, help me put away these groceries," she shook off the matter and got up to busy herself unloading her shopping bags, "the taxman isn't at the door this very moment. I've been meaning to talk to you anyway about the boardinghouse," she said, a lilt coming into her voice. "In a little while we can maybe open it for business again, Griff and Hoop and luck willing. That would help out the provider considerably, don't you think?"

The provider, such as I was, dumping the seasonal fare of rutabagas and turnips into the vegetable bin, for once did not know what to say. Finally words found their way out. "Grace, lovesome, you give every appearance of listening, but are you hearing? We're strapped. Driven to the wall in our finances. Trapped in this fancy poorhouse with Ajax on the door, however you want to put it." A stray potato had got away, and I fired it into the bin. "We have only just been getting by on my salary, and there is no money lying around to pay preposterously high property taxes that are due now, *now,* not in a little while, and — what did you say?"

"Now who's hard of hearing, honeybun?" She reached over from the canned goods cupboard and prodded my shoulder. "I said, it's a good thing I have some tucked away."

"You do? I mean, do you. How much?"

Hearing the sum, I nearly swooned in relief. "My dear, you are a treasure in more ways than one. If the boardinghouse isn't taxed like the Waldorf Astoria, that amount should tide us over, this time. But how did you ever . . . ?"

She dimpled becomingly. "Remember when we'd arrive in Venice or Marseilles or one of those places and you'd send me to the exchange window to trade in some of our American money while you tracked down newspapers? Now, this is not to criticize in any way, darling, but given your spending habits, I thought it might not hurt to put aside a certain amount each time before cashing the rest in for the foreign money. I'd slip it into the bottom compartment of my purse, where husbands always fear to go." Sweet reason prevailed in her gaze at me. "You'd be surprised how much it added up to in a year."

"Amazed, is more like it," I said fervently.

"Under this roof, then, we're all of us saved," my miraculous wife mused, folding away her shopping bags. "Hoop and Griff don't own any more property than the soles of their shoes, and His Nibs passed his along to us, the old smarty." The offending tax notice lay open on the kitchen table, where she gave it the Butte eye. "But most people aren't as lucky as we are, are they. Just imagine how hard it must be in Dublin Gulch and Finntown and the rest when the postman comes today and — Morrie? You seem lost in thought."

"No. Perhaps finding something, actually."

9

"Oh, hell, Morgie, it's been tried before," Armbrister objected, shrugging like someone tired to death of the litany. "It'd be like shooting at the moon, trying to hit Anaconda with that. Every damn time the issue gets brought up, the votes are never there in Ulcer Gulch, am I right, Jared?"

"But what if —" I spun out my idea at greater length, my pair of listeners leaning to take it in even though we were in the quiet confines of the editor's office, away from the newsroom's racket of phones going off and typewriters accelerating toward deadline. With a train to catch, Jared kept checking his watch; Ulcer Gulch waits for no man, his expression said. But he heard me out to the final word before saying, "That's a brainstorm if there ever was one, Professor. It's a long shot, but maybe worth a try. Jake, what do you think?"

The glum editor still did not think much

of it. "I still say we'd only be whistling Beulah, same old tune that never gets anywhere. You can dig up whatever you want on Anaconda, and they just throw it back at you and buy off enough politicians, excuse my language, Jared, until the matter goes away again."

"But there's digging, and then there's digging," I invoked what must be a Butte truism. "All we need is to hit just this little bit of, mmm, paydirt" — what on earth would we do without analogies? — "and then we can refine things."

"Sounds to me like a show of color," Jared decided with a miner's phrase beyond any I could have come up with. "I'll see what I can find out in the capitol." Putting on his overcoat and heading out the door, he called over his shoulder: "You do the homework at this end, Professor, and we'll figure out what it adds up to. Good hunting."

Jared reported back after his legislative week, this time with Rab at his side practically purring with intrigue.

"Sure enough, one of my colleagues" — the political life was drawing him in enough that he no longer said that with any irony — "knew how to get the dirt. He's Williamson's man in the Senate, actually. Likes to joke that he's the cow herder of the place. He checked with Williamson, and from the sound of it, what we're after took some asking around in the major's old Harvard crowd back east, but somebody knew somebody else who knew to the decimal point how much Anaconda has been raking in. You can see why they hide the figure."

Armbrister and I waited with shrinking patience while, unconsciously or not, Jared tugged at his short ear as though the profit had come out of miners' hides, looked at Rab for the courage needed after what he was about to say, and finally said it. "Last year, it was twenty million dollars."

"Imagine," Rab murmured, although none of us could really picture a fortune of that size — even Henry Ford, industriously spewing out Model Ts every minute on his famous assembly line, was probably a pauper compared to that — accruing in the copper company coffers like clockwork.

Dazzled as we all were, Jared wasted no time prompting me. "Your turn. What did you come up with at the assessor's office?"

What Grace came up with, actually. Carrying off this part of my scheme like a trouper, she drew no particular attention at it, merely a boardinghouse owner — better yet, a widow, as she still was on the county's assessment and tax records — come to see if there was not some horrible mistake about the tax bill on her humble property. And when directed to the ledgers to see for herself, naturally such a person would timidly open those from the very front, where it could hardly be her fault that the alphabet delivered the A's.

"The Anaconda Copper Mining Company last year paid taxes in the grand sum of" — I could not resist a slight dramatic pause — "thirteen thousand, three hundred forty-six dollars."

"The pikers," Rab did the arithmetic with a schoolteacher's rapidity.

"Jumping Jesus!" Armbrister's eyes suddenly were alight beneath the green eyeshade. "That's peanuts! It's only, only — Morgie?"

"Seven ten-thousandths of one percent, rounded off."

Jared banged a fist into his palm, the sound like a shot. "In other words, the Hill is assessed like it's a pile of worthless rocks while it pours out tons of money to Anaconda. And the company gets away with taxes the size of a gnat's eyelash."

"Excellent analogy," I filed the phrase away for a forthcoming editorial. "And well done in your reconnaissance, Senator."

"You too, Professor. We've got the numbers, but it's still only half the battle." He gave me the mock command, although with our fate and the *Thunder*'s behind it. "Rally the troops."

"Oh, boy, Morrie, I dunno about this. What do you say, Hoop?"

"Be a big step."

"Righto."

"Real big."

"All that is involved is for the pair of you to become the owners of record," I patiently laid out the idea again.

"That's all, huh? Sounds like plenty."

"As I've said, it would only be temporary. Just while Jared and I are at this."

"Except you want to tell everybody in Montana about it."

"Well, yes, more or less."

That did nothing to erase so much as a single wrinkle of concern from the two old bald heads. Griff looked at Hoop, and Hoop at Griff, then both together at Grace, listening with her arms crossed determinedly. "Up to you, Mrs. Morgan. It's your piece of property. We'll do what Morrie wants if you say so, but —"

There was a catch in her voice, but she said it. "Whatever it takes. The boarding-

212

house is yours."

I always want my battles in life to be bloodless. In the periodic tricky situations that somehow find me, and I them, so far I had managed that, although with some escapes narrower than was comfortable. Never far from my mind was my margin of safety from the Chicago gambling mob, but the more immediate concern was the behavior of the Anaconda Copper Mining Company. Believe me when I say I'd had enough of window men and goons during my previous spell in Butte. Since then, people had been gunned down in broad daylight on the Hill for the temerity of challenging the mighty corporation. And there was the murky set of circumstances that cost cocky Quinlan his life. Yet even while conscious that newsprint was no more bulletproof than my own flesh, I did feel shielded by the *Thunder* and its ability to make a noise in the world; that and Jared's steely political presence. So, while Voltaire was never more trenchant than when he said God always sides with the big battalions, numbers of another sort might be deployed for a certain kind of stealthy victory in this different kind of battle, something told me. Handled right, arithmetic can be quite a weapon. For if my

213

brainstorm worked, we might suddenly have a majority of the state of Montana on our side.

The heady buzz in the newsroom could be felt, like the thick hum of bees in clover, when it became known that Jared, Armbrister, and I were about to launch a new editorial campaign against the masters of the copper collar. Jared stationed himself in Helena to contend with reaction in the legislative halls, while the other two of us huddled, I suppose, like conspirators, guarding the first of our surprises until it was safely set into type.

"You need to be ready for the *Post* to kick and scream," Armbrister warned, veteran of many arrows in his own journalistic hide. "The SOBs."

"I know."

"They'll call Pluvius every name in the book and make the same old argument Anaconda always does. It's probably in overset, they dust it off and run it at the slightest hint of something like this. The bastards."

"I know, I know."

"Fire away, then." Leaving me alone with my typewriter, the editor raised his voice to the watching staff, "Let's crack our knuckles and get to work, folks. We're not going to make history by running blank pages in the rest of the damn paper."

As the regular newsroom commotion resumed, my fingers found the typewriter keys, old friends of the mind. And down the coarse strife-scarred streets of Butte, above the dark honeycomb of mineshafts beneath the copper-ruled city, from an all-wise portrait above the Reading Room door came the unabashed inspiration that lends words lasting power: "Devise, wit! Write, pen!"

I typed like a man possessed. If Shakespeare was not enough, Cavaretta passed by with his account of the latest bone-crushing accident in the depths of the Hill, telling me savagely, "Go get them, Morgie."

When I handed in the editorial, deadline looming, Armbrister read it through without putting a pencil to it. "That ought to do the job. We'll give it a screamer," by which he meant an inch-high headline, in newspapering terms an absolute shout for readers' attention.

PLIGHT OF PROPERTY OWNERS.
ALL EXCEPT ONE.

A taxing situation exists within the boundaries of the Treasure State, in more ways than one. It is as indelible as a seemingly

215

innocent line from the Bible: Foxes have holes and birds of the air have nests. Let us suppose you own a modest house nestled on no more space than it needs, and your neighbor owns a gigantic business atop the most bountiful hill in the world. Good citizen that you are, you pay full taxes on your property, while what does that neighbor pay? The answer, alas, does not hew to biblical justice of any kind:

Next to nothing.

The hole in the taxation system that the foxes of the Anaconda Copper Mining Company have added to their vast den of mines has let them hide the pittance they pay, compared to the fortune they earn.

Then came the magic numbers, adding up to the fact that in the course of a mining year, it took a mere six hours — or as Armbrister gleefully had it set it in boldface, **six hours** — of Anaconda's profits to cover its property tax bill.

Reaction at the *Post,* and no doubt at certain desks high in the Hennessy Building, was a predictable tantrum. Scriptoris squealed in print at the word t-a-x and pulled out the old argument Jared and Armbrister groaned over in unison, that it was

216

only to be expected that domiciles which otherwise put no product into the world should pay on a different basis than productive property which already contributed to community prosperity, and furthermore any penny wrongly wrung out of the Anaconda Company would take away from wages for the workingman, et cetera. That, and calling me, in my Pluvius persona, a hysterical jackass.

"Ouch, Morrie," Grace said as the *Post* screed got passed around the supper table. "It makes it sound as if I'm married to someone who has taken leave of his senses."

"Never fear, that's merely what we expected. The stars are now aligned for our next phase of the battle. That's if" — I swept a look past Sandison, who was chewing an antelope cutlet and keeping his own counsel, to Hoop and Griff — "our two secret weapons are willing and able."

Their forks paused in midair, the pair looked at each other for a long moment before saying anything. "It's like Rudy says," said the one, "you got to chuck it in the laundry and see what comes out in the wash." It took me a moment to identify Kipling as translated by Griff, but no time at all to take to heart what Hoop then uttered. "Ready as I'll ever be, this side of the grave."

10

And as planned, the next day's *Thunder* featured, in the top-of-the-page spot where my editorial customarily held forth, an extended "Voices of the Hill."

I worked in the mines for all of my life that amounted to anything, and on my first day in the Nevada Bonanza my three names, Maynard Emlyn Hooper, got barbered down to one, Hoop. Ten years old, I was. Starting out as putter boy, fetching tools and feeding the mules and so forth all the way down in the old Boney. I wasn't so poorly off as Huck Finn with that no-good Pap of his, but my old man was what you might call seasonal, going off somewhere for months on end and leaving my mother and us six kids to get by as best we could. It's funny about life — the only way I could see to go up in the world was down there in the hard rock where it was hotter than the hinges of Hell. I stuck with it, and by the time I was fourteen, I was as much a miner as anybody, following the ore from one place to the next.

Which is how I lit into Butte from the silver diggings in Alta, Utah, where the boss was Marcus Daly. Mark Daly could see into the ground deeper than any other man, and I figured he was worth tagging along with when he came here to the Hill to have a look. I was on the crew in the Anaconda, a good enough mine but nothing special as far as anybody knew, when he had us blast into some "new material," as it was called, at the 300-foot level. I was standing right there when he picked up a chunk of ore with copper showing all through it and turned to the foreman and said, "Mike, we've got it!" That was the making of Butte, the largest deposit of copper in the world, and it set a lot of us up to stay and be miners here. It was not a bad life then. Marcus Daly always got along with the union, and things were pretty peaceful on the Hill. It was a sad day for Butte when he let the Anaconda get away from him and the ownership changed from day to night.

Later on, I was in the shape-up when the first shaft of the Neversweat was being opened, and this fellow came up to me and said, "You look like you know which end of an eight-pound sledge to hold. Want a partner?" And that was Griff. We got ourselves known as a flash team with the hammer and steel, before drilling changed over to the air pressure machines. We was never out of work in the mines together, in the Lucky Jim, the Shamrock, the Frisco, and a bunch of others. We seen a lot. Men hurt or killed, right near us. We're only alive because we worked the earlier shift at the Speculator, before the big fire trapped all those men.

You get a little old, though, and the work gets to be too much for you. These days, Griff and me are new in the occupation of owning a boardinghouse — first thing we've ever owned besides our mining helmets and the clothes on our backs. But we're in a spot. We don't see how we can make a go of it, what with the taxes on the property. It just seems to us a strange situation, where working people have to be hit so heavy while we know perfectly well the biggest company in the state can afford to pay up but doesn't. It makes a person wonder how things got so upside down.

There, I crowed to myself as soon as I felt

221

the vibration of the press whirling those words into the world: If, reader of the *Thunder,* Hoop's tale does not speak to your heart, it is made of harder ore than the Hill's.

Grace served up the fondest of smiles that suppertime and Sandison gruffly congratulated Hoop — alongside, Griff beamed as if the credit were just as much his — who shyly maintained that the newspaper piece was nothing much, "just some gab Morrie took down on paper."

Sandison glanced over at me with amusement. "The moving finger having writ, ay? And moves on to what, Morgan?"

"You shall see," I said, like the magician withholding the rabbit in the hat. "In Jared we trust."

If I thought that would satisfy Sam Sandison, I had another think coming. Grace and I were on our way up to bed when we heard him call from his library lair, "Step in here a minute, Pluvius. Excuse us, madam. I'll return him to you in working order." Rolling her eyes, Grace mouthed, "Don't stay too late," and headed on upstairs.

He had his back to me when I stepped in, shelving a scattering of the books that lived in piles around the room. "The Creation story of Butte in Hoop's own words," he said over his shoulder. "Very moving. Damn near biblical. Anaconda's rag had better think twice before ripping into a poor old miner who has everyone's sympathy, hadn't it." He turned half around, eyeing me over a ridge of shoulder. "Clever."

"Why, thank you, Sandy. Even better, it's true. Principally."

"Wipe the feathers off your whiskers." He gave me The Look. "What if they find out about the boardinghouse shenanigan?"

"I prefer to call it a ploy," I protested, a bit for show. "Merely a necessary tactic. A mild subterfuge. Well, you see my point, I'm sure." The Look did not bear that out. "Sandy, I assure you we are being very careful to stick to the letter of the law. Hoop and Griff are the owners of record ever since a down payment which, let me finish, took place at least on paper, and in time to come, they will simply fail to make their payments, and the property reverts to Grace, under her previous name." I whisked my hands together as if that took care of that. "It was the one way I could think of to bring the battle down to the level of the reading public's wallets. Was I wrong?"

He grunted neutrally. Clomping to his desk, he picked up a volume of *Appleton's*

Cyclopædia of American Biography, the famous edition with no fewer than forty-seven fraudulent entries, rather coincidentally, and glancing at the empty spot on the shelf and deciding it was too much trouble to cross the room again, added it to a pile. "All right, you have the snake by the tail, let us say. What now?"

"The next step is Jared's," I said with confidence. "It's all in the plan."

The *Post* temporized frantically after Hoop's tale of tax distress, practically inventing new dance steps to get around the issue. Scriptoris, showing the strain, dodged off into the generality that property assessments were purely a local matter overseen by a duly elected assessor, ignoring the fact that Anaconda's handpicked candidate for that office always strangely won and prospered in life thereafter.

Meanwhile, letters to the editor sympathetic to the plight of Hoop and Griff poured in to the *Thunder.* "Here's another doozy, lords and ladies," Armbrister trumpeted across the newsroom, plucking the prize from the overflowing mail basket. " 'Why must the rest of us be soaked while Anaconda floats above it all? Drown the reptile in fair taxation!' " Over the cheers and guffaws, he called over to me, "They're doing your job for you, Morgie, bless their angry souls."

Not to the extent I might have wished, as it turned out on what would go down in *Thunder* history as the red-letter day.

The elated editor and I were debating whether to pull an AOT piece out of over-set and settle for that or fill the editorial hole with a fresh Pluvius offering on the plight of the Hoops of the world, when Jared Evans made his appearance, still in his senatorial suit and tie but also wearing a warrior's conquering grin. At the jerk of his head, Armbrister and I stepped out into the editor's sanctum with him.

"We're ready," Jared told us, tired but exultant. "It took so much arm-twisting that half the legislature look like pretzels, but the votes are lined up and the governor will sign it." His eyes met mine, the message there before he spoke it. "Let's tell the world, copper is going to start paying its way. Get out the big type, Jacob."

Armbrister checked the clock and grimaced. "It'll have to be damn fast, Morgie."

"Duly noted."

I raced to my typewriter, flexed my fingers,

prayed to the gods of the alphabet, and began.

The time has come. For far too long, the Treasure State has been robbed of a source of its natural wealth — the jealously guarded profits of the mining industry. As this newspaper has chronicled, under the influence of the Anaconda Company and its Wall Street owners the tax burden has fallen almost entirely on the home owner — which is to say, the miner, the store-keeper, the rancher, the farmer, all of the citizenry shut out of the narrow corridors of power in Helena and unable to prevail in local elections where a certain key candidate proves to be bought and paid for by the company.

Does this mean there is nothing to be done, and Montana is forever doomed to have its mineral treasure extracted nearly tax-free while its citizenry must pay in full to support roads, schools, and other necessities of civil society? Absolutely not. To remedy this fiscal injustice, the Thunder is proud to propose a plan as simple as it is fair. Even as we go to press and these words reach your eyes, Senator Jared Evans is preparing to introduce a measure that will put to a statewide vote the creation of a tax commission to review the levels of revenue from all — all — segments of society. . . .

It was here that Jared's twist came in — a lovely double snare, really — for Anaconda and its political puppets; the war may have cost him the bottom of an ear, but it certainly taught him the art of ambush. Precisely according to the plan he, Rab, Armbrister, and I worked out one night at the Purity, only legislators willing to openly wear the copper collar — even the dimmest of politicians had to choke at that — could oppose letting voters have their say on something that hit home in every pocketbook, and once approved, a tax commission was the ready route to a state levy on mining properties or, lo, even profits. And not coincidentally, a seat on that cocked-and-loaded commission to be appointed by the governor was quietly reserved, with a wink and a handshake, for Senator Evans of the city of Butte. It was almost enough to make an editorial writer swoon. At one swoop, Jared's proposed legislation — and the philippic I was composing as fast as my fingers could fly — took the tax iniquity out of the hands of the company's stooges in the legislature and assessor's offices. Abracadabra, and one link of the copper collar was gone. I would have cheered myself hoarse if I hadn't been so busy writing.

I pounded out the last of the editorial just as Armbrister shouted "Copyboy! Make it snappy, damn it!" As he and Jared gave my words one last careful look, he said aside to me, "Needs a grabber, Morgie, see what you can come up with." Wheeling back to my typewriter, almost without thinking I produced:

WHAT IS TO BE DONE?

That hurried headline seemed to fit the case, the copyboy went scrambling away to the typesetter with the finished result, and like mountaineers who had scaled a treacherous escarpment, the jubilant three of us — editor, publisher, and editorialist — slapped one another on the back in the rare alpine air of success.

Then the strangest thing. No word was heard from the *Post* in response, rebuttal, refutation, anything. A day passed, another, two more, then three, and it was as if Scriptoris had taken no notice of a proposal that would shake Anaconda in its giant boots, and all in the world the *Post* was concerned about were the old standbys, potholes, and patriotism.

"I don't like it." Armbrister tossed the latest namby-pamby example in the trash with the rest of the week's worth. "They're too quiet over there. The sunuvabitches."

"I'll take it," Jared said with relief. "While they've got their heads stuck in Afghanistan or wherever you call it, we're building support for the tax commission vote all the time. The Stockmen's Association is lined up to pass a resolution — we can thank Williamson for that, the Farm Bureau will follow suit, and, get this, every lodge in Butte, from the Moose to the Knights of Columbus, is with us. Not to mention these." He fondly patted the overflowing mail basket.

Even the saturnine editor had to admit things appeared to be going well, although not before snapping the question to me, "The boardinghouse boys — they making sure to do their part?"

I assured him Griff and Hoop were going through the motions of new property owners, and with them, motions were loudly noticeable. They enthusiastically spoke of having the boardinghouse open — with Grace's consent, of course — for the summer turnover, when numbers of miners returned to families in the old country and newcomers drawn by the smoky beacon of the stacks of the Neversweat arrived to take their place. I saw no reason to add that Hoop and Griff, for company's sake, still slept and ate at the manse.

Thus it was that I left work at the end of one of those heady days of editorial cloud-walking in the best of moods, humming the "America" reel from the Burns celebration as I started home. Spring was providing more definite indicators than Sandison's sniff sorting the Hill smoke from pleasant airs to come; any tree that managed to survive in Butte was showing buds, nature's assertion that hope springs eternal. Caught up in the season and my even sunnier mood, I did not pay particular mind when my usual route was interrupted by a broken water main, which had turned the street into a pond.

As a glum municipal crew tried to stem the flood, I detoured through an alley that brought me out on an unfamiliar backstreet. The prime business on the block, from the look of it an original bucket-of-blood saloon, now announced itself as the MILE-HIGH BILLIARDS AND PINOCHLE SOCIAL CLUB, making me chuckle at the resourcefulness of speakeasies. Although the enterprise evidently had not yet opened for the evening, out front a hawk-nosed man in a bowler hat was holding forth to a uniformed policeman, gesturing in frustration at the purported social club. He broke off at the sight of me.

"Well, well. Speak of the devil." Swaggering up to me, he thrust his face practically into mine. "Couldn't resist dropping by" — he jerked his head toward the speakeasy — "to see how business is, huh?"

"You are mistaken," I sputtered, drawing back from his intrusion. "I'm a, a property owner and a taxpayer and a fully employed —"

"The mistake's all yours, Highliner," he sneered the word, "showing your face around here in broad daylight. Rub our noses in it, I suppose you think, strutting around collecting your bootlegging swag like a real businessman. We'll see about that." Hawknose flashed a badge and practically purred, "Let's run him in, Murph."

"No, wait, I'm not —" The uniformed policeman, the burly sort called a harness bull, clamped me by the biceps. "Shut your yap and come on along to the station house."

There, the desk sergeant sat back in shock.

231

"Jaysis, Davis, you'll be arresting the pope next."

"If I catch him running booze right under our noses, you better bet I will." The hawk-nosed detective cut off my attempt to protest that I had been doing no such thing. "Book him on something or other — 'spitting on the sidewalk' will do until I can come up with better charges — and toss him in the drunk tank. We'll see how he likes his customers for company."

The view from behind bars was a disturbing one. The world abruptly striped with iron, smelling bad, and rife with company of dubious character. My cell mates were a pale, bony man still wearing a full-length apron that marked him as a dishwasher, traditional occupation of drunks, and a stouter individual with the characteristic stoop of a miner. The aproned one had the shakes. In a cracked voice he asked me, "Got a flask on you, buddy?"

"Sorry, I'm not equipped."

"Dressed like that and you don't carry a drink of no kind? What are you, some kind of camel?"

The other inmate, marginally less unsteady, ogled me with a slowly dawning expression. "Say. You ain't — ?"

"You're right, I'm not."

"We unnerstand, don't worry. A guy starts owning up, it can get to be a bad habit, can't it." Shielding his mouth with his hand, he whispered something to his jail mate. The shaky one said, "Ooh." The other continued, low enough not be heard outside the cell, "He gives the cops fits." They both took a wobbly step back in tribute. "You can have the lower bunk."

I lay down and put my hat over my eyes, to try to let this nightmare pass. Of all the people on the planet I could resemble, why did it have to be the kingpin of a gang of bootleggers? True, the Highliner seemed to run a masterfully efficient operation, judging by that tempting cache of cash I had glimpsed at the warehouse, but he still was a lawbreaker, even if the law was a supremely stupid one. If I had to have a twin, why not Charlie Chaplin or George Bernard Shaw or some other personality the world would heap with riches and esteem instead of perilous misapprehensions? Finally worn out by the traffic of such thoughts and aided by the considerate *shh*s of my cell mates to each other, I drifted off to the only escape at hand, slumber.

I awoke on the jail bed to Sandison frowning through the bars at me. "Turn him loose," he wearily told the hawk-nosed detective at his side. "I know him like a bad habit."

"If he's not the Highliner," the detective protested, "then who is he?"

"My butler, you fool." Sandison scowled at me. "The next time I send you downtown for cigars, do you think you can stay out of trouble?"

"I'll make every effort."

We left the jail, the clangor of the nearest mines on the Hill following us as we headed home in the dusk. After the first wordless block or so, Sandison glanced at me. "What's the matter? Your jailbird phase make you forget how to talk?"

" 'Butler,' Sandy?" I gave him a look. "You could just as easily have said I'm your land-lord."

"*Tch tch,* hurt feelings? Maybe I should have left you in there with the bedbugs and barflies."

"How did you know I was incarcerated?"

"The boy. Snickelfritz or whatever you call him."

"Russian Famine, in reality. Thank heaven he watches out for me."

"Someone needs to, Morgan. You seem to

be a walking lightning rod." An observation of the sort from the Earl of Hell did not lift my spirits any. "The whippersnapper came tearing into the library to find me, saying he'd been delivering newspapers to the jail as usual when he spotted you back there in the drunk tank. 'Must've got into that libation stuff,' he told me." Sandison's upper half shook with amusement. "Sharp lad."

"Jail, Morrie. That's not good."

"Grace, it could have happened to anyone of my general appearance under the circumstances."

"I thought you just said it was a million-to-one chance that you happen to be the spitting image of this Highliner person."

"Paradoxical, but true."

She softened the next with a bit of a smile, but concern was behind it. "I don't remember that part in the wedding vows."

"Only because 'for better and for worse' sounds less dire," I muttered, undressing for bed. Already in her nightie, Grace undid her braid and shook her hair for brushing. She watched me in the dresser mirror while silently counting her strokes. Much too disturbed to settle in for the night, I paced the floor in my slippers and pajamas, trying to reach some conclusion. If my stint in jail was upsetting to Grace, the shotgun blast from the other side of the law in my first encounter with the Highliner's shadow world of bootlegging would be decidedly more so, were I to tell her the whole thing. Yet it would hardly be right to leave her wondering what manner of mannequin she was married to. The remedy was drastic, but had to be swallowed. Going to Grace, I nuzzled her cheek as the hairbrush paused in mid-stroke. "I have something to tell you, darling."

What a picture we made as a couple, caught there in the mirror's reflection, she as violet-eyed and pleasant-faced as a maiden in a Dutch painting and I in my set expression of determination, my beard practically bristling with resolve as I announced my decision. "I am going down to the barbershop tomorrow and have it shaved off."

Grace took in my mirrored image before finally saying, "Let me be sure I'm following this development. You intend to make the earthshaking change to clean-shaven in order to not look . . . paradoxical?"

"Exactly. More or less."

She pursed her lips coquettishly. "Naturally I'll miss the whiskers. But of course, you must do what you think is right."

■ ■ ■ ■

Sacrificing a beard may sound easy, but believe me, it is more than a matter of lather and razor. There is an attachment that goes beyond the follicles. My crop of whiskers had been carefully grown during our honeymoon year, and thus was a kind of keepsake of that romantic time. And a cultivated beard had proved to be a successful disguise on our travels, permitting me to pass with impunity even through the Chicago train station, in proximity to the gambling mob and its window men. No, shaving it off would be like losing an old friend, one who had served well. My reflection in the downtown store windows was more than a little guilty, the upper part of my face apologizing to the lower half. Why couldn't the damnable Highliner shave his? A mute question, as Hoop and Griff would have called it, and I trudged on toward the barbershop.

I was passing the *Thunder* building when Armbrister thrust his head out the office window. "Morgie! Damn it, man, we've been looking high and low for you."

"I'll be in later," I called back, "I'm on my way to a tonsorial appointment."

"Never mind that, get yourself up here right this minute. We've got big trouble."

When I entered the newsroom, the entire staff was clustered around Armbrister's desk. He was scowling down into what I could tell was our contraband early copy of the day's *Post,* the ink practically dripping from it. "All right, everybody. Hold on to your hats and listen to this."

THE TRUTH COMES OUT. IN RED.

What is black and white and red all over?

The usual punch line, cue the guffaw, is a newspaper, read to the fullest extent of the pun and readerly endurance. But there is a wholly unfunny answer when the gazette in question is the daily issuance of ominous noise that calls itself the *Thunder.* For it has revealed its true colors, and those are, in the anthem of revolutionaries awaiting their chance, deepest red.

"Whaaat? Have they gone loony?" Hoots and groans and profanities chorused until Armbrister held up a hand. "It gets worse."

Consider this: The *Thunder*'s latest jeremiad against the existing order in the mining industry — which is to say the capitalistic system — was brazenly head-lined **What Is To Be Done?** Which was, let's don't mince words, the exact question of Lenin, the Bolshevik leader, with which he titled his published blueprint for undermining the existing order in Russia and seizing power for his ruthless socialistic coterie. It is all there, the plan for the dictatorship of the proletariat, and it surfaces now on American soil with the coaxing of a supposedly legitimate newspaper. The telltale phrase is a code for Bolshevism, nothing less and nothing more.

That was met with stunned silence. My head felt as if it were going to burst.
Armbrister read on.

The Red menace takes various forms — anarchist bombs and bullets, on-the-job sabotage by the Industrial Workers of the World (the so-called Wobblies; may they wobble back to their holes) that this industrial community only lately has rid itself of through apt governmental prosecutions and direct action — but here is a new and insidious manifestation, striking at the profits that pay the wages that provide prosperity. As the mouthpiece for the radical element in the miners' union, the *Thunder* is slickly setting the tune for nothing less than the soviet of Butte.

It's enough to make an honest patriot see red and hurl those bespoiled batches of newsprint being peddled on the street into the nearest trash can, isn't it.

There was more, much more. All of it invective, expertly done. The blood seemed to have drained out of the *Thunder* staff; I am sure I had turned pale as a ghost.

When Armbrister finally recited the last iota of innuendo, he removed his eyeshade and mopped his brow. The younger staff members glanced around nervously. Mary Margaret Houlihan moved her lips in prayer.

As for me, I had an awful feeling in my gut. From lede to end, Scriptoris never saw the day when he could deploy language in so deadly a fashion. In the stunned silence of my colleagues, I asked, "How . . . how is it signed?"

With extreme distaste, Armbrister read off the editorial signature beneath the diatribe: " 'Cutlass.' "

Of course. It would be.

Cutlass, as I too well knew, was the byline and trademark of the newspaperman more familiarly called Cutthroat Cartwright, the most famous and feared columnist in the savage pages of Chicago journalism. Just the thought of him anywhere in my vicinity made my head hurt.

Cecil Cartwright had claimed early fame in the Spanish-American War for writing dispatches under fire during the charge up San Juan Hill by Teddy Roosevelt and his Rough Riders, and parlayed that into the safer but still combative career of sportswriter. Meaner than Ring Lardner and shrewder than Damon Runyon, he scourged anyone he set his sights on — I'd immediately recognized touches such as "cue the guffaw" and "let's don't mince words" as characteristic of his cold-eyed, cold-hearted style. The fact that the Anaconda Company had imported him to wage editorial battle with the *Thunder* was bad enough, to judge by our stunned newsroom. But his arrival to Butte brought with it an even worse threat to me. Cartwright's latest notch in his belt was breaking the story of the Black Sox scandal, and should it somehow come to his attention that his word-slinging counterpart across town, a rival to be eliminated by innuendo or whatever else it took, happened to be the mysterious Montana bettor who had outguessed the World Series fixers and won a fortune, he would leak that news back to the Chicago gambling mob as surely as water runs downhill. So I was in deep, deep trouble if Cutthroat, as I would always think of him, ever saw through me and my beard.

At the moment, the urgent need was to rally the shell-shocked *Thunder* staff. Putting up a show of confidence as bold as it was illusory, I addressed the silent ring of faces around me, Armbrister's worried one foremost.

"Never fear. Tomorrow Pluvius will respond in kind, fang and claw."

"My, you are a marvel," Grace greeted me, beard and all. "You've grown another one already."

"I'm more fond of it than I knew."

"I'm glad. It makes you stand out." Before I could blink that away, she was giving me a kiss and asking, "And how was your day at the paper?"

"Heart-stopping. You'll hear more than enough about it at supper."

The mealtime consensus was that the Cutlass editorial was deadly. Coming to the "soviet of Butte" phrase in the *Post* I had forced myself to buy on the way home, Griff observed to Hoop, "That's pretty strong, ain't it." In her turn at it, Grace gasped — "Bolshevik! Oh, Morrie, how awful!" — and wrung her hands until I put a calming one atop hers and repeated my ill-founded assurance that I would take care of the matter on the morrow. For his part, Sandison scanned the invective with a series of grunts but otherwise stayed dangerously quiet. As we rose from the table, however, he gave me a sharp glance and I followed him to his library quarters as if magnetized.

"Good grief, so-called wordsmith," he wasted no time, "you handed them the billy club to beat you into the ground with. 'Red menace,' hah," he practically spat out, "but you left yourself wide open for that one, didn't you. Jared Evans can't help but be utterly sick when this reaches Helena and the louts in the legislature, can he. What were you thinking, man?"

"Sandy," I sounded as miserable as I felt, "I was writing at deadline speed and the connection of 'What is to be done?' to Lenin's infernal revolutionary tract simply never occurred to me."

"You'd better race the deadline for wriggling out of the straitjacket this Cutlass character slapped on you." Irritably he reared back, his paunch bulging as he considered me, down the formidable slope of himself. "Well? What are you going to do about it, mad dog Marxist. Skedaddle off the newspaper, so it can say you're out of the picture and the revolution isn't coming to Butte after all?"

"Quite the opposite." I repeated to him my last-ditch vow to the *Thunder* staff that I would parry Cutlass's slashing attack. "Toward that end, may I borrow this" — I indicated to his library trove that surrounded us on all walls — "for the evening?"

"I should hope so," Sandison drawled as if it were his idea all along. "You need all the help you can get, Pluvius." Grumbling to himself, he lumbered to a shelf and plucked out *Paradise Lost,* the beautiful edition with Gustave Doré illustrations. "Myself, I'm retiring for the night with Milton as company. There's a man who savvied 'confusion worse confounded.' You might read him sometime yourself. Heh."

With that, I was left alone with the silent legion of books standing at attention all around me, tier upon tier of the world's finest literature. I draped my suit coat over the back of Sandison's oversize chair and tried to decide where to begin, on a search through so many pages. What I was after had to be somewhere in the riches of this room. It had to be.

I still was hunting, groggy and haggard in the small hours of the night, when Grace tapped on the door and came in before I could respond. Rubbing the sleep from her eyes, she peered worriedly at me and the books piled in the pool of light given by the desk lamp. "Aren't you coming to bed at all?"

"Sleep isn't the answer," I mumbled, not looking up from the open pages.

I heard her slippers shuffle on the carpet as she crossed the room, and then she was beside me, hefting *War and Peace* from the stack at my side, weighing her words along with it. "Morrie? I realize you're in a fix and looking for a way out of it, but I have to ask." Strain thinned the usual lilt out of her voice. "You aren't trying to read yourself to death, are you?"

Until right then I had never considered an overfill of books as one of the mortal varieties of fate. There are worse. But that was not my mission. "No, darling," I answered hoarsely. "I'm trying to raise the *Thunder* from the dead."

However, the newsroom the next day was like a tomb when I dragged in, so exhausted I could hardly see straight. All eyes were on me, although that changed as soon as the reporters who had covered the newsprint conflagration incited by the Cutlass editorial straggled to the editor's desk with their eyewitness accounts. They'd had the sickening experience of watching their own words go up in smoke while mobs, doubtless spurred on by Anaconda operatives, seized stacks of *Thunder*s from outnumbered newsboys and chanted "Burn the Bolshie rag!" while turning the newspapers into bonfires on street corners. Naturally Armbrister in hearing these painful reports was long-faced as an undertaker whose dog had died, but when the last reporter had his dispirited say, the editor had his. "Don't bring me a laundry list, get me a story, damn it," he instructed with an intensity that made heads snap back even among those of us merely listening in. "Pull up your knickers, the whole bunch of you," he barked — which happened to include Mary Margaret Houlihan, pressed into service in the scramble to cover the firestorm of anti-*Thunder* thuggery — "and sit down with Matthews on rewrite and give him what you've got, one by one, like with any other assignment. I know this story hits you in the gut, but we're going to pull it together and front-page the sunuvabitch like it's the lede of the Bible, everybody savvy that? Now get at it."

Everyone else in the newsroom, including me, walked a wide circle around Armbrister after that outburst. Not to my surprise, Jared came in practically on my heels, redeploying himself from the legislative fight in Helena to try to rally the *Thunder* troops in the crisis my editorial had caused. Noble fellow, he did not assess blame, although his expression was much like it must have been under fire from German snipers. After a brief exchange with Armbrister that won a dour nod of the green eyeshade, our publisher called the staff together, with the exception of the reporters working with the rewrite man typing at machine-gun pace in the rear of the room.

"Chin up, everybody," Jared started right

in on what we faced. "Anaconda has tried this old stunt on us before, playing the Red card. It didn't work then because there were always the Wobblies raising hell and the union looked sane in comparison. Now we have to slug it out on the Bolshie issue, so we will." Smacking a fist into his palm, he turned to me. "I hope you're loaded for bear, Professor." In my sleepless near trance, Grace's image of Anaconda as a carnival bear dangerous when unmuzzled so transfixed me that the roomful of *Thunder* staff began to shift uneasily before I thought to respond.

"I've . . ." I had to swallow that croak and start again, "I've found what is needed. I'll put it to use."

Depend on it, Armbrister rapped out, "You need to make it prontissimo. We're coming up on —"

"— yes, yes, deadline." Without another word, I started across the newsroom to my typewriter, trying not to totter. Armbrister and Jared shadowed me as if I might fall and break, the latter asking in my ear, "Professor, are you sure you can write straight? You look like you've been dragged by the eyeballs."

"Just get me coffee. Lots of it."

They hovered around me like handlers tending a boxer in a corner of the ring, Armbrister snatching each finished page from me to read in one gulp and cry, "That's the stuff!" before thrusting it to the copyboy to run it to the back shop, while Jared kept replenishing my coffee until I practically sloshed. But when the last sheet of paper was ripped from my typewriter and dispatched for typesetting, the *Thunder* had spoken.

WHAT IS TO BE DONE?
COME CLEAN, THAT'S WHAT.

Yesterday, the copper mouthpiece known as the *Daily Post* sounded a note of shrill hysteria, inciting mob action against, of all innocent targets, newsboys. Those bonfires of *Thunder* bundles are only the flicker of the conflagration the *Post* and its Anaconda masters hope to set off, however. The corporate potentates and their journalistic janissaries are resorting to one of the oldest and ugliest tactics, guilt by association. Let's examine again the inflammatory charges made against this newspaper and its purportedly notorious editorial, **What Is To Be Done?**

"Which was, let's don't mince words," the *Post* blustered, "the exact question of Lenin, the Bolshevik leader, with which he titled his published blueprint for undermining the existing order in Russia and seizing power for his ruthless socialistic coterie. It is all there, the plan for the dictatorship of the proletariat, and it surfaces now on American soil with the coaxing of a supposedly legitimate newspaper. The telltale phrase is a code for Bolshevism, nothing less and nothing more."

Oh, really?

The *Post* accuser-in-charge must not be much of a reader. One only has to delve into that acknowledged masterpiece of Russian and world literature, *Anna Karenina,* written long before Bolsheviks ever existed to serve as bogeymen, to come across this supposedly sinister catchphrase uttered time and again by the cast of characters as a cry of the Russian soul to the heavens: Oblonsky in despair over his debauched life, Levin — Tolstoy's country squire alter ego — in guilt over the political paralysis of his privileged class, and most tellingly, Anna Karenina herself in torment over a marriage that is coming apart. If the Robespierre of the

Russian revolution, V. I. Lenin, plucked a similar plaint out of the air three decades later, it only shows how common the expression is, down to the current day. To charge that anyone uttering it in print — Tolstoy, we are humbly in your company — is espousing Bolshevism is like saying the dictionary is full of words radicals use.

At that point of the piece, having fought off the worst Cutlass could throw, it was time to fight back, and I did so with vehemence.

The *Post* and its insinuating editorialist likely cannot be counted on to come clean about their true purpose, so the *Thunder* is happy to do it for them. If there is anything "Red" about this episode, it is the red-handed attempt to scapegoat a rival. This is the kind of propaganda that produces class warfare, pogroms, lynchings, and in this ridiculously contrived mob outburst, the bullying of blameless newsboys and destruction of their wares. Such malicious instigation is the venom of hate throughout the worst of history. The antidote is truth, and here it is: the only revolution this newspaper advocates is the overthrow of Anaconda's unconfessed influence over the state of Montana's tax system.

In short, a person could survey every liars' club from here to Chicago and not find a bigger falsehood than that in the *Post*'s false diatribe of yesterday.

— PLUVIUS

"That ought to hold them awhile," Jared exulted, and the staff cheered as the press began to roll with our boldly headlined shot back at Cutthroat Cartwright and the higher snakes on the top floor of the Hennessy Building.

"My, aren't we glad Sandy had books by all those Russians," Grace said.

"Maybe you're learning your trade, Morgan," Sandison granted. "That Chicago gibe was a nice touch. Heh, heh."

True to Jared's prediction, the *Thunder*'s retaliatory blast did give the *Post* cause for pause. Its editorials for the next some days were confined to topics such as streetlights and stray dogs — and to our relief, the corner bonfires of *Thunders* were quenched when Cutlass wasn't furnishing the matches. Our own philippics, in Jared's choice word, kept up the drumbeat on taxes, taxes, taxes, though I was exceedingly careful not to give Cutthroat Cartwright another opening; the "Red menace" episode had been too narrow an escape. Newspaper life seemed to have settled down to the usual journalistic rivalry, our reporters resorting to every wile to scoop theirs, our newsboys outshouting theirs with catchier headlines. Yet there was a feeling in the air, distinct as the ink-and-nicotine atmosphere in the *Thunder* newsroom, that in the ongoing struggle with Anaconda, it was our move next.

Rab precipitated it.

On Saturday furlough from the hoosegow school, she and Russian Famine accompanied Jared when he dropped by to brief Armbrister and me on that week's legislative progress toward the vital statewide vote on the tax commission matter. "It's slower than digging the Panama Canal, but we're getting there," he vouched. "The bill survived the committee hearings despite all the company's Ulcer Gulch stooges tried to do to it, and now it comes to the floor. We win there, and all it takes is the governor's signature."

And many thousand voters' X's, I thought but didn't say. Jared was inhaling the smell of victory, Rab bright and keen at his side, and even Armbrister for once came out from under his cloud. Maybe we all caught exuberance from Famine, darting to the society desk where Mary Margaret Houlihan, possessed of a sweet tooth, kept a jar of gumdrops free for the taking, and helped himself to his customary handful. Back in high spirits myself — there is nothing like a close call to sharpen one's zest for life — I caught his eye and when the others were lost in conversation, I clinked the brass knuckles in my pocket as though I were jingling loose change. Grinning conspiratorially at the sound, the newsboy bounded off to the back room for his bag and bundle of *Thunder*s.

"He thinks you're the cat's meow, Mr. Morgan," Rab observed. "All I hear is how much he wants to be like you."

Touched by that, "He's one of a kind himself" was as much as I could say.

"Maybe the kid is getting us more readers than we are, bless his buttons." Armbrister really was in a sunny mood. "Circulation's up, day by day."

"That's the stuff," I chortled.

"The more the merrier," Jared said jubilantly.

"All well and good," the feminine voice of

reason abridged us, "but aren't you just preaching to the choir?"

We three men buttoned our lips like caught schoolboys taking our scolding and reluctantly faced around to its authority. It was up to Jared to ask warily, "How so, Rab?"

She poised for a moment before settling to the corner of the editor's desk, in the attitude of a canny abbess revealing the Gospel. "You're selling papers like mad here in town, but what does that prove? Butte people mostly have their minds already made up about Anaconda and the miners, they've had to for years, haven't they." She was not waiting to hear the male view of things. "What about other places? Every voter in the state is going to have a say on the tax issue, but how many of them have any chance to read Mr. Morgan's editorials, unless they pick them up out of the tumbleweeds?" Having made her point, she crossed her arms on her bosom and looked at us sternly.

Jared recovered first. "As much as I hate to admit it, she's right. I practically wallpaper the legislature with the *Thunder* when I can, but go downtown in Helena and there's Anaconda's local propaganda sheet being sold on every corner."

"We've looked at this up, down, and sideways," Armbrister protested. "Shipping bundles of papers around the state by train costs a fortune — the Anaconda bastards see to that with the railroads, you can just bet. And it's slower than the Second Coming, anyway." He shrugged fatalistically. "We're putting out a Butte newspaper, Jared, we can't snap our fingers and change that."

Maybe we couldn't, but someone could. In spite of myself, the phrase *What is to be done?* again raised a clamor in my brain, demanding answer. To quiet it, I entered the discussion Jared and Armbrister were having.

"If, as the Braille salesman said to the Cyclops, you'll turn a blind eye, I believe I can arrange to have truckloads distributed to other towns."

"At how much per delivery?" Armbrister demanded.

"As low as it goes. Don't ask me more."

"Truckloads?" exclaimed Jared. "How?"

"Blind eye, remember? Have the bundles waiting under a tarpaulin on the loading dock tonight."

"There, see?" Rab said as if it had all been foretold.

Armbrister was dubiously doing arithmetic on a sheaf of copy paper. "We'd need to double our press run."

Jared looked at me, then at the pleased pussycat that was Rab, then at me again. He set his jaw and said, "Let's go for broke."

"*Hsst.* Over here, Smitty."

"Boss! Almost didn't see you there in the shadows." The thickset bootlegger veered off from entering the warehouse and joined me in the dark alley. "I thought you wasn't coming back until next week."

"Change of plans," I intoned in what I hoped was a passable Highliner voice.

"I bet I know. You don't want them dumb duck hunters catching on to your comings and goings." He peeked around the corner until satisfied there was no sign of an ambush vehicle and someone riding shotgun, literally. "Coast's clear. Ain't you coming in to tell the boys what's what, like always?"

"I'm in a hurry, I have to leave it to you." Smitty swelled in importance. "The trucks on the Whiskey Gap run —"

"Boy, that works so slick, boss, you'd think it was a regular highway out there in nowhere."

"— the trucks are empty on the way north, am I right?"

"Sure they are, so we can load them to the gills when they get to Canada."

"Tell the boys here's what I want done on the trips from now on." I recited it as he listened closely. When I was through, he wore a puzzled expression.

"Just plain old newspapers, is this?"

"Hardly plain." I thought fast. "More like an extra, only they can't call it that every day. You know how people snap those up to see what has happened. Think how many more drinks that will add up to while customers sit there taking in the news."

"Oh, I get it." Smitty brushed the shoulder of my overcoat in case any speck had dared to light on it. "You bet, we'll drop papers at every speakeasy from here to Canada. What a humdinger of an idea, boss."

Fresh from that unblemished performance as the Highliner and riding high in the newsroom on account of the *Thunder*'s miraculously doubled circulation, I hummed my way up the front walk after work the next day. Even Ajax on the door knocker looked less forbidding than usual. "Grace," I called cheerily as I stepped in, for once unconcerned about whatever mischief the house had wreaked on itself during my hours away. "I'm home, darling. Yoo-hoo."

No answer. Or did I hear a low moan somewhere?

"Grace?" With growing apprehension I headed for the kitchen, the silence at that end of the long hallway now more ominous than any sound.

I burst in, then stepped back at the sight of her, seated at the kitchen table as if dumped there. Her face was smeared white. The calamine lotion she was slathering on her arms barely covered the red welts from wrist to elbow. Stopping to scratch like fury, she looked at me woefully through her tragic white mask.

"Morrie," she said in an awful tone, "you're giving me hives."

"I just got here," I said in confusion.

"You know what I'm talking about." She strenuously banged the bottom of the calamine bottle with the palm of her hand for more of the soothing lotion, which unfortunately for me could not be taken internally.

"Grace" — I circled in as close as I dared, knowing better than to touch her — "I have no idea what brought this on."

"Your, your past history," she half whispered as if in agony. I blanched. She went on miserably, "There was a knock on the

259

door after you left for work this morning. Who else but the railroad drayman, saying our trunk had turned up finally. Hurrah, I thought, but when he brought it in, I saw it wasn't ours" — she gritted her teeth and dug at both elbows before going on — "and figured it had to be the one you'd lost when you first came to Butte."

I had lamented the loss of that trunk, with all my earthly belongings in it, for a year and a half, but right then I wished it had vanished forever.

"Then I thought," Grace was struggling to tell the rest, "I don't know what I thought, but I peeked in the trunk and there were some clothes and things but mostly books. I picked up the one on top, wanting to surprise you with it when you came home — it was something or other in Latin —"

"Julius Caesar's *Gallic Wars*," I said numbly, knowing what was coming.

"— and when I opened it out of curiosity, there it was on the flyleaf, wasn't it. 'To Morgan. Merry Christmas 1908 in any language. Forever yours, Rose.' " She looked at me furiously. "Another wife, have we here?" She scratched at herself so hard it hurt to watch. "And that wasn't all."

"No, but I can expl—"

"Newspaper clippings of a prizefighter.

Who looked for all the world like a younger you, but with some name I never heard of." This woman I so loved, the mending spirit of my life, gazed at me through her wretched mask of lotion and asked the question I had hoped would never come. "Who are you, if you're not Morris Morgan?"

12

Morgan Llewellyn, of course. Although for someone left as much in the dark about my past as Grace, there was no "of course" to it, unfortunately. More like a plaintive owl hoot *"Who?"*

In desperation I set out to explain that the prizefighter was not me but my late brother Casper "the Capper" Llewellyn, onetime lightweight champion of the world, and Rose was not my wife but his, and therefore merely my sister-in-law — "You must believe me, Rose is the sort who would sign 'Forever Yours' on a Montgomery Ward catalog order" — and that certain unforeseen circumstances back in Chicago had made it imperative for me to change my name. With interruptions accompanied by Grace's furious scratching, the story came out in fits and starts. Even so, she soon enough grasped that a fixed championship fight, the gambling mob's wrath that did in

Casper, and the necessity for Rose and me to flee together to Montana were involved.

When I was finished, or at least out of words, the woman I had never wanted to hurt looked at me in a heartbreaking way. "Morrie, you are a magnet for trouble," she despaired. "If all this happened a dozen years ago, why are the gamblers still after you?"

"Long memories and short tempers." I thought it best not to add that a suspicious World Series bet worth a junior fortune was enough to stir both of those.

My hopes went up while she deliberated as if to herself. "I can understand that much, I suppose." Butte as well as Chicago certainly held examples of such behavior, after all. Then, though, she spoke with more agitation than even hives could bring about. "But to marry me under" — was I imagining, or did the red of her eyes increase like the glow of coals as she sought the most damning phrase — "false pretenses! Who am I supposed to be, let alone you, with a phony name that I'm not even sure I can spell?"

"I, ah, apologize for the discrepancy," I gingerly tried soothing her. "But people alter names all the time."

"Oh, really? Since when, impostor?"

263

"Since, well, let's say Mark Twain. It is well known he was born Samuel Langhorne Clemens, and if that doesn't constitute an alteration —"

"Morrie, he was a writer," she said through her teeth, "of course he made things up. I'm talking about honest citizens."

"Then what about a vice president of the United States?"

"Now you're telling me that pickle-puss Calvin Coolidge is not actually Calvin Coolidge?"

"I'm not prepared to speak to that," I backed off markedly. "I refer to an earlier officeholder — Henry Wilson, who served under the presidency of Ulysses S. Grant, 1873 to 1875, I believe the dates were. The poor man began life as Jeremiah Jones Colbath. So, you see, there is precedent for improving on one's given na—"

"I see, all right. And I don't care what some forgotten mucky-muck back in the time of Useless Grant called himself, what matters to me is the husband I thought was Morrie Morgan but who turns out to be Morgan Llewellyn, if he is even telling the truth about that, and with a price on his hide besides." Tear tracks glistened on the calamine mask of her face. "I never expected life with you to be all strawberries and cream. I went through enough with Arthur to know a marriage isn't like that. But to find out that you're not at all who I thought you were —" Her voice trembled and broke. "Why couldn't you have told me before now?"

"Because I was afraid of something like this."

"Did you think I wouldn't forgive you?"

"You could start now," I said hopefully.

"Ooh, you. Morrie, I can't take it," she moaned. "I cannot live with someone who goes through life like, like" — she scratched more furiously than ever — "a chameleon on a barber pole." As ominously as I could hear them coming, her next words hit me worse than blows. "I'm going back to the boardinghouse. You can have your mansion and your shenanigans and your names, and see if I care."

The door-banging commotion of her departure drew Sandison out of his book-lined stronghold, the drumbeat of boots preceding the familiar bulk and beard into the drawing room where I waited despondently for the next round I was bound to lose. Before he had time to do more than scowl at me, Griff and Hoop appeared behind him, suitcases in hand.

"Um, uh," Griff stammered, and could manage no further utterance.

Hoop croaked out: "What he means is —"

"I know," I acknowledged the valises they were holding as guiltily as robbers making a getaway.

"It's nothing against you, Morrie," they practically chorused.

"That's welcome news."

"We're sort of attached to Mrs. Morgan, is all."

"Understood."

"We aren't taking sides, you know."

"Of course not."

"It's not for us to judge whose fault it is when a woman walks out on a man or anything."

"Just go."

"Righto."

They shuffled to the door. "It's been nice, Mr. Sandison." He grunted in response as they gimped out to join Grace at the boardinghouse.

"The last two rats on the ghost ship, are we?" Sandison rumbled in the oppressive silence of the house. "What did you do to the poor woman, Morgan?"

"Nothing that can be corrected without going back in history, I fear," I said in agita-

266

tion, pacing back and forth on the Turkish rug.

"That bad, hmm?" He crooked a finger for me to follow him into the library. "What a shame. I liked that Grace," his words kept after me as the desk chair groaned under his bulk. "Reminded me of Dora. Had a mind of her own. Not every woman does." No, mainly the ones who repeatedly tossed me in the reject bin. Rose and Grace. Womanhood unbridled, when it came to my efforts to be a reliable mate in life. Caught up in self-pity as I was, it took me a moment for Sandison's change of tone to register and stop me in my tracks. "Tell me," he was saying quietly, "the whole thing."

I did. My true name. The fixed-fight scheme, when Casper yielded his lightweight championship of the world — "Just parking it until the return bout," he reasoned — that worked all too well. The unabated fury of the Chicago gambling mob after it figured out we had won a fortune betting on the opponent. My beloved brother's long walk off a short pier into Lake Michigan, as the gamblers took their revenge and looked around for more. The pose of Rose and myself as sister and brother in our Marias Coulee concealment, her as a housekeeper and me as teacher in the one-room school. My impulsive return to Montana after nearly ten years' absence, only to become enmeshed in the 1919 chapter of struggle between the miners and Anaconda and thence shadowed incessantly by company goons suspicious of my identity. Even I had to admit, it added up to quite a story. If confession was good for the soul, mine should now have been so freshly scrubbed it shone.

Stroking his beard like a pet, my listener said not a word until I was done. "Gamblers. Bad company," he *tch-tch*ed, the man who had sent people swinging from the end of a rope for looking sideways at his cows. He heaved himself around in his chair to face me directly. "Back there in '19, I wondered why you rated goons trailing you around more than anyone else in this demented town."

"Yes, well, at least that pair of imbeciles long since departed Montana for the sake of their health. As prescribed by the Wobblies, whom they were managing to annoy when they weren't after me like bloodhounds."

Sandison eyed me thoughtfully while I awaited whatever wise counsel he could offer to a wifeless, overworked, underpaid editorialist operating under an alias beyond an assumed name. Instead, what I received was:

"Morgan? 'Twixt thee and me, you don't happen to be this Highliner character, by any chance?"

13

I have to admit it: the iambic beat of " 'Twixt thee and me, you don't happen to be" as uttered by Sandison came like the opening of a new chapter of myself. As if some turn of plot had sprung loose from the most imaginative of his books there in their wise ranks surrounding us in the circular room and, in the surprise coil of a sterling tale, captured the story line of my existence. Imagine what that would mean. My telling of the episode in the booze warehouse is shown to be a charade, and I stand revealed as the bootlegging mastermind I was taken for. Possessor of a daring secret existence such as that of the Scarlet Pimpernel during the French Revolution. Avenger in the mask of a people's hero who causes chaos in the despotic haciendas of the rich and mighty, as per Zorro. Dual personality with an interchangeable identity in the manner of Dr. Jekyll and Mr. Hyde

— no, that goes much too far. In this doffing of disguise, I simply emerge in my own telling as the Highliner whose appearance I already shared, with access to a safe crammed with cash, a legion of willing henchmen, and a ready-made legend. What a wonder the human chronicle is, how one's character can be rewritten so thrillingly in the space of a page.

"What," I parried Sandison's all too poetic inquiry, "makes you ask?"

His gaze never veered from me in the least. "Let's review. Back in Chicago you were Morgan Llewellyn, then you show up out here miraculously transformed into Morris Morgan, and you're also Pluvius along the way. I just thought I'd check to see if I'm staying current."

I held the moment. Then slipped back to the plain print of reality. "I am irremediably me, Sandy. Morgan Llewellyn, from birth on. A fallible being like any other. With a few too many names to my name, perhaps," I joked feebly.

"Hmmp." The man whose own tags included String 'em Up Sam and the Earl of Hell frowned at me. "Too bad if you're not this notorious bootlegger. It'd give you a reliable livelihood." Sighing heavily, he folded his hands on his stomach and sat back in the ringing silence of a house empty except for the two of us. "What's for supper?"

Dual identity divides a person in more ways than one. I'd had long practice at being Morris Morgan, with Morgan Llewellyn put aside like an uncomfortable memory, and while that rearrangement of myself always took some toll on the nervous system, my assumed role in life was a safe bet as long as no one knew I was acting, so to speak, under an alias. Now the two individuals who meant most to me were aware of my change of name and the unflattering reason behind it, and while their reactions were worlds apart, the result was the same. Still volcanic as she flung things into her suitcase to leave, Grace erupted as I had tried one last time to assuage her. "You can call yourself Confucius for all I care, I am having no part of it. I refuse to look like a silly goose for marrying someone whose right name I had no least idea of. And if you know what's good for you, you won't tell anyone either." In his turn, Sandison merely drawled, "I suppose what you call yourself is your own business. Just remember what happened to Billy the Kid."

So, unexposed except to the bleakness of

existence without Grace — and the challenges of bachelor life with Sandison — all I knew to do was to keep on as before at the *Thunder*. One thing about a newspaper office, behavior that would get you thrown out on your ear elsewhere in society is winked at as long as your fingers can still find the right typewriter keys. "Something happen to your dog, Morgie?" was the extent of Armbrister's fellow feeling toward me in my low mood. I felt an actual sense of relief when the *Post*'s editorials sharpened again with Cutlass calling my anti-Anaconda diatribes warmed-over cabbage in a cracked dish while I called his contributions the antics of an organ-grinder's monkey on a copper chain. That kind of contest seemed safer than the domestic gauntlet I had just been put through.

Life had no more tricks up its sleeve until the day Sandison announced he would be late for supper — "The library trustees got it into their fool heads to have a meeting; bad habit of theirs" — and rather than face the empty house alone, I stayed on at work, thinking up Pluvius stratagems and losing track of the time.

Dusk had given way to the lit windows of storefronts when I belatedly set out for home, into the teeth of a squall. Maneuvering through the sidewalk traffic of pedestrians ducking their heads as they hurried out of the weather, what popped to my mind was Edward Bulwer-Lytton's hackneyed phrase in a justly obscure novel, "It was a dark and stormy night . . ." Well, it was. Energized by the wind, rain streaked the darkness, and as I climbed the street toward the Ajax end of town, each corner streetlamp was a silver cone of raindrops.

By then, the only other storm-adrift soul in sight was a delivery van driver who had pulled to the curb and was bent over at a fender, apparently checking a tire. Slogging past with my head down against the chilly wind and rain, I suddenly felt something much, much colder at the back of my neck, unmistakably the business end of a gun. An authoritative voice ordered, "Get in the back of the truck. Fast."

Rather than have my head blown off, I clambered up the bumper step and stumbled into the blackness of the van. My captor followed swiftly, yanking the door shut behind him. "Sit down," he snapped, "and don't try any monkey business while I get a light going." Managing to grope my way to a crate of some sort to sink onto, I tried to formulate a plan of action, not easy to do with the memory of that shotgun blast from undiscriminating bootleggers filling my mind. Mistaken identity could be a mortal error, a trigger squeeze away, if I made the wrong move. Meanwhile this assailant, kidnapper, whatever he proved to be, lit a carbide lamp such as was used in the mines. With the aid of its glow, my eyes adjusted to the dim interior of the van. Stacked around me were egg crates, sans eggs. In the full light of the lamp, I found myself looking at a near replica of myself.

"You're" — I swallowed — "him."

"And you're not," said the Highliner, keeping the pistol casually but steadily aimed straight at me. "Although there seems to be some confusion about that."

"Please understand," I tried to keep a quaver out of my voice, "I did not set out to pose as you. It just happened."

"Right out of the blue, I suppose."

"Absolutely."

"Isn't that something." He whistled through his teeth. "You're just strolling along innocent as a lamb, two or three times, when all of a sudden Smitty and the boys, not to mention certain others, somehow get the notion you are me, eh?"

With a flick of the gun, he cut off my protestation that such was exactly the case, and in the abrupt silence we sat studying each other. This was unnervingly like confronting myself in a full-length mirror. Upon close inspection, and mine of him was nearly microscopic in intensity, the Highliner was more solidly built than I was, but the pounds I had put on in the traveling year with Grace enforced the resemblance. My beard was dark chestnut to his cinnamon brown, but again, similar enough that it took more than a casual look to tell the difference. Our taste in clothes was not identical — tweed for me, serge evidently his preference — but overcoats concealed that. And as if we shared a forehead like Siamese twins, both of us chose snappy fedoras that pulled down low over the brow, a rakish effect I had liked until now.

"Interesting how close we are in looks, isn't it," he broke my trance.

"Breathtaking."

"Morris Morgan," he tried the name on his tongue. "Easy one to remember, if you're forgetful."

This was risky territory, but since we were there anyway, I tried: "Inasmuch as you know mine, this might go more easily if I had a name to call you."

He responded coolly, "Not in this life, friend." Maybe it was my imagination, but his trigger finger seemed to twitch with those words. Oh, how I wished Chekhov had shot a toe off in a hunting accident, so he'd not been so eager to proclaim the theatrical dictum that when a gun appears onstage, it must ultimately be fired. The weapon I was facing, however this scene played out, plainly was in the hand of someone with a dramatic enough reason to use it, ridding himself of a troublesome double. One who was in no way bulletproof. To delay that outcome, I stammered, "How did you know I'm . . . me?"

"It didn't take any stroke of genius," he scoffed. "That stunt of loading the trucks with newspapers got me to thinking about who a brainstorm like that would come from. This Pluvius character stands out as being pretty clever, wouldn't you say?"

"That depends," I said dispiritedly. "If he were as smart as he sometimes thinks he is, he would not right now be incarcerated in a Golden Eggs delivery van."

What may have been a fleeting smile moved in his beard. "Speaking of that kind of thing, how'd you like your taste of jail hospitality?"

No sooner had I blurted, "How did you find out —" than he shrugged as if there were nothing to it. "I have my ways of keeping track of what the cops are up to." I recalled the startled desk sergeant. "Anyway, better you than me in the slammer. They let you out. Me, they'd throw away the key."

Still unable to keep my eyes off the unwavering gun, I ventured, "I hope you appreciate the favor."

His gaze as steady as the weapon, the Highliner studied me, the moments ticking by. Out in the dark, the wind howled and the rain pounded as though we were in some stormy cell of hell. Finally, he spoke. "You didn't spill about the warehouse. You could have, you know. Cut a deal. Given them the boys and the booze, to let you off."

I answered stiffly, "I am not a stool pigeon or whatever you call it."

"Canary, songbird," he reeled off, "fink, squealer, snitch —"

"I get the idea."

"You're not as enterprising as you could be, are you."

That stung. "All I want is to mind my own business."

"Which is putting a hornet up Anaconda's nose." He shook his head. "There are easier ways to make a living. Bootlegging, for one."

Suum cuique," I said before I thought. The gun lifting by an inch indicated rapid translation would be a good idea. "To each

278

his own."

Once more, his expression softened under the beard. "You're an odd duck, Morgan. And that probably makes us two of a kind, in more than looks." He fondled the gun. "Am I right that you won't try anything funny?"

"Nothing even close, I assure you."

The pistol disappeared into a handy pocket and I breathed easier. "Do you mind telling me how is it that you, or I, or we, are so recognizable to the world at large?"

The Highliner laughed, the dry kind with no mirth in it. "Don't you know? That propaganda sheet, the *Post*, ran a likeness of me and a big story, back 'round Thanksgiving. Anaconda doesn't like to see anybody make a dollar besides them. How'd you miss something like that?"

"I was, ah, traveling."

"That answers that." His voice even had a similar timbre to mine, and he had picked up the pattern of my diction with the ease of an actor; this person was a chameleon in his own right. "I kept trying to figure out why you showed up all of a sudden and Smitty and the boys couldn't get over what a whirlwind I am." He leaned forward and tapped my knee. "There at the warehouse — you passed up the chance to walk off

279

with a bundle of money. How come? Some kind of Holy Joe, are you?"

"Not noticeably. The temptation was tempered, so to speak, by the prospect of you dogging my trail every step of the way."

His laugh this time was silky with danger. "You're not wrong about that." Another tap on my knee. "Fill me in on something, so I look as smart around the warehouse as I'm supposed to be. Where'd that Whiskey Gap idea come from?"

"Ocular logic."

"That or a lucky guess?" The Highliner sat back, tipping his fedora up a fraction in a minor salute. "Either way, it's been perfect for us — we run trucks through there day and night. I ought to thank you some way." He gestured royally to what was stacked around us. "Would you like a crate of hooch?"

"No, I would not. But if you really want to do me a favor —"

"Yes? What?"

"Shave."

He chuckled. "Nothing doing. The boys would think I chickened out, gotten scared of the other gangs."

I despaired. "Then you won't part with a beard, and I can't. Tweedledum and Tweedledee."

"Can't?" That quick, he was gazing at me as if through a gunsight. "There's something more on your mind than barbering. Spill it."

I drew in breath. This slick bootlegging operative had granted me reprieve, and in all conscience, I had to do the same for him. "While we're in the trading mode, I should warn you — you're not the only one with people on the lookout for you."

"Is that a fact," he let out with a world-weary sigh. "It must be our irresistible good looks."

"If only it were that simple." I told him my own twofold story, the Chicago gambling mob's ire over the long-ago prizefight ready to be fanned anew if the big World Series bet was traced to me.

When I was done, the Highliner whistled through his teeth again. "Man, you're a case. I thought bootlegging was complicated. Thanks for tipping me off, I'll put the boys on the lookout for stray hoodlums." I felt better on that score, for the first time since Cutthroat Cartwright arrived. That lasted until the next words I heard. "What are you going to do to keep breathing? Don't you carry?"

"Carry — ? Oh. A gun. No." How much better off humankind would be had gunpowder never been invented and combat was waged with more civilized weapons. Such as brass knuckles. "Chicago pinkie rings," I tried to sound tough but had to pat hard through my layers of clothing to make the telltale jingle.

The Highliner rolled his eyes. "Sure, those are really great up against some gink armed to the teeth and more than arm's length from you. But if that's how you want to plan your funeral, it's your choice."

With that decided, he leaned toward me, authority in every whisker as he made the terms of our mutual existence clear. "Here's the deal, Morgan. I'm not saying anything to the boys about you. Nothing to be gained from that. Just don't abuse the privilege of being a spitting image." I shook my head. "And you'll keep your trap shut about the warehouse and these trucks and so on." I nodded my head. The Highliner gave me a last keen look, then winked roguishly as if at himself in a mirror. Reaching into one of the crates, he pulled out a bottle of Canadian rye and uncorked it with a flourish. Offering a swig, he said with that silky laugh: "After you. We have to make a toast — Confusion to our enemies, eh?"

14

The boardinghouse looked a bit worse for wear, Butte weather to blame, but otherwise the hillside residence with its distinctive sign — CUTLETS AND COVERLETS — OR IF YOU'RE NOT WELSH: BOARD AND ROOM — appeared much the same as when I first arrived into this vexing city, in need of food and shelter. I had led what I thought was an eventful life before coming to this address, but what an amount more had been squeezed in between that first knock on the blue-painted door and mine now.

"Yes?" Grace's pleasant lilt came first as she answered the door. That immediately changed to "Oh, no, you don't," as soon as she saw it was me, along with the taxi driver who was laboring up the sidewalk with the trunk. "You can't come crawling back here with all your belongings and think you can kiss and make up and everything will be like it was before." Pushing me aside, she called to the driver struggling with his load. "Put that back in the taxi."

"Grace, that's not my trunk, it's *our* trunk. From our trip. The railroad evidently ran out of places to sidetrack it."

"Why didn't you say so." She called to the taxi driver again. "Leave it and take him with you."

"But I need my things from it."

Grace puffed her cheeks, bottling up stronger language before she said, "Morrie, you have turned into the most exasperating human being. Why couldn't you get your junk out of there ahead of time?"

"It's locked. The key is on your Portuguese charm bracelet, remember?"

"So it is."

"Aren't you going to go get it?"

"I'm debating."

The hackie spoke up from where he stood puffing. "Could you folks have this fight inside on your own time, maybe?"

Between us, he and I wrestled the trunk into the boardinghouse with Grace hovering over our every move. I gave him some money and told him to come back in half an hour. Fifteen minutes, Grace truncated that. Off she stormed, her golden braid bouncing, to fetch the key. Hoop and Griff edged out of the parlor where they had been listening, chorused "How you doing, Morrie?" and "What do you know for sure, Morrie?" and fled to the far reaches of the house.

In no time, Grace flew back, unlocked the trunk, and flung open the lid. She snapped a glance at me where I stood watching her with yearning. "Well? What are you waiting for?"

"You look recovered. From the hives, I mean."

"No thanks to you. Get busy on your stuff."

What stood open in front of us was more than a trunkful of mingled belongings, it was every memory of our glorious honeymoon year. With my throat tight, I began sorting out my clothing and the other contents — books to me, trinkets to her, we agreed on at least that much — until I came across a creamy souvenir program from a performance of the Lipizzaner riding academy. "Remember Vienna? Those magnificent horses white as ermine?"

"Don't start that kind of thing, please." Her violet eyes were shiny with near tears. It was all I could do not to take her in my arms and —

Suddenly there were footsteps on the stairs, and the stairwell practically filled with a rangy figure who had a Roman nose and a centurion chin and a full head of black wavy hair. Pausing midway down, he scrutinized the two of us and the strew of belongings on the parlor floor. In an Italian baritone, he asked: "Is he bother you, mizzus?"

"Nothing to worry about, Giorgio, thank you."

Giving me a sharp look that took inches off my height, he turned back up the stairwell. "At your service."

I stared at the broad back disappearing at the top of the stairs. "Who in the world is that?"

"Who do you think? The new boarder. Giorgio Mazzini. He's a powderman on the graveyard shift at the Neversweat."

An Adonis on the premises; another arrow into my heart. Glumly I added opera formal wear to my stack. Time was running out on me and I had to speak my piece. "Grace, you must listen. I've reached an understanding with the Highliner. He'll see to it that the police won't pick me up at random and his men will be on the lookout for thugs from out of town — that's a help, wouldn't you say?"

"Oh my, yes," she said too sweetly. "Now you're in with bootleggers, but still on the outs with gamblers and this Cutthroat menace and whatever goons Anaconda may decide to sic on you. You're practically a walking insurance policy, Morrie."

"You don't sound very reassured."

"Imagine that." Drawing a breath through her teeth, she steeled herself for what she was about to say. "Now it's your turn to listen. If" — she doggedly erased that — "*when* I take you to court, as I'll need to because of the properties" — her arm-flung gesture somehow took in territory from the parlor to Horse Thief Row; the fact caught up with me that I was half owner of the boardinghouse, as she was of the mansion — "and everything, it will all have to come out about you. About," she faltered, but went on in a low voice, "Morgan Llewellyn and so on. You have to be ready for some rough treatment from any judge."

"The one in front of me now counts the most," I said humbly.

Her eyes glistening again, she turned her face away from me to the clock. "You'd better get busy on the trunk. Your time is about up."

It was my turn to draw a determined breath. "There's something else that has to be sorted out, now or never. My position at the *Thunder*. Jared and Armbrister can't keep me on if I'm being dragged through a scandal in court; the *Post* will shout it from every street corner. I have to ask you to wait a little while before starting legal proceedings." I hurried the rest as she started to protest. "We're not that far from turning the tide against Anaconda — I swear to you, we're not."

There was a third presence with us now. In the spot of honor on the sideboard was propped the wedding photograph of the ever so young Grace and her Arthur. My predecessor, foursquare in his roomy suit and expansive mustache; even on that matrimonial day, doomed to leave her a widow, when the unsafe conditions in the mines produced the Speculator conflagration. Now Grace rested her gaze on that fateful photo, as did I. Finally, she nodded, all the agreement I needed. She said again, "Go get them, the snakes. Now you'd better hurry, I hear your taxi."

Each with an armful of my clothes and books, the driver and I loaded into the flivver for a silent ride up the slope to Ajax Avenue. Leaving behind half my heart, the put-upon woman who was still my wife until divorce or annulment or some other form of dissolution caught up with me, and one Giorgio Mazzini, powderman, which was to say dynamiter. Without intelligence enough to blow his nose, if I was any judge of humanity, but built like a stallion and with that Mediterranean name full of lip-puckering vowels. Worse yet, it no doubt was his legitimate one.

"What are you going to do with yourself now that you're an involuntary bachelor, join a Lonely Hearts Club?"

"Not funny, Sandy. I'm still a married man." Conscious of his stern gaze, I roamed uneasily around the library tower. Conversation with Sandison in his lair somehow could cause the prickling sensation that pages were mysteriously turning in some certain book on the surrounding shelves, with the escaping spirit of the printed tale suffusing the atmosphere of the cylindrical room. In this case, alas for me, the literary presence seemed to be the inexorable Grand Inquisitor from *The Brothers Karamazov*. Facing the judgmental figure leaning back in his desk chair with his arms folded and his beard resting on his chest, I tried not to sink into Russian fatalism while telling him Grace and I, for the time being, had reached an understanding that there would be no legal separation.

"An understanding? That must have been some reach." He lurched up straight in his chair, sighing a mighty sigh. "I don't know about you, but I miss having a woman around. They're good for a lot of things. Look at us now," he glumly continued this train of thought, "a pair of wild cards, with no queens in the deck. I tell you, Morgan, or Llewellyn, I should say, poor representatives of the human race as we've been, what would I have amounted to without Dora and you without Grace?" He shuddered.

To cut the gloom before it became as thick as borscht, I protested that he was being overly hard on himself, implying myself as well, and chided, *"There's a fascination frantic / in a ruin that's romantic."*

He bared his teeth at the jingle from *The Mikado,* as I figured he would, but it worked in distracting him from lugubrious memorializing. Dora Sandison had been a force to be reckoned with when I'd had to schedule the Gilbert and Sullivan Libretto Study Group around other bevies of enthusiasts that met in the public library basement, besieging both of us with queenly demands on behalf of her musical idols. Thinking back on that, Sandison now looked almost contrite. "I probably shouldn't have called it the Giblet and Mulligan Society."

That pretty much ended that, as he turned with a grunt to the latest fine edition waiting in the package from a rare book dealer and I to the encyclopedic demands of the house. The manse was balky with only the pair of us as residents. It sorely missed the ministrations of Hoop and Griff, not to mention the presiding influence of Grace. Fortunately the kitchen was not hostile territory to me — I had picked up certain culinary skills in the course of life and I was a whiz at washing dishes — but the grocery shopping and a dozen other unaccustomed chores kept me hopping. As for the rest of the domicile, he and I truly were like captain and mate trying to keep the hulk afloat after the crew had abandoned ship. Samuel Sandison had not spent his life as boss of cowboys and librarians for nothing; his approach to upkeep consisted of pointing out to me things that I was then expected to fix.

And so I was not as surprised as I might have been to hear an explosive "Damn, what next?" from the hall bathroom on a not untypical day when I was about to leave for the newspaper office.

He materialized in the hallway in suspenders and flapping shirttail, looking aggrieved. "The sink is plugged. Better tend to it or the place will turn into a swamp."

I groaned and went to find the rubber-cupped plunger called a plumber's friend. When I returned, Sandison was still circulating, dressed now and gathering a book here and a hat there, grumbling all the while — "It's a hell of a note when a man can't even wash his face" — before heading out to the public library. Consequently I was at the nasty task of suctioning out whatever had clogged the drain, idly mulling whether the appropriate verb was *plunging* or *plungering,* when the door knocker banged urgently. "I'll get it," Sandison growled as he passed, "you keep at the damnable plumbing."

"Package," an unfamiliar voice was heard over the sink sounds. "Are you Morgan?"

"Ha. Not by a long shot. You're not our regular postman — where's O'Malley?"

"He's down with the croup."

"Sturdy lad like him? This country is going soft. Are you sure the name on that parcel isn't Sandison?"

"Sure I'm sure. I have to give it to somebody named Morgan."

"If you're going to be silly about it." Sandison called to me, and I abandoned the plunger and started for the front doorway where he hadn't budged, still incredulous that the postman did not have somewhere on his person a package containing a valuable book as usual. Shaking his head and agonizing for me to come, the postman jumpily clutched what appeared to be a wrapped box, about the size of a cracker tin. All I could think was that Grace must have mailed something of mine overlooked in the trunk. As I approached, the man in postal uniform yanked a pistol from the open back of the box and hissed, "This is for you, Bolshie pig!"

The first bullet nearly parted my hair, Sandison having batted the gun as if annoyed with a fly. The shooter fired wildly again and again, into the floor and ceiling, while the two of them grappled like wrestlers and I ducked and dodged from one side of their mad struggle to the next, trying vainly to get my hands on the weapon. They knocked the hat rack over, coats sent flying, and shattered the hall mirror as they reeled from wall to wall in the narrow confines. Sandison had the weight advantage but was twice the other's age, and the assailant possessed the determination of a bug-eyed fanatic. Somehow he momentarily twisted loose and spun to point the gun at me, this time at close range. A split second became eternity as I could see death coming. But as the shooter yelped, "Take that, pinko!" and pulled the trigger, Sandison lurched onto him like a falling tree and intercepted the bullet meant for me.

"Sandy!" I cried as I at last wrenched the revolver free, with him gasping in pain but still upright and wrestling the cursing gunman. In a supreme surge of strength, he grabbed the man in a headlock and with a supreme effort of his powerful arms, wrenched his neck until it snapped. The two of them crashed to the floor together.

Tossing the gun out of reach, I frantically did what I could to stanch the blood turning one entire side of Sandison's torso red. Neighbors who had heard the shots and called the police were by now poking cautiously through the doorway to assess the body-strewn scene. "Help is on its way, Sandy, don't give up, please don't," I babbled as he lay on his back, laboring to breathe.

Chest heaving, Sandison turned his shaggy head to the dead man beside him. "That'll teach you," he wheezed. Then he lost consciousness.

It took extra stretcher bearers to transport Sandison from the ambulance into St. Jude's Hospital and immediately the operating room. For what seemed ages, I paced the waiting room, nuns in white gliding by me with faces as composed as plaster saints.

Half-sick from the medicinal atmosphere, I questioned myself over and over. Had I cavalierly brought this on? Put Sandison's life at gravest risk by rash words on a sheet of newsprint? Shouldn't I have listened to the common wisdom about this roiling cauldron of a place, "They play rough in Butte"? Impervious fool, me. Yet, how can you outguess fate, if it walks up your front steps gripping a pistol? My thoughts twisted and turned as the waiting dragged on. At last, a gray-haired doctor wearing half-moon glasses appeared in the corridor.

I nearly collapsed in relief when he told me Sandison would pull through. "He's already awake and complaining to the nursing sisters — that's a good sign. But," the professional tone went to the next level, "we need to keep him for the next some days, whether or not it's popular with him." Pausing, the medical man peered at me over his specs. "Ready for the story element?"

"I'm sorry, the — ?"

"There is one every time someone survives a shooting, you know. 'An inch the other way,'" the doctor mimicked, "'and the bullet would have killed him dead as a doornail.'" He chuckled mirthlessly. "In this case, it happens to be true. The shot just missed his heart, by some miracle. But then" — he glanced down the corridor, where a white flock of nurses was wheeling in someone groaning on a gurney — "I could have given that diagnosis as soon as I saw who the patient was, couldn't I." Another dry chuckle. "String 'em Up Sam isn't going to be done in by one chunk of lead. Excuse me, I have to go back to work."

And I had to recount to the police the entire shooting episode. The gunman turned out to be a minor hooligan, known more for his lack of smarts than anything else. Not inclined to investigate now that the criminal was a cadaver, the police wrote him off as a political crackpot who saw Red where I and my editorials were concerned. To which I could only say a silent *Maybe*. He might have been some maddened newspaper reader or he might have been in the hire of Anaconda to act like one. Either way, it came to the same. The worse equation was that now I had been shot at by two out of three, the out-of-town bootleggers and the local foes of the *Thunder*. In the shooting gallery that my life was threatening to become, that left only the Chicago gambling mobsters, who had yet to try their aim.

15

I stood at the window of the hospital room with my hands clasped behind my back. Above the brooding horizon of grimy ground and stark headframes, smoke ribboned from the seven stacks of the Neversweat, the Hill's own cloud formation. As happened every eight hours, regular as the spin of the earth, the gullied streets turned into glaciers of people as a shift changed at the mines, the Cornishmen flowing to the Centerville neighborhood, the Italians to Meaderville — oh, why couldn't the interloper Giorgio Mazzini have taken lodging there? — the Irish cascading to Dublin Gulch, the Welsh and Serbians and Finns and Norwegians to their own enclaves. As clear as a historical diorama, they showed me the house of labor, these workingmen whose hard-rock toil had been a foundation of the union movement championed by Jared Evans and others like him. I knew, too, from his fraught experience as the mine-workers' leader and the evidence of my own eyes and ears in my travels, that the timbers of that house, although still standing, had been cracking and crumbling under corporate and government pressure for nearly half a century. I'd have hazarded a bet that historians of the future would describe the American Industrial Revolution as more truly an industrial civil war, driven mainly by the management side determined to incorporate and rule. In the West, the battles on many fronts were disheartening. The Colorado conflicts at the mines in Ludlow and Cripple Creek ended in violence, deaths, and suppression. On the coast, the Seattle general strike flared and went out, and in Everett a boatload of strikers, including suspected Wobblies, came under mortal gunfire from authorities on shore. The list went on, with this copper-rich, copper-cursed city inscribed on it in blood time and again. And my own efforts in the union cause, that of Jared and the men streaming to and from work on the Hill, had brought on the latest fusillade.

My mood spoke for me. "I should simply leave. The *Thunder* and Butte and Montana, maybe even America. Take passage for Tasmania. Trouble finds me too easily here."

Shifting in the high bed with a mighty groan — from the tone of it, caused as much by me as the pain of his wound — Sandison dismissed my plaint. "Don't talk nonsense. Running away won't make up for that pistol-packing moron."

"Maybe not, but —"

"Besides, you can't leave. I need you to pitch in so the Butte Public Library doesn't fall to pieces while I'm out of commission."

"You do? I mean, do you?"

"Use your head, man. You're the only one besides me who knows the ins and outs of the whole place. All you have to do is duck in there now and then and say I told you to tell the staff thus and such. They're a good bunch, they'll follow orders." Flat on his back, he still managed to give me a lofty look. "While you're at it, you might pack home the ledger that has the payroll and the book budget and so on in it. We could just as well tend to that at our own convenience."

"Mmm." To make sure what I was in for, I dropped my voice and inquired: "By any chance, does that ledger perhaps need some mending? From the inside?"

The hospital bed shook. "Damn it, it hurts when I laugh." The fierce white eyebrows doing their work, he confronted my question. "I knew you were a ring-tailed wonder when I first hired you. Call it instinct. Or dumb luck."

Right then a nun appeared in the doorway, holding a bedpan. "The call of nature will have to wait," he impatiently instructed her. "I'm doing other business."

She vanished, and he resumed on me. "Anyhow, handling numbers like hot potatoes isn't my strong suit, never has been, and you've got a trick mind for it, so why not put it to use, eh?" He must have seen my own eyebrows hoisting. "Yes, of course, thickhead. If the idiot board of trustees happened to snoop into the ledger, they could get the wrong idea. You know how it is."

Did I ever. In my time as his assistant when one of my countless assignments was to balance the bookkeeping, I had no choice but to unravel the Samuel Sandison approach to library administration. The madness to his method, it might jocularly be called, if shunting funds from where they belonged to where he wanted them could be considered a joke. For it had become clear to me back then, bit by bit, that there never seemed to be quite as much library staff as was budgeted for, the shortfall ingeniously made up by shuttling someone from task to task — namely, me — so the unspent wages could gravitate down the ledger columns to entries labeled *Miscellaneous book purchases.* The migration did not stop there, I realized when I undertook an inventory of his trove on loan to the institution, those magnificent books that would still be around a century and more from now, that were the heart of the Butte Public Library's "finest collection west of Chicago." The old rogue was slipping "miscellaneous" purchases into his *SSS*-bookplated holdings; there was a paste pot on his office desk just as there was at home, after all.

Well, how severely can you judge a person whose crime is a passion for the very best that literature has to offer? And who like a generous Midas sets out the timeless volumes on open shelves for the reading public to share? In my previous incarnation as the Butte Public Library's jack-of-all-trades, I had kept a wise silence about its librarian juggling the books, so to speak. But now I hesitated.

"Sandy, I already have a job. One that is perfectly aboveboard," I said pointedly, "and which keeps me so busy I meet myself coming and going. On top of that, there's the house threatening to fall down on our heads, and —" I broke off at the huge sigh heaved by the patient flat on his back. "None of which counts, does it. You saved my life."

"In bad fiction, this is the point at which the one who saved the life says, 'Pshaw, it was nothing,' " Sandison drawled. "That's twaddle. Dime-novel stuff. Undying gratitude from you will suit me fine, Morgan. Now, get over there to the library. And don't forget the ledger."

I must concede, spending whatever time I could afford at the familiar old granite grandiosity with BUTTE PUBLIC LIBRARY PROUDLY incised over one of its twin arches of entrance and LUX EX LIBRIS over the other was gratifying. The staff enthusiastically welcomed me back — always with the exception of Miss Runyon, the Medusa of the main desk — and never questioned my grant of authority from Sandison. With my experience, whatever knotty matter of scheduling or personnel presented itself, I could resolve. And if I may say so, more quickly and decisively than Sandison customarily did, with his habit of tugging at his beard and muttering, "I'll let you know before doomsday." Still, adding that to my editorial exertions at the *Thunder,* plus regularly visiting Sandison in the hospital, where he now kept the ledger in a bedside drawer the way other people keep a Bible, lent credence to Grace's analogy of a chameleon on a barber pole. More often than not, I reached home late at night, ignored whatever complaint the manse had developed that day, and dropped straight to bed, too exhausted even to crack open a book.

Then came the morning when I was awakened by loud knocking, which I assumed was the furnace or a water boiler signaling disaster, and I moaned and turned over under the covers. As the commotion mounted, I realized the front door knocker was to blame.

Groggily checking at the window — there was just enough daylight to see — I looked down on the unmistakable heads of Hoop and Griff. Spotting me, one of them called out, "Don't worry none, Morrie. We're unarmed." The other one cackled.

Still in my pajamas and wondering what their reappearance portended, I met them at the door. Griff lost no time enlightening me, Hoop nodding along. "Mrs. Morgan figured you could stand a little help with the shack now and again." They had with them the bulging tool bag that showed hard use in the mines, much like themselves.

With alacrity I showed them in and told

them to start anywhere. They shrugged off my gratitude as they clanked down the hallway, one of them saying over his shoulder, "We got nothing better to do anyway. Giorgio can take care of things at the boardinghouse." The other one cackled again.

How I burned to ask just what the extent of his caretaking was.

As usual, later that day I made time to go by St. Jude's and look in on Sandison. A visitor already stood posted by his bedside. Grace.

"Ah. Hello."

"The same to you, man of many names." In visiting clothes, she looked as fetching as she had on our honeymoon promenade around the world.

"Heh. Don't make me call in the sisters of mercy to form a cordon between you two." Sandison was sitting up in bed by now, still bandaged around his middle like a mummy. "Madam, this husband of yours — as I understand he still is — at least is not dull to be around, you have to grant him that."

"Nice try, Samuel." Grace gave him a chilly smile, and to me simply the chill. "His thrilling approach to life includes marrying a woman under a false name. That kind of excitement I can do without."

"Grace, I have explained the extenuating circumstance."

"It didn't extenuate by itself, Morrie."

Heaving himself higher on his stack of pillows, sultan holding court, Sandison mournfully came out with, "I wish Dora were here. She'd sort this out so quick your heads would swim."

The specter of Dora Sandison regulating our lives did give both of us pause. Grace recovered quicker than I. "I simply came to pay my respects," she turned to the patient, "I hope you're well soon. The wrong one of you is in for repairs." So saying, she marched out of the hospital room.

With just his eyes, Sandison told me to quit standing there like a fool and follow her.

"Grace, one minute, please." I caught up with her in the waiting room. "I wanted to thank you for the loan of Hoop and Griff."

"Charity begins at home." Halting, she took the opportunity to confront me again. Even the dimple that ordinarily was a beauty mark looked fierce. "Don't think that was any kind of a favor to you. The less upkeep you have to do, the faster you can finish the job at the newspaper and I can be rid of you as a husband, understand?"

"Implicitly. But —"

A nurse wearing a majestic wimple, evidently a senior nun, sailed past us like a resolute angel. In her wake, Grace unexpectedly giggled. "You and him among the holy. Life is too funny sometimes."

"There, see? We can agree on that much. And if you will just give me another chance —"

"Oh, no, you don't," she bristled again, enough that I backed up a step. This was like trying to pet a lioness. "With your record," she blazed, "what does another chance amount to but another headache? Ever since we came back to Butte, you've been up to your neck in fix after fix. Thrown in jail because you look like some other disreputable character. Then that stupid trunk of yours. Now it's gunplay, is it. What will you get yourself into next, Morrie?"

"A maniac brandishing a revolver wasn't my idea," I couldn't help pointing out.

"Fine, but it's just one more proof that trouble finds you like rain goes in a barrel, isn't it. No, stop, please, don't make sad eyes at me." Her own were blinking back something. "If you're worried I'm going to divorce you sooner than later, you needn't get yourself worked up like this." How could I help it, with a Giorgio tending the home

306

fires that had been the hearth of my happiness? "I gave you my word," Grace flung at me as she stalked toward the hospital exit, "which is better than some I could mention."

Wifeless and without even the grumpy company of Sandison until the hospital ever discharged him, I had only the silent, empty manse to see me off each gray morning and to come home to each long night. Something had changed in me; something in the weight of life. For more of my years than I cared to count, solitude seemed to be my full measure spooned out by fate. Ever since Casper. Ever since Rose. It was hard, alone, but I thought I had myself resolutely sorted out, reconciled to my own company in the experience of living, independence strapped firmly on me. Now, though, I longed for Grace as if part of myself were missing. I even yearned for Hoop and Griff making a racket in the precincts of the house. One's own footsteps, the only parlance in the emptiness between hyphens of carpet, are a sad stutter of existence hour upon hour.

The newspaper office saved me from myself, the rescue vessel moored within reach of the isle of Ajax, thanks be. What was it about being met daily by Armbrister's brisk number of column inches of editorial space I had to fill; hearing the staccato of typewriters start up, each as distinctive as a telegrapher's rhythm, as rewrite men and headline writers set to work on the nightside's stories; answering shouted queries such as "Morgie, is it Freud or Jung they call 'the mechanic of dreams'?" — what did I find in the din of deadlines and wisecracks and calamities and trivia and pronounced personalities on the page and off that captured me so?

Chapters of the earthly saga, I suppose, old as the alphabet. Humanity's never-ending tale of who did what to whom, when and where, and if told right, how and why. The *Thunder,* with Armbrister's bloodhound knowledge of Butte and Jared's foxy tactics against Anaconda, was set up as well as a newspaper could be to pursue that hallowed goal of journalism, to comfort the afflicted and afflict the comfortable. If I live into eternity, I shall still think daily news and opinion set in type for all to read is honorable work. Although that belief was severely tested by the example of Cutthroat Cartwright.

16

Ever wondered where schemers come from? Do they breed in stagnant pools as mosquitoes do? That would explain the pestilential cloud of political agitation, reckless charges, and editorial sophistry hanging over the Thunder. Underneath all the buzz, the scheme is the same old one of stealthy attack on the American system of productivity, the envy of the world — at least those parts of it not colored in pink or red.

— CUTLASS

"Hoo hoo. Cartwright has a touch, you have to admit."

"You bet. So does a skinning knife."

"Sophistry, I don't think we had that in school. Hey, Morgie! What's this sophistry guff your opposite number is so worked up about?"

"Mmm, a style of argumentation that goes

back to the Greeks. The root —"

"Yeah, yeah, always look to the root, we know."

"— is the verb that means playing subtle tricks."

"About like bluffing in poker, huh? Keep up the sophus-pocus, champ, you've got Cartwright looking at his hole card."

If our high-spirited staff had a taste for no-holds-barred editorial brawling, our grimacing editor sometimes had a bellyful of being slandered.

"Damn it, can't you come up with something that will shut that windbag's yap for a while?" Armbrister demanded of me, flinging Cutlass's latest into the wastebasket. "I'm sick of us being called every name under the sun."

Taking up the challenge at my typewriter, I soon placed on Armbrister's desk a sheet of paper he snatched up for a look, then put down as if it might bite him.

The *Post* having descended to entomological depths in its latest diatribe — if anyone's head is buzzing with buggy ideas, it is that of the Anaconda-paid prattler who calls himself Cutlass — all that needs be said is consider the source and beware the frass.

— PLUVIUS

"Frass?" Armbrister reluctantly tried out the word. "Never heard of it. What monkey language is that in?"

"English." He gave me a sour look. "By way of German, naturally."

"Naturally. What the hell does it mean?"

"Insect excrement."

For a space of several seconds, Armbrister found nothing to say. At length, he let out: "I had a hunch it was something like that." He ground his teeth, the way editors will, picked up the sheet of paper in a gingerly fashion that had it hovering over the wastebasket where Cutlass's invective ended up, then thrust it at me. "Run it."

Thank heavens, my barbs could drive Cartwright into wounded silence for short periods, while he and his invisible bosses on the top floor of the Hennessy Building contrived some new attack. More than a few of my *Thunder* colleagues celebrated each such absence of Cutlass's slash and thrust — "Guess who's gone fishing today" — in tried-and-true journalistic fashion, by going out for a drink after work. "C'mon, Morgie, join us," Cavaretta all but took me

311

by the arm on one such occasion, while Sibley of the city hall beat and several others, including Mary Margaret Houlihan beckoning in a frisky way, as they formed up at the doorway. I was half out of my typing chair before I remembered. For me to show up in a speakeasy, dead ringer for the Highliner that I seemed forever doomed, destined, fated to be, was to invite complications not even I could imagine. "Really, I . . . I can't," I said lamely. "I'm expected at the house."

"Okey-doke, pal." Cavaretta slapped my shoulder and went to join the others. "But the invitation stands, anytime."

The happy mob of them went out, while I did meaningless things such as squaring paper and pencils on my desk until they were clear of the building. Quiet descended so completely I could feel it on my skin, the newspaper office deserted except for the night editor and a couple of rewrite men silently editing copy at the far end of the room. In my trance of solitude, I hadn't seen the overcoated figure standing against the wall by Armbrister's glass cage of office.

"You have a lonesome cat these days, Professor?"

Sharply coming to, I told Jared I didn't know what he meant, although I did. What business was it of anybody, if the human race and for that matter the feline held nothing for me these nights?

Keeping his voice low, the publisher here strangely after hours came over to me, purpose in his gaze. "I saw that kind of stare on men in the trenches, my friend. Come on, get your things on. I'll walk you at least partway to that house that's expecting you so wonderfully much."

Side by side, the two of us joined the downtown flock of other home-goers, secretaries from the tall buildings and clerks from the storefronts, Welsh miners coming off shift and singing the way to their neighborhood near Grace's boardinghouse, messengers and delivery boys hopping trolleys now that their day on foot was done. Summer had found Butte at last, but there was still a mild nip in the air on clear evenings such as this, a new moon free of clouds standing over the work-lit Hill. Walking with Jared Evans was just short of a march, this man who had led other men under killing conditions and since had added the political weight of the state. Was the ghost of Teddy Roosevelt watching from somewhere? We had not gone a block before the soldier-senator beside me spoke his mind.

"You and the missus are on the outs, I gather."

I suppressed a groan. "Does it show on me that much?"

He tapped the side of his nose significantly. "Rab smelled it in the air. Don't ask me how, I'm only a male."

"As am I, so all I can tell you is, Grace has moved out."

"And Sandison's not healed up yet, so you're all by your lonesome in that moose of a house."

"That is the case," I conceded.

We waited for a spate of Model Ts to putt-putt through the next intersection, then as we crossed, he brought out: "It's not much of a guess you have time on your hands these evenings, so I wondered —"

"Jared, no." This time I did groan; I could not face day and night jeopardy, even for him. "I dare not get involved any more deeply in union matters. One lead-coated message from Anaconda" — at that, he winced as if dodging a bullet himself — "if that's what it was, is enough."

Jared looked at me levelly, frank as the moon. "That's not what I was thinking, believe it or not." He lowered his voice as he had done in the newspaper office. "Rab and I need your help. With Russian Famine."

I blurted, "Is he in some kind of trouble?"

"The worst," he said whimsically. "He's growing up. Remember what a holy mess that was, for any of us?"

Looking off ahead to where the street started to climb, Jared continued: "He's not really ours to raise as if our word is law, worse luck. Can't adopt him because he's still legally the ward of that uncle of his who used to go round with a pushcart sharpening knives, remember him?" A rueful shake of the head. "The old devil was pretty sharp himself, scooting back to Poland when he saw that Rab and I would look out for the boy. But never mind that, we just want to do the best we can for Famine, and that's where you come in." Jared marched the words out of himself at a pace as determined as his strides. "He's at that restless age. Not saying much, but you can tell there's more going on in him than he knows what to do with. So, we wondered if you might pitch in and find something to keep him occupied."

I was listening hard, but still had trouble believing my ears at Jared's next words. "Say, boxing lessons."

I stopped short, under a streetlamp casting a cone of light like a net. "Wh-what makes you think I'm capable?"

Jared turned to me in surprise. "Rab again. She picked up the notion, back when you were her schoolteacher, that you knew a little something about boxing. Said you could square away with the eighth-grade galoots smartly enough, it kept them in order."

I breathed again.

Man to man, Jared confided: "She'd rather you gave him Latin lessons, wherever she got that from." He grinned ever so slightly. "I had to point out to her, Russian Famine has trouble sitting still for English." Then, more soberly: "That's a tough bunch he's around at the detention school, and then there are the *Post* newsboys. We just want him to be able to stick up for himself if push comes to shove, as it generally does in this town."

"All well and good," I sighed. "And I happen to know a right cross from a left hook. But honestly, I am no pugilist myself. I don't see what good I can —"

"You're a teacher. You can do anything."

The blunt force of that statement took my words away. Jared Evans reached out a hand and shook mine, a pact beneath the moon as old as brotherhood between men.

"It's settled then, Professor. You'll show Famine how to handle his dukes." And he strode away at that marching pace, into the night.

■ ■ ■ ■

Cautious as I was in answering the door since the postal gunman, Russian Famine was shuffling his feet like a nervous suitor by the time I let him in the following evening. "Hiya, sir," he said with a swallow, stepping in as if across hot coals. "Some house," his voice sounded shrunken. "You live here all by yourself?"

"For the time being," I put the best face on that.

"I'd be spooked." That hit home, in more ways than one. The manse yawned around us, growing bigger with the night. What does it say about the human nervous system that one of us had been more at ease springing around atop bookshelves at the public library, and the other of us thought less of cajoling a hundred people into a dance called America, than either of us felt at the prospect of spending time in a lonely house?

While I was hanging up Famine's jacket and cap, he turned so fidgety that I expected he was about to ask the way to the bathroom, but no. "Where'd the old fella get plugged?"

Uncomfortably, I indicated on my rib cage the approximate spot of Sandison's wound.

Famine shook his head, hair flopping. "Unh-uh, where was he at? Is there blood-stains?"

"As much as I hate to disappoint you, it happened right where we're standing."

"Aw."

Taking pity, I pointed to the bullet holes overhead. He brightened. "That's better!" After counting the ceiling perforations to himself, he gave me an awkward glance. "You didn't get a lick in on the guy with your brassies or nothing?"

That question in other forms had circled me ever since, but it took a boy to ask it. With a tight throat, I related that I was down the hall when the shooting started, but Sandison managed to land a blow.

"The Earl of Hell bashed him one? Awright!" I could see in his eyes he was imagining the scene down to the last detail, then the frown coming. "So how'd he get plugged?"

Truth can be such a difficult master. "He stepped in front of a bullet. Meant for me."

"No kidding?" The boy looked at me a new way. "You're a lucky duck."

"I suppose I am," I said huskily. "Let's get on with the boxing lesson, shall we?" He trailed me into the drawing room, where I had shoved the furniture back for us to maneuver. When I produced boxing gloves for us both, he shuffled uncertainly again. "I dunno," he mumbled, eyeing the mitts, each larger than his head. "How'm I supposed to wallop anybody with them things?"

"That's what we're about to work on, how to wallop without being walloped. These are the tools of the trade in learning that."

"If you say so," he said dubiously.

I had him strip off his shirt, as I did mine, true to ring tradition, and at once regretted it. In his undershirt, he was the definition of skinny; no more meat on him than a sprat, as the old saying goes. But Jared was right, he was growing, his legs and arms ahead of the rest of him. Where there's reach, there's hope.

As I was tying his gloves on, my fingers knowing how almost without me, he gnawed his lip before looking up at me and making it known, "I better own up — I got my doubts about this boxing stuff."

"Now's the time to voice them," I said, as if I hadn't just bypassed my own. "Such as?"

"Sure it isn't a fancy way of getting beaten up?"

I sucked in a breath. "Famine, we want to keep that from happening. That's why I am going to have to teach very carefully and you are going to have to learn very thoroughly."

He twisted and turned before coming out with it. "See, what I like to do when a scrap comes up is run."

He made sure I understood. " 'Stead of a fight. I'm awful good at running."

That was not so far from the philosophy that had governed certain chapters of my own life. Run away and live to fight another day; not for nothing is that the most poetic of strategies. And I had seen him bolt off at full speed, swift as a zephyr. What was I doing, what were his supposed protectors Jared and Rab doing, in upsetting the defense nature had given him?

"Sometimes the circumstances are such," I tried to sound convincing to both of us, "that you simply can't get away. Or choose not to. You don't want the *Post* newsies to take away your corner, you said."

"Yeah, that's the trouble," he said darkly. "Can't run and be there too."

"And in the oldest story there is, that's why hands are sometimes made into fists," I said as I pulled on boxing gloves for the first time in a dozen years. "And ultimately why we're at this. The first thing is to guard against having your block knocked off, as I believe the hoosegow school approach is, hmm? Here, watch me protect my head.

Elbows in, forearms up, see how my gloves shield my face?" Gloved hands dangling almost to his knees during my demonstration, Famine studied the matter before reluctantly nodding. "All right, now it's your turn," I encouraged. "As they say in the funny papers, put 'em up."

He did so in a way that made me drop my guard as though I'd seen a ghost.

"What's the matter?" he asked, peering at me over the leather moons of his gloves. "Ain't this the same as you done it?"

"You're left-handed."

"Person's gotta be one or the other, don't he?"

"It's an advantage," I somehow found the words, overtaken as I was by the flood of memory. "Be sinister to be dextrous."

"Huh?"

"Merely a saying in Latin about the left and right hands. Never mind," I murmured, still hurtled back to a boxing ring where the young fighter facing me was nearly my mirror image, except for his cocky grin and the bit of footwork he was practicing. Casper and his left hook, as I sparred with him to develop that surprise punch. "I got it down pat, Morrie. Squash the bug" — the ball of his left foot digging in — "give a hug" — the left arm and shoulder coming around as if in sudden embrace — "hit the lug" — whapping me half across the ring as his fist connected. Casper's little rhyme and sinister hand, the left, put away opponent after opponent who literally did not know what hit them. As if at the sound of the bell at the start of a round, I came out of my trance, back in the company of a scrawny boy whom life was apt to rain blows on if I did not do something about it. "Famine, we are going to concentrate on one particular maneuver. Here, watch."

Time after time I put him through the motions, footwork, shoulder and arm and fist working as one, until we were both panting and could hardly hold our gloves up. Even so, he was reluctant when I called a halt and began to strip off our mitts. "When am I ever gonna get a real punch in?"

"Tomorrow night."

"Oof!"

"Sorry. Didn't mean to bust you one when you wasn't ready."

"No, no, surprise is a permissible tactic, within limits. I was thinking when I should have been ducking. Always dangerous. Let's work on that left hook some more. The last one was more of a haymaker, which is why I wasn't looking for it."

"Here goes. Squash the bug . . ."

"That's correct."

"Give a hug . . ."

"Yes, good."

"Hit the lug." *Smack.*

"Yes, well, I felt that one on the jaw, definitely. You're showing progress."

"Better be. Running's easier."

"All right, now let's spar a little before you throw the next one. Gloves up, remember." Bobbing and weaving, I circled him as he pawed back, instinct of defending what I held dear gaining possession of me. Take that, Mazzini!

"Ouch!"

"Oops, sorry, Famine. I got carried away."

"Ain't it about my turn to whack back?"

"Arguably. Give it a try. Keep that foot planted, good, good, shoulder and arm and fist ready, now! *Ow!* Casper would be proud."

"Huh? Who?"

"Someone familiar with a left hook, is all. Let's call it a night."

Sparring partners that we were, one of us sharpening reflexes long dormant and the other learning moves of a past champion, Russian Famine and I took on our foes.

"Nailed 'im," he reported proudly when

323

the next *Post* newsboy tried to hijack his corner. "Right in the kisser."

I must have scored similarly with some editorial blow, judging by what transpired one evening after Famine had shed his gloves and gone home. The house now silent, I was doing a bit of bookkeeping in Sandison's ledger — the Butte Public Library budget was a miracle of levitation in his design, and if I did not keep things in balance to his satisfaction I was sure to hear about it — when the door knocker banged like a shot in the night.

Thinking it wise to put on brass knuckles first, I opened the door the barest crack and peeped out. Sleek as a sheikh, there stood a personage who could only be Cutthroat Cartwright.

"Moe sent me," he parodied the speakeasy "Open, Sesame," which had practically become the national password since Prohibition. Dressed in the brazen elegance that announced Chicago — snappy hat, tailored pinstripe suit, and two-tone perforated oxfords, reading from top to bottom — he gazed cavalierly in at me through the narrow opening as though I were the wiseacre in the matter. "Come on, buddy, where's your western hospitality? We need to have a chitchat."

The horns of a dilemma can come at a person, as that limited but effective poet Cheyne put it, *as hooked and blood-bright / as surprise in a bullfight.* And at the moment I had a paralyzing case of surprise. Which to do? Close the door on the importunate face, brassy as Ajax's, with something like "You must have the wrong address, this isn't the Fraternal Home for Character Assassins"? Or let the unwelcome visitor in as an opportunity to size up the opposition?

Falling in between is not at all a good course, yet that is what I ended up doing. Trying to deliver an austere "Sorry, I don't speak snake language," I let the door swing too wide. Or perhaps it opened of its own accord, under the influence of that forceful gaze and wardrobe. Before I could muster myself and almost before I could slip brass knuckles out of sight into my side pocket, in strode the journalistic slasher called Cutlass, handing me his hat to hang up. He had the sheen of a big fish among minnows. I knew I must be careful not to be swallowed.

Taking in everything at a glance, the acre of house and me, he launched right in. "Fancy digs. How do you rate a setup like this on a scribbler's pay? Rich wife?"

"Providence of another sort," I said stiffly.

"Good old Providence. What would we do without the old dame?" Looking every inch the John Held Jr. caricature that topped his famous column in the Chicago *Herald* — cannonball head, pencil-line mustache, calculating eyes, and mouth set for the last word — the unwelcome visitor at once glimpsed the floor-to-ceiling books in Sandison's lair and went and peered in. He gave a low whistle. "No wonder you were able to shoot down my try at nailing your *Thunder* bunch as a nest of pinkos, with all this ammunition. Nice job you did, incidentally." A sardonic gleam as he turned to me. "Although I'll bet a lot of those books are in Lenin's library too, don't you think?"

I burst out, "If you're here to show off your bag of dirty tricks, Cartwright, you can just —"

"Call me Cutty," he insisted smoothly. "What do you go by?"

I drew up short at the sudden jeweler's squint he was giving me, as if trying to evaluate past my beard. "Morgan will do."

"Be that way," he shrugged off my rebuff. He cocked an ear, then the other. "Quiet as a mausoleum in here, isn't it. No wife at all? Only you rattling around in this barn?"

Just that quick, he had me caught in a race with myself, fielding domestic questions to fend off worse ones. "She's away." All too much truth in that. "I have a boarder but he's incapacitated, as I'm sure you know."

"That's right!" exclaimed the journalistic cutthroat who was not going to hear a chummy "Cutty" out of me. "The leading citizen who got plunked instead of you. What did I hear the unlucky chump is in this two-bit town," he pondered, "the old gray mare?"

"He's not mayor," I immediately disparaged that. Too late realizing, with my heart fluttering, that I had just shown I was familiar with that flat Chicago pronunciation of it. And given myself away, that fast? If so, Cartwright showed no sign, blandly waiting for me to go on. Not quite through clenched teeth, I managed, "Samuel Sandison is the Butte public librarian, the best anywhere."

"How about that. From the sound of it, near immortal but not bulletproof," he toyed with that philosophically while my heart did a bigger skip at his employment of that last word. "That beats most of us, wouldn't you say?" Casually tilting his head back, he gandered at the bullet holes overhead as if beholding the ceiling of the Sistine Chapel. "So here we are at the scene of the crime, hmm? They must be lousy shots in Butte." He laughed. Jocular he was not. That laugh would have soured milk.

Still stargazing, he confided, "You came out of it lucky in more ways than one, buddy. The *Post* was going to plaster that little ruckus on the front page, drag you through all the mud it could, and the *Thunder* along with it. I made them spike the story."

Dry-throated, I managed to respond: "I don't suppose your generosity comes at a price or anything like that."

He waved that off with just his fingers. "The little stuff comes free."

"Or maybe," it was time I pushed back, "that story would have raised a few too many questions about who might have hired the gunman."

"Conceivably," he nodded on every syllable, meanwhile giving me a lidded look. "Anyway, I made it known they shouldn't be trying to bump you off, if they were. You're worth more alive than dead, Morgan. Not everybody who takes on the Anaconda Copper Mining Company can say that."

However much of that was true, I managed to digest enough to say I supposed I should be flattered. "State your business, Cutthroat."

"All in good time," he passed that off in the manner of one man of the world to another. "We ought to get to know each other a little, don't you think? Journalistic blood brothers that we are." Parking his hands, thumbs sticking out, in the pockets of his expensively tailored suit, he did a perfect version of a Windy City alderman. "Back where I'm from, we gen'lly start things off wid a drink togedda."

Like the lord of the manor — well, I was — I responded, "If you don't mind Old Ballycleuch."

His surprise showed. "You must have one hell of a bootlegger." The Burns birthday libation from Sandison's bottom desk drawer to the rescue, I poured what I hoped were proper proportions to oil Cartwright's tongue and not mine. We sat down across from each other in the cavernous living room, like characters in a sketch, and he toasted, mock or not, "Remember the *Maine*!" I didn't like the way he kept looking at me. "Morgan," he tasted the name along with the scotch. "You don't wrap yourself around that glass like an Irishman and you're not snotty enough to be English. Welsh, right?"

"Unavoidably. Now, as to why you're —"

He sat forward suddenly. "The way you

329

sling words, you must have had quite an education. Where?"

"At my father's knee and other low joints," I resorted to the mossy joke as if running out of patience. "Are we going to keep on like this all night?"

"This *is* a nice scotch," he held up his glass admiringly. "And you're good with the razzmatazz."

My blood turned to hot water at Casper's old word for clever boxing. "I mean, that's a real talent, slugging away at Anaconda the way you do, day after day," said my caller in a knowing tone, while I took refuge behind my drink. Cartwright leaned toward me even more, as if about to spring. "I'll level with you. They're worried up there on the top floor of the Hennessy Building. They don't like the looks of that wild jackass Evans in the legislature and whatever you rabble-rousers are up to with the *Thunder.* You're in a position to call the shots," he smirked toward the bullet holes in the ceiling, "for a change."

"Speak plain," I bluffed, "I'm still hard of hearing from the last guest."

"Quit."

That was plain enough. "Leave the *Thunder*? Just like that?"

"In the name of a higher wage, why not?

Newspapermen have been doing it since Ben Franklin invented penny-pinching. You could move along to the *Post,* let's say, for the sake of argument. That long-eared editor of yours jumped like that, didn't he, just the other direction."

I'd intended for my silence to make Cartwright talkative, but now it was working too well. Giving my beard the jeweler's squint again, he was saying with a rough laugh, "I have to hand it to you, Morgan, you're hard to read behind that bush. It reminds me of those pushcart peddlers, whiskers all over them, we used to have on Maxwell Street when I was a cub reporter working that part of town." He curled a grin at mention of Chicago's toughest neighborhood, while I cringed inwardly. The West Side fight clubs there were where Casper learned his trade, the razzmatazz of the boxing ring. Where his likeness, so like my own, had appeared on prizefight posters on every brick wall. Where the Llewellyn countenance probably was still on fading poster board up some alley or another.

"Those old Maxies were hard to dicker with, too," Cartwright was finishing his smirking reminiscence while I rigidly sat, trying not to look like myself. "But they'd strike a bargain in the end."

I shook my head, mainly to unclog my voice box. Cartwright read an answer into that and heaved a sigh. "Okay, no go on packing your talents across town. But you could investigate retirement, better yet, hmm?" His eyes locked with mine. "Maybe Providence would come around again, like Christmas." He drilled the point home. "Brighten up, Morgan. All you have to do is nothing. You can be prosperously self-unemployed."

Now I had to say something. What came out was, "Drink up. The house limit is one."

The justly named Cutthroat sized me up one last time. "You *are* full of razzmatazz, aren'tcha." Tossing down the rest of his drink in one swallow, he got to his feet. "Anyhoo, pard," now he was comradely, as if we were old campaigners bivouacked around a campfire, "the offer stands. Think it over." He didn't bother to wink, but might as well have. "By the light of day, I'll bet you see I'm right, buddy."

That echoed in me after he was gone and I was alone in the house. To some extent, he was right. Journalistic blood brothers we inescapably were. Buddies we were not.

17

"I see the bats and owls haven't moved in quite yet."

Even Sandison's growl about my less than inspired housekeeping was welcome, just to have him out of the hospital and back in the manse for companionship, such as it was. Whatever might be the fit description of a crabby wild-bearded shooting victim stalking through the place in cowboy boots, deafening silence was the farthest thing from it. His wound still nagged him, a fact he acknowledged only by grunting through set teeth whenever he sat down or stood up. The absence of Grace, and for that matter Hoop and Griff, told grievously on the pair of us as we went about domestic life only fractionally, the way bachelors do. I cooked as necessary, Sandison ate without comment. Nobody dusted, swept, or mopped on any regular basis; no offense to my dear wife, but never had I missed Rose and her housekeeping skills so much.

Say for Sandison, however, grumblesome and moody as he was, he was not unfair on larger matters. Try as he might, he could find no fault with my juggling of the public library's ledger in his absence — "One thing about you, Morgan, you know the meaning of legerdemain, heh, heh" — or for the most part, my handling of scheduling and personnel matters. He nonetheless was chafing to get back to bossing the Butte Public Library from top to bottom himself, which I daily had to restrain him from. "Sister Magdalena" — she of the majestic wimple — "instructed me you are to take it easy until your side is completely healed, no exceptions."

"Sister Magdalena holds the firm belief men can't blow their noses without hurting themselves," he could only mutter to that, listing to one side as he sulked off to his book-lined lair down the hall. Fortunately I'd had the foresight to simply stack on his desk the book parcels that arrived while he was hospitalized, and after heaving himself around in his chair until his side hurt least, he would settle in there like some Rip Van Winkle catching up on Christmases by opening the packages and turning the pages as carefully as a boy. Many a morning I left him engrossed in some fine edition of Turgenev or Blake or Balzac or Whitman, and would find him at the end of the day dozing in peace over the open book.

There was no such peacefulness in my working hours, as I grappled daily with what Cutthroat Cartwright threw at the *Thunder* and Jared and the tax commission plan, which the *Post* continued to imply — although not in so many words, since my desperate defusing of the "What Is To Be Done?" imbroglio — was a union-conceived plan to undermine capitalism and cause the crash of America into Russia-like rubble. I am happy to say he equally had to fend with what I flung in Anaconda's direction. Thank heaven Theodore Roosevelt's unrestrained enthusiasms had included smiting his foes with that Latinate billy club, "malefactors of great wealth"; my typing fingers continued to play every tune I could think of that hit the notes of the tax burden maleficently heaped on the honest citizens of the Treasure State while the copper colossus paid hardly pennies. Pluvius and Cutlass, we were hammer and tong, day after day as the newspaper war was shouted out in the streets of Butte by our newsboys and theirs.

Howsomever, as Griff would have said,

the weak point, if there was one in Jared's plan of attack, was the amount of time it was taking. The statewide vote could not be held until autumn, a special election set for the first Tuesday of September. Propitiously, the day after Labor Day, a conjunction that made Cutlass howl to high heaven in print, but Jared and his Ulcer Gulch allies had managed it somehow, perhaps by black magic. Pluvius didn't ask. In any case, the showdown date was months off yet, an interval that made me uneasy. Caught up in the heat of competition, the *Thunder* staff gleefully produced news pages that shone with sharp writing and keen coverage and seemed exhilarated by the fight in which our typewriters and telephones served as artillery. But Armbrister and I, going over my editorials, which somehow had to keep up the barrage until election day, exchanged glances now and then that said, without ever daring to utter the word aloud, *stalemate.*

The one clear victory of this time was Russian Famine's. I jumped up when I saw him slip into the office from the back shop with his newspaper bag jauntily slung at his side, grinning despite another split lip. "Done it," he boasted, grabbing his daily allotment of gumdrops from the candy jar and popping one into his mouth. "A dumb Postie jumped me again. He got some licks in, but it ended up I cleaned his clock good." Seasoned pugilist though he now was, he could not help giggling at the next. "He never seen the left hook coming."

"Nicely done, Capper," I said without thinking, my tongue slipping back more than a dozen years.

"Huh?"

"I merely meant, I wish I had been there to watch you at it."

The giggles contending with his attempt at nonchalance, Famine imparted: "Jared says he's real proud of me, sticking up for myself like that. Mrs. Evans scolded me, you know how they do," now speaking man to man about the ways of women. "But I think she was kind of tickled, too."

"As are we all," I told him warmly, "when the side that deserves to wins."

"It happened out of the blue" is one of those phrases worn smooth to cliché, I realize, but a wording of that sort endures because there is no better way to say it.

Consequently, I was enjoying myself on the steps of the public library, having ducked out for a breath of air that agreeable June forenoon — by the calendar, summer was not yet here, but it felt like it — while filling in for Sandison on some minor directorial matter, when I noticed something odd taking place on the Hill. More precisely, in the otherwise clear blue sky above the dominant rise of ground. One after another, the plumes of smoke from the seven stacks of the Neversweat were diminishing to nothing as each drifted off and vanished. Along with that, as though the disappearing smoke were taking the usual machinery noise with it, the Hill quieted steadily down as I stood watching until it fell silent.

In that ominous moment, I strained to hear the dreaded whistles signaling for medical aid, but there was not even that sound. Puzzled, I pulled out my watch and checked. Right on schedule it was time for the change of shifts, but ordinarily that did not stop the throb of mining operations at all.

By now people in the street had stopped to look questioningly up at the earthen height humped on Butte's back and the silent headframes spearing the sky, and my feet had found their way down the library steps almost without my knowing it. As I hastened through the downtown streets, trolleys still clanged and automobiles yet honked, but there was a sense of the city slowing, like some great clock running down. Repeatedly asking storekeepers who had come out to stare or shoppers bolting for home what was happening, invariably such answer as I received was along the lines of "Something at the mines." But what, what? The last few blocks to the *Thunder* office, I broke into a mad dash.

I found the newsroom going crazy, half the staff shouting into telephones, the others typing madly, Cavaretta trying to handle two phones at once. Plainly the *Thunder* was putting out an extra, hitting the streets with the news behind the sudden silence of the Hill. I panted into Armbrister's office, where he and Jared stood together like men stricken.

"Another accident?" I asked, gasping for breath. "You called the men out?"

Ashen-faced, Jared shook his head. "Not a walkout. This is a lockout."

The news was worse than I could have imagined. In a ploy of its own, the Anaconda Company had declared an impasse in the wage negotiations and informed Quinlan's stunned successor at the bargaining table that from this day forward, mining operations were shut down until the union accepted a pay cut of more than twenty percent. At a stroke, the past two years' gain in ten thousand paychecks was gone, the tenaciously won "lost" dollar per day lost again. Quin must have been howling curses in his grave.

The rest of us — Jared, myself, Armbrister when he wasn't shouting to the news staff or the back room to hurry up with the extra; the *Thunder* had an entire city waiting for it — were flummoxed. "They can do that, without so much as a by-your-leave?" I struggled out of my daze. "Doesn't the government care whether half of the world's copper supply is choked off or not?"

"Professor," Jared responded bleakly, "if the country was at war, Washington wouldn't let the company bigwigs —"

"The plutocrat sunuvabitches," Armbrister improved on one of my recent editorial epithets with his own.

"— get away with it for one minute. But production regulations and the like were thrown out the window right away after the Armistice." Jared's tone was more bitter than I had ever heard it. "Now 'normalcy' is back, haven't you heard, and its high priest is Harding."

"Here in our parish, it's Cutlass, worse yet," Armbrister bluntly spoke what I was thinking. "And pardon my French, Morgie, but we're down the crapper and he's on the hole." That distressing analogy aside, the day's development did make it all the more evident why the powers that be in the Hennessy Building imported Cutthroat Cartwright. They had been preparing to escalate the battle with us from the very first volley over the taxation issue. I felt sick. However, worse off by far was Jared, in his public role as the instigator in all this. He turned half away from Armbrister's words as though physically struck by them. "A strike is one thing, hell, Butte's been through those how many times and lived to tell the tale," the relentless editor went on even as he checked around and shouted, "Roll it, Charlie!" to the pressman waiting in the back room doorway. "But this is the same stunt the company pulled in '03, isn't it, and we all know how that turned out. Three weeks of shutdown until the only sign of life anywhere in the state was grass growing in the streets, and the copper bastards got everything they wanted."

"You want us to cave, just like that?" Jared rounded on him with a steely look. "Give up the dollar in wages, and pull back on the tax vote, which is what is really behind this? I hired you for this because I thought you had guts, Jake."

"Guts, hell," Armbrister flared back, "brains are the shortage in this mess."

"Boys," I instinctively stepped between them as if breaking up a schoolyard fight, "if they could see this up in the Hennessy Building, they'd fall out of their chairs laughing."

"Right, right. Sorry, sorry," they muttered back and forth. The floor trembled under us as the press began to roll and the lockout Extra literally began to thunder into existence. Sheepishly, Armbrister took off his eyeshade and rubbed his forehead. "At least we got the damn paper out."

"And it's a good job well done," Jared told him. "The same as you and the professor do every day." He began pacing the narrow confines of the office, like a sentry on high alert at his post. "All right, my rod and my staff," he rallied the pair of us. "Let's put our thinking caps on, as Rab would say. We have to try to stick this out, and time is maybe on our side for once. Anaconda can't let the Hill stay shut too long, or some outfit in Arizona or Chile or somewhere will start digging copper like mad to meet market demand. The powers that be, up in the Hennessy and higher, have got to be looking over their shoulders at that, however pigheaded they are toward us."

342

"Sounds like their weak spot," Armbrister agreed, as did I.

"It's not going to be easy, keeping spirits up," Jared calculated like the veteran of union battles he was, "since we couldn't prepare for this. But we've got one advantage ahead." Very much the publisher at this moment, he pointed to the calendar board, where potential stories ahead were marked in red.

I still didn't follow, but Armbrister stirred as if about to be hit by a hunch.

"That's right, Jake," Jared encouraged that response, "it's a while yet to Miners Day. That'll help the town hold out." A ghost of a smile visited him. "Show me any miner who isn't going to want to march this year to demonstrate to Anaconda we can't be pushed around."

How right he was, if past experience was any guide at all. Miners Day was Butte's version of New Orleans's Mardi Gras, Venice's Carnevale, Munich's Oktoberfest, of all such gala holidays from the daily strains of life, a civic celebration giving mineworkers a chance to march in their thousands under peaceable conditions, the various lodges and brotherhoods and sisterhoods to show off their regalia, businesses to build floats to wow and woo customers, on and

343

on through the ranks of all those with local pride or some cause to flaunt. It was a spectacle, a declaration, a civic rite, a coming together of the nationalities of the Constantinople of the Rockies, all that and more. I oh so vividly remembered watching — no, there was not time for that memory now as Jared in his authoritative way was going on, "The Hennessy Building jaybirds think they're so clever, how'd they overlook that? We're one up on them until the big day, anyway."

"I shall remind them of it so incessantly they'll hear it in their sleep," I promised to do my editorial utmost.

"That's the stuff." What remained of the smile hovered another moment as he gave the mock instruction, "Give Cutlass a dose of bayonet."

"It's still going to be a damned hard slog from now till then, Jared," Armbrister warned. "You know how things get when the mines aren't running. Butte goes on its back like a beetle."

Jared knew that only too well, his face told, but he remained grimly resolved. "Every family on the Hill has lived on short rations before." Under the weight of command in such circumstances, his voice went low and reflective. "One thing about it,

Dublin Gulch and Finntown and the rest"
— he solemnly named off his vital constitu-
encies, as union leader and senator — "are
used to misery. We'll see how Wall Street
likes the taste of it."

At least the newsboys prospered as the
lockout took hold, with headlines raging
back and forth over the dead quiet of the
Hill. My editorials were variations on a
theme, practically operatic in orchestration,
back and forth from characterizing Anaconda as the cold-blooded money-grubbing
untrustworthy reptilian corporate monster
it behaved like — this was no time to spare
the adjectives — and sounding every note
of hope and defiance I could think of, for a
citizenry under economic siege to hearken
to. Or so we hoped. Jared and his union
council were busy keeping the anger banked
in the miners' neighborhoods, helped by
the newspaper running pleas and pledges in
various tongues that echoed those of "Voices
of the Hill," only with much graver accents.
And while the *Thunder* lived up to its name,
Cutlass dueled with my offerings by employ-
ing every dirty trick known to journalism,
from quotes out of context to implications
that Pluvius was, of all things, a hired gun
of the writing sort, bought and paid for so

richly he lived in a mansion while posing as a tribune of the people. "He ought to have to live in this overgrown bunkhouse," Sandison said to that.

As Armbrister bleakly forecast, Butte did slow to a crawl without the rhythm of the mines in its daily life. Men whose hands knew nothing but work had to find time-killing pursuits. The public library was jammed daylong, I reported to Sandison, and I would have bet good money that Smitty and crew were telling the Highliner the same about speakeasies. Nor did it escape me that with everything shut down, a certain Neversweat powderman with a Roman profile now had nothing to do but idle around under the same boardinghouse roof as the attractive woman who was very much my wife, still. The animal.

Even in those first days, a widespread unease, something like the brink of fever before some terrible illness, could be sensed in the conversations in the streets and the way people glanced up at the stock-still equipment of the mines and quickly down again. The pinch of lost wages had been endured before by the families of the Hill during strikes, but, according to the oldest hands on the *Thunder,* Armbrister profanely included, there was a feeling in the air that this time was nothing like anything before. A strike was one thing, workers withholding their labor, the only real weapon they possessed. A lockout was chillingly different. The contrast, say, between a queue waiting at the doorstep for the right invitation to come in, and a slammed and barred door. Between negotiation and coercion; between callused hand and merciless fist.

The one bright spot on the horizon remained Miners Day, and as vowed, in my editorials I drummed away at reminding our readership that, more than ever, Butte's own holiday must serve as the occasion to celebrate the unity of the house of labor and show the copper bosses that the spirit of ten thousand mineworkers was not broken. Take *that*, Cutlass. I did my best to have my typewriter keys echo the sound of a mile of men on the march, Jared's confident goal for turnout on the great day.

This was the hard going for my fingers, every mention of that midsummer high point of life in the proud mining community bringing such a surge of emotions in me. Two years before, watching the parade together from a private aerie and then a trolley ride to the attractions of the amusement park called Columbia Gardens had been Grace's and my first "date," to use that modern term for the onset of courtship, those first breathless hours of shy glances and modestly exchanged confidences.

What a picture we made, I in my best suit and checked vest the least of it, Grace resplendently filling out an aquamarine dress with a sea shimmer to it, her hair done up in a circlet braid with a swooping ribbon-sprigged summer hat topping even the gold of that crown upon a crown — an enchanting vision time could not dim. Although it flickered the following day, when my new-found darling suffered an outbreak of second thoughts and hives. *I tossed and turned all night trying to figure out who am I with when I'm with you,* she'd wailed through her mask of calamine lotion while trying not to scratch. *Take yesterday. One minute I'm on the arm of someone I enjoy thoroughly, and the next, you're gambling away money like you're feeding the chickens.* Actually only a bet on Russian Famine in a footrace, which I pointed out in vain was a sure thing. Thank heavens, hives and much else had been overcome in the subsequent course of our romance, leading to matrimony and our year of wonder, of traveling the world on a cloud.

Descending from a cloud brings an awful jolt, however, and I already was not at my best while trying to compose yet another Miners Day piece, several days into the lockout, when Armbrister came by my typewriter stand and dropped a freshly inked *Post* with a plop. "Take a look at this, and then slit my wrists for me."

I stared down at the headline shrieking across the top of the front page.

**Anaconda Takes Steps
Against Miners Day Threats**

And below was worse.

The Anaconda Copper Mining Company, citing grave threats against life and property, today announced the hiring of extra guards to be deployed around company headquarters and other properties during the forthcoming Miners Day observance. "We have reason to believe radical elements may use the parade as an occasion to incite violence," a company spokesman declared, "making necessary certain protective steps."

Questioned whether the guards would be armed, the company spokesman said: "All necessary measures will be taken."

It went on in the same sickening way. The mayor was quoted as calling on the miners to forgo the traditional parade in this time of tension. The chief of police was quoted as warning the public at large that he did not have enough men on the force to quell major trouble if it erupted. Anaconda and its *Post* lackeys had not missed a trick.

Topping it off was a front-page editorial — front-page! — by Cutlass piously expressing the hope that cooler heads would prevail on the union side, but if not, the consequences clearly would fall on those who instigated trouble. "Those who mistake the temple of prosperity for the Bastille," the fiend wrote.

"Cute, isn't it," Armbrister said dolefully over my shoulder. "Just nicely letting everybody know there'll be goons with guns if the union doesn't scrap the Miners Day parade."

The threat sent a chill cold as ice through me. "Has Jared seen — ?"

"I called him at union headquarters. He'll be here as soon as he picks himself up off the floor."

It wasn't long before we were joined by our Sisyphus of a publisher, who indeed looked as if the rock had rolled down the hill on him. Alert to trouble, the newsroom watched the three of us huddle over the flagrant *Post* front page spread on the desk

350

in Armbrister's goldfish bowl of an office.

His voice tight, Jared began, "I'm afraid" — the first time I had ever heard that word from him, even in such a context — "they've got us. I can't put our people in a fix like that, where a hothead on either side can set off a shooting war." He looked ready to spit out something bitter, and did. "Anaconda doesn't mind that, it would just as soon live on blood as copper."

"What about troops," I reluctantly came up with, "to keep the peace?"

Jared shook his head. "This governor won't want to do that. He's too new in office, and while he's mostly with us against Anaconda, he won't stick his neck out farther than he already has on the tax vote." The other two of us followed his dispirited gaze back down to the threatening headline. "This raises absolute hell with us in trying to hold on against the lockout, but we've got to scrap the parade, I don't see any way around it."

"Conniving bastards," said Armbrister. "Bastard," he corrected himself, for this had Cutlass written all over it in more ways than one. Dread in his every feature, he shook his head at the retreat the *Thunder* now had to lead. "Better get started putting the best face on it you can, Morgie, so —"

351

The editor broke off, scowling as he always did at unfamiliar faces in his newsroom. "Who the hell are these, the oldest living candidates for the Lonely Hearts Club?"

No, they were not lovelorn ancients come to place matrimonial ads, they were Hoop and Griff. Each wearing a suit and tie, like themselves a bit threadbare but serviceable, and clutching in both hands nice hats, homburgs I never would have suspected they possessed. Behaving as though they were in church, they gazed around the newsroom meekly as they padded past surprised reporters.

Coming up to us in the editor's office, they nodded a little greeting as if we were all in the same pew, and paused to consider, one to another.

"You better tell them. It's pretty much your idea."

"It's just as much yours. You go ahead."

"No, no, be my guest."

"Righto. What this is" — Griff addressing the blinking trio of us — "we couldn't help but hear the *Post* newsboys yelling their tonsils out about what the snakes are up to now." He shook his head at Anaconda's latest injustice, Hoop following suit. "We'd miss the Miners Day parade, something awful. Marching in that is the last thing we've got of our life on the Hill, if you know what I mean." The seamed old face, duplicated by the work-worn one next to it, spoke memorably to that. "So Hoop and me got to thinking, how about the Fourth of July?"

While I was a moment behind on that, Jared looked like he'd been hit by the Book of Revelation. "The American Legion parade? Pull a fast one on Anaconda and the mayor?"

Armbrister's face lit up all the way to the green of his eyeshade. "Hell yes, that's it! The Legion is always scrambling for bunches to march with them besides the DAR and the GAR and kiddies with sparklers."

He had scarcely finished before Jared let out a whoop that brought up heads all around the newsroom. "Not even Anaconda can let itself be known for a Fourth of July massacre," our tactician said with a smack of his fist in his palm. "I'll bet my bottom dollar they have to rein in any bloodthirsty goons if we're out there strutting our stuff like true Americans."

By then I could see it as plainly as reveille in some grand dream, the men of the Hill stepping forth as if from some monumental shift change to form the tighter ranks of comrades in arms. Montana always rallied to the colors, famously so, contributing more than its share of manpower in time of war — there was no doubt about it, every mining neighborhood of every nationality would have veterans who were in the Great War or served in the Philippines insurrection or in Mexico against Villa. What a sight it would be, the army of the Hill stretching behind the Legionnaires in their service caps and the Grand Army of the Republic aged remnant in their Union blue and the Daughters of the American Revolution costumed as Betsy Ross in multiple. Carried away, I whapped Jared on the back hard enough to startle him. "And you, Sergeant Evans, must wear your uniform and be out front, like a good soldier."

Laughing, he said Rab might have to let it out a little for him, but by God, he would wear it to the fullest. Exuberance then got the best of him. "You old devils," he seized Griff and Hoop each by a shoulder, "are going to be right there in the front rank of the honor guard." Modest as church mice, they shuffled their feet and declared in duet that would sure take care of their wanting to march, all right.

As publisher and editor feverishly began trading further ideas about how to turn the

Fourth of July into Miners Day come early — Armbrister already was envisioning a *Thunder* special section headlined **Butte Marches for Loyalty and Country;** "Let the readers catch on, loyalty to what," he chortled — Griff and Hoop edged toward the door, turning their hats in their hands. Before they could make their exit, I caught up with them to rid myself of the question tickling at the back of my mind. "Why are you dressed to the teeth?"

"Oh, this." Hoop looked down as if just noticing his suit and tie. "You explain, Griff."

"Sure thing. Giorgio is taking us to the matinee of the Eyetalian opera company that's in town."

I had an awful premonition. "Grace — Mrs. Morgan as well?"

"Well, yeah, sure. He's got to invite one and all, don't he, that's only manners."

"*Polly-atchy,* they're doing," Hoop chimed in. "Something about a clown who bawls a lot. Should be better than it sounds."

The despicable creature Mazzini, copying me culturally as the way to the heart of my wife? What next? With an effort I got hold of myself. "Please tell her for me I love —" Sudden emotion choked me. "Just say I miss her."

"We'll pass that along," they chorused heartily. Their expressions adding, for all the good it would do.

At the end of that day when so much was happening, perhaps it was ordained that I would coincide at the front steps of the manse with O'Malley the postman, who'd had an abjectly apologetic air ever since the intrusion of his gun-wielding impostor. "I hope himself is on the mend," he said anxiously while handing over a package somewhat larger and lighter than the usual book box, and I assured him Sandison's recuperation was taking its course as well as its time.

When I duly took the parcel in to Sandison, he lifted it with a frown. "What the blazes is this, cotton batting? I was expecting the collected Burns with Rowlandson engravings."

After dubiously hoisting the package a few more times and giving it another grumble or two, he got around to slitting it open. Inside was a slouch hat, the kind with the brim rakishly turned all the way up on one side. I recognized the style at once, which was not the same as grasping its significance.

"Sandy," I exclaimed, "you mean to tell me you were a Rough Rider?"

"Don't I wish," he intoned distantly, turning the hat over in his hands. "Dora wouldn't let me. 'Who's going to run the ranch if you trot off like a patriotic fool?' she said. Good enough question. But I gave some horses, and three of my top hands signed on with Roosevelt after he begged me for some good men to take to Cuba. That damned Teddy. Hard to say no to." Wincing, he managed to lift an arm enough to try the hat on. "Well? How's it look?"

"Dashing enough to conquer Cuba by itself," I replied, not terribly far off the truth. Indeed, with it on, Montana's Earl of Hell looked like the very manifestation of wild and woolly triumph in the Spanish-American War, the grizzled rider of the range who might have led the famous charge up San Juan Hill if Teddy Roosevelt had gotten out of the way.

"Hah." Trying to hide his pleasure, Sandison shucked open the envelope that had come with the apparent gift. Reading the accompanying letter, he began to laugh and gasp with pain at the same time. "Get an eyeful of this, Morgan. You never know what'll come around the corner in this life, ay?"

With various loops and flourishes of phrase, the missive invited none other than

Samuel S. Sandison, valued patron and old pard when mounted patriots were called to the colors, to join their presence on the occasion of the twenty-second annual gathering of the 1st United States Volunteer Cavalry — better known as the Rough Riders — this year to be held in Butte on the Fourth of July, to serve as an honorary member of their honor guard — a bit redundant, that — and thereby ride at the head of their mounted contingent in the parade.

"Now I do feel guilty," I lamented after reading over his shoulder.

"Why? You been up to something?"

"Well, I mean, if it had not been for that shooting intended for me, you could ride with them."

"Where do you get your logic from, the bughouse?" he said peevishly. "I'm not an invalid, I'm merely laid up." With a sharp grunt, he took the hat off, admired it, and clapped it back on. "Of course I'm going to ride with them. Heh. Watch and see."

No amount of argument could budge him from that, and so I did the next best thing. Which was to turn it into news for the *Thunder*.

Jared was back in the office the next day

plotting out the paper's parade coverage with Armbrister, Rab along probably because she could not be kept away. When I joined them and reported that, thanks to Sandison, we knew the Rough Riders were coming to town, Armbrister swore mightily before catching himself and asking Rab to excuse him all to hell. "That's just what Cutlass needs, an excuse to ramble on about his famous dispatch from San Juan Hill and his dear old friend, Teddy Roosevelt. Front-page feature, up top of the parade coverage. That's where I'd play it, you can damn well bet."

Thrown by his reaction, I lamely said, "If it helps any, Sandy was on a first-name basis with him, too. Theodore, that is."

Jared's eyebrows shot up at that, while Rab looked intrigued. "You know that for a fact? How's he ever chums with Roosevelt?" Armbrister asked doubtfully. "The Earl of Hell has never seemed to me the political type."

"They were, ah, lynchers together, back in their cattleman days."

"Oh, swell. What a perfect story peg — dishonoring a dead president on the Fourth of July. Got any more bright ideas, Morgie?"

"Actually, I do. Sandison is going to ride

359

at the head of the Rough Riders color guard, at their invitation — what's wrong with a story about that?

"String 'em Up Sam is going to lead the Rough Riders? That's more like it." Armbrister had that look of reading print in the air. " **'Vigilante Rides Again with the Rough Bunch.'** Sensational!"

I coughed. "That is a word that does not sit well with him. Were that headline to appear, he would promptly be in here chastising you, perhaps physically."

"Touchy about the old days of the Montana necktie, is he. All right, then — **'Pioneer Figure Saddles Up with the Rough Riders.'** We'll run it as a parade sidebar." The energized editor stopped suddenly. "I've got a better idea. Cross your fingers, everybody." His already were, in that hex sign that signaled a hunch, and the other three of us guardedly waited for this latest brainstorm to strike.

"Here's what we'll do. Stick a reporter right in there with the Rough Riders. Horseback interviews, that's the ticket." Again, print in the air that only an editor could see: " 'By Our Mounted Correspondent.' Can you beat that for a byline? We'll scoop the sonofabitching *Post,* right out in plain sight, and Cartwright and his crew won't be

360

able to do a thing about it."

"Sounds good to me," Jared immediately signed off on the idea, Rab clapping in approval.

"Very enterprising," I approved heartily. I swept a look around the newsroom for anyone who looked fit for horsemanship. "One of the young ones, I suppose. Sibley, perhaps? Or Cavaretta? He's the daring type —"

"Nope. You."

My skin prickled. I suppose I was not allergic to horses in the strictly medical sense, but the thought of parading through the city on the back of one had much the same ill effect. I tried to laugh. "Jacob, sorry, but I am not an equestrian."

"Oh, but Mr. Morgan, you're much too modest!" Rab stuck her pretty nose in. "At Marias Coulee, you had to ride horseback to go anywhere, remember? We schoolgirls thought you had a very nice seat." She giggled, all too innocently. "Of the horsemanship kind."

"Necessity is not the same as aptitude, Rab," I tried to evade that ambush.

Armbrister was not hearing anything but the gallop of story in his head. "It'll be a peach of a feature. I'll have Sammy set up his camera across from the Hennessy Building, so he gets a terrific shot of you riding right past Anaconda's doorstep. Let Cutlass try to top that."

"Jake, no, really, I —" My protest was drowned out by his shout for the photographer.

"Jared?" I was running out of names to plead to.

"I'm infantry, remember?" Poker-faced, he tugged at his short ear. "I leave the cavalry up to you, Professor." Wasn't that just like a politician, my aggrieved look told him, and words to that effect would have followed had not Armbrister got me by the arm and dragged me off to hatch his plan with the photographer. The two of them plotted his assignment out on the wall map of downtown Butte while I tried to blink out of my daze.

"Easy one. See you at the Hennessy corner, Morgie," the cameraman said, and went back to his poker game, as Armbrister impatiently overrode my last-ditch protests against becoming the *Thunder*'s mounted correspondent. "You're buddy-buddy with Sandison, he'll be right in the thick of the mounted bunch, that makes you the natural one to tag along with him and do the story. What the hell, all you have to do is get up on a horse —"

18

— And ride through the downtown streets
lined by a whooping crowd, with bands
blaring and Fords backfiring and boys on
bicycles wild as Cossacks, while simultaneously keeping track of Samuel Sandison
and interviewing his Rough Rider cohorts,
all of it without falling out of the saddle
and killing myself, my hunch-playing editor
might just as well have added to his instructions.

The Fourth of July began with the usual
bangs, firecrackers going off in fusillades
that added to my jumpy nerves. As parade
time drew nearer, things got under way at
the manse, with Sandison clomping around
in his best cowboy boots, digging out his
old leather chaps that shined from use and
a pair of sharp-roweled spurs, and topping
it all off with the Rough Rider hat. Thus assembled, he cocked a look to where I stood
waiting on one foot and then the other, back

and forth between dreading my horseback assignment and wanting to get it over with. "Am I seeing right? Are you going looking like an undertaker?"

Miffed, I protested that my blue serge suit, sober tie, and dove-gray vest marked me as a member of the press. "Besides, I bought a Stetson."

"Bonnet on a rooster," he wrote off my new hat, meanwhile lumbering to his library lair for what he said was the one last thing he needed.

He came out strapping on a gun belt with a six-shooter, the large old kind called a hog leg, in the holster.

I stared. "Where did that come from?"

"The Colt Firearms Company in Hartford, Connecticut, where do you think?"

"I meant — is that a good idea? With Anaconda's armed goons on hand? Isn't carrying a gun possibly giving them an excuse to —"

"Morgan" — he rolled his eyes toward the bullet holes in the ceiling — "I am the one who got shot merely for hanging around with you, remember? I don't want that to happen again. Nor," this came with a full serving of growl and scowl, "do I necessarily want it to happen to you for hanging around with me, if some idiot with an old

364

grudge decides to take it out on me and my riders. Anaconda or anyone else, this is to give them second thoughts." The gun belt circling his girth like the equator, he rested his hand on the prominent handle of the Colt .45 as if it was a natural fit. "I have a reputation to uphold in this damn town," he said, with all the austere dignity expected of the Butte public librarian. Then came the gleam of the Earl of Hell, reflected from his vigilante days. "More than one."

Inasmuch as a good many of the Rough Riders shipped their own mounts in by boxcar, their encampment was down by the stockyards, where Sandison and I duly delivered ourselves by taxi before parade time. "You can just about bet most of them slept in a feather bed somewhere uptown," he shrewdly guessed as we approached the camp, "then scuttled down here for a breakfast of beans around a campfire." The cluster of weather-beaten tents carried the tang of both a military bivouac and a cattle roundup, as did the Rough Riders themselves, actually. Hip-sprung men of a certain type stood around fire circles talking in slow cadences and, likely as not, spitting tobacco juice onto the sizzling embers. I was itching to pull out my notepad and jot down just how their slouch hats and loosely knotted neckerchiefs — bandannas, I mentally corrected myself — and blue flannel uniform shirts made them look like exhibits from an earlier age. "A Frederic Remington museum diorama come to life," was the phrase that suggested itself. But given the squints and odd looks aimed at Sandison and me as we passed through, him in his ranching getup of forty years ago and I in my city clothes and clean Stetson, I kept my reportorial materiel in my pocket.

There was a similar gang of blue-shirted figures ahead at the stockyards, some fence-sitting, some peering between corral poles to where horses were being wrangled with considerable commotion and dust. Lanky and akimbo and in some drawling world of their own, these hardened military cowhands or cowboy-soldiers did not look any friendlier than the set at the tents, so I felt compelled to ask Sandison a little tentatively, "Who will be our, ah, riding companions?"

"Who do you think," he grunted in answer, stepping up his stride, his chaps flapping, as we neared the corral. "The James brothers."

"Very funny, Sandy. I suppose Butch Cassidy and the Hole in the Wall Gang will be joining us later?"

"What's funny about it?" Sandison huffed, giving me a look. "Leonard James and his kid brother, Claude, both rode for me on the ranch from the time they were green saddle punks. Had to teach the young scamps every blasted thing about cowboying." He shook his head reminiscently. "Same with Tinsley, another pea in that pod."

"Related to them, is he?" I took the implication to be.

"For crying out loud, Morgan, where do you get these ideas? He's colored."

I surrendered to the situation, whatever it was going to be, and simply stuck as close as possible while Sandison surveyed the dusty scene in the corral. He was grumbling, "I got carried away with that silly little war. Should never have let the three of them off the ranch to go fight Spaniards. Lost the whole batch to that old humbug, Buffalo Bill, afterward."

My expression must have told him I was not keeping up with these particulars.

"The Wild West Show, dolt. After the charge up San Juan Hill and the tripe written by your colleague Cartwright" — he looked hard at me — "Bill Cody turned that cactus circus of his into Buffalo Bill's Wild

West and Congress of Rough Riders of the World."

Ducking behind a corral post, I busily scribbled this down while Sandison went back to scanning the swirl of lasso-swinging wranglers and dodgy mounts.

"Heh." The tone of that made me look up, right into those eyes the blue of glacier ice. "I don't know about you," although it hardly took a guess in this regard, "but I haven't been on a horse since" — he gave me a complicit look — "that time with you."

I swallowed hard. That excursion, in my first Butte chapter of life, had been an unforgettable one, in the valley to the west where his ranch once stretched from horizon to horizon. Not knowing what his intentions were, I had ridden in a sweat of fear as he led me to the hanging tree where his reputation as the Strangler had been earned. Where rustlers were strung up, vigilante style, by him and doubtless the same ranch hands we were to meet with today. His anguished words echoed in me yet. "What gets into a man, Morgan, to set himself up as an executioner?" I am no stranger to redemption myself — possibly even a periodic visitor — but I had never witnessed a person turning his soul inside out as Samuel Sandison did that day. It all flooded back, overwhelming me again. And with that, my assignment, my presence, seemed out of place in his world of cowhands and cattle and horses and lasting consequences of decisions taken decades ago.

"Sandy," I breathed out, "this is beyond me. I really don't have any business intruding into your reunion with your riders, and I'll just go back uptown and watch the parade from some convenient —"

Sandison held up a stopping hand. Casting his eyes to the heavens, he intoned, "God of fools, here is a newspaperman with an opportunity to ride with the men who made Theodore Roosevelt president of the United States, and he's scared of a little thing like climbing on a horse. Take him now, his work on earth is done."

Wounded, I muttered, "You don't have to be like that about it. I'll stay."

"That's better. I knew you had it in you, somewhere." Scanning the horse-wrangling again, Sandison grunted with satisfaction. "Aha. Here come our cowboys."

Indeed, out the corral gate and toward us came three riders, the ones on the outside of the triptych each leading a saddled horse, which, I realized with a tightening in the seat of my pants, must be the mounts for Sandison and myself.

"Good to see you again, boys," drawled Sandison as they rode up to us.

"Sam," the James brother introduced as Leonard acknowledged him, nodding an inch. The one called Claude, saving energy along with words, merely nodded half an inch. It was left to Tinsley, his smile a burst of enamel and gold in the dark face, to come out with, "How you been doing, boss?"

"Surviving," the answer came as a heavy sigh, together with a weighty glance at me.

"Packing a Peacemaker these days?" Tinsley expressed the curiosity showing on all three Rough Riders, at Sandison's prominent firearm. "Butte that tough a place?"

"You might be surprised," Sandison responded in the same weary tone before indicating me again. "Morgan writes for the newspaper. He's going to ride along with us and talk to you boys about your heroic exploits, heh, heh."

Studying me for what seemed long moments, Leonard and Tinsley at last nodded; Claude did not make the effort. "Got horses for you," Leonard said as though we might not have noticed the large animals standing practically atop us. "Prince and Blaze, from the show string. One of the boys in camp was gonna take whichever one you didn't choose, Sam, but he'll have to bum one somewhere else, looks like."

"Pick a mount, Morgan." Sandison's booming generosity was no help. Other than the camels Grace and I posed on at the Sphinx to have our picture taken, I had not been astraddle an animal in recent times and would gladly have continued that way. In this situation, however, I was stuck with the fact that horsemanship of some degree was required. All I thought I knew about horses was ears. If the ears stood straight up, I reasoned, the equine was probably spirited. Prince was a well-named sorrel, high-headed and regal, with erect ears that twitched as though batting away flies. Spirited I did not want. That left Blaze, a bay-colored steed that appeared sleepily disinterested in us and our doings. Since the animal did not appear to be any ball of fire — more as if its flame had gone out — I was at the point of foolishly asking about its name when some fortunate tic of memory suggested that the splotch of white from the horse's nostrils up to its languid ears was the sort called blaze face. "I'll try this one," I took the plunge.

"Let's go, buckaroos," said Sandison, swinging onto the sorrel with a painful groan before my foot even found the stirrup. Climbing as much as mounting, I scrambled into the saddle atop Blaze with the James brothers and Tinsley watching impassively, and we joined the ranks of blue-shirted Rough Riders prancing to where the parade was forming up at the west edge of the business district.

Half of Butte seemed to be there, milling into place to march down Broadway, the other half of the populace already lining the blocks ahead in joyous anticipation. The American Legionnaires at the very front in their doughboy outfits and earlier uniforms looked a bit staggered at the long, long line of marchers filling in behind them. American flags were everywhere, the air undulating with red, white, and blue. Right in with the unit of children in Uncle Sam and Miss Liberty costumes, I spotted Rab in command of our roughneck newsboys from the detention school; their newspaper bags were innocently turned inside out so the *Thunder* logotype could not be seen, and at their front, holding high the banner YOU SHALL KNOW THE TRUTH AND THE TRUTH SHALL MAKE YOU FREE, were Russian Famine on one end, giving his restlessness something to do, and on the other the angelic urchin Punky, doubtless to keep his hands out of people's pockets.

Since horseback troupes best brought up

the rear of the parade — "the manure matter," Sandison gave all the explanation needed — we rode past innumerable contingents on the way to our position, the Daughters of the American Revolution in dowager ranks and the Grand Army of the Republic veterans lame but game beneath battle flags from Gettysburg and Antietam and other hallowed fields of conflict, and then the Hill began to make its showing, the Miners Band glorious in the green of its uniforms and the gold and silver of its instruments, the blocks-long files of miners who had served their country headed by Jared, more leaderly than ever in his Army uniform, giving me a wink of confidence as Blaze and I passed, succeeded shortly by ear-to-ear grins from Griff and Hoop in the Welsh honor guard.

But then a sight I could have done without, as we passed the Irish and Cornish and kilted Scots and approached the Italian segment of miners. The flag-bearer of their red, white, and green alongside the Stars and Stripes was none other than the damnable dynamiter, Giorgio Mazzini, doubtless chosen for height, might, and proud bearing. Why oh why couldn't Grace's current boarder have been some ordinary Mustache Pete instead of a Roman god?

Fortunately or not, I had little time to brood on that. "Fall in!" came the call from the gray-bearded captain of the Rough Riders, and we accordingly turned our horses and waited for the Miners Band to strike up first "The Star-Spangled Banner" and then the union anthem. Impelled by a certain kind of frown from Sandison, I managed to squeeze Blaze and me between the Jameses' mounts, the better to interview the brothers — or at least the one capable of speech — while we rode. At last came the first stirring notes of "The Song of the Hill," the long line of marchers accordioned into motion, and we were under way.

It took me a block or so to figure out how best to handle reins, pencil, and notepad all at the same time, but finally I felt ready and, turning to Leonard, casually asked over the *clop-clop* of our horses' hooves: "How is Buffalo Bill these days?"

"Still dead."

I mentally kicked myself; the name of P. T. Barnum, long deceased, was on a circus apparently for eternity, wasn't it. "His, ah, showmanship cannot be interred with him, of course," I hastily accorded promotional immortality to William F. Cody as well. "I meant, how is the Wild West Show and —" I peeked at my earlier notation "— Congress of Rough Riders of the World faring?"

About the same as practically forever, Leonard allowed as how. "Can't print tickets fast enough." As I listened to this slow testimonial, it dawned on me how veteran he and the other two were, in all senses of the word. Up close, the seamed faces of Sandison's "young scamps" were a reminder that more than two decades had passed since Teddy Roosevelt rallied men like these in the conquest of Cuba. Surreptitiously I wrote down *crow's-feet around the eyes* while trying to think what a mounted correspondent ought to ask next. "Mmm, what is the most memorable place you've ever been with the Buffalo Bill show?"

Leonard considered the matter for so long I wondered if he had forgotten he was expected to answer. At last, though, he drawled, "St. Pete was a humdinger. Wouldn't you say, Claude?" The other James brother inclined his head a fraction.

"St. Petersburg? What a coincidence! I remember it fondly myself." My confidence as a roving reporter went up a peg, with my interview subject and me in concord about that burgeoning but oh so pleasant Florida city, where during our travel year Grace first dipped a toe into an ocean, the tropical breeze through the palms like a murmur of benediction on newlyweds. My sigh holding volumes about those balmy days and nights, I put the next question: "In the winter, I hope?"

"As wintry as it gets in St. Pete," came the taciturn response. "Right, Claude?"

"Isn't that climate something." Thinking of the proximity to Cuba and the heroics of the Rough Riders in the so-called splendid little war, I asked, "Did performing there have a different feel to you, with that sort of audience?"

"You said a mouthful. People about went crazy," the talker of the James brothers rationed out. "The big cheese hisself was there, gave ol' Bill a toad-stabber of some kind to welcome us to town."

Before I could ask the exact nature of the ceremonial sword, presumably presented by the mayor, the tale picked up speed.

"We put on the show like we usually done, riding and whooping and shooting in the air and making that San Juan Hill charge. Do that right at the audience, hell for leather, and it gets their attention, for sure. But those St. Peterkins, as we called 'em, was standing on their seats and yelling their heads off at every little thing we did. Never saw nothing like it, hey, Claude?"

"It must have been quite an experience," I

furnished as encouragement to keep him talking and his silent sibling nodding, meanwhile writing furiously on my pad and somehow manipulating the reins enough to remind drowsy Blaze that I still was a passenger, and also trying to keep a concerned eye on Sandison where he rode, favoring his wounded side by leaning so sharply in the saddle, it looked like his horse was tipping over. When he wasn't wincing with pain, he seemed to be thoroughly enjoying himself, patting his gun butt meaningfully whenever some old-timer in the crowd yelped out, "String 'em up, Sam!" or some other tribute. And the Rough Riders proved to be a popular feature as well, met by the chant that first greeted their 1898 military triumph, "The boys in blue always come through!" as we progressed. Somewhere in back of us, a Rough Rider regularly sounded the blood-stirring bugle call that echoed the famous charge up San Juan Hill. The role of mounted correspondent beginning to fit me, I brightly posed a next question to my interviewee: "So, was there anything else particularly memorable about St. Petersburg?"

Leonard thought back some more, glancing to Claude for help, evidently the telepathic sort. "Well, yeah, there was. Before we pulled out of town, people was dancing the kickapoo, right and left."

"Excuse me? The — ?"

"The Indians we had with us in the show at the time was Kickapoos, from back east around Chicago. They'd do their war dance, and the St. Peterkins had never seen nothing like it, had they. So next thing, people was dancing something like it in the nightclubs. Called it the kickapoo."

The vision of Floridians cavorting like savages was mildly entertaining but I couldn't see how to use it, and moved on to other questions about taking the Wild West et cetera from city to city. Before long, however, the parade was winding through the heart of the business district and I hadn't yet interviewed Tinsley, so I turned Blaze to one side to let the James brothers pass, profusely thanking Leonard for his observations. He shrugged as though it had been nothing. It was the other one, Claude, who half turned in his saddle and laconically said over his shoulder:

"Like they say in St. Pete, *da svidanya.*"

Cursing myself up and down and Armbrister for good measure, I frantically flipped through my notepad and began trying to recast my supposed reportorial notes from an imagined setting of sand beaches and whispering palms to the snowy clime of Cossacks and czar.

With my haphazard grip on the reins during this, Blaze came close to joining the crowd on the sidewalk, before Sandison reached over to catch the bridle and steer us back into the parade. He gave me The Look. "I hate to interrupt genius at work, but you can't turn things over to the horse, Morgan."

Protesting weakly that I had merely been collecting my thoughts, I was stopped in mid-sentence by what lay ahead, past the lopsided outline of Sandison. We were approaching the public library, closed for the day, its gray granite edifice a composition of light and shadow, with a wash of sunshine on the magnificent entranceway and Gothic tower and accompanying balcony. There, alone on the balcony, Grace was poised, watching the parade like a solitary queen.

"What — why — how did she get up there?"

"Ay?" Spotting her, Sandison tipped his slouch hat as though gallantry were his middle name, and she waved back while somehow managing not to acknowledge my existence. "The poor woman needed a place to watch from, on her own the way she is. Just because you and she are on the outs, you can't expect her to live under a rock, can you?"

That fairly closely described how I envisioned her existence without me, matching mine without her. Swallowing hard, I made no answer but tried to keep my eyes from meeting her watching ones, there on the snug balcony where the pair of us had spectated the parade in the golden time of our courtship.

"Back to work," I croaked to Sandison as my estranged wife, stately as a ship's figurehead, passed from view behind us. Mustering myself, I managed to navigate my drifty animal into position alongside Tinsley and his mount.

"I hope ol' Leonard and Claude didn't fill you too full of hooey afore I get a chance to," he greeted me with a radiant smile. As wiry and talkative as the James boys were long on height and short on words, Tinsley had the nonchalant ease of a veteran interviewee. First name, Alonzo. Originally a buffalo soldier, which was to say, he explained at some length, a member of the colored cavalry formed after the Civil War and sent to the Southwest "to fight Apaches and Comanches and whatnot." I wrote as steadily as he volunteered information. "Soldiering is what brung me to Montana,

380

see. Afore I latched on riding for the boss there at the Triple S, I finished out my Tenth Cavalry 'listment as a corporal at Fort Assinniboine, up by Canada. Company C, that was," he leaned back in his saddle reminiscently, "under ol' Lieutenant Pishing."

Conscientious reporter that I was trying to will myself into, I requested, "Would you spell that, please?"

"A-S-S —"

"No, your commanding officer's name."

"Lemme think. P . . . E . . . R . . . S-H-I-N-G."

I stared at those letters as written down. "I don't suppose his first name and middle initial could possibly be John J."

"Yup, that's the gentleman. Ol' Black Jack, he was known as, from officering with us dark-complexioned troopers."

I felt light-headed, and not just from the elevation of being horseback. "Corporal Tinsley. Alonzo. Are you telling me you have ridden with both a president of the United States and the supreme commander of the American forces in the Great War?"

Gold teeth flashed. "That's about what it comes down to. Don't know why I'm such an attraction."

My elation at this newsworthy element of

his life in the saddle was about to receive another boost. Just then we happened to be approaching the *Daily Post* building, a virtual front-row seat for watching the parade, and up there in a second-floor window, unmistakable among the spectating heads, was the Cutlass himself. Big as life, Cutthroat Cartwright was surveying the parade scene with that superior air of a predator looking over the pickings. My eye caught his, and he stared unremittingly as I cantered past with the Rough Riders. I could tell, he knew perfectly well what I was up to. I resisted the impulse to rub it in by tipping my Stetson to him, but my canary-swallowing smile probably did the job.

Activated anew by the smell of competition, I got busy probing Tinsley's memory of his famous cavalry commanders. Pershing as a prairie hussar, for instance? Cool under combat as his famous icy demeanor would imply, was he? "Can't rightly speak to that," my buffalo soldier informant surprised me. "Combat is stretching it some, as to what Fort Assinniboine duty amounted to. It was more like herding Indians. See, 'bout all we did was scoop some loose Crees over the line into Canada. They'd get kicked out of there, we'd round 'em up, mostly women and kids, get 'em in a line of march and scoop 'em back across the border. Anyways, that happened just a number of times. Wasn't none of it what you would call real cavalry fighting." Chuckling, he waved his hat to cheering onlookers high in the Finlen Hotel. " 'Course, San Juan wasn't, either."

My pencil jabbed through the paper. "Wha . . . what did you say?"

Blandly he recited that the San Juan battle had been no kind of a cavalry charge and he ought to know, he was there.

"But" — I twitched the reins so agitatedly that Blaze turned his head to see what my trouble was — "I was under the impression —"

"— the Rough Riders made some kind of yippy-yi-yay cavalry charge up San Juan Hill?" Tinsley gave an amused snort. "It beats me, but I guess there must've been newspapers somewhere that wrote it up that way — the ones Buffalo Bill read, at least." He smiled slyly about the fake charge that thrilled audiences of the Wild West Show, then sobered. "Nothing against your line of work, unnerstand, but reporters was a dime a dozen in the Cuba campaign, and some of 'em worth about that, too. The one tagging along with us colored troops was so drunk most of the time, he didn't know if

383

we was afoot or horseback." Would that it could have happened to Cecil Cartwright, I despaired, instead of his career-making dispatch under fire.

Dropping his voice, Tinsley glanced across to where Sandison was holding forth to the James brothers about something. "Anyways, Claude and Leonard don't much like being teased about it, but we was all dismounts in Cuba. Yup, that's right," he responded to my jaw dropping further, "on foot in spite of being the First Volunteer Cavalry — I guess the higher-ups figgered the volunteer part was all was needed." He wagged his head at the ways of the military. "Nobody much had a horse except Colonel Teddy."

Groaning inwardly, I rebuked myself again for leaping to conclusions. Just because a military unit formed as the Rough Riders had charged the heights of San Juan did not automatically mean they had done so on horseback, sabers flashing and guidon flying, as my imagination would have it. No wonder Cutthroat Cartwright was not down here with the blue-shirted procession; he knew all the rough riding they had done was in a Wild West Show. Off the top of his head, he could write a piece about old parading cavalrymen, such as they were, that would leave mine in the figurative dust.

Swallowing my disappointment, I thanked Tinsley for his time and nudged Blaze off to one side of our clopping contingent to try to think. How did I get into this fix? Why couldn't I be sitting comfortably at a typewriter tapping out invective about copper bosses, instead of trapped in a saddle as a mounted correspondent with no thrilling horseback tale to cap off my article? Time was running out, too. The parade had turned onto Granite Street and would soon be passing the Hennessy Building, where the *Thunder* photographer was set up to shoot me, as the phrasing was. Not one I liked, the less so as Sandison now rode across to where I was, leaning his wounded side in my direction, discomfort and stubbornness vying in his expression, as he wanted to know, "Getting it all down like Tennyson with the charge of the Light Brigade?"

"The plot of this is somewhat harder to follow," I said faintly.

"Ay? Buck up, Morgan. You've had a good ride with the boys, you're about to have your picture in the paper, people will read whatever folderol you come up with. What are you complaining about?"

Satisfied that he had put things in perspective, Sandison stayed stirrup to stirrup with me as, down the block in front of us, cohort after cohort of defiantly singing miners marched past the lofty headquarters of the Anaconda Copper Mining Company. What a scene that moment of the parade was as a thousand voices lifted in the verse, *"Down there deep we're all one kind, / All one blood, all of one mind / I back you and you back me, / All one song in unity."* Flags waved, pinwheels spun on sticks children held like lollipops, the sun shone bright on a Butte free of strife for the course of a day. And tomorrow, I knew even without the sage glint in Sandison's eye, the civil war of labor and capital would resume, I would shed my temporary mantle of mounted correspondent and resume editorial battle with the *Post,* the calendar page would be turned, with each of us one day nearer our destiny.

But right now, my role in life was to look as presentable as possible astride a clip-clopping horse while portraiture occurred. Catercorner from the Hennessy Building, the photographer Sammy waited beside his big box camera on a tripod, gesturing urgently to make sure I saw him and was ready. Gruffly saying he didn't want to break the camera, Sandison dropped back out of range. "Don't forget to smile at the birdy, laddie."

A smile became out of the question, however, as I spotted a number of bruisers strung out along the entire front of the Hennessy Building, positioned against the wall and the display windows with their hands over their private parts in the manner of museum guards and other functionaries who stand around for hours on end. Unquestionably, these had to be the extra goons making good on Anaconda's threat to station guards at all company property, in this case merely for show around the infamous top-floor headquarters. Of a type I would not like to meet in a dark alley, the Anaconda operatives favored gabardine suits; as Hill lore had it, blood was more easily sponged off that than softer fabrics. In the holiday crowd, they stood out like gray wolves.

After my initial alarm, I realized the scene was actually peaceful, no guns on display or evident inclination toward any, and with the long file of miners having marched past without incident, apt to stay that way. Blind Heinie's newsstand was situated right across the sidewalk from where the most prominent of the goons had made their presence known alongside the department store's big windows, and as the sightless old news vendor entertained himself by slapping his thighs in rhythm with the Miners Band's distant rendition of "When You and I Were Young, Maggie," the nearest gabardined thugs were idly nodding along. Breathing a sigh of relief, I sat up tall as I could in the saddle to be ready for Sammy's camera. The throng lining the sidewalk *ooh*ed and *ahh*ed at the prospect of being in the picture, meanwhile making guesses about my importance. "I bet he's some relative of Buffalo Bill's. Look at that set of whiskers on him." Trying to live up to all the attention, I patted Blaze's neck, fiddled with the reins, straightened my hat. At least some of Armbrister's hunch was paying off as, goons notwithstanding, the main display window with HENNESSY'S DEPARTMENT STORE in large golden lettering made a fetching backdrop, mannequins in cloche hats and flapper dresses indolently holding teacups, the mischievous implication there that since Prohibition had come in, "tea shops" served gin that way. Bobbing in and out from behind his viewfinder, Sammy called across the street to me, "Slow down a little, Morgie. I want to get the shot just as you pass the window."

Blaze and I never made it past. As if in a strange dream, I still see the individual who looked like a drunken bum, appearing from

the far side of Blind Heinie's newsstand,
suddenly plunge through the other onlookers and come stumbling out of the crowd to
intercept us with something held like a
bouquet. But no, too late I saw it was a
rolled newspaper he had lit with a match,
and with it flaming like a torch, he made a
last running lurch and thrust the burning
paper under Blaze's tail.

Put yourself in the poor horse's place.
Driven wild by its singed hind part, my
steed left the earth, and came down frantically swapping ends, bucking and kicking.
His gyrations whirled us onto the sidewalk,
scattering onlookers and goons alike. My
panicky cries of "Whoa! *Whoa!*" fell on deaf
horse ears. As if we were in a steeplechase,
Blaze's next jump aimed straight for the
maidenly tea or gin party, as the case may
have been, crashing us through the big
display window.

Flappers flew, teacups sailed. Ducking
falling glass, I was low as a jockey, clamping
to the saddle for all I was worth. Now that
we were in the store, in the ladies' wear
department to be exact, Blaze seemed not
to know where to go next, very much like a
baffled shopper. My repeated chorus of
*whoa*s finally having some effect, he halted
in the aisle of the lingerie section, still snort-

ing and quivering and his ears up like sharp flanges, but no longer determined to buck us both off the face of the earth. Holding the reins taut just in case, I cautiously felt around on myself and could find nothing broken. Remarkably, my hat still was on my head.

"Ride him on out! C'mon, the horse knows the way now!" The commotion in back of me was from Leonard and Claude and Tinsley, their own horses' heads curiously poking through what had been the window. In truth, I didn't know what else to do, and at my urging, Blaze rather delicately picked his way through fallen flappers and other window-dressing and rejoined the street as if hopping a ditch.

The scene outside the store was a shambles I gradually made sense of. What had been the parade was a blue knot of Rough Riders, whooping to one another as they caught up with what had happened. Nearer, leaning more precariously yet in his saddle, Sandison had the culprit at gunpoint, the six-shooter aimed squarely between the man's eyes as he babbled that somebody he had never seen before paid him to play a prank, was all. The squad of goons had backed off to a discreet distance, evidently wanting no part of any trouble they hadn't started. Policemen belatedly elbowed through the crowd. The more familiar blue uniforms of my riding companions surrounded me.

"You all right, pard? Man, we've seen some stunt riding, but that one takes the cake." Tinsley and Leonard were singing my praises — and Blaze's — while Claude mutely slapped me on the back. More to the point, I realized, was the remark from Sammy hustling past with his camera and tripod. "Got a good one of you flying through that window. Better come on, if we're gonna make deadline."

Somewhat worse for wear when I showed up at the *Thunder* office on foot — Blaze being restored with high honors to the Wild West Show string — I was fussed over by Armbrister, but meanwhile steered to my typewriter. I did my best to concentrate, to make sense of my notes, to think straight like a good reporter should, but it felt hopeless; my mind was a blur. Thank heavens my fingers seemed to know what they were doing.

Armbrister nearly wore out the floor, pacing as he waited to grab each page. After the last tap of a typewriter key, I fell back in my chair, exhausted, awaiting his verdict. Eyeshade aimed down into my story like the beak of a clucking bird, he mumbled the sentences rapidly to himself until finally swatting me with the sheaf of pages. "Terrific lede. 'I rode with the James brothers — up to the point where my horse and I went into Hennessy's department store.' Let that bastard Cartwright top that! And the bit about Russians dancing the kickapoo, great stuff. That's what a hunch can do for you, Morgie. Copyboy!"

In no time, the newsroom trembled with the start-up of the press, and we along with the rest of the *Thunder* staff could hardly bear the wait to see what a similar rumble of machinery was producing across town. At last our contraband early copy of the *Post* was rushed in. Armbrister speedily scanned the pages as only a journalist could, then, with an odd expression, he passed the paper to me to do the same.

There was not one word in the *Post* about the Rough Riders.

19

"I still can't believe it. It isn't like Cutthroat Cartwright to miss out that way. He ought to have snapped up the Rough Riders story like a wolf licking his chops."

"Are you going to natter about that all night?" None the worse for wear — unlike me — after the day's horseback adventures, Sandison was heartily tucking into his plateload of scalloped potatoes and veal parmigiana; stiff and sore as I was, cooking had to be done. Also for supper were the *Thunder* and the *Post* spread around on the table, more like a long wharf than ever with just the two of us docked at one end. "I don't know what's the matter with you. You achieve a whatchamacallit, swoop —"

" 'Scoop' is the honored journalistic term."

"— and you sit around maundering about why the other fellow didn't get it instead of you. Can't stand good luck, ay? Pass the spuds."

"I am only saying, it's mysterious."

"Yes, yes, the dog that didn't bark, we've all read our Sherlock Holmes, never mind. It'll become clear or it won't." With that profundity, he turned back to the *Thunder* front page, with the splashy headline **Bronc Goes on Hennessy Shopping Spree** and accompanying photograph. I still had trouble believing the evident daredevil in the saddle was me. "Not that I mean to criticize," Sandison pontificated, studying the photo, "but when the pony takes to the air like that, you really should hang on to the saddle horn instead of your hat."

"I must remember that the next time I mount up on Pegasus." That retort flew by him, as he returned to the newspaper while forking down his meal, sturdy as a Viking while I ached from the bottom up. It occurred to me that in all the confusion and deadline rush, I had not managed to express my appreciation for his holding the flame-wielding culprit at gunpoint. "Ah, thank you for riding shotgun, so to speak."

"Hmm?" He barely glanced up. "Seemed like a good idea if you were anywhere in the vicinity." Favoring his side, he reached for his coffee cup with a wince. "What is it about you? I spent my whole ranch life around people armed to the teeth and never got shot."

"You would think," I said wearily, "guns should be as allergic to me as I am to them. Balance of nature, that sort of thing."

This drew me the observation that I was an optimist, which did not seem to qualify as a compliment in Sandison lexicon. Pushing his practically gleaming plate away and untucking his napkin, he leaned back with a groan and addressed the ceiling. "I know what I'd do, though, if a bunch of idiots was gunning for me and setting fire to my horse and so on."

You sit up and pay attention when the Earl of Hell offers advice on matters of that sort.

"I'd let it be known something nasty could happen to them as well as to me," he drawled, lowering his gaze as if sighting in on me. "Someone in particular, to get their attention."

"Threaten Cartwright, you mean."

"An eye for an eye. Right there in the Bible, heh."

I swallowed hard. "Sandy, I don't think I have it in me to even the score that way. Do I look remotely homicidal?" A sigh from across the table answered that. "Cutlass is unfortunately as sharp as that damnable pen name. He would know in a flash I was bluffing."

"Think straighter than that, man. All sorts of unpleasant things might happen to someone like him that aren't necessarily fatal." He steepled his fingers, evidently pondering the list. "Butte after dark can be a lively place," he plucked an example. "A person could accidentally get into an altercation with someone rowdy. A muscular miner or two, for instance." His gaze lofted off again. "I'm only saying, that could be pointed out to the pertinent person."

Now I was the one pondering, deeply. The bearded old figure across the table had taken a bullet for me and similarly performed heroically in the horseback episode. He could hardly be blamed for wanting to head off any more such incidents. Even besides him, everyone else near and dear to me — Grace, Jared and Rab, Russian Famine, Hoop and Griff, the embattled *Thunder* staff — was bearing some kind of brunt of Anaconda's machinations. And there was always the ghost of Quin, the question mark hovering around his death.

The more I thought about it, the straighter the thinking became, as Sandison prescribed. Why should Cutthroat Cartwright waltz into town to do Anaconda's dirty work and be left spotless? My verdict did not come easily, but it came.

"I'll put the matter to Jared Evans — he no doubt has some way of getting the message across to Cartwright that he had better watch his step," I met Sandison's terms with all the determination I could muster. "I take your point, about being on the receiving end of gunshots and equine high jinks and all. *Satis superque.*"

For whatever reason — would I ever understand the outsize bear-like book-loving string-'em-up personality across from me? — the Latin tickled him into a rollicking belly laugh. " 'Enough and more than enough,' " he wheezed. "Well said, my boy. You have a touch when you half try."

In high good humor now, he poured himself some more coffee and did the same for me, rather a stretch for his usual contribution to our mealtimes. "By the way, figure me into breakfast tomorrow. Bacon and three or four eggs and a stack of hotcakes will do."

Seeing my surprise at this departure from his routine of breakfasting only with his books, he said defensively, "Don't drop your teeth. A man has to stoke up a bit to get back on the job, doesn't he?"

"Back on the — ? You don't mean downtown, surely."

"Unless it's been moved in my absence, that's where the public library is."

"But you're still nursing your wound."

"Am not," he said crossly. He tried unsuccessfully to sit up straight without wincing. "Bit of a stitch in my side, is all."

"Minutes ago you were describing that to me as a nearly lethal bullet."

"You're worse than Dora ever was for nagging," he grumbled. "Don't you see, I have to get down there and tend to the collection. There's a board of trustees meeting coming up and I need to have things patted into place."

I saw, all right, as if a veil had been lifted by a corner. He had to make sure the mingled budgetary funds that steadily nourished the finest book collection west of Chicago — and thanks to the judicious use of the paste pot in his office, grew the number of rare volumes with his SSS bookplate in them — did not show any loose ends. "It's time I picked up the reins again," he said smoothly. "Though I'm sure you did the best you could filling in for me."

Buried in that was the fact that he would go to any length for his beloved books, even entrusting their care to me. No matter how cantankerously he put it, I was deeply moved. So much so that I could no longer hold the secret in. With the help of seemingly casual sips of coffee, I began: "As long as we are unburdening ourselves about such matters —"

"Is that what we're doing? You could have fooled me."

"— I have a confession to make. That winning wager I made on the fixed World Series. I, ah, bet your book collection. The inventory I did for the public library, I mean. Butte bookies are used to strange collateral."

"Of course you did, nitwit. How else were you going to put up a stake like that?"

My coffee nearly went into my beard. I sputtered, "You knew? All along?"

"That's the trouble with you bunkhouse geniuses," he waved away my soul-baring disclosure. "You think nobody else has a clue about what's going on."

"You — you're not angry?"

"If I lost my temper every time you did something, I'd be going off like Old Faithful, wouldn't I." He heaved himself to his feet. "Better get your beauty rest, bronc buster. You don't get to show off in a parade every day. Tomorrow you have to get down to business and give that Chicago scissorbill something to think about. Heh, heh."

■ ■ ■ ■

Despite its name, the Purity Cafeteria seemed to me the apt spot to inaugurate playing dirty with Cutthroat Cartwright, in council with Jared and, of course, Rab, amid the hurly-burly of food fetching and wholesale dining where we would not be suspected of anything except runaway appetites. Sandison informed me he would be putting in late hours at the public library for some time to come, so I was furloughed from supper duty at the manse anyway. Perfectly free to follow the edict of the Earldom of Hell, if I had the courage. I was nervous, not to say a novice, at plotting of this sort. Threatening harm to another human being, even an Anaconda hired gun — I had to regard Cutlass as such, just as much as if he were blazing away at me, so to speak, with pistol and torch — did not come naturally to me. A show of brass knuckles when danger stared at me face-to-face had always been as far as I was prepared to go. Now, though, the Highliner's authoritative, "If that's how you want to plan your funeral, it's your choice" rang in me like the opening bell of a boxing match. Wasn't I merely counter-punching, in the effective style of a certain lightweight champion of the world? Casper never shrank from hitting back, and he won nearly every time. Nearly.

Beaming, the plump bow-tied proprietor greeted me as an old customer the moment I entered the Purity. "I hope you brought your appetite. You're in luck, tonight's special is Dublin Gulch filet," by which he meant corned beef and cabbage. He knew his business in more ways than one, having made peace with the fact that Butte was a union town by posting prominent notices that the enterprise hired only members of the Cooks and Dishwashers Brotherhood, and always welcoming Jared and other union leaders as though he were an honorary member of their number. Accordingly, the cafeteria was where the Hill ate when it went downtown for an evening out, and it took me a minute to spy Jared and Rab in the crowded room, she naturally spotting me first and waving like a student who knew the answer. I could certainly have used one.

I waited until the three of us had been through the serving line and were seated with heaped plates of corned beef and cabbage before broaching the topic of Cutthroat Cartwright. Rab listened sharpeared as if she were at a keyhole, while Jared chewed on his Irish filet mignon as well as what I was saying in roundabout fashion. When I was done citing Sandison and counterpunching and otherwise trying to put the best appearance on the topic, he asked, poker-faced, "So what is it you and Sam the Strangler want us to do, Professor? Drop Cartwright down a glory hole some dark night?"

"Mr. Morgan!" Thrilled as a schoolgirl but trying to stay proper as a teacher, Rab examined me with fresh eyes. "You really want" — detention school language came to the fore at a time like this — "his block knocked clean off?"

"No, no, I didn't say that," I protested guiltily. This conversation was veering uncomfortably close to the memory of my brother's long walk off a short pier. "I'm merely suggesting giving Cutthroat a taste of what might happen to him if he keeps trying to live up to his nickname at my expense. It would be good for him." Not to mention, for me.

Veteran of life-and-death battles far beyond my experience, Jared considered the mission. "Tempting to give him the works, though, isn't it. Twice now the ones he fronts for have tried to put you where you'd be pushing up daisies. That's asking for it." When Rab, her conspiratorial nature notwithstanding, had to exclaim at that, he winked it away. "Trench talk, is all. You should have heard us sit around in the mud all the time and discuss what we'd like to do to the Kaiser, too."

Glancing around casually one more time to make sure we were not being overheard, he got down to business. "It sounds to me, Professor, that you're prescribing a dose of muscle for our friend Cartwright."

"Uhm, within reason. A taste."

"Tsk," he pulled that oh-so-straight face again, "where ever will I find lugs of that kind in Butte? I'll have to look long and hard, don't you think? Especially in Dublin Gulch around Quin's old neighborhood." He brushed his hands. "It's settled. He wants to play tough, we'll show that conniving —"

"No army language now that you're a senator, remember," Rab sweetly admonished.

"Chicago scissorbill," I filled the blank for him.

"— that, too," Jared blithely added the term to the military pile, "that he can't use you for target practice." He leaned across the table toward me, reaching aside for Rab's wrist as he did so to hold her attention in more ways than one. "Professor, we're going to need you and your editorials more than ever," his words were quiet and stronger for that. "Hard times are coming fast now. People did themselves proud thumbing their nose at the lockout yesterday, but it won't be long until kids start going hungry and women are scavenging coal down by the tracks and the men start to get antsy about no work and no pay." I thought he could not have summed up the gamble any better: "Anaconda holds the cards — we have to stay in the game any way we can until they fold."

"Or there's a draw," Rab anted her two bits in. "Rome was not won in a day, a wise teacher I once had used to say."

Sudden interest in my corned beef and cabbage let me duck that, while Jared sighed mightily. "Up against the cardsharp I'm married to and some earful in Latin, am I. Lucky thing Russian Famine is on my side — throw that left hook until it makes them dizzy, isn't that the ticket, Professor?"

"By the way," curiosity was getting the better of me, "where is our star athlete? Surely he hasn't lost his appetite?"

With a little crimp of concern between her eyes, Rab checked the large wall clock with PURITY IS SURETY FOR GOOD FOOD! across its face. "Selling his papers down to the last scrap, I expect. But it's not like him to miss a mea—"

Just then the proprietor came bustling toward us from the front of the cafeteria, and inasmuch as I was going to be a regular customer, I tried to get ready whatever compliment corned beef and cabbage was owed.

"Your boy!" he cried as he came up to our table. "He's outside, somebody worked him over!"

We rushed out, Rab in the lead. Sagging against the building as if on his last legs was Russian Famine, clothes torn, face bruised and nose running with a mix of blood and snot, and his *Thunder* newspaper bag showing dirty footprints where it had been stomped on.

Before we could even ask, he spat out through bloody lips the word *Posties*. Painfully he wiped his lips. "Bigger 'n me. Three of 'em run me off my corner. One of 'em held me and the other two whaled me." He did not quite meet the gaze of the furious Rab, freshly attacking him with a wetted handkerchief to dab away blood and such, or Jared's deep frown. "They didn't like it that we was in the parade."

I asked weakly, "The left hook didn't . . . ?"

405

The beat-up boy shrugged thin shoulders. "Wasn't enough," he reported, trying to hold back tears. "I'd no sooner get one of 'em knocked down good than the other two'd pile in on me from the other side."

Three against one were simply too high odds, all right, yet I felt I had failed him. Rab was inveighing against the *Post*'s junior auxiliary of brutes and vowing to give the chief of police a piece of her mind about hoodlumism running wild in the streets when Jared, hands on knees as he leaned down to the beating victim, spoke up.

"You did the best you could, we know that. Now it's time to get you out of the line of fire, trooper. We'll put you on the carriage route."

"That?"

The boy's quick cry of despair was painful to hear, but Jared's reasoning was hard to argue with. The *Thunder* was most swiftly delivered to newsstands and cigar stores and similar vendors in the middle of downtown by way of a baby carriage stacked full of newspapers, a trick Armbrister had picked up on one of his journalistic stops. That safe route literally would save Famine's hide, with no bloody corners to be fought over. Wiping his nose with the back of his hand, the teary youngster mumbled something.

Rab was instantly attentive. "What? Famine, tell us."

"Makes me feel like a sissy."

"Never mind." That came firmly from Jared. "The carriage route will keep you on the job, and that's what counts, right?" Famine mumbled, "Whatever you say goes." Jared rewarded him with an encouraging grip on the shoulder, then decisively turned to me. "And we'll move on that other matter prontissimo, Professor," he said grimly. "It's time the other side licked a wound or two."

Sick at heart over Russian Famine's beating, feeling I had let him down in the boxing lessons, I knew nothing to do but watch and wait for some better turn of fortune in the days that followed. It was a tense time, with the feel of something major about to happen, some storm about to break, but there was no telling when. After the mile-high, mile-deep amplitude of the Fourth of July parade, Butte fell as quiet as if it had temporarily lost its voice. The mute mines of the lockout stood as empty as ever, an apprehensive stillness blanketing the neighborhoods as foraging food for the table and scrounging coal for the stove became the daily challenges of households without paychecks. Even speakeasies were subdued, according to my newsroom colleagues, where clots of miners speculated in low tones what would befall them if the union could not withstand Anaconda's ruthless shutdown. Out in the prairie towns and tawny ranchlands, the standoff was being watched as a prelude to the statewide vote on Jared Evans's brainchild, the tax commission that at long last would fix a price tag onto Montana's copper collar. High stakes, great issues, which to my and Armbrister's surprise the *Post* continued to tiptoe past in the immediate days after the parade, an editorial quietus from Cutlass as baffling as his passing up the chance to ripely reminisce about Teddy Roosevelt and the Rough Riders' conquest of San Juan Hill.

At first I wondered whether my foe had indeed met his fate in a bottomless mine pit, but when I cautiously sounded out Jared on that, he only smiled mysteriously and said, "Don't concern yourself, the scissorbill is still in one piece." The battle of words had only paused, in short. Meanwhile, I actually had leisure to write AOT editorials about matters other than the eternal battle over the Richest Hill on Earth — "spitwads," Armbrister cackled over such offerings, just enough impact to them to annoy the opposition with our persistent presence.

In this lull, Sandison alone seemed to thrive, resuming his post at the public library like a potentate returning from exile. "He's here at all hours," Smithers of the periodical desk confided to me when I stopped by to check on the impatient patient, "and not the least little thing anywhere in the building escapes him, I tell you." Imagining Miss Runyon like a rabbit under the gaze of a hawk, I tried to keep a straight face. Smithers, a lively sort, was in his element as confidant. "And get this. When the janitor left the other night, he heard our man Sandison in his office singing 'The Bluebells of Scotland.' Out loud! It's a changed place around here, Morrie."

So was the manse, a changed place not necessarily for the better without my sole companion clomping around in old boots and pajamas early and late.

Often now it was near midnight when I would hear a taxi putt-putting up to the front door, and the sounds of someone more than sizable retiring for the night. At breakfast, Sandison would eat heartily as a cowboy, questioning me about any sign of Anaconda weakening on the lockout and grunting whenever I asked him the state of his health or that of the Butte Public Library, then off he went, still listing several degrees to his wounded side but as functioning as a locomotive. Leaving me with the echoing house and its principality of unoccupied rooms, as if I were some fairy-tale figure under a strange spell. Prince of an empty manse, with his princess fled.

"It's you, is it." Answering my knock, Grace peeped the door open as warily as if I were about to storm the boardinghouse. "The famous trick rider. What brings you to our humble neighborhood?"

"I came to see if I can help out."

"I can't think how," the reply came swifter than swift. "We don't need any fights fixed or names fiddled with, thanks just the same."

I flinched, but did not give up. "Grace, please. Couldn't a little money be put to use, perhaps?"

Her expression warmed one degree, from skepticism to suspicion. "I hate to ask, but is it honestly gotten?"

"Positively." I reached in my pocket and produced the thin fold of bills. "Sandy had a fit of conscience and upped his rent somewhat. That's where this comes from, I swear on a hill of Bibles."

Keeping one hand on the doorknob, Grace still eyed the money dubiously. "He opened his wallet, just like that? Tell me another."

"I prompted him a wee bit," I admitted. Which prompting, in truth, had been met by the Sandisonian grumble, "When I gave you this place, I didn't expect you to turn into a gouging landlord. Oh, well, leave it to you to get blood out of a Scotchman. Here."

Back and forth between being shrewd landlady and aggrieved spouse, Grace bit her underlip, but the next thing I knew, the cash had vanished into her apron pocket. "All right then. It will come in handy. Good day, Morrie."

"Wait. I wanted to ask —" What I wanted went beyond words, to the essence of man and woman and life altogether, the constellation of chance that draws us one to another out of the lonely depths of night. Try speaking that to an unwilling listener, especially one you are only nominally married to. I instead pleaded: "Can I come in? Only for a minute? I feel like a leper, standing out here."

Wordlessly she swung the door open and pointed to the parlor. "Make it quick. What was it you wanted to ask?"

"If I can borrow Hoop and Griff. The

kitchen drain is leaking again."

"I'll send them first thing in the morning." She looked at me questioningly. "Is that all, I hope?"

"Did you enjoy the parade?"

Grace closed her eyes as if seeking strength. "You. Can you not get it into your head, Morrie, that you can't come mooning around here and win me back with sweet nothings? Too much has happened." Blinking now, the violet of her gaze hazed a little with moisture, she said huskily, "Just go. Please."

"Grace, can't we —" Such a thumping broke out overhead, I feared for the ceiling. "What's making the awful racket?"

"Oh, that," she said as though the commotion were nothing. "Giorgio at his exercises. He does jumping jacks. Lifts a dumbbell."

I somehow held my tongue about the aptness of that word associated with the Mazzini creature. My turn to be highly suspicious.

"How is he paying his rent? There are no wages these days."

"On the cuff. You would let him do the same," she maintained entirely inaccurately. "He can catch up on the rent when the mines are running again."

"Not much of a provider until that day ever comes, is he," I took what little satisfaction jealousy would allow me.

The jumping or dumbbelling or whatever it was went on above us as we stood looking at each other helplessly. Grace was the first to say anything. "Morrie, what's going to happen? I don't mean with us. That's —" She washed her hands of the topic. "The lockout and all, what can make Anaconda ever back down?"

"Jared and I are putting every effort to it." Unspoken was the fact that our every effort so far had left the greatest copper mines in the world shut tight as a drum.

Tight-lipped, she nodded. From her expression, I could tell that there luckily was not more.

My mood weighed down by wife, lockout, Cutlass, manse, and anything else that came to mind, I retreated from the boardinghouse one more time. Deep in brooding as I started home without even Sandison to look forward to, I let traffic thoroughly pass so the next turn of events would not be, say, getting run over by a Golden Eggs truck.

As I crossed the street thinking the coast was clear, traffic of an unanticipated sort emerged as a pram came trundling out of

Venus Alley, simultaneous with a covey of streetwalkers sashaying to their posts for the night. Bent low behind the laden baby carriage, pushing for all he was worth on the uphill street while the ladies of the evening kidded the pants off him, in a manner of speaking, was a depressed Russian Famine. Misery famously loving company, on impulse I changed direction to accompany him as he distributed the *Thunder*.

"Hiya, sir," he greeted me disconsolately, his ears burning. "Come to hear the canaries sing?"

"Ooh la la, what's under that beard, hon?" a buxom redhead in minimum street apparel squealed at the sight of me. "I bet you been just waiting for the barbershop special."

Quite sure she did not mean a shave and a haircut, I declined the offer, to a round of catcalls from the Venus Alley sisterhood as they stationed themselves along the block. My ears now the red ones, I joined Famine in a concerted stint of pushing that propelled the buggy and us out of the red light district into a calmer neighborhood of speakeasies and funeral parlors.

As the street turned less precipitous, I let him commandeer the conveyance by himself again. Brushing my hands, I asked as cheerily as I could, "The daughters of Venus aside, how goes the carriage route? At least, you only have to drop the papers at each place and collect for them, am I right?"

"Yeah," he said grudgingly. "It's slow nickels instead of fast dimes, though," he gave the classic response of the frustrated earner.

I had to smile. "Sometimes something comes along and changes that. Luck, for a better word." He eyed me as if it had better hurry up. "Do you mind if I walk with you? I'd like the company."

"Nah. Help yourself." Strenuous as his task was, he managed to jounce along typically, every part of him on the move. I fell into step, and that seemed to loosen his mood. "You get that way, too, huh?"

I was startled. "Pardon?"

"Down in the dumps," he specified. "You sorta look like you lost your best friend."

An apt enough description of the situation with Grace. "Yes, well," I alibied, "I have some things on my mind and I suppose it shows." I shifted the conversation. "I've been meaning to ask, to offer, really." Guilty as I felt, this was hard to get out. "Wouldn't you like more boxing lessons? A left hook isn't the only weapon to be had."

"It sure ain't," he blurted, glancing sideways at me in apology. "Sir, sorry as all get out, but I'm gonna call it quits on the boxing." He added bitterly, " 'Least until I get some meat on my bones and any muscles."

"Famine, we've been through this," I tried to lift his spirits. "You're blessed with speed."

"So's jackrabbits, and all kinds of things get them," he said in the same dark mood.

"Mine isn't the only case of the dumps, hmm?" I jogged him lightly. "I'll tell you what, let's make a bargain to quit feeling sorry for ourselves the rest of your route. Then we can go back to being worrywarts. Agreed?"

That got a rise out of him. "I ain't no —" He caught himself. "Yeah, well, maybe I do have too much stuff on my mind, like you say you do. How we supposed to get rid of that?"

"Let's talk about something else. Tell me," I flipped my fedora off my head and held it the way a magician holds a hat full of magic, "if I could pull out Russian Famine, grown and muscled and with meat on his bones, what more would you want to be?"

The old schoolhouse trick worked. The boy brightened, and in between dashes to deliver stacks of newspapers while I held the baby buggy from rolling half a mile downhill, he confided that his great dream in life was to be a trainman, on the famous silk trains that rushed the delicate cargo from the port of Seattle across the breadth of the country to the mills of New Jersey. "Run the locomotive, how about," he enthused during one scampering return, pushing the lightened carriage so fast I had to skip to keep up. "Highball 'er as fast as she'd go," his imagination was already up in the cab of a cannonball express, whistle screeching as the wheels pounded the rails, no other sound on earth like it. I had to concede it was a dream with a certain appeal. He confided out of the side of his mouth, "Them trains got the right of way all across the country, you know. Don't stop for crossings or nothing, just let 'er rip. Wouldn't that be something?"

I could agree with that. Yet the vision of another young dreamer with extraordinary physical skills would not leave me. Casper had wanted to be a street preacher in Chicago's Bughouse Square before awakening to his body's possibilities. "Don't take this wrong, my friend," experience spoke up in me, "but you are destined for higher things than that."

"Awful nice of you to say so, sir," he sobered, coming down to earth where the wheels of the baby carriage met the hard streets of Butte, "but that don't help getting chased off my corner and putting up with the hussies."

Before I could try to buck him up from that, we were at the last stop, Blind Heinie's newsstand outside the Hennessy Building. "I'm kinda late," Famine apologized, with a look at me as he hurriedly scooped newspapers from the bottom of the baby carriage and stacked them within practiced reach of the grizzled old man.

"*Alles* forgive, *Jungchen*," the news vendor assured him with a guttural chuckle. As I went on my way and Russian Famine trundled the carriage back on the same route we had come, the sweet words lingered in my ear, the benediction we all seek in the winding journey of life, young and old alike.

It is a measure of how low my domestic subsistence had sunk that a cafeteria became my salvation. Bachelor life soon drove me to regularly staying on late at the newspaper and then eating at the Purity before facing another evening alone at home, to call the manse that. Even with the city on hard times, there was definitely no lack of clientele because fetching a meal for oneself felt like a bargain whether or not it actually added up to one. I suppose it was not a good sign — bachelor habit setting deep — that every suppertime without fail I headed directly for the counter where pasties were stacked in a warming pan and fed myself as mindlessly as a dray horse going to a feed-bag.

Thus came the evening when I was dishing up my favorite fare, a plump, crusty pasty and the Purity's tasty gravy, when I felt a presence. The way a shadow across your path can cause a sudden chill. Or a window man can be sensed rather than seen. I turned my head ever so slightly.

Practically next to me, there stood Cartwright, with a cutthroat smile that more than lived up to that nickname. Slick dresser that he was, he had on a pearl-gray suit and matching vest with a silken lavender tie that was more properly a cravat. Before I could react to his sudden presence, he slapped me on the shoulder and said in a louder voice than necessary, "How's the world treating you, buddy?"

Nudging his tray up to mine, he looked over the meal line offerings as if I weren't the real thing on his menu. "Pork chop sandwich?" he whistled in disbelief. "They eat anything in this burg, don't they?" Then ever so casually, he dropped all pretense.

"You danced circles around me with that editorial today, I have to hand it to you. Sheer razzmatazz. You're one whiz at word-slinging, you are."

I made to move away, leaving him with the rebuff: "Really, we have nothing to say to each other except in print." But he plucked at my sleeve, smiling all the while.

"Oh, I think we do," his voice practically oozed fellowship. "Especially since this seems to be the only way at you." He flexed his upper parts, the cannonball head to one side then the other, as if working kinks out of his neck. "Boy oh boy, that Evans of yours knows his stuff. A couple of Irish miners, both of them pretty far above my weight class, pushed me around a little the other night. I was given the impression you're a privileged character, and if anything happened to you, I'd get plenty more of the same." He gave me another unwelcome pat on the shoulder. "There, see? We have a lot in common. We both want to keep breathing. And it'd surprise you how well that can pay."

His close presence was making me uncomfortable, as well as his gall in trying to bribe me in public. "You can save some of that breath. I told you before, I'm not for sale."

The damnable man laughed as if we were

420

sharing the best joke. "You don't know your own worth, my friend. You can name your own price. What could be sweeter?"

"Strychnine."

I uttered that in spite of the vision of my satchel stuffed with money once more. The Anaconda Copper Mining Company had even more of it to spare than did Chicago gamblers.

Cartwright's eyes hardened, although he kept up the deadly geniality. "Butte rules take some getting used to," he lamented. "These miners don't know when they're licked. But you're not that kind of dumb cluck. Cash in while you can. Throw some moolah at that rundown monastery you live in. Go on a nice long trip somewhere." He cocked a look at me. "Morgan? You still with me? What the devil are you doing?"

"Merely humming 'Flight of the Bumblebee' while waiting for a nuisance to go away."

He snickered. "Smarting off isn't going to help. Come on, get with it. People already think you sold out, so you might as well." I looked sharply at him. "Just the two of us palsy-walsy in public like this does the trick," he said almost sympathetically. "Word gets around, you know."

A rapid glance around the dining room

verified that all too well; people were watching us, too many of them with the rough cut of miners. Up at the front, the proprietor was monitoring matters with a double-chinned frown. As sure as anything, even if the word did not spread some other way, he would inform Jared of my seeming duplicity. Jared I might explain this away to, but others, the union core and the faithful readership of the *Thunder,* would be left with a distinctly wrong impression: that I had sold out to the other side.

"Just in case you need any more convincing," Cartwright leaned in as if the conversation had reached the confidential point, "there are some, shall we say, Anaconda associates out in the crowd. They're making sure people notice us being chummy." My knees went weak. Goons, even in here? "Naw, don't bother to look around," my antagonist advised in a cheery tone. "If they're doing their job, you can't spot them. Window men, we call types like that back in Chicago — who knows what the term is out here in the sticks, huh?"

The next blow came as a casual afterthought. "Oh, and by the way, they tail me to make sure I don't meet with any kind of accident." Cartwright rocked back on his heels. "We're really some pair, aren't we, you and me? Two newspaper guys who get to call the shots on something that counts, for a change. Cream rises to the top, why not?" The spiel was practically purring out of him now. "The only trouble is, we've worked ourselves to a draw. I can't touch you, and your union henchmen can't touch me. A standoff like that" — he spread his hands as if juggling — "you may as well take what you can get and retire in style. Well, that's the setup anyway." He beamed me a final smile that his eyes had nothing to do with. "You know where to find me when you want to cut yourself a nice fat deal. Don't let me keep you from your meal, pal."

I found my voice as he started to turn to go.

"Wait."

"Cutty" — he perked up at my use of that — "have you tried the Butte specialty, a pasty?" With that, I lifted my plate and mashed it squarely into his chest where cravat, vest, and suit met.

For an incredulous moment Cartwright gaped at the dripping mess of gravy, mashed potatoes, and such plastered on his chest, while I rid myself of the plate. "You —" He drew back to hit me, but froze at the sight of my brass knuckles. Rather, the flash of brass as I whipped them from my side pockets in immediate readiness stopped him cold, but then he simply stared as I held my stance. Instinctively I had dropped into the fighting pose practiced with Russian Famine. Casper's old pose.

As the Purity proprietor bustled toward us with a moonfaced grin, calling to the kitchen for someone to bring a mop, Cartwright backed off, but he was not the kind to give much ground. Still eyeing me, he said silkily, "Handy with your mitts, are you. You're full of surprises, Morgan. But round one isn't the whole fight, you know. Better wise up and think over my offer." Dabbing at his ruinously splotched suit with a napkin, he gave me one last smooth smile. "It still stands."

"I hear you had quite a chat with Cutlass." Jared was waiting when I next arrived at work, after the weekend, with Armbrister attentively on hand.

"He trapped me," I sighed. I explained that in true Cutthroat fashion he wanted to make it appear that the two of us were in cahoots, obviously bought off. The pursed expressions on my listeners caused me to pause. "Which I hope did not work whatsoever."

Jared faced me squarely. "Professor, I

424

don't doubt your word. Besides, Rab would beat up on me if I did. You were caught in a bad situation, as you say, and you wiggled out of it, by all reports. Good enough." Now he paused. "Although you might have tossed that grub on him a little sooner."

He cut off my protest. "That's that, all right? We've got other things to worry about. I'm heading to Helena to hold the governor's hand, he's getting the heebie-jeebies about when the lockout is ever going to end. Can't really blame him, I'm having a few of those myself." He said it in droll enough fashion, for a man who had turned himself into a lightning rod under the menacing cloud of Anaconda. "Hold the fort, gents," he left us with, off to catch the train to Ulcer Gulch.

Armbrister still was looking sour about Cartwright. "Conniving bastard to do that to you," he gave the matter one last mutter. "All right, let's get back to making hay. I've been busy with Cavaretta, trying to figure out new ways to say no progress on the lockout. Please tell your suffering editor you aren't stuck for editorial ammo, too."

"Have no fear." By staying late as much as I had, I'd managed to work ahead; there was at least that to be said for doldrums at the manse. "I have blasts of various velocity against Anaconda ready to go in overset, slugged for each day this week. I wanted to surprise you with some good news for a change."

Turning into Generalissimo Prontissimo, he shooed me off to fetch them for him immediately. "Morgie, nothing you do surprises me. Let's see the little wonders, so I can slap headlines on them and get them set. Damn," he said with relish, "it's going to be nice to get back to tearing the hide off the *Post,* no more spitwads."

But when both newspapers rolled off the presses the next day, I was the one who felt as if I were missing some skin. I had written an editorial I quite liked, to the effect that the smokeless skies over the tight-shut Hill were a clear indication of Anaconda's undue power, concluding:

> When one lordly company can turn the actual atmosphere of an entire city, of a whole state, on and off at will, it is the very reverse of heavenly. It is satanic.
>
> — PLUVIUS

As if by divination, the *Post* trotted out an old argument in favor of the smudge of belching smokestacks, of course with a certain Chicago flourish:

There are certain starry-eyed types who seem to believe that the Hill will produce its copper just by wishing, instead of basic economics. We've said it before, we'll say it again, we'll repeat it until the daydreamers grow ears as long as the jackass variety: the scent of smoke from working factories, such as the Hill's when the costs of labor and the rewards of corporate investment are in economic balance, is the smell of money, wages, prosperity. You only have to be smart enough to sniff.

— CUTLASS

"The scissorbill seems to have looked out the window at the blue sky the same time you did," Sandison needlessly pointed out to me when I fumed to him over the sparring editorials, round one handily to Cartwright. "Either that or he's reading your mind, heh."

That began the longest week of my newspaper career. In humiliating Cutthroat Cartwright the way I did at the Purity, I apparently roused him to the peak of his not inconsiderable journalistic talents. Day after day, edition after edition, my carefully thought-out editorials looked lame in comparison to his masterpieces of anticipation; suddenly his were the thunderous dispatches to the readers of Butte. Talk about humiliation. I felt almost as if I had been called onstage by a sly magician, told to shuffle a deck of cards and cut them, and every time he named off my bottom card without looking. Razzmatazz had deserted me and found a home with him. I won't say I was cowed by Cartwright's supernatural show of ability, but for the first time I had to wonder if I belonged in the wordslinging profession.

In that frame of mind, I came home from the newspaper one otherwise fine day to find the front-porch drainpipe being lustily repaired. "What do you know for sure, Morrie?" Griff called out heartily. Too heartily. "Isn't this weather something?" Hoop followed that with, just as full of false cheer.

My mood sank farther toward my shoe tops. If rheumatic old miners were feeling sorry for me, I had to be even worse off than I'd thought. Brooding my way past the pair of them, I stopped on impulse. "You're regular readers of the *Thunder,* am I right?"

"Oh, yeah, sure. Most definitely," came the chorus.

"And you're familiar with the *Post* since the advent of Cutlass, yes?"

They cautiously admitted to looking at the Anaconda rag now and then.

"So you've no doubt been following his most recent editorials."

They looked back and forth uneasily. "Been on kind of a tear, hasn't he," Hoop finally came up with. "Strutting his stuff, a person would have to say," Griff added.

"And mine, lately?"

"A little falling off, maybe," said Griff.

"Just a little. Got to read close to see it," said Hoop.

"So much for vox populi," I muttered, and went on up the steps. They glanced up as I passed, the last word coming from Griff:

"You asked."

At the *Thunder,* Armbrister wasn't saying anything, although the gloom evident beneath the green eyeshade bespoke plenty. When Jared returned from trying to settle down the governor, he looked unsettled himself by the *Thunder*'s recent editorial performance.

"We're gradually losing ground, Professor," an understatement if there ever was one. "I'm hearing mutters from the Hill that maybe we've pushed Anaconda too far. What's wrong with the company making enough money to pay people to work, even some of the miners who've stuck with the union through thick and thin are asking me." He rubbed his short ear as if such questioning had done the damage. "I'm sensing we don't have much time to turn this around," he said somberly. "Morrie" — his use of my actual name said volumes about how serious a fix we were in — "I don't have to tell you to do your best. But pull out all the stops in taking on this Cartwright hoodoo, all right?"

Sound advice, but I knew nothing to do but compile another several days' worth of my most imaginative efforts to be typeset, Armbrister outdoing himself with the flaming headlines he added. At the end of that awful week, though, I took home with me to Sandison, Ajax, and the manse the paralyzing sense that Cutlass could outguess, outmaneuver, outwrite me anytime he wanted. And that was not the worst.

Sunday morning, the plump weekend newspapers spread around Sandison and me at the breakfast table. Prominent of course was the editorial matchup, mine yet another dogged invocation of the spirit of Teddy Roosevelt against malefactors of great wealth, and Cutlass's, alas, mocking a certain unnamed critic of the American way of business who blew the same limited tune on the same tin whistle time after time. I brooded into my coffee while Sandison was sopping up syrup with the last of his hotcakes and squinting critically at the side-by-side editorials. "Foxed you again, it looks like," he unnecessarily announced. "He's on quite a streak." A prim eater for someone of his girth, he dabbed with his napkin lest any trace of breakfast find its way into his beard. "What's this Cutlass character look like?"

Bitterly I described the Chicago sheen of the man, outdressing me as well as outguessing me.

"Hmm. Hmm." I looked at him curiously. "Think I spotted him in the Reading Room yesterday," Sandison drawled. "Took his hat off to read — didn't strike me as the Butte type who wanders in to kill time until the speakeasies open. After he left, I went down and asked Miss Runyon what he'd looked up. She didn't pay me any mind at first, claimed he was obviously a gentleman in town on business. Silly old bat." He snorted. "She thinks any male who gives her the time of day is Prince Charming. Had to tell her he looked to me like he might be a snipper. That sent her flying off to what he'd asked for, which turned out to be in the bound newspapers." His frosty eyebrows raised the dreaded question before he did. "The *Chicago Tribune* for July 1909. Mean anything to you?"

My life, was all.

20

This turn of events hit me where it hurt most. Why oh why hadn't I seen it coming? Cartwright was blocked from causing me grievous harm himself, or Jared's men would do the same to him. But it became something terribly different if some third party — say, the Chicago gambling mob — were to target me. And the Windy City underworld style in these things was to make it perfectly plain who had done the target practice; it was a matter of bragging rights. No, Cartwright would be in the clear, and with twenty-twenty hindsight I saw how he was getting there. In the Purity when he squared off against me, the boxing stance I instinctively adopted not only set him back on his heels, it set him to thinking. It had taken him a while, but he figured out who that reminded him of, and a trip to the library refreshed his memory of a certain boxer who had been lightweight champion of the world and, worse, fitted me into the picture: the fixed fight, Casper's well-known fate at the hands of the gamblers, and the gossip in the sporting circles Cartwright drew on for his column, that the other Llewellyn brother had got away but if the mob ever caught up with him, it was curtains.

And that did not even include a notorious World Series bet that had fleeced the same gambling crowd a second time. I was a dead man twice over, if Cartwright tipped them off to my whereabouts.

"You look green around the gills," observed Sandison. "Anything a poor librarian can do to help?"

"I'll — I'll let you know, Sandy." I got to my feet, trying not to totter. "I have to think."

I went straight upstairs and dropped flat on the bed. The prone position maybe did not promote thinking, but it at least kept me from acting on my first impulse, which was to get on the next train out of town. Not for the first time had I come to this point of decision. You would think self-preservation made the choice definite, yet running was not the ready answer it had been too often in the past. Lying there, the ceiling of the manse over me like some blank plaster map, I thought of all I would be leaving behind for good. Grace. Sandison. Jared and Rab. Russian Famine. Armbrister and the newsroom. And Butte itself. This tortured, boastful, inventive, grudge-ridden, wise-cracking city built not upon bedrock but copper ore was impossible to banish, like some wayward family member you can't help but keep in touch with. If Butte fairly often got under everyone's skin, including mine, the heart is located there as well as the spleen. Not to mention the red blood. No, there had to be some other answer than steel rails for the mortally tight spot I was in. If only I could come up with it.

They were waiting for me when I reached the *Thunder* newsroom the next day. Through the cubbyhole office's pane of glass I could see Armbrister looking agitated, Jared determined, Rab tense as a cat.

"Are your ears burning?" Jared said the instant I stepped in, their eyes fixed on me. "We've been trying our double damnedest to figure something out." Union leader, publisher, senator, all his burdens of command weighed on his words. "Such as, how come you lost your touch at writing rings around Cartwright all of a sudden."

"I've spent a sleepless night on that myself," I replied tonelessly.

"Cutlass, pah," Rab said with contempt. "I'd call him something else."

"Purple-prose bastard," Armbrister provided in the next breath. Even more wound up than usual, he paced behind his desk as if caged. "Not to excuse what he's been doing to Morgie lately, but the SOB has been a show-off right from the start. Christamighty, I was just a cub reporter in Denver when his Rough Riders dispatch came in, and I'll never forget it. 'Outlined against a tropical azure sky,' " he parroted, " 'they rode like horsemen of the Apocalypse, not four in number but a cavalry charging into history, wreaking destruction and defeat on the Cuban forces atop San Juan Hill.' It made every front page in America." He stopped short, green gaze leveled at the other three of us. "The hell of it is, I'd have run the damn thing, too, that fast," he said with a snap of his fingers. "Anyway, that's what we're up against and we'd better quit beating around the bush and figure out —"

"Say that again," I blurted. "Back there at the start."

"What, purple-prose —"

"No, the other. The lede."

Armbrister looked at me askance, but

436

recited it again. "If you're trying to pick up some tricks from him, it's a little late."

I let that pass. Jared stirred, patience at an end, Rab biting her lip against what was coming. "Let's get to the main thing. Go ahead, Jacob, you came up with it."

A picture of reluctance, Armbrister hesitated in facing around to me but said what he had to. "Cutlass outguesses your every move lately. If it were checkers, you'd be cleaned off the board. Are you thinking what we are?"

"Inescapably," I sighed.

Veteran of journalistic shenanigans that he was, he spelled it out. "No one is that good a guesser, not even this Cutthroat bird. Somebody's tipping off the *Post*."

"Snitching, I'd call that," said Rab indignantly.

"Spying," Jared bleakly defined it.

Armbrister swore a short blue streak, then threw up his hands in frustration. "How can it be? I handpicked the entire staff." Through the office window he scanned the newsroom, every man and woman head down at their tasks, trying to picture to himself who out there amid the busy typewriters and jangling phones of news gathering — stalwart Cavaretta, Sibley the go-getter, coy Mary Margaret Houlihan,

Matthews the old hand on rewrite, twenty others — could conceivably be the traitor. Very slowly he turned to Jared. "I ought to have my tongue scraped for saying this, but it needs to be said. Everyone but Morgie here."

The Scarlet Pimpernel moment again. Myself rewritten. Only, this time the secret existence, the hidden identity, stands forth in a far different light. This time the chameleon on the barber pole, in Grace's unfortunately immortal phrase, is shown to be desperately trying to save his skin, as it were. How many pages back in the chronicle of time does such a mask, as dramatically alluring to don as those of tragedy and comedy, have to be put on? Merely to the chapter break after the episode in the Purity Cafeteria, when quicker than the eye can follow on the page, the chameleon gets cold feet and turns a subdued color. Cartwright is contacted, a price is named, a deal done, and the *Thunder*'s editorials take a dive, in boxing parlance. Always intriguing to see oneself cast in a new role.

Ah, well. Enough of make-believe. I faced my jury of three — Armbrister edgy, Jared alert, Rab frozen — and spoke from the heart. "I hope no one really thinks that I spend part of my time writing my soul out for the *Thunder,* and the other part slipping information that makes me look like a fool."

"There, see?" Rab couldn't contain herself. "Morris Morgan is a better man than that, I'd bet my life on it."

Jared did not go that far, but he was earnest in his verdict. "Relax, Professor. Even you aren't that much of a Houdini."

"I didn't mean to accuse you," Armbrister backtracked in a mutter, "it just drives me up the wall that anybody in this newsroom is in cahoots with Cartwright."

"Thank you for the votes of confidence," I said without irony. "Besides, I know who our informer is."

There was a moment of silent goggling at me, before Armbrister beat Jared and Rab to speech. "Why in the name of Pete didn't you say so? Just point the finger. I'll fire whoever it is so fast he won't know what hit him."

I drew the deepest breath possible. "Unfortunately, the solution isn't that simple."

It fell to Jared to ask: "Why not?"

"Because . . . because . . ." — the words did not want to come — "the spy is Russian Famine."

21

"Mr. Morgan, y-you" — Rab, stricken, shocked, next thing to speechless for once but not for long — "you have to be wrong. I can't believe it. I won't."

Jared, equally jolted, was more to the point. "Are you sure?"

"Unfortunately so," I spoke with the firm conviction that a sleepless night of thinking can lead to. "It has to be him. No one else comes and goes so readily, in time to tip off Cutlass to what I've written, day after day."

"But a milk-tooth kid like him?" Armbrister burst out. "How in hell does he do it?"

"That is yet to be determined. And if we simply accuse him, he may swear with all his heart it wasn't him. Rab, do you agree?" Governess of the boy empire of fibbers — to say the least — at the detention school, she could only nod mutely. "To put it in starkest terms," I said with reluctance, "we have to catch him at it."

The three of them glanced at one another, then read my face before the words came. "Let me."

When the *Thunder* rolled off the press as usual that afternoon, Rab and Jared made themselves absent so as not to give away what we were up to, and Armbrister wasn't any more scowly than ever when Russian Famine beelined in from the back shop to the gumdrop jar, mumbling "Hiya" as he passed me, and like a wraith, he was gone again to load his baby carriage with newspapers. I slipped out of the newsroom immediately after, mentally mapping out his route. And down on the street, as the newsboys spilled out of the back shop with their shouldered bags bulging to head for their corners and one came pushing his newspaper-laden pram, I turned myself into a window man.

My disguise, sudden as it was, couldn't be much; Armbrister's derby instead of my fedora, a casual jacket borrowed from a mystified Cavaretta instead of my customary suit coat, several pats of Mary Margaret Houlihan's face powder to gray my beard. My hope was that from a distance I would blend into the downtown shopping crowd, should Famine catch a glimpse of me. That and ducking and dodging from store window to store window like a crazyhouse of mirrors.

From the *Thunder* building Famine dug hard to propel his load, the delivery route stretching literally up the Hill, the tilted streets that were the apron of the higher elevation where the black steel headframes stood silent above the shut mines. The course was also a rise through society, from the newspaper's disreputable neighborhood to that pinnacle of Butte majesty, the Hennessy Building, block by block. It kept me busy adjusting, bearing out all too well Grace's chameleon-on-a-barber-pole accusation. In Venus Alley, where Famine deposited *Thunder*s on the stoop of each brothel — interesting that reading material was in such demand — I had to meld with some other lingerers, my hat on the back of my head as if out for a good time, giving the appearance of shopping the painted-up women smiling and whistling down from the windows. Next a slight step up in respectability, or not, the cigar stores — so called — that essentially were speakeasies with a tobacco aroma. As Famine made his deliveries, setting the brake on the carriage and darting into each drinking establishment with papers under his arm, I followed him from across the street, keeping a careful distance and successfully loitering unseen until he reached the most notorious of the lot, the M&M. Just as the boy sped to the doorway, he ran smack into Smitty, exiting. I felt the shock of their collision in my every bone.

"Hey, kiddo, what's the rush?" I heard the burly bootlegger ask genially as I spun to feign interest in the nearest shop window, which, to my horror, held the casket display of the C. R. Peterson Modern Mortuary and Funeral Home. And in there, scant feet away, long face pursed as he shined up the coffins with a rag and linseed oil, stood Peterson, "Creeping Pete" himself, my former employer. Foreboding hit me like lightning. When I moved on as quickly as possible from representing his funereal establishment at wakes, he had practically wept in trying to persuade me to stay on and keep up the handholding and sympathetic imbibing at those weepfests in Dublin Gulch. "You're the best at it I've ever had, and there's never any end to the Irish kicking the bucket," he'd pleaded futilely. Now his back was mostly to me as he lugubriously polished his merchandise, but the second he turned around, I was caught there, framed full-face in the window, looking for all the world like an importuning job seeker, and I absolutely knew he would rush out with a glad cry. Meanwhile, stunned as I was, I overheard Smitty joshing the carrier of the *Thunder,* "News too hot to hold on to, that it?"

"Making my rounds, is all," Famine said with injured dignity.

That brought a belly laugh. "Know what? That's two of us." From the sound of it, Smitty must have been feeling flush after his day of collecting from speakeasies to add to the stash in the warehouse and dug into his pocket. "Here, buy yourself a sody pop."

"A whole buck! Gee, thanks!"

There was the bang of a door as Famine rushed into the M&M, which meant he would be right back out and I would be in his line of sight, while a whistled tune growing louder indicated Smitty was crossing the street in my direction. Creeping Pete had stepped back to scrutinize the sheen on a brass-handled casket, his eyes fixed on the accoutrements with undertakerly concern, but he had only to lift his head and there I was. In my paralyzed brain rang the prospective chorus of being discovered by not one, not two, but three sets of eyes:

"Sir! You been following me?"

"Boss! Boy, you're everywhere, huh?"

"Morgan! You've come back to work, thank heaven."

Instead, something miraculous occurred. I saw by the reflection in the funeral home window Russian Famine come charging out of the cigar store, stop short at what he saw, and shout, "Hey, mister! You dropped some bullets!"

"Hah?" Smitty turned back, recrossing the street with alacrity. "Oh, yeah, thanks, kid. Them are just some reloads — I mean, goodluck charms I carry loose in my pocket."

Famine's yell straightened up Creeping Pete with a start, craning his neck and peering right over the top of me to see what the commotion up the street was.

And, head down and hunched over, I made myself scarce with the gait of a man who had just remembered an appointment around the corner.

There, breathing freely at last, much the wiser about the pitfalls that went with being a window man, I made myself think through the carriage route Famine was pursuing, from start to end. I was certain he hadn't delivered stolen information either at a brothel or one of the speakeasies, he zipped in and out of those places too fast to hold a conversation with anyone. Besides, those venues did not fit well with Cutthroat Cartwright's elegant manner of machinations. Ahead, as far as I knew, were only deliveries to the colored doorman at the Hirbour apartment building and the last stop, Blind Heinie's newsstand. Neither of those seemed a likely *Post* operative. Maybe I was flatly wrong and the youngster we all thought so highly of was not the culprit smuggling the inside skinny, as he'd have put it, to the other journalistic camp. Yet the fact stood that Cutlass was gleaning enough information from somewhere to rip me to pieces day by day. That thought spurred me on, sending me trotting up the alley that intersected the last leg of the carriage route.

The apartment building doorman, I saw by peeking around the alley corner, was kidding Russian Famine much as Smitty had, and the boy was grinning his ears off. No subversion there, surely. After a minute, he left a bundle of papers, and with the energy of a colt in the homestretch, began pushing the baby carriage up the last block at a rattling pace. Here I had a rapid calculation to do. Blind Heinie's newsstand was located around the corner of the Hennessy Building, its department store side, and so I shortcut through the store to where I knew I'd have a good view, unseen. Hurrying through the aisles past curious clerks, I quickly enough reached the ladies' wear section and all but sprinted to the very same display window — the cloche-hatted mannequins, a bit worse for wear, had resumed their teacup gin party — by which Blaze and I had unorthodoxly entered the store.

Luck was with me, I was in the nick of time to peek past the flapper dresses and see Famine park the buggy alongside the newsstand and heft out his remaining newspapers, quite a stack. Blind Heinie greeted him with something jolly I could not hear, and Famine grinned nervously. I watched him neatly arrange the pile of papers within the vendor's easy reach, then, something I hadn't remembered from the earlier time I accompanied him to the newsstand hutch, Famine bundled half a dozen *Thunder*s with butcher's twine. His fingers were quick, but not quicker than the eye. And so I saw the deed done. Watched him slip the narrow folded pages of overset proofs into the middle of the bundle before knotting it.

Now I knew, and almost wished I didn't. Blind Heinie counted out some money by feel from the upturned hat he used as a cash register and handed it to Famine, then the boy spy of the *Thunder* and — this part hurt even worse — betrayer of my editorial efforts went off pushing the empty baby carriage with one hand. Tempting as it was to rush out and confront him, caught red-handed, on a further hunch I held to my post at the display window. But no longer alone.

"May we help you with something?" a stentorian voice addressed me from behind.

I glanced over my shoulder to the floor-walker, boutonniere and all, evidently summoned by an alarmed clerk. "I think not. I'm merely . . . window shopping."

"Most people do that from outside," he said down his nose. Suspicious but uncertain, he persisted: "Interested in dressing the little lady, are you?"

"I suppose, when the alternative isn't possible. I mean, no." Nothing was happening at the newsstand except Blind Heinie digging in his ear with a finger. Ominous silence behind me growing by the second, I could feel the stare of the floorwalker. My own gaze unremittingly at hem level past the soiree of shapely mannequins, I was desperate not to be thrown out of the store just yet. "Actually, what I am interested in" — it was a reach, but I got there — "are the teacups."

"The cups, did you say?"

"Naturally. I'm the purchasing agent for

the Purity Cafeteria and we're always on the lookout" — keeping my eyes fixed on the newsstand — "for appropriate cupware."

"I see." Cautiously the floorwalker asked, "How many?"

"Five hundred. Saucers, too, of course."

The floorwalker was, well, floored. "That's a considerable order. I'd have to check our inventory, but if we don't have that many in stock, I'm sure we can order —"

While he was speaking, my hunch paid off. A shirtsleeved office worker in a celluloid collar tight enough to choke, an Anaconda minion if I had ever seen one, appeared at the newsstand, said a word or two to Blind Heinie as he dropped coins into the upturned hat, grabbed up the twine-tied little bundle of *Thunder*s, and vanished. Upstairs to the top floor, where the contents of the overset editorial proofs would be conveyed immediately to Cartwright at the *Post.*

"I just remembered," I whirled so abruptly the floorwalker, startled, reeled back, "the Purity may also need demitasse cups. I must go check."

"But don't you want to put in your order for —" his voice faded plaintively behind me as I hustled down the aisle. By hotfooting through the department store and racing back down the alley from the apartment building, I had hope of cutting off Famine as he headed back to the *Thunder* building with the empty pram.

It worked too well. As I whirled around the corner nearest the C. R. Peterson Modern Mortuary and Funeral Home, boy and buggy were trundling down the street directly at me. Famine practically screeched to a stop, my face giving me away. I read his guilty expression as all the confession needed. Stunned, we both were further startled by an urgent tapping on the showroom window of the funeral home. Caskets forgotten, Creeping Pete was showing actual animation, gesturing vigorously for me to stay where I was while he came out. I tried to wave him off and simultaneously deal with Russian Famine. The youngster wasn't waiting for what I had to say. I heard again the sentence I had fantasized, only this time, full of anguish, it was not a question.

"Sir! You been following me."

"I had to. Famine, listen —"

"Morgan!" Creeping Pete popped out of the funeral home with a glad cry, alighting between us on the sidewalk, rubbing his hands together in professional habit. "You're back! I knew you'd end up here. I have three wakes in need of a cryer and —"

Seeing his chance, Russian Famine turned tail and bolted. As he fled, the abandoned baby buggy rolled down the steep sidewalk, accelerating rapidly straight at a befuddled Creeping Pete. With an "Oof!" he caught the runaway pram squarely in his middle, long torso splayed across it and arms clutching around it protectively, unaware there was no baby in it. "I didn't know you were a family man, Morgan," he panted. "Is this some sort of domestic dispute?"

"I'll explain some other time," I said, taking off after the running boy. "Park it in the garage with the hearse, please, someone will be by for it." Dodging past honking automobiles, I raced after my quarry, already a block away. "Famine, wait!" I called as loudly as I could while running. "I only want to talk to you!"

He streaked out of sight.

Worse, I knew exactly where he was going.

22

There may be a trek through a neighborhood of hell — I hope never to find out —
similar to the abandoned part of the Hill.
The dead zone, where the violated earth
had yielded up all its treasure of copper.
Gray waste heaps lay like nightmare dunes
that knew no shifting sands, inert forever.
Glory holes gaped at random in what bare
ground remained on the steep hillside. Up
top, the gallows frame of the Muckaroo
mine reared against the sky, westernmost of
the stark dozens of such headframes, si-
lenced by the lockout, scattered across the
crest of the Hill like strange spawn of
Eiffel's Parisian tower. Luck willing, those
might operate again, but the Muckaroo
never would. "They shut the Muck a while
back," the boyish voice echoed in me as I
puffed my way up the winding haul road.
There had been no time to enlist Jared and
Rab nor anyone else, I alone had been

confided in by an acrobatic gremlin grinning down from atop high-standing bookshelves that he climbed only dead headframes. My heart pounded with the knowledge of what a distraught and shattered youngster might do, scaling the steelwork tower girder by girder, handhold by foothold. He could fall. He could jump.

The abandoned mine yard was fenced with sharp wire, high and formidable enough that at first I wondered whether Russian Famine had merely been bragging in saying the Muckaroo was his pick for climbing gymnastics. Wildly scanning around, I spied the narrow opening, boy size, where a gatepost had separated from the guardhouse. It was going to be the tightest of fits for me, but there was no choice. Alternately grunting and sucking in my breath to make myself as lean as possible, I squeezed sideways through the narrow gap, regretting the consequences to my suit.

"Famine!" I shouted as soon as I wriggled in. The sound echoed emptily off the silent mine works. Bustling with hundreds of men who descended into the honeycomb of ore tunnels the last time I was unwillingly here, now the Muckaroo was a ghost town where no one had ever lived, only labored.

The haunting last testament of this, I

came face-to-face with as I rushed across the yard to the mineshaft, passing the long building that housed the lamp room where the miners, and I among them one unforgettable time, started each shift by equipping themselves with helmet lamps and other gear for working in the deepest mine tunnels on earth. Griff had been my guide in that adventure, and it was he who pointed out the markings as high as a person could reach on the outer wall of the building. "Them's the dead," he'd said simply and unmistakably. Chiseled into the brickwork were sharp but neat up-and-down strokes, one for each miner killed in the treacherous copper labyrinth below, with a diagonal slash completing each set of five. Every Butte mine with a fatal accident on its record, he told me, which was to say every Butte mine, displayed such gouges of death somewhere on the premises, tribute from the surviving miners to their fellow workers that no mine management dared touch. It raced through my mind that someone like Quin was doubly interred, in a cemetery grave and a groove chiseled as carefully as a jeweler's cut. By the raw toll on the wall, an even dozen lives had been sacrificed to the Muckaroo, and it had to be my mission to make sure there was no unlucky thirteenth.

Hastening around the corner from the lamp room, I stopped short at the spectacle of the headframe rearing over me, the spider-leg stanchions and the bracing girders at crazily ingenious angles thrusting like a colossal bridge truss with no roadway but the sky. Looking straight up to the top dizzied me, not a promising development. The steel-webbed tower stood perhaps no more than a hundred feet high, but with my apprehension of heights it appeared more like a thousand. Up there, where I could not see clearly past the crisscross of thick girders, the winding wheel that had lifted the elevator cages bearing men and copper ore was surrounded by a small platform, which could be reached by a steel ladder. But if I knew the climber involved, he spurned the ladder and was somewhere in the maze of steelwork supports, the better to defy gravity.

I cupped my hands and called, "Famine, I know you're up there. Come down, please, so we can talk this over. On firm ground."

Only the wind in the steel frame answered.

A feeling of extreme dread setting in, this time I hollered louder. "If you're afraid of what Jared and Mrs. Evans will do to you, don't be. I'll speak up for you. You won't be punished, I promise. We're all merely concerned for you. Shall I say it again? Come. On. Down."

Again, I was dickering with the wind.

"Very well," the shout I had desperately wanted not to make, "then I'm coming up."

That brought a strawy head of hair, startling against the black of the metal, into sight around a girder directly back under the platform. Good grief, he had climbed the entire vertical steel maze and tucked himself into an angle-iron support, to call it that, his back against the sloping strutwork and his feet idly braced against the nearest upright, like a sailor resting amid the stays and shrouds of a topmast. Open air was on every side of him, all the long way to the ground.

"Sir," he anxiously called down as though it was only good manners, "don't bother. I'm just gonna jump and kill myself anyhow."

I put a shaky hand on the cold steel of a ladder barely wide enough to stand on, calling out as I did so, "Not until I come up and we have a talk."

The fair head shook vigorously at me not to. I hesitated with hand and foot still on the narrow ladder, but the threat to jump did not renew itself just yet.

"You trying to kill yourself, too, sir?" he

scolded instead. "You told me you don't like high places, and ain't none in Butte higher than a gallus frame, everybody knows that."

There was all too much truth in what he said, my twanging nerves informed me. Even from ground level there at the Mucka-roo mineshaft, the city sprawled below the Hill as if it had run out of breath trying to climb to our elevation. "What's the sense of you getting up here and falling off," Russian Famine's maddening logic persisted, "just because I'm gonna?"

Rather than answer that, I began to climb, each steel rung slick under my city shoes, telling myself over and over not to look down and carrying on aloud a one-sided conversation to the effect that neither of us needed to fall off — as if that were insurance against it — and we simply had to settle things face-to-face, the situation was not as bad as he thought, and so on. I was gambling that my precarious ascent would keep him watching rather than drive him to leaping, a theory that might hold until I was up even with him. Then something else would have to be devised, and I had no idea what.

The wind worried me, for both our sakes. My hat sailed off, probably to downtown. As if that were an omen, a hint of what the forces of nature could idly do, I was nearly halfway up the spider-spin of ladder when the spasm hit, clamping me to the rung I was on. *Acro,* from the Greek for "high above" or "topmost," and *phobia,* which needs no definition other than "sheer fear." Holding to my resolve not to look down, instead I glanced upward, just the flick of an eye, to see how much farther it was to the top, and the void above loomed as a blue canyon impossible to climb. My hands clenched on the cold steel of the ladder and my feet would not lift. Clinging there, I would have been a victim of muscle failure and gravity, had it not been for the voice from on high.

"You don't want to be stopping like that, sir, you'll tucker out from holding on. If you're gonna climb, you got to keep climbing."

"J-j-just resting," I hoarsely called back to the anxious onlooker somewhere overhead. Where I summoned the strength from, there is no knowing, but with an overwhelming effort of will I forced a hand free and pulled myself to the next rung, my feet shakily following.

Then another.

And another.

Counting to give my mind something to

fasten onto, it was another thirty-three rungs before I finally drew level with the spot beneath the platform where the boy was squirreled away in the strut braces, looking quite at home perched on a six-inch-wide girder. "Do you mind," I wheezed, hugging the ladder with both arms, "if I climb up on the platform and we can talk from there?"

Acrobat to acrophobe, Famine eyed me. "Looks like you better. Told you it was high up here."

Arms aching as if they were going to fall off, I pulled myself onto the planked platform belly-first and lay there like an exhausted swimmer reaching a raft. Squirming into position to peer over the lip of the platform at the boy tucked away in the angles of the supports, six or eight feet below, I managed to say, "You didn't have to run from me. There's nothing to be afraid of, I swear to you."

"That's you talking," he replied miserably, shifting on his steel beam in a way that made my heart lurch. "I seen that look on your face when you caught up with me from Heinie's. Jared and Mrs. are gonna be even worse. They won't raise me no more," he choked on that. "I'll be back to getting by on the street or else in the hoosegow school forever." Involuntary tears streaking his face, he shook his head decisively. "Huh-uh, I might as well be dead."

"Just . . . just listen, Famine, please" — if only I could keep him talking instead of leaping, falling — "Mrs. Evans and Jared won't throw you out, I swear to you. The carriage route was not a good idea for you, that's our doing, not yours. We'll find something else for you to do, how about? Honestly, you can patch things up with everybody, starting now." Blood was rushing to my head as I hung my face over the edge of the platform and I was seeing spots before my eyes, but at least the youngster was hearing me out, however dubiously. "What we want to know is who put you up to it. That's the only person who needs to be dealt with."

"Huh. That's easy. The flashy guy with the cookie duster, who else?"

Cutthroat Cartwright never better defined.

"He told me there wasn't no harm to it," Famine unburdened himself. "All it was is whatchacallit, something like garbage — them long sheets of paper in the wastebasket."

The spoilage! Of course! The smeary proofs tossed away as the compositor adjusted inking on overset such as my editorials. Smeary but mainly legible. "People was gonna read 'em anyway in a couple of hours, he said."

"One person, anyway," I said grimly. "There's still something I don't understand. How did you get those out of the back shop without being caught?"

"Punky. He'll swipe anything for gumdrops."

The detention school cherub who could steal the puff ball off a dandelion. Enough said.

"But why?" This was pressing him, but the question would not stay in me. "If you needed money so badly, you could have come to Jared or me."

"Wasn't the money itself," came the downcast answer.

"What, then?"

"You know."

"Famine, I swear I don't."

"Knuckies."

"Brass knuckles? What do those have to do with —" I broke off, remembering the beating he had taken from the posse of *Post* newsboys.

"I wanted to get my own," he said bleakly. "Stick up for myself and not get the stuffing beat out of me for a change." He glanced at me as if that required an apology. "A left hook's no good against a bunch."

My head swimming from altitude and revelation, the words jumped out of me without my needing to think. "Why didn't you say that's what you wanted so badly? If you promise not to jump, I'll share mine with you."

The boy shifted in surprise, not a movement I wanted to see on his perch with no inch to spare. "You're woofing me."

"No, I'll prove it." Awkward as it was while lying flat, I dug in my side pocket, the pair of brass knuckles clinking. I withdrew one and held it out over the platform edge for him to see.

Staring at the object of desire, Famine even so looked like he didn't trust the proposition. "You'd be short one knuckie, and those are 'spensive. How come you'd do that?"

"First of all, because you're worth it, and secondly, I need you to do a couple of things for me that only you can do."

His expression was still dubious. I tried to sound as guttural as Blind Heinie. "All is forgive, young friend."

It worked, to the extent he twitched at the touch of those words. I persisted, "Do we have a deal?"

It seemed an eternity before he nodded,

then stipulated: "Toss me the knuckie first."
Reading my face, he flashed me a challenging look. "For luck."

This I had not counted on; Russian Famine's street boy tenet, hard learned, that life
would have to prove it still wanted him. I
gulped, making myself swallow any argument to the contrary. If he was willing to
trust luck, I would need to, too.

"All right, then. The moment it leaves my
hand, it's yours, Famine. You have to catch
it or —" We both were aware of the mineshaft directly under us, where the article
could fall nearly a mile into the ground.
"Ready, are you?"

He tensed on the narrow girder, looping
an arm around the upright strutwork and
holding a hand out toward me for the toss.
Good grief, it was his right hand he was going to catch with. Luck did not dare make a
slip with him. "You bet," his voice was high
but determined. "Let 'er fly."

The metal weapon spun in the air, the
brass glistening, before the boy stretched to
a heart-stopping length and snatched it.

"There now," I burst out in relief. "With
that on, you won't even need the left hook."

His arm grip holding him safe, almost
shyly he tried on the brass knuckles. With
his other hand he stroked the knobs as if

feeling their magic power to change a life, then gazed squarely up at me. "Hunky and dory, sir. You kept your end of the deal. What's the couple of things on mine?"

"Carry a message. And find someone for me. We have to get started." Squirming toward the ladder to lower myself onto it, I caught a glimpse of the ground an awful distance below and my body refused to move. "Famine?" My voice worked, barely. "Make that three things. The truth of the matter is, I need help getting down."

"Awright. I'm coming over. Gimme your hand."

23

At the end of that longest day, the restless city settling for the night as much as it ever did, I approached the darkened boarding-house. Immediately I was filled with long-ing, remorse, regret, all the shades of emo-tion that come with loss. Be that as it may. The next challenge had to be faced, then and there.

Hearing me let myself in, Grace appeared at the top of the stairs in her rose-colored dressing gown, my favorite. Blinking against the light of the dining room chandelier I had switched on, she said as if my presence might bring on a fresh outbreak of hives: "That had to be you, nuisance. What now?"

My gaze up at her should have said it all, but just in case, I wreathed the words with all I could, spoken from the heart. "I am here to reclaim my beautiful bride."

A flush to match her gown arose in Grace's cheeks as my intention registered on her. She scratched an arm nervously. "Morrie, we've been through this and through this. You can't just dance in here in the middle of the night and expect us to go back to being" — she faltered for the term — "lovebirds."

"No, and we both know a prime reason for that, don't we." I could hardly contain myself. Actually, I couldn't. "Where is the swine?"

"The which?"

I was as determined as I had ever been in my life. The Italian gigolo was about to get a taste of my brass knuckle if it came to that. Backing away from the stairwell to give myself sparring room, I roared, "Mazzini! Get down here now. We're going to have this out."

In the ringing silence, nothing ensued at first except Grace peering down at me in astonishment. Then came the sound of shuffling footsteps in the upstairs hallway behind her. Braced for battle, I motioned for Grace to stand aside, which she mutely did, as I waited for the wife-stealing cur to show himself.

Only to be confronted by not one figure but two.

"Keeping kind of late hours, aren't you, Morrie?" said Griff.

"Not that we can't get back to sleep when you're done yelling at the top of your voice," said Hoop.

It was Grace's turn. "And you'll have to shout even louder to reach Mr. Mazzini. He's in Genoa. His stay was up some time ago and he's gone home to his wife and five children."

"Ah." I cleared my throat in embarrassment. "Good place for him." The pair at the top of the stairs in underwear tops and pajama bottoms shook their heads in unison and shuffled back to bed, while the third member concentrated her frown at me. "Grace," I saw nothing to do but start over, "I have much to tell you."

"Do you. Who will be doing the talking, Morgan Llewellyn or Morrie Morgan or some deceiver yet to be invented?"

"Can you please come down, so I don't have to do all this with a crick in my neck?"

She hesitated, our fate as a married couple in the balance, and something in the air between us tipped it. Wordlessly she descended the stairs, her dressing gown swishing. Mesmerized, I could not help hearing in my head Robert Herrick's yearning poem, *Whenas in silks my Julia goes / Then, then (methinks) how sweetly flows / That liquefaction of her clothes.* Thoughts of that

467

sort ended abruptly when my vision of liquefaction planted herself a safe distance from me, arms crossed and eyes snapping. "Well, I'm here."

With a pleading look, I ushered her to the dining room table, the electric chandelier overhead glowing gamely in the Butte night. Neither of us saying anything, we sat there as of old, she in her place nearest the kitchen, I in the star boarder's spot across from her, her Arthur watching eternally from the wedding photograph on the sideboard. I mustered myself. "There have been developments."

"My, my. There generally are with you."

If ever there was a guarded listener, it was Grace, but at least she was listening. Where to start? "It will be in the paper tomorrow," I plunged in, "the *Thunder* is putting out an Extra. The lockout is over."

Jared made the announcement, at my prompting after closeting himself in Armbrister's office for a significant phone call to the top floor of the Hennessy Building. The negotiation went on for some minutes, helped by the ammunition I had given him, and he emerged with the solemn look of a plenipotentiary who had settled for an armistice when victory was too costly for both sides. Dutifully he gave me a little salute and called the staff together.

"Folks, here's the size of it. Anaconda has agreed to end the lockout, at the start of first shift tomorrow." At the first whoops and Armbrister's bray to the back shop to be ready for an Extra, he held up his hands. "That's the good part, and then there's this. To get the men back to work, the union had to take a pay cut." The newsroom went quiet and tense as he mustered the rest. "Fifty cents an hour. I hate that like poison, but something had to be done to get the Hill working again. I promise you this," he pledged as if taking an oath of office, "we'll fight like hell to get the full dollar back in the next go-round."

He paused, the strain showing. "So we didn't get all we wanted, but neither did Anaconda." In a corner of my mind, I could hear Rab, always wiser than her years, forecasting a draw. "They're gambling that they can defeat the tax commission measure," Jared forced the words out, "and it's about fifty-fifty that they may be right. What they don't know," his voice lifted, "is that if it goes down this time, the governor and I will tinker with it a little and get it back on the ballot at the regular election next year. We'll keep doing that over the long haul until we get something passed that reins in Anaconda, by damn."

Looking around at the intent faces surrounding him, that most unsentimental man choked up. "I want to thank every one of you for working your hearts and guts out the way you have. Sometimes it's been a rough ride" — he managed to crack a thin grin in my direction — "but this is a different town because of you and the *Thunder.* And," his voice rose and steadied, "we're not done yet. This newspaper started from nowhere, and we've got this far." He made the same vowing fist Quin showed the world of corporate rulers. "We'll keep on, putting out the best damn paper Butte has ever seen."

Armbrister clapped first, then the others, the entire newsroom in a thunder of ovation.

"That's good news, of course," Grace allowed, still cautious. "But you're still up against that awful Cartwright."

"Ah, him."

Some hours before, the Purity was busying up with home-goers grabbing a quick bite at the end of the workday, the proprietor ringing up profits as if the cash register were a set of chimes, and watching worriedly when Cartwright made his appearance. The self-styled Cutlass sauntered to my table in his usual swanky manner, although I saw him cautiously eyeing the plate of spaghetti and meatballs in front of me; I was famished after the headframe experience. "So now you don't mind being seen with me in this joint?" he said with bravado but staying just out of range. "Change of heart, pal?"

"Let's restrict ourselves to the cranium, shall we?" He looked at me speculatively. "Sit down, Cutthroat."

"Do I need to wear a bib?"

"Not unless you burp haphazardly."

He snickered and took a seat across from me. "I have to hand it to you, you've got more moves than a weather vane, Morgan." Lazily he let drop what I knew was coming. "If you don't mind my using your first name."

"So you are capable of legwork when you're not pandering in print for Anaconda. I suppose that's in your favor."

"I must be slipping, though," he shook his head at himself. "It took longer to click than it should have, who you reminded me of. But when it finally did, it was plain as day — you're the ghost of your brother. Same build plus a little, same phiz somewhere under that beard, same way of putting up your dukes." Confidently he leaned toward me, grinning in triumph. "Same razzmatazz. In certain circles back in civilization" — he meant Chicago — "they still talk about that fixed fight the Llewellyn brothers pulled off. And you know what?" He raised an index finger as though inspiration had just hit. "I've heard rumors, back there, of a pretty big bet somebody out in this direction snagged from the big boys, on the Sox World Series. Somebody who knows a fix when he sees one, would be my guess. Boy oh boy, Llewellyn," he laughed, "you like to live dangerously, don't you."

"Actually, no."

"Well, you sure give a good imitation of it." He slapped the flat of his hand on the table. "Let's get down to business. That scarecrow of a kid said you're ready to make a deal. It's about time. What's your price for putting Pluvius to rest for good?"

"Nothing."

Genuinely taken aback, Cartwright stared at me as though I were betraying the hired-gun brotherhood. "Don't be a chump. Take the long green and go buy yourself a new life. Anaconda expects to pay, plenty."

I speared a meatball and dabbed it in spaghetti sauce, just to further unnerve him, then set aside the morsel and fork on my plate. "You misinterpret. I have no payoff coming because I'm not going anywhere. It's Cutlass who is. Yet tonight."

"Have you gone nuts?" His voice rising in register, he slapped the table harder this time. "I'm calling the shots here. Sure, I can't order up a funeral for you myself because of that damned Evans bunch. But if I drop word to the right people who got burned on the Sox Series, they'll be happy to do it for me. Get hold of yourself, wise guy, before —"

"I wonder, Cartwright," I interrupted, "whether you know the story of the Laconians, from whom we get the word *laconic.* It goes like this. During the Peloponnesian War, the Macedonians threatened Laconia with an ultimatum to surrender. 'If we prevail in battle, we will kill every man, woman, and child.' The Laconians sent back a one-word message. 'If.' "

"That's cute," he sneered. "But what makes you think you can get away with that answer?"

"Because, if you were to tip off my whereabouts to certain gambling interests in Chicago, I will provide documentation from a number of Rough Riders that your San Juan Hill dispatch was an utter fraud."

To my satisfaction, I have to admit, the

pencil-thin mustache twitched like cat whiskers finding danger.

"As you with me, there was something I couldn't quite figure out," I kept right on before he could say anything. "Why you shied away from the Rough Riders angle in the parade coverage. You didn't dare make a peep while they were in town, did you, for fear they'd remember you and your famous dispatch all too well." I watched to make sure this was having its effect on the suddenly less sleek figure across the table, and it was, every word.

"Roosevelt's men won the battle on foot," I went on remorselessly, "not galloping up the slope under an azure sky like horsemen of the Apocalypse, *tsk*. Which indicates, wouldn't you say, that you weren't even there. The only high ground you were on during the charge up San Juan Hill was the height of deceit."

If looks could kill, he would have done me in then and there. "What happened, I wonder," I went on. "A bit too much Cuban rum the night before, perhaps? It was easier to hang around the cable office and send in your supposed scoop when word that the Rough Riders had won trickled in? Am I getting the story right? Close enough, I see."

Cartwright managed to find his voice.

"You're bluffing."

"Care to try me?"

I saw him waver, then concede. "Casper was the best counter-puncher I ever saw," he said thinly. "You must have picked it up from him." He paused, by the look of him still tempted to remind me of my brother's fate.

"Just in case," I headed that off, "I have left instructions, should anything happen to me, that all the proof needed to ruin your career will be —"

"Skip it, Llewellyn, we've all read that in cheap novels." He cocked a resigned look at me. "Out with it. What do you want from me?"

"You should have read a little further, Cutthroat. Absence and silence, of course, in that order. Must I spell it out? You go back to Chicago, right now, and never mention me to the gambling mob."

Cartwright let out his breath in a soundless whistle. "You'd make a helluva poker player." Following that up, he made a gesture of throwing in his cards. "I fold. May I go now?"

"Nearly. First, I am going to threaten you with brass knuckles" — one hand's worth, anyway — "and loudly tell you to get out of

Butte and never return. And you will comply."

"Theatrics, is it," he groaned, looking around the cafeteria at the audience of miners and others already watching us. "It figures." Turning back to me with a doleful expression, the most feared columnist in America shook his head regretfully. "You're ruining a good newspaper war, you know."

"I fervently hope so."

He couldn't resist. "Lapdog of the Bolshies."

Nor could I. "Purveyor of puerile nonsense."

"Fancy-pants fabulist."

"Windy City windbag."

"There, see?" Cutlass to the last, he spread his hands persuasively. "We could have had a lot of fun with each other yet." One glance at me dispelled that. "All right, all right. Put on your pinky ring, let's get this over with." He started up from his chair, but paused midway. "There's something I still don't get. You've got me bottled up. But what's to stop the right people in Chicago from stumbling onto you, like I did, and then it's your death warrant even if I didn't have anything to do with it?"

"Can't you tell?" I said, rising to my feet and slipping on the brass knuckles as Cutthroat Cartwright and I prepared to part for good. "I'm bulletproof."

"How can you be any such thing?" said Grace in disbelief now as I told her the same. "I hate to side with that Cartwright creature on anything, but why on earth can't the gamblers still come after you?"

"Not if they know what's good for them."

Beeping its horn once but that told enough, the Golden Eggs truck pulled up in front of the manse at dusk. The neighbors on Horse Thief Row may have wondered why, instead of a delivery from the van, I was delivering myself to it by climbing in the back.

The Highliner had vacated the driver's seat and awaited me there amid the egg cases concealing the bootleg load. No gun in sight this time, to my relief.

As ever, the pair of us took in each other's likeness, as if looking into a mirror with a slight waver in the glass. After some moments of this, he tipped his fedora up an inch and gave me a rogue's wink. "So, twinsy. I don't know how you do it, but that kid found me. Thank God he's not a cop."

"Never underestimate the abilities of newsboys," I said fervently.

"What's up?" His gaze locked with mine,

as though reading my mind. "This is just a guess, but do you need somebody bumped off?"

"I appreciate the thought, but that's not quite it." No one could hear us, but I dropped my voice, the moment seemed to require it. "What I really want done" — I took a decisive breath — "is for you to become me. In certain quarters."

His head turned sharply to one side, the Highliner heard out my fuller explanation. When I finished, he made sure: "That's all you want? Just run a bluff on some boobs back in Chi?"

"It would be exceedingly helpful."

He stroked his beard while thinking the matter through. "Pretty sharp of you. That has its advantages for both of us, doesn't it. You get to be just plain Morris Morgan, and I get to be someone with a reputation attached, in case anybody gets nosy about my 'real' name, eh?"

"An identity switch, yes. That's precisely what I have in mind."

"This moniker I'm supposed to take on," he checked, "how's that spelled?"

"Double L," I recited, "E, W, E, double L, Y, N. The Welsh are an inventive race."

"I'll try live up to that," he said drily. "So here's the deal, then." Leaning forward, he tapped my knee to signal mutual trust. "I'll have a few of the boys spread the word around Chicago that any mobster who sets foot into Montana for any reason will go back out in a box six feet long. Message signed, sealed, and delivered by Morgan Llewellyn, better known as the Highliner." The fleeting smile moved in his beard, no doubt reflecting my own. "That suit you, chum?"

"A perfect fit."

"There you have it," I concluded, Grace sitting spellbound, glued to her chair during every word of my tale. "Oh, except for one thing." I couldn't help a note of regret in letting her know, "Pluvius is no more, alas. It is time for me to move on from the newspaper. Cavaretta will take on the editorial writing, he's a good choice." I drew a difficult breath. "I shall miss the *Thunder*" — the truest way to say it was also the hardest — "like a lost brother."

For hopeful spells during my telling of it all, she had been the Grace I so happily trotted the world with, bright eyed, thoroughly attuned, avid for what came next. Now her face fell. "I'd rather take a beating than have to say this, but that's always been the trouble, you. Something goes off in your head, and the next thing, there you are again, free as a bird and with about the same means of support."

"Grace, wait. Before we deal with moving on, there's something I must say. It matters more than anything." It welled out of me. "You are my all. I will love you until — I don't know what. The pyramids turn upside down. The stars lose their twinkle. The last breath is out of me. The —"

"Stop! That'll do." She caught her breath. "You are a case, Morrie." She studied me fiercely, her expression a mask of exasperation until, at last, the dimple crept in. "That's not all bad, I suppose."

Before my hopes could soar, she too spoke her heart. "Well and good, everything you've told me. And you're such a temptation when you're not up to some shenanigan, there's nobody in the world I'd rather be with. But there's still the matter of" — she sorted a moment for the right name — "Morris Morgan's habits. If you've left the newspaper, how are you going to, you know." She bit her lip before saying it. "Provide."

I said humbly, "You are looking at the new city librarian of Butte."

Grace covered her mouth with her hand as if to slap down astonishment.

"Sandy," my own incredulity burst forth when the man himself announced that thunderclap, along with his casual gruff remark that he had the place shaped up enough by now that even I could not make a mess of the Butte Public Library and the finest book collection west of Chicago, so it was time for him to sit back and write his memoir, "I don't mean to accuse you of plotting, heaven knows. But did you plan this from the very start? With the manse and all?"

Here came The Look, the blue gaze over the cloud of beard. "Did you just now figure that out, dunce?" He shifted in his throne-like desk chair to fuss with the latest rare book arrival — Boswell's *Life of Samuel Johnson,* ripe for plucking for a certain kind of memoir, no doubt — all the while shaking his head and clucking to himself. "You're slowing down, Morgan. Heh, heh."

"Sandison has some sway with the library board," I said innocently in response to Grace's flabbergasted look.

Recovering, she warned me by manner and word: "Morrie, you're leaving something out, I can tell."

"Ah, that," I sighed. "Sandison has them over a barrel. It's either me in the job or, as I believe he told the trustees in somewhat plainer terms, every book in the public library with his nameplate in it goes goodbye." I paused, leaving her practically teetering toward the next revelation. "The salary is such that we may actually be able to meet the demands of the manse." I threw up my hands to show her I had nothing up my sleeve. "So you see, I am gainfully employed in spite of myself."

At that bit of honesty, she started around the table to me, her eyes shining. Just as swiftly I was up and toward her. We met halfway.

Grace being Grace, she made doubly sure, scanning my face, beard, eyes, deeper than any of those. "You've really turned over a new leaf?"

"Better than that, Mrs. Morgan." I moved to take her in my arms. "Book upon book of them."

THE END

482

ABOUT THE AUTHOR

Ivan Doig was born in Montana and grew up along the Rocky Mountain Front, the dramatic landscape that has inspired much of his writing. A former ranch hand, newspaperman, and magazine editor, with a Ph.D. in history, Doig is the author of eleven previous novels, most recently *Work Song* and *The Bartender's Tale*, and three works of nonfiction, including his classic first book, the memoir *This House of Sky*. He has been a National Book Award finalist and has received the Wallace Stegner Award, a Distinguished Achievement Award from the Western Literature Association, and multiple PNBA and MPBA Book Awards, among other honors. He lives in Seattle.

The employees of Thorndike Press hope you have enjoyed this Large Print book. All our Thorndike, Wheeler, and Kennebec Large Print titles are designed for easy reading, and all our books are made to last. Other Thorndike Press Large Print books are available at your library, through selected bookstores, or directly from us.

For information about titles, please call:
(800) 223-1244

or visit our Web site at:
http://gale.cengage.com/thorndike

To share your comments, please write:
Publisher
Thorndike Press
10 Water St., Suite 310
Waterville, ME 04901